SEDUCING NOLAN

She wrapped her fingers around him, knowing without knowing that touching him this way was right; then tightened her grip. She closed her eyes and moved her hand up, then down, following a rhythm as instinctive as breathing. She ached, longing to match the movements with her hips. He did.

She couldn't reach his mouth, so she lifted his shirt with her free hand and kissed the center of his chest. She turned her head to the right and found his nipple. She flicked her tongue, teasing him with her mouth as he had her.

He grabbed her wrist that disappeared down the front of his breeches. He squeezed so tightly, she gasped at the pressure. "Stop. Please, Jewel," he gritted out between his teeth.

She gazed at his face, taken aback by the dazed glow in his eyes. Though his features strained as if he were in pain, she could tell he didn't want her to stop—far from it. A small smile tugged at her lips.

"Lie with me," she whispered.

THE
Pirate's
JEWEL

CHERYL HOWE

LEISURE BOOKS NEW YORK CITY

To my dad, Les Howe.
Thanks for introducing me to
historical romance novels and sailing.

A LEISURE BOOK®

March 2004

Published by

Dorchester Publishing Co., Inc.
200 Madison Avenue
New York, NY 10016

ISBN 0-8439-5305-5

The name "Leisure Books" and the stylized "L" with design are trademarks of Dorchester Publishing Co., Inc.

Printed in the United States of America.

Visit us on the web at www.dorchesterpub.com.

THE
Pirate's
JEWEL

Chapter One

Charles Town, South Carolina, 1775

How could all her dreams have come to this?

Jewel Sanderson glanced across the tavern filled with patrons taking their noon-time meal. At a small table next to the wall sat her future husband picking through his uneaten stew. She quickly averted her gaze, unable to accept the inevitable. With a tray of empty tankards balanced on her hip, she crossed the crowded room and put as much distance between Latimer Payne and herself as possible.

She set the tray on the long bar without bothering to wipe away the perpetual puddle of ale that warped the varnish. Marriage was her only option and Latimer Payne her only prospect. After five years without a word from him, it was past time she accepted the fact that her father wasn't coming back. The memories she clung to— a moonlit battle, a pirate's map, a golden swashbuckler of a father with eyes the same green as her own—had withered to nothing more than the diaphanous dreams of a lonely adolescent. She was no longer a girl and had to look her choices square in the eye.

If it weren't for the blasted map she kept wrapped in a silk handkerchief beneath her mattress, maybe she would have realized her father's vow to return was as false as the one he'd made to her mother: to ensure her welfare and that of the unborn Jewel when he'd deposited them in Charles Town all those years ago. He'd not bothered to honor his promise then; there was little room left to believe he would now.

Jewel glanced back to the table where Latimer Payne sat, where her mother slipped into the empty chair opposite him. Jewel stuck the wet rag in her apron pocket, not caring if it soaked all the way through to her best dress. She had to stop her mother from delivering her to the man by sundown.

Reaching the table, Jewel forced a smile. "May I bring you another ale, Master Payne?"

He didn't stand at her approach. Not that Jewel expected him to court her—the thought actually caused an involuntary shudder. Everyone involved knew this was no more than a business arrangement. Latimer needed a housekeeper and mother for his five children, and Jewel needed a protector. Or at least that was what her mother had decided. Jewel disagreed. Still, she understood what drove her mother. The woman's greatest fear was that Jewel would lose her heart to the wrong man and find herself in the same strait she had: unmarried, pregnant, alone.

"*Jewel.*" Her mother's strained tone snapped Jewel back to the present. Worry knitted the woman's brow and had aged her since this morning. "Latimer is concerned about the trouble we're having with our customers. He doesn't think it proper for a maid to be around men of such temperament."

Payne brought a pinch of snuff to his long nose and

2

sniffed loudly. After a vigorous fit of sneezing, he cleared his throat. "Such violent outbursts are a sure sign of a choleric humor. Too much yellow bile. A good cupping would do them well."

Jewel tried to keep her smile from becoming a grimace. Latimer Payne had asked for her hand after he treated her, free of charge, for a burn she had on her arm from the kitchen fire. He had heated a glass cup, placed it on the burn, and when the hot cup raised a blister, he'd lanced it. The burn did heal, but the blister got infected.

"Perhaps some of your fine treatment would cure them of the ailment, sir," suggested Jewel. Maybe if he were busy with other patients, he'd forget about her.

Latimer took a long swig of ale. He lifted his mug and handed it to her mother. "Another if you would, Mistress Sanderson."

Jewel's mother got up with the tankard in her hand. Before she left to do Master Payne's bidding, she gave Jewel a warning look. Her displeasure Jewel could tolerate, but the pleading she saw in response to her own gaze forced her to stay when she wanted only to snatch the mug from her mother's hand and fetch Payne's ale herself.

Payne gestured toward the empty chair. "Sit. You look pale."

"Thank you, but I have customers."

He cleared his throat. "Those men, the choleric ones, they aren't the type of patients I take on. Their violent temperaments make them too difficult to control. Brute force is all they understand."

Jewel nodded, slightly nauseous. Marriage to this man would give her the chance to have a life of relative comfort. She'd be much better off than her mother. Even the taint of illegitimacy would be lessened with her securely yoked to an upstanding citizen. . . .

3

And it would permanently smother the last breath of the woman she knew she was meant to be. If only she knew that the map her father left led to an actual treasure, her choice would be simple. The idea of persuading a captain to help her locate it, then have nothing to pay him with except herself was unappealing, but with her father's prolonged absence and the inevitability of her marriage to a man she found slightly revolting, allying herself with a stranger might not be such a bad option. Unfortunately, the fact that her father had never returned also led her to the conclusion that his map held no real value. Perhaps the treasure had already been found. Perhaps her father had merely provided the map because he'd wanted to escape her pleas to go with him.

Jewel picked up Payne's crockery bowl, which remained half-full of stew that had obviously grown cold. "I need to see to my customers."

"Of course, see to your customers. But don't take too long to accept my suit. The element here is more stimulating than is proper for a woman. Take that gentleman who just walked in the door. He's sure to cause trouble."

Jewel followed Latimer's gaze. The gentleman in question stood at the far end of the room, in shadow. Jewel blinked, trying to place the familiarity she felt. The way he filled the door frame, his height, his presence—all singled him out from the men around him. But . . . after all this time, it couldn't be him. Her father? A rush of hope swelled from her chest and filled her throat. She couldn't breathe, much less speak.

Latimer sniffed loudly. "Too much blood. Sanguine humor. Full-blooded and bloodthirsty. Stay away from him."

Jewel set the bowl she held down with a clank, plucked at the ties of her apron, and left it all lying on Latimer's table. She heard Payne's sputtering protests as she darted between a bank of tables and long benches,

4

ignored calls for her attention from impatient patrons, her focus only on the stranger. No doubt desperation conjured the impossible, but a hopeful flutter under her rib cage swore she wasn't wrong.

The new arrival stepped more solidly into the tavern and Jewel's determined stride faltered. His hair was dark, not blond. A tide of disappointment threatened to whisk her off her feet. Just when she had convinced herself of her foolishness for believing her father would return for her, a glimpse of a stranger could bring it all back. The fresh loss cut her anew, a hot knife through her heart.

She continued her approach, knowing she'd appear even more foolish if she abruptly retreated. To hide her despair, she tilted her chin up slightly. Her show of false confidence brought her gaze to his face. She was surprised by what she saw.

He was uncommonly handsome. Jet eyebrows framed blue, vibrant eyes. A full mouth softened his strong jaw and conspired to make his rough features almost beautiful. Jewel's stare touched him from head to toe. He was tall, lean and muscular all the way down to the taut calves emphasized by his knee-length breeches. When her eyes returned to his face, he scowled at her obvious admiration.

Recognition hit her like a cold blast of air off the ocean. Her desperate wishes were answered—though not by her father but the man who'd accompanied him on his fateful visit so long ago. She stared at his features with undisguised intensity, teetering on the edge of doubt. As she tried to remember this man's face, he looked familiar and strange at the same time. His name came to mind.

"Nolan?" It felt right on her tongue.

His curt nod confirmed her shaky memory but warned he wasn't as pleased to see her again as she was him.

Even so, Jewel breathed a sigh of relief. Fate had intervened. Not only had her father finally come for her, his timing proved dramatic. Perhaps he waited outside. She glanced over Nolan's shoulder and out onto the busy street. Before she could speak, he directed her to the edge of a long table away from the other customers.

He laid his tricorn hat on a clear spot between empty tankards and piled bowls crusted with dried stew. Jewel reached for the dirty dishes, a comment about a busy noonday on the tip of her tongue. Simple speech seemed a difficult task, though, in this physical presence of a dream come to life.

She resisted the urge to glance at Latimer. The fact that he probably hadn't vanished into thin air like the villain from a fairy tale once the curse was broken didn't mean her father wasn't waiting on a ship in the nearby harbor.

Nolan shoved aside plates along with a half-eaten loaf of bread and gestured for her to sit. His stern gaze didn't invite argument. Though his manner was commanding, she took note that he patiently stood until she found her seat across the bench. With her shoulders high, she gripped her ale-soaked gray wool skirts and spread them as if she wore voluminous silk the colors of spring. He knew she was more than just a lowly barmaid without family or status; she was the daughter of a notorious pirate and a woman who held the key to a treasure.

He straddled the polished oak bench, then removed his gloves. "I see you remember—"

"Oh, I remember." Jewel's nerves stretched at Nolan's decidedly unfriendly manner. A fluttering of her heart in a sensation close to fear forced her to purse her lips to stop their tremor. "I never told a soul about that night. I'd almost begun to believe I dreamed it."

She studied Nolan, trying to reassure herself of his familiarity. But he wasn't familiar. If he'd not scowled, she might not have recognized him at all. He was no longer the awkward youth who had challenged her father the night the treasure map had been given to her for safekeeping. At the time, she'd thought him not much older than herself. Now he seemed like a seasoned man far beyond her years. Suddenly, he was more threat than friend.

The memory of their first meeting resurrected itself with more clarity and fervor as she studied Nolan's blue eyes and tight jaw. His scowl was the same, though he was now clean-shaven. And his navy coat and pressed fawn breeches belonged to a gentleman. He even wore white stockings. Perhaps it was a disguise.

"I've come for the map. Do you still have it?" Nolan's tan skin had faded to pale olive, leaving the mysterious boy she remembered as merely a serious man.

She leaned across the table. Her excitement in meeting the only other person who knew of her father's last visit temporarily allowed her to forget the outcome of their encounter. "I see you recovered from your wound," she whispered. "If you and my father are still at odds, you'll not find help from me."

A muscle jumped in his jaw, and he absently rubbed a spot beneath his left shoulder. "The wound became infected. I almost died. Your father nursed me back to health. Kind of him, since he was the one who saw fit to imbed his dagger in my chest in the first place."

"You didn't want him to give his map to me. I remember that."

"The map belongs to me. It's my grandfather's treasure, not Bellamy's. He stole the map from me when I was too young and stupid to do anything about it. Even so, I'm willing to pay you for it—and for your silence all these years. You couldn't imagine what men would do to gain the map to Captain Kent's lost treasure."

Jewel had heard of Captain Kent's treasure, as had

everyone. The pirate had been hanged without revealing its location. For the last seventy years, treasure hunters had scoured the coast looking for that hidden booty rumored to be worth over one million pounds—a sum Jewel had trouble even imagining. Her father and Nolan had argued over the ownership of the map she now guarded, but neither had mentioned that it was the key to that famous lost treasure. Jewel wiped away beads of perspiration suddenly rising on her forehead. Thank goodness she had resisted the urge to confide in someone, or she might have lost the map to a ruthless opportunist!

She glanced up at Nolan, hoping to persuade herself he was lying. His dark, serious gaze sparked another flood of memories: Nolan, sheathing his sword when the thrown dagger brought him down. Her father, explaining his reasons for wounding the boy he called his protégé. Their apparent friendship before that.

Sudden doubt threatened to topple Jewel's dreams of escape, but she pushed it away. Mere moments ago her frantic wish had been instantly answered. For nothing, not even her own doubts, would she let Nolan slip through her fingers. She'd leave this place and find both the treasure and her father.

A wary expression crossed Nolan's face before he dropped his gaze to the oak table, effectively silencing her. A hush descended on the disjointed chatter in the tavern.

Jewel studied the tables around them, sure someone had overheard them mention the treasure. Instead, a group of British soldiers strolled past, chilling her more than a random eavesdropper could have. The blue-coated naval officer wasn't an uncommon site, but the five redcoated marines who accompanied him, bayoneted muskets slung over their shoulders, could only mean trouble. These men hadn't arrived for a late afternoon meal.

"Are they after you?" Jewel leaned across the table and whispered to Nolan.

He spared her a brief glance. "No. I don't think so. Not yet, anyway."

Jewel watched the British move around the tavern, not bothering to hide the fact that they were checking the faces of the patrons. Harvey, the tavern's owner, sat at a table sharing an ale with a group of regulars. He didn't appear eager or willing to greet them.

Jewel glanced at Nolan again, who sneaked cautious glimpses of the soldiers. Though he dressed like a gentleman, she'd not be surprised in the least to discover he had a price on his head. And the longer he stayed in the same room with representatives of law and order, the more likely his identity was to be discovered.

She stood. "I'm going to see what they want. Leave once I've distracted them." She mouthed the last words. The possibility that she'd not see him for another five years was a risk she would take. He'd do her no good behind bars; less dangling from a noose.

Nolan's grip on her wrist surprised her with its suddenness. "Sit down. Do nothing."

She tugged, but he didn't budge in his restraint. "I have customers, sir. I'd appreciate you keeping your hands to yourself." She spoke loud enough for everyone to hear.

The British turned to see what was going on. Their smirks proved they found the exchange amusing. Nolan released his grip and averted his face, but not before he gave her a scathing glance. To ensure the British focus stayed on her, Jewel sauntered in the soldiers' direction, an inviting smile on her lips.

"Gentlemen. Welcome to the Quail and Queen. Shall I find you a table and bring you a tankard?"

The smile from a tall, wigged marine deepened to a leer. Jewel speculated he was an officer by the quality of his red uniform and the fact that he carried a sword. "I think I'd prefer what he thought he was getting," the man said.

Jewel returned his smile but ignored the innuendo, gesturing to a table discreetly and abruptly vacated. "Please, have a seat and I'll take your order."

The older, heavyset naval officer who was obviously in charge cleared his throat. "That won't be necessary. We didn't come to partake of your fine establishment." His tone was pleasant enough, if condescending. He swept the room again with his eyes. "Just a friendly visit to let the good people of Charles Town know that the Royal Navy is glad to be of service."

"Thank you, sir. That's good to know." She affected a polite nod. She wanted to glance back to see if Nolan had slipped away, but she dared not bring any attention to him. "Is there anything else we can do to be of service to you this fine afternoon?" She just wanted them gone before Nolan and her father got nervous and escaped Charles Town without her.

The marine officer's wicked laugh forced her to realize her blunder.

"I'm so glad you asked. Sometimes these situations can be awkward. May I request the pleasure of your company later?"

"Leave it alone, Devlin. Solicit strumpets on your own time," said the naval officer. "We need a full crew before we set off to the beastly West Indies."

Jewel stiffened. A glance at Harvey showed he had no intention of coming to her aid this time. She'd been propositioned before, of course, but this time she felt unnerved and very much alone.

"Thank you, sir, for such a kind invitation, but I must decline," she said.

The marine officer continued to grin and glanced over Jewel's head. "Ah, your other gentleman friend. He doesn't seem pleased. But not to worry. I can assure you, your interests will be better served with me—and I have plenty of friends not unlike myself who don't mind loosening their considerable purse strings for a pretty woman."

She followed the officer's gaze. Nolan was still there, staring at them with open hostility. What was he doing?

The officer tilted his head. "Are you afraid of him? You've no need for that." He reached out and caressed her cheek.

Jewel stepped away. "If you don't wish food or drink, I'll say good day, gentlemen." Escape at this point was her best option, but the officer's hand dropped to her shoulder.

"Release her." Nolan's voice loomed behind her and held an edge that made Jewel's stomach clench.

The officer did as he asked, but only to place his right hand on the hilt of his sword. "And who might you be, sir? Do you have some claim on the"—he cleared his throat—"lady?"

The naval officer intervened. "All right. Enough of this, Devlin. We have our orders, and I intend to see they are carried out. Leave the man the strumpet. We have other stops to make."

Nolan stepped forward. "I believe Miss Sanderson deserves an apology."

The heavyset naval officer blinked, as if he'd been dunked underwater. The marine officer pressed the back of his hand to his mouth in an obvious attempt to hide a smile. "I agree wholeheartedly," he said. "This fair maiden is so much more than a mere strumpet. Really, Lieutenant Greeley. Speak up." The musket-toting marines straightened and indiscreetly repositioned their weapons.

Lieutenant Greeley's bulbous face reddened, and the set of his shoulders proved he was angry rather than taken aback. He addressed Nolan: "Step aside, sir. You're in the presence of His Majesty's officers. We shan't be ordered about by the likes of you."

"His *Majesty's officers*? As such, I would think you would have the proper respect for a lady. I might not hold such an esteemed title, but I have enough sense to know when a woman wishes to be left alone."

Devlin stepped forward. "You backwoods colonial—"

Jewel stepped between the men. "Please. This is all my fault. My friend and I just had a bit of a quarrel. I lost my temper with him, I suppose. I didn't mean to give you gentlemen the wrong impression. My sincere apologies."

To her relief, Nolan apparently came to his senses and took a step back. The younger officer held his gaze, not as eager to back down. His hazel eyes held a note of animosity that seemed to go far beyond what the situation warranted.

"Very well, then," Greeley spoke up. "Mind yourself from now on, girl. Let's be off." He strode past. Everyone followed but Devlin, who held his ground.

"I believe the strumpet has wish to rethink her choice of patrons." The way the man continued to stare at Nolan warned Jewel that the standoff had gone past the simple matter of her preference. Neither man had an advantage in height or build but the way the officer tilted his chin and looked down his long nose warned he was confident he would come out on top.

"Stop referring to her in that way." Though Nolan hadn't advanced, his posture showed he'd not back down again.

"It's an honest mistake. Let the gentleman be on his way," Jewel said. She barely stopped herself from entreating Nolan by name.

"Devlin, come along! You might be used to taking command of our land excursions, but this expedition has been assigned to me. You're wasting my time with your antics. That's an order!" Greeley called.

Devlin swung his gaze to the other officer, then relaxed his stance and bowed to Jewel. "I pray we'll see each other again soon—and under less trying circumstances."

He gave Nolan one last scathing glance and followed the soldiers out. The entire room gave a collective sigh of relief; everyone except Nolan, who still stared at the door.

Harvey and her mother were immediately at Jewel's side, both with a heated string of recriminations laced with breathless worry.

"Jewel, there are certain customers you shouldn't approach. How many times have I told you that?" Her mother gripped her shoulders and studied her as if the contact with the soldiers might have bruised her in some way.

Harvey held out his hand to Nolan. "Let me buy you a drink, sir. It's not healthy to be so obvious in your politics these days, but I thank you for speaking up on behalf of my barmaid."

Nolan nodded, but there was little warmth in the gesture. "No need for thanks. I'd just like one last word with Miss Sanderson before I'm on my way."

Her mother and Harvey exchanged glances, then handed Jewel over. Must they be so obvious? she wondered. Apparently, her mother had sized up Nolan as a better prospect than Latimer—whom Jewel had almost forgotten. She glanced Payne's way and he waved her over. She shook her head to his silent request, and he sank into his chair a little lower.

Jewel followed Nolan back to their table.

"He'll be back, you know."

"Hopefully we'll both be long gone by then. Why didn't you leave?"

"I don't like it that you have to fend for yourself that way. I imagined you with better protection over the years."

His blue gaze met hers, and she could tell he was disturbed by his encounter with the officer. Not for himself, or the imminent danger he'd put himself in, but for her. And by the frown in his eyes and the tight lines around his mouth, the continued threat he thought her to be in.

She had the sudden realization that not only didn't he intend to take her to her father, he didn't intend to take her from the Quail and Queen at all. "What's this about, Nolan? Where is my father, and why hasn't he come for me?"

Nolan played with the fingers of his brown leather gloves. "Bellamy *won't* be coming for you." He paused, and his hesitation revealed that he was as uncomfortable delivering the news as she was hearing it. The weight of what remained unsaid hung between them: Her father had never planned to come for her. Nolan cleared his throat. "I shall pay you handsomely for the map. You can leave this tavern and never look back."

He might as well have reached out and tugged her single braid as hard as he could. Her eyes felt hot and wide. "Why? Why did my father lie to me? Why did he give me the map in the first place if he never intended to return?" Betrayal swooped down on her like a large black bird with sharp talons. Her father had filled her full of false hope and empty promises, exactly as he had her mother. Why would he do such a cruel thing to a child?

Nolan's gaze seemed startled. Her voice must have

14

given away her flood of anguish. He set his gloves down and splayed his hands flat on the table, apparently bracing himself. "It's not that he doesn't want to come for you. It's that he can't."

She tried to smile to ease his obvious discomfort, but that didn't work so she dropped her gaze instead, sparing him the bitterness she knew shone in her eyes. "He wasn't ever coming back, was he?"

Nolan thrust a handkerchief at her. "He was detained."

She intended to push the unadorned linen cloth back to him, letting him know that her slight tremble came from anger. The way he continued to gaze at her with real concern choked her throat with unwanted emotion. She didn't want to cry in front of him, but realizing that she'd hung her hopes on a lie was not sitting well. She brought the cloth to her nose and sniffed. It smelled of salt, tobacco and warm male. Finally, she wrestled her sorrow into place enough to continue the conversation. "Is my father in prison?"

"No. Please don't cry. You're better off without him in your life."

Jewel sniffed, but her eyes were painfully dry. And wide open. The smell of stale beer and burnt bread that filled the room could not be erased by Nolan's warm scent. She glanced back at Latimer, who glared in her direction. The British presence in the tavern today warned not only that Harvey's fears regarding the threat of war held merits, but also her mother's fears about her continuing to work in the tavern.

"Believe me, I won't be better off." When Jewel turned back to Nolan, she noticed he'd followed her gaze to Latimer's table.

Nolan's scowl, along with his willingness to confront the armed military men, reminded Jewel of what Latimer had called him when he walked through the door: bloodthirsty. She turned back to see Latimer cowed, studying the contents of his tankard.

"Who's he?" Nolan's stare skewered poor Latimer.

"A customer." Admitting he was her only prospective groom was too embarrassing.

"Why was he staring at you like that? I don't like how your mother lets your customers treat you." Nolan turned his accusing gaze on her.

Though she'd been more than a little pleased he had come to her rescue earlier, she now found his tone too assuming. Nor did he seem eager to provide any real information about her father. She meant to set him straight. "Nothing would have come of that exchange with the officer if you hadn't intervened. And Latimer thinks he wants to marry me."

"That's not the stare of a suitor. That man thinks he has some right to you. You deserve better than that—from him or anyone else."

"But I've rarely gotten it." His kind words were merely that: words. Nothing would change once he walked out of her life without revealing her father's whereabouts or how to find the treasure, except that she'd have less hope for a better life than before. "I've heard nothing from my father or you in all these years. If you were so concerned for me, you could have sent word."

"You don't know how I've made your life my concern." Despite his clipped words, she knew she'd hit her mark when he glanced away. He quickly recovered from his moment of discomfort and returned his gaze to hers, stiff but composed. "I want the treasure for the revolution, not my own personal gain. War is inevitable, and you'd be wise to take my offer."

Nolan was right, of course. Still, she wasn't sure she could trust him. She desperately wanted to. "I promised my father I'd keep the map for him. Please, tell me where he is. What's become of him?"

Nolan tapped his thumb on the table. "I haven't seen him in some time."

There was something he wasn't telling her, and she was afraid she knew what it was. If her father had forgotten about her, she'd rather know. "Did he say he wasn't coming?"

Nolan stilled his tapping thumb. "Not exactly. But, I assure you he won't come."

Her suspicions increased that he was hiding something about her father. "I well remember the argument you two had at our last meeting. I won't be a pawn, Nolan."

His lips curled in a tight, closemouth smile. "*You* remember? I have the scar to remind me of it. Nor am I the one who made you a pawn."

Jewel clasped her hands in her lap and made her decision. Though she was tempted to take Nolan's offer, his mere presence proved she hadn't been as foolish as she thought in pinning her hopes on the map. "You won't get anything from me until I see my father."

"Bellamy's dead."

Nolan's unblinking stare, the way he held her gaze, the way his jaw jumped after he spoke: all told Jewel it was the truth. The tips of her fingers to the roots of her hair went numb with shock. She remained snared in Nolan's harsh gaze, unable to even blink.

It occurred to her briefly that he'd had something to do with her father's demise, but the anguish she saw in his eyes banished the thought. Besides, how could he face her if he were responsible?

As the weight of his words settled around her heart, grief was not what she felt. That would be for the sudden loss of someone you knew. The anguish she felt was for the loss of a part of herself, the part that would never

17

know a father. Bellamy Leggett had died without giving her so much as an hour of his time. A hot tear rolled down her cheek, reminding her that she hadn't stopped existing like her dreams had.

"How did he die?"

Nolan sat forward. "I'm sorry." He spoke to her clasped hands rather than to her face, and his gentle tone was more unnerving than his anger had been. "I wanted to spare you. He died at sea."

She wiped her cheeks. "Did he ever say anything about me?"

Nolan hesitated. Her unwavering gaze forced him to look up. She would never have a father, but if she knew he had thought of her, it might allow her to feel the grief she should while whisking away her sire's betrayal.

"He mentioned you often. He wanted to come for you, but his life was too dangerous. Let me buy the map from you. Bellamy wanted me to find the treasure."

The grief finally came, but it only worsened the shock. Jewel felt as if her life would never be right. With all her childhood plans irrevocably smashed, she felt like she was floating, unattached to anything.

Nolan reached across the table to touch her hand. "Let me help you, Jewel."

The weight of his warm hand resting on hers grounded her, gave her reason to hope. She lifted her gaze to his. His deep blue eyes burned with sincerity. No one had ever looked at her like that before. He truly wanted to help. "I want to go with you to find the treasure."

A crash startled them both. Nolan quickly withdrew his hand in a swift, guilty motion. Latimer Payne stormed past and out the door without a backward glance at the chair he had overturned. Jewel's fate was sealed. She had to ally herself with Nolan. Her only other option had just been closed. And all Jewel felt was a tremendous flood of relief.

All traces of compassion melted behind Nolan's scowl. "That's not possible. I'll leave you with enough coin to ensure your security, and more than triple that once I find the treasure. Take what I'm offering now—there is a chance I might never find the actual treasure. The map isn't clear."

Jewel leaned forward to touch his arm. "That settles it then. I've studied the map every night since my father gave it to me. If you take me in the right direction, I know I'll be able to recognize where the treasure is buried."

Nolan pulled away without the slightest effort to be discreet. "Absolutely not. Be sensible. Sell me the map."

Jewel laughed. If she could be sensible, she would have married a man who would give her a stable future. "My birth is questionable. I have no family besides my mother. And I just ran off the only man who would consider marrying me. You're all I have, and I can't let you leave without me." She looked down at the handkerchief she had been rubbing between her fingers. She had always known she was illegitimate but had never dared say it out loud. Of course, the pity and hostility she had experienced over the years had never let her forget.

She glanced up at Nolan, afraid she would see condemnation in his features as well. His scowl softened. She let out the breath she hadn't realized she held. If anyone could understand her, Nolan could; they shared secrets. "I don't want you to feel sorry for me, I just want your help. If I'll never have my father's name, I'll find his treasure."

Nolan's eyes narrowed. "*My* treasure. It was never Bellamy's."

She changed tack. "I'm not denying that, but I've

guarded the map all these years. I deserve to be a part of finding the treasure. Please be reasonable." Jewel kept her tone pleasant, even cajoling, but it didn't seem to do a thing to soften his stance. A muscle jumped in his jaw, belying the coolness in his gaze.

"You're a woman."

Jewel ceased her efforts to win the battle bloodlessly and lunged at his weak spot. "But I have the map."

Nolan didn't flinch. "I won't take you with me."

She had to fight not to wilt under his unyielding stare. Instead, she raised her chin, matching his determination with her own. "Then you won't have the map."

He leaned back, rubbed his chin and studied her. It was obvious he hadn't counted on such resistance. "You're not a little girl anymore." He paused, as if taking in that fact. "But you're still as foolish and naive as the night we first met."

She clasped her hands on the table, not letting him know his comment stung. Maybe it was foolish to hang on to a dream, but the dream was all she had. "You don't know anything of me."

He smiled. It strained his mouth and eyes rather than softened either. "I can see that." He tapped the table again. "I'm doing you a favor by offering to pay you for the map before I've found the actual treasure."

"You're not giving me a choice."

His eyes turned harsh, as if he saw something he didn't like. "You don't know what I've given you."

Jewel got angry. "Then explain it to me! Just because I'm a tavern girl doesn't mean you have the right to dictate my life. After all, *you* are a pirate."

"I'm not a pirate anymore," he said through gritted teeth.

But his ferocity was unconvincing. Jewel asked: "Why? What happened? What happened between you and my father after you left here?" Perhaps she'd been too hasty in absolving him for responsibility in her father's death.

He picked up his gloves. "A curious young woman is a dangerous thing."

She blinked, not liking the chill in his voice. "For who? You? I have a right to know."

"You should think before you speak." Nolan stood. "I hope you'll change your mind about selling me the map. Take my offer or you'll be left with nothing."

Jewel stood, too, letting him know she had no intention of backing down. Her father's map was important. "But you forget: I have the map. Sail without me and *you* will be the one left with nothing."

Nolan put on his gloves and hat. "You don't know what to do with it." He stared at her, waiting.

She stared back. Going with Nolan to find the treasure would change her fate. She had to prove to herself, as well as Nolan, that she was a woman of her own means, master of her own destiny.

His anger was palpable. "You have more than your father's eyes, Jewel. I hope it doesn't bring you to a similar end." Then Nolan walked out the door without a good-bye.

Jewel wasn't insulted. She'd see him again. Nolan's parting words were both compliment and inspiration. What would her father do if he were in her predicament? He would force Nolan to see reason. Over the years, she had prepared herself to be a useful member of her father's crew. Growing up in a tavern had hardened her in ways that would make other women her age swoon. Nolan would not win their battle of wills. And if she discovered Nolan had done anything to harm her father, Jewel would show him she had indeed inherited more than her father's eyes.

Chapter Two

Nolan paused at the door of the worst tavern in Charles Town, painted as it was the color of blood. Located in a small alley east of Bay Street, the Maiden's Head didn't even have an address. A small version of a ship's figurehead sprang from a windowless brick building marking the entrance. Two street lamps at the turnoff had been shattered, leaving the carved image of a woman muted by shadow. Nolan stared at the woman's bare breasts and the black hair that fell to her waist.

He glanced away, disturbed that he'd been momentarily intrigued by the sight of the poorly carved statue. Five years had passed since he had set foot in a place like the Maiden's Head. He straightened his jacket, secure in the knowledge that he'd become a different man. This establishment would not change that.

The moment he pushed open the heavy door, several patrons paused in throwing back their tankards to stare. Nolan met the wall of hostility with a fierce gaze, swept off his stiff tricorn hat and entered the thieves' den.

He searched the room for John Wayland. Exposed

beams crisscrossed one wall and lined the ceiling. Smoke from the fire at the far end of the tavern strained the plaster in between those beams. Brick made up the other two walls, and there was a long bar at the back. After stepping in from the crisp spring night, heat from the sweating sailors and the flames hit Nolan like a fist.

He reached for his handkerchief, intent on wiping his brow, but realized he had left it with Jewel. He wished he could discard her memory as easily. She had not been at all what he expected. He remembered her as a wide-eyed little girl who had made him long for home. Barely out of his teens, he'd already become bored with the women he met in the drinking dens and alleys of the Caribbean. Though she'd worked at the Quail and Queen even then, Jewel had reminded him of the boy he might have been if he hadn't run away from home at fourteen. A strange combination of adolescent lust and a man's protectiveness had overcome him and urged him to challenge an opponent he couldn't beat. His reward had been a dagger in the shoulder.

Had he been expecting gratitude five years later? Perhaps he had. Perhaps he'd thought she would come to realize her father was a liar and had only used her. The man had even used her to ensure Nolan's obedience. Bellamy had promised to spread word of the map's location if Nolan tried to leave his crew again. By that time it had become clear to both Bellamy and Nolan that Captain Kent's map couldn't be read by just anyone, themselves included. Kent's cryptic directions held secrets to which his grandson wasn't privy. Fear of what would become of Jewel had kept Nolan in line for a short while. But it also had necessitated the impetuous Bellamy's own downfall.

Nolan searched the crowd again, looking the fiercest men straight in the eye. Strangely, he felt more comfortable with these armed pirates than Bellamy's offspring. He now gladly sought the worst his former profession had to offer, if only to prove how much he had changed.

Unfortunately, the identifying scar running from the corner of Wayland's eye to the tip of his nose did not render him distinguishable in this lot. Missing eyes and noses were common among the weathered faces. Piracy had a tendency to wear down a man as traffic did the cobblestones on Bay Street. Bellamy was the exception. He still loomed larger than life every time Nolan thought of him.

Nolan walked to the bar and ordered ale. He took an ungentlemanly gulp, which prompted some of the hostile stares to slide away. He leaned against the bar, scanning the dimly lit tables on the fringes of the room. Wayland sat in the corner with his back to the wall. A shadow covered part of his face. When Wayland turned, catching Nolan's gaze, light reflected off his glass eye. With a subtle nod, the pirate summoned Nolan over. Nolan ordered two more ales before complying.

Wayland grinned, and Nolan noticed he had lost a few more teeth. "I like the way you walked in here, lad. Ye've the gait of a captain."

Nolan sat down and pushed a pewter mug in front of the pirate. "Since you knew I was in Charles Town, I'll assume you know how I got here." He leaned forward, and both Wayland's artificial ice-blue eye and his true dark brown one came into view. The mismatched glass eye was Wayland's prized possession. Nolan had been there when he had snatched it from an unlucky victim. Most men, even other pirates, crossed themselves when they saw the freakish eye. Nolan was glad he'd remembered and didn't flinch.

Wayland studied him. "Aye. I heard you got yourself a ship and a crew. The *Integrity*. What do you plan to be doing with her?"

Nolan shrugged out of his coat, the sweltering heat in the enclosed room winning over propriety. "I intend to privateer. War's inevitable."

"A privateer. Hmph. I guess that's why you're using the name Kenton instead of Kent."

"It was my father's name." Nolan hadn't heard the name Kent in so long, it no longer made him drop his gaze in shame. His last few years of sober repentance had finally convinced his father that he was truly a pious reverend's offspring rather than the spawn of the most notorious pirate of the last century. Of course, his father was likely writhing in his recently turned grave. He wouldn't believe that Nolan had used his inheritance to buy a ship merely to join the coming revolution any more than Wayland did.

Nolan might have let his father's wishes to deny the family's tainted past hold sway even in death if not for the worn leather book on the occult he'd found in the man's possessions. If the cover had ever declared an author or title, it had long since been worn away. Inside, the print had smeared and faded as if the pages had been pored over for hours on end. Why his devoutly religious father had a book that spoke of mystical connections between astrology and varying alphabets, notes in his own hand in the margins, led Nolan to only one conclusion: He too had an interest in the notorious Captain Kent's legacy.

"Where will you get your letter of marque?" The unmistakable note of disgust in Wayland's question showed what he thought of privateers. He tipped his head, assessing Nolan with his good eye. "Will it be England? Is that why you changed your name? Sucking up to the bloody crown, hoping they'll forget they hung a Kent not so long ago?"

Nolan drank from his tankard. "No, I remember what English justice did to my grandfather. I wouldn't sail for them even if they pressed me in chains. I've been promised a letter of marque from Massachusetts. They'll start issuing them any day now."

"Massachusetts is no country. Sounds like piracy to me, lad." Wayland eyed Nolan with pleasure.

Nolan forced himself not to flinch. Perhaps a slight thrill surged through him at this taste of his old life, but the horrors of those days still gave him nightmares. All he need do was recall the time that Bellamy nailed a particular captain's foot to the deck when he hadn't heeded the raising of the black flag quickly enough.

"Extreme violence, torture, death? I have no stomach for that. I'll admit I've given in again to the lure of the sea, but you know how I felt about piracy. About Bellamy's practices."

"Bah. Bellamy wasn't as bad as most. You just had to show you had some ballocks if you wanted to stay afloat. He didn't kill one woman he raped. Set 'em all on shore nice and gentle-like. Hell, I'll wager he didn't even have to rape half—most of them high-bred ladies came to him practically purring."

Nolan shook his head and stared into his ale. After he'd returned home from his stint with Bellamy, his father could barely look at him. He'd thought his son had participated in every sordid crime attributed to pirates. Nolan's own grandfather had been rumored to take women as well as plunder from the merchant ships he captured. Once they'd served their purpose and required more care than they were worth, he'd tossed them overboard to drown or be eaten by sharks.

"Privateers operate under a different set of rules. We only take ships that are sanctioned in our letter of marque. And harming the passengers or crew of said vessels is not part of the game." Nolan glanced up to see Wayland's amused gaze. He said, "I'm returning to the sea because of something I believe in beyond my own selfish lusts. It's not just about freedom for the few who can take it by strength and violence. It's about freedom for an entire nation."

"I like to see that passion in you, Nolan. The sea is in your blood, like it was in your grandfather's." Wayland took a pewter flask from his coat pocket. The once red garment had turned the color of dirty brick. Even the coat's original cut was altered by disuse, but Nolan had the distinct impression it once had been part of a British soldier's uniform. Obviously not content with his ale, the pirate took a long swig from the dented flask. He offered the container to Nolan, who winced at the slight whiff: kill-devil, a vile but potent rum from Barbados.

Wayland chuckled, then tucked the flask back in his pocket. "I say pirating is the only true life that's free, but you make a strong argument for the patriot's cause. I think I'll join you."

Nolan tried not to laugh outright. Wayland would terrorize his crew more than the British. He shook his head, grinning. "I don't think you could tolerate the rules of a privateering vessel."

The barmaid set down drinks Nolan hadn't ordered. Before he could tell her so, Wayland grabbed her wrist. "Meet the captain of the *Integrity*, Kat. Nolan, this is Katie. Say hello to my friend properly, love. I'd wager he's been real lonely these last few years."

The dark-haired barmaid giggled and plopped herself in Nolan's lap, throwing her arms around his neck. Her curves fit him in all the right places. "Nice to meet you, Nolan. I get off at midnight."

Wayland had guessed correctly: Nolan had been very lonely since he gave up pirating. Katie felt warm and soft in his arms, reminding him of all he had tried so hard to forget. He even liked the cloying fragrance of her heavy perfume because it smelled exclusively feminine.

He craned his neck away. If he caught the scent of her long cascading hair, he'd be lost despite himself. "Sorry, I'm leaving at dawn. Maybe the next time I'm in Charles Town."

"We can make it quick if you like, love." Katie settled herself deeper in his lap.

Nolan's sharp inhalation garnered another scratchy laugh from Wayland. He had lost his taste for tavern wenches when he still wore an earring, but Katie felt too good to ignore. A sensation, a dangerous one, one he had learned to instantly douse, sparked in Nolan's groin. He quickly gripped her corseted waist and put the woman on her feet.

"Another time." He tipped her a shilling, double the price of the ales. She walked away with hips swaying and a wink over her shoulder.

Wayland rested his chin on his hand and studied Nolan. "Don't like women anymore, lad?"

Nolan smiled. "I'm more selective than I used to be."

Wayland shrugged. "As long as you still like 'em. I don't want to be sailing with no one I have to be watching me bum around."

Nolan laughed. He had forgotten how good it felt. He'd also forgotten how good it felt to act freely. He doubted he could offend Wayland if he tried. "You don't have to worry because you're not coming with me."

Wayland grinned. "You'll need me. And you're lucky, I'm in between captains. After being with Bellamy all those years, it's hard to take orders from a lesser man. But I'll be proud to sail with you. Bellamy thought of you as a son."

Nolan's smile faded. "No, he didn't."

"Still, he taught you well. You were the best, as good as Bellamy his—"

"I don't think you'll like the kind of ship I'll be running. My concern is with fighting the British, not loot and plunder." Nolan shook off his previous ease. Over the years of reform, he'd focused exclusively on the brutality of his former life. He'd never intentionally taken a woman against her will, but he now wondered if he'd been too into his cups to notice when fear was the cause for lack of resistance. Probably he was inherently more gentle than the rest—not that the trait was impressive considering the competition—and the women in question sensed that.

Nor had he killed without cause, but he'd broken a few bones on Bellamy's command, all in the name of building a reputation. Nolan couldn't afford to let himself act freely, no matter how appealing. The abandonment of one restraint so easily led to another.

"Who's your carpenter?" asked Wayland.

Nolan sipped his third ale with more caution. "You won't know him. He just finished his apprenticeship with one of the finest ship builders in Boston."

Wayland made a mulelike sound through closed lips. "He's been in battle then?"

Nolan wasn't about to reveal how green his crew was. "I don't want any pirates on my ship. My goal is to harass the British whenever possible. I told you before, I'm not concerned with plunder and I don't want anyone on my ship who is."

Wayland winked his brown eye. "Captain Kent's treasure concerns you, or you wouldn't have gone to see Bellamy's girl today."

Nolan stopped his surprise from reaching his features, though it gripped him by the throat. He should have known that was why Wayland had sent him a note requesting this meeting.

The pirate smiled widely, apparently unconcerned with his lack of teeth. "Didn't know for sure what happened to that map, but you made me sure. I'm going with you."

Nolan glanced over his shoulder. His old instincts returned. He wondered if Wayland had allies stationed nearby. In this crowd, it would be easy to slip a dagger between his ribs and carry him out into the alley without anyone noticing or even caring if they did. In an old habit he'd sworn he'd rid himself of, he eased his hand to a dagger that wasn't there. To come to a place like this unarmed had been stupid.

"Leave her alone," he said with enough threat to compensate for being unarmed.

Wayland waved his hand in a gesture of dismissal. "I won't hurt the chit. And you don't have to look around like I have mates to jump you as soon as you get on the street. I know I can't read the map without you. If I could, we would have found the treasure with Bellamy."

Nolan leaned back, but he was far from relaxed. He had not handled his confrontation with Jewel well. Her stubbornness had knocked him off guard. That, and the unexpected surge of guilt temporarily capsizing him when he stared into her clear green eyes. He had thought protecting her from her father was a sort of gift, but he'd not considered the life he'd abandoned her to. Was the man who'd left in a rage actually a suitor, or was he something more sordid? And no doubt that British officer would be back. The man covered his aggression with polite language, but the colonies had been prayed upon by wolves in sheep's fine aristocratic clothing for years. The Quail and Queen reigned far superior in its clientele than this den, but arrangements forced upon women with no family were not uncommon even in the finest of establishments.

Jewel's predicament was not entirely his fault, Nolan forcibly reminded himself. Relieving her of the map would be better for her all around. He'd move her to a safe place while helping her find a situation that was less compromising . . . and less dangerous. If Wayland had been watching, someone else might have too.

Wayland's raspy words punctuated Nolan's last thought. "Don't scowl so, lad. You're too young for that. Always the serious one, you were."

Nolan took another sip of ale and watched Wayland over the rim. From here on out, he had to live as if the war he'd been anticipating had already begun. Only, he'd be battling more than just the British.

Wayland emptied his tankard, then chased the ale with a swig from his flask. "Why wouldn't the girl give you the map?" he asked.

Nolan hesitated, thinking before he spoke. Being with his family in Boston had softened him, but now he was back in a realm where every move, every word had to be guarded. He wasn't about to give out any more information that might put Jewel in danger. "What makes you think she didn't?"

Wayland laughed. " 'Cause when I mentioned her, you looked like you had a bowsprit stuck up your arse. Did you tell her her dad's dead?"

Nolan nodded but couldn't stop himself from glancing down at the table. God, how Bellamy would love to know that after all these years, he still couldn't hide his emotions.

Wayland raised the brow of his good eye. "Maybe that's why she won't give you the map."

Nolan leaned back, struggling to look relaxed when he really wanted to grab Wayland's tattered jacket and haul him across the table. "I didn't tell her how he died."

"Hmm. Must have been hard for you to see her. She looks like Bellamy, don't you think?"

Nolan was trying not to think of how she looked at all. It was better when he remembered her as a child, when his adolescent admiration had sparked nothing more than images of long, stolen glances and heated moments holding hands. Now she was a woman who might or might not be experienced. If her flirtatious handling of the British officer didn't convince him, the way she'd challenged Nolan while looking directly into his eyes made him think so. Unfortunately, that didn't seem to diminish his attraction. After five years of marriage-minded society virgins, a woman who knew what a man was about had become fresh and enticing all over again.

"She favors her mother."

Wayland rubbed his chin. "The eyes. Surely you saw him in the eyes. That's an unusual shade of green."

"Bellamy was a monster. All I saw in his eyes were greed and death."

Wayland made the sign of the cross, an act that seemed superstitious rather than pious. "Don't speak ill of the dead, lad." He raised his hands in surrender. "Though I ain't harboring no ill will against you. Can't be two cocks in the ring without trouble."

Nolan rubbed his forehead. The pungent flavor of the past was as strong as the day he'd left Nassau. Hiding out for years hadn't softened it at all. "If you want to join me, you have to follow my rules. No more talk of Bellamy or piracy. Those days are gone. I'm going to be a privateer, and my loyalty is to the Colonies."

"I'll join you. But I won't lie to you. My loyalty lies with finding the treasure—and I want my share. I'll follow your orders 'cause you're the captain, but I'll leave the moralizing to you, Nolan."

Nolan wasn't sure if he had won or lost the confrontation. He really had no choice. He couldn't leave Wayland in Charles Town now that the man knew about Jewel. Besides, Wayland was the finest carpenter he had ever known. In battle, his young recruit would be useless. Wayland had experience and knowledge. And, on board the *Integrity*, Nolan could keep him under his thumb. It was always better to keep your enemies close.

He downed the rest of his ale and stood. "I expect you aboard the *Integrity* at dawn. Do you want to come with me now, or will I see you in the morning?"

Wayland winked. "You'll see me in the morning. I have a few good-byes to say, if you know what I mean."

Nolan put on his gloves. "I'll talk to Jewel again and try to get the map from her before we leave. I'll approach her differently this time." Not that he knew what his approach would be, but he had to have the map. He no longer had the luxury of waiting Jewel out. For the second time in their acquaintance, her life was at stake and only Nolan could protect her.

Wayland tilted his head, studying him. "Got a soft spot for Bellamy's chit, do you?"

Nolan wished. A soft spot would be a lot easier to handle. "I have to get the map, don't I?" He grabbed his coat and punched his arm into the sleeve, acutely aware of Wayland's scrutiny.

"Aye. And I bet you know just how to get the map, don't you, Nolan? You always had a way with the ladies." The pirate downed his ale and signaled the barmaid for another.

"Things have changed."

Wayland grinned. "But you haven't."

Nolan turned and walked away. Let Wayland think what he wanted. Maybe he would get so drunk he'd forget about their little visit.

Not bloody likely.

Chapter Three

Nolan secured the skiff and hauled himself up the rope ladder dangling near the water. "Mr. Tyrell," he shouted as he cleared the railing. "Raise anchor. We're setting sail within the half hour. There's a press gang on shore."

They had no choice but to leave without the map. He had not set a single foot upon Queen Street's cobblestoned surface before he'd turned back at the sight of three marines dragging a man toward the wharf. No doubt that was what the British visit to the Quail and Queen had been about yesterday: They'd been searching for deserters, as well as men to take the place of any missing crew members who weren't located. It was not an uncommon occurrence.

Unfortunately, Nolan's anchorage wasn't remote enough to spare him from being included in such a search. He couldn't chance being discovered with a vessel outfitted for war instead of trade. Until he had a letter of marque, his vessel could cause him to be charged with treason or piracy.

Nolan tugged on the lines that lifted the skiff out of

the water. He didn't turn to locate his eager lieutenant. Parker Tyrell had a knack of gravitating to him.

"That's illegal. How can they do that?" The man's voice said behind him.

With the help of the block and tackle, the skiff reached the ship's railing in a few yanks. Parker helped Nolan haul the small boat over the side.

"They're doing it. I don't imagine it's too hard to find a Tory magistrate to back their press warrants."

"It's war, then. The press is only legal during war."

Nolan hoped he had learned to hide his emotions better than Parker. They were not but a handful of years apart in age, but he felt ancient in his former pupil's presence.

"I don't know if it's war, but I want to get the hell out of here before I find out from a British press gang. Take a deep breath, Lieutenant. We have a long road ahead of us."

Parker pushed back the heavy strand of blond hair that had come loose from his perfect queue, then straightened his already straight coat. What the man lacked in experience, he made up in enthusiasm. His painfully neat appearance and boyishly pretty face always reassured Nolan. No one would ever mistake him for a pirate.

"Aye, Captain. I'll ready the ship to sail." Parker had to sidestep Wayland to go about his duties. Wayland held his ground while Parker deviated from his path. The telling moment confirmed Nolan's fears: Wayland fit with the *Integrity*'s crew as well as Blackbeard's ghost would fit at one of Nolan's father's Sunday services, severed head in hand.

"I know fifty men with more experience than that whelp," the pirate said, strolling toward Nolan with his hands in his pockets. He had not taken any of Nolan's suggestions to tie back his long stringy hair, remove his earring or wear an eye patch. Even though a black patch conjured up visions of pirates, it was better than the alternative. A hollow eye socket was better than the alternative.

"I imagine all the men you know are either British deserters, pirates or both. Parker's not as young as he looks. He's also honest."

Nolan strode to the navigator's station, hoping Wayland wouldn't follow. Without a master sailor, Nolan had to do the navigation himself: another skill obtained from Bellamy. His old mentor had created a wonderful captain in Nolan, but an awful man. Nolan had spent the last five years of his life correcting the damage.

When he reached the small cabin used for navigation situated on the main deck, Wayland squeezed in behind him. Nolan unfurled a large map, smoothing out the wrinkles with the palm of his hand. He picked up a set of dividers, marking the fastest route back to Boston.

"You haven't lost your touch, Nolan. A born sailor you are. That lieutenant of yours isn't much younger than you, but he doesn't have near what you have. And honesty won't keep us from getting killed, lad."

Nolan concentrated on his calculations, ignoring the pirate. The discipline gained in his theological studies these past years had enhanced his navigational skills rather than leaving them rusty. And his stint as schoolmaster had given him much-needed patience, something he'd require to deal with Wayland now without losing his temper. Nolan's father had been disappointed when Nolan returned from the university with his ministerial degree in hand yet not eager to follow in his footsteps and be ordained, but establishing a school for those of the merchant class who desired higher education for their sons and couldn't afford a private tutor mollified him somewhat. He'd even stopped commenting on Nolan's occasional visits to the harbor to gaze longingly at the ships.

"You're welcome to leave if you don't approve of my crew," he said to Wayland in his calm yet stern schoolmaster voice.

"No, lad, I wouldn't leave you. It's plain to me you need more help than I expected." The old pirate slapped Nolan on the back, hard. His gaunt frame belied his strength. "So, did you get the map?"

Nolan straightened. "No. The British were swarming the docks, picking up anyone they could find to impress. I thought it best we leave—for now." Besides, this would give Jewel time to realize he wouldn't be swayed into taking her with him. Though he hated to leave her at the mercy of the life she'd been handed, and though he feared his defense of her had only encouraged the British officer to be more aggressive the next time he saw her, she seemed to be able to handle herself well enough. Nolan was the one who'd almost ignited the situation by not maintaining a cool head. She'd sent him packing without the thing he'd come for.

Wayland rubbed his gray, stubbled chin. "Maybe I should talk to the chit."

The pencil in Nolan's hand snapped. "Stay away from her."

Wayland held up his hands in surrender. "Didn't know it was like that between you two. I just planned to talk to her, not purchase her services."

"What do you know about Bellamy's daughter?" Nolan braced himself for the worst. He'd not wanted to think the British officer had reason to proposition her so openly. Thinking she was available to all of Charles Town startled Nolan with a surge of violence.

"Calm down, boy. You're going to hurt yourself. Don't know nothing but what you told me. I haven't been in Charles Town near a fortnight myself."

"Then don't spread malicious gossip that will cause

the girl harm. She's not safe with the map as it is."
Wayland laughed. "My lips are as tight as a dead man's
grip. Always have been, so don't go accusing me of
causing the girl trouble. I'm not the one who—"

Nolan slammed his finger in the drawer as he stowed
his instruments. "Damn!"

Wayland crossed his arms over his chest and leaned
against the curved planks of the cabin. "I can see you're
upset about not getting the map. Sounds like Bellamy's
girl's a little tougher than you expected. Instead of treating her like a pampered miss, we should send someone
with a little backbone. I met this fella in an alley off
Bay Street—"

"If you breathe a word about her to anyone, I promise
I'll gut you." Nolan took a step around the desk to shake
Wayland in the event the man thought it an idle threat.
Wayland's knowing smirk stopped him. Nolan unballed
the fist he hadn't realized he'd readied and calmly returned to the task of rolling up his map. How easily he'd
reverted to his old ways made his hands shake. "I don't
want her hurt. A soon as I get the map from her—and
I will, once she realizes her options are limited—I'm
going to move her to Boston so she can start a new life."
He hadn't intended to bring Jewel to his mother and her
entourage of Presbyterian matrons, but the idea seemed
the only way to guarantee her safety.

He turned to leave, but Wayland blocked the door. He
had a grin on his face Nolan didn't like.

"I think that's real gentlemanly of you, the way you're
taking such care with the chit. But I warn you: I think
she might have some of her sire in her. It might take
more than a little coin to get the map."

Pushing past Wayland would be effortless, but Nolan
wasn't about to start physically bullying his crew. He
didn't have to. His authority came from respect, honor

and a common goal. Yet those things had no meaning for John Wayland. Maybe that was why Nolan had the strong desire to wipe the smirk off the pirate's face with something he did understand—violence.

Yet the man was right: Jewel wanted more than money. Not unlike other women her age, she aimed to boost herself from her circumstances. Of course, in Jewel's case an honorable proposition wasn't likely, even if she did claim to have a suitor. She'd apparently shunned the idea of marriage for another romantic delusion regarding buried treasures and pirates. Though Nolan could understand the misconception easily enough—he'd been snared in the same way when he'd first found his grandfather's map—he'd not let Jewel be devastated by her own illusions. And the surest way to accomplish that was to take the map from her once and for all. Not that she'd thank him for it.

He jerked his head up, reminding himself a second time that he didn't want her gratitude. Wayland propped himself against the closed portal, apparently enraptured with the sight of his turmoil. Unable to tolerate the mangled pirate's knowing smirk, Nolan shoved past him to escape the small cabin and his own thoughts.

He took a deep breath when he reached the main deck. The sound of sails rippling in the wind invigorated him. A breeze lifted his hair and cooled the back of his neck. He tamped down his temper, but the effect was short-lived.

Wayland dogged his heels. "Hey, lad, if you show the girl what you're made of, you'll get her where you want her. Young girls like a *firm hand*." He winked, as if Nolan didn't immediately get a clear picture of his meaning.

"Mr. Wayland, you will address me as Captain Kenton. If you want me to show you what I'm made of, I'll be glad to keelhaul you once we're at sea. Right now

39

we're all rather busy." Nolan gritted his teeth. "See to your duties."

"Aye, Captain—but I suspect you're going to have your hands full once we set sail."

Nolan didn't stop Wayland when the man strolled to the bow and found a comfortable position to sun himself instead of helping haul up sails. Though many of his crew were inexperienced seamen, a trait Nolan had overlooked, he would rather perform the physical labor himself than tolerate the pirate's presence. Teaching his eager crew all they needed to know would be easier than finding experienced seamen who'd never given in to the lure of smuggling or piracy at least once or twice. Not that it wasn't possible, just not probable.

As the *Integrity* reached the open sea, Nolan's troubled thoughts faded. Under the task of helping his crew learn the ropes, even the slow going due to the men's inexperience didn't detract from Nolan's pleasure at being under a rippling sail and fighting a changing wind. His happiness proved short-lived, however, when a British man-of-war on their starboard easily overtook them.

A speaking trumpet was used by the captain of the *Neptune* with a request to come aboard. Nolan took it for what it was: a command rather than a request. Considering the skill of his crew, outmaneuvering the British was not an option. Besides, tension ran high since Lexington and Concord. Any further resistance shown by Colonials was likely to ignite an incident. Though Nolan was anxious for war, he didn't want to be the fuse that set it off.

The Second Continental Congress had recently convened and provisions for an army would be one of its main topics. In a meeting with the Sons of Liberty before he'd departed to retrieve the map, Nolan agreed that restraint would be best until the more conservative colonies could be brought into the line of thinking of the more radical Massachusetts. Many held out hope for a peaceful reconciliation with England while others, like Nolan, already realized an armed conflict was the only solution.

Wayland marched up to Nolan, distracting him from his study of the *Neptune*. Even if he had not been persuaded to refrain from open hostility, the firepower of the British vessel would have dissuaded him from taking them on. The man-of-war outgunned him thirty-six cannons to eighteen.

"What the hell ye be doing? I woke up from me nap to find a warship cuddled up next to us. Man your cannons, boy," yelled Wayland directly into Nolan's ear.

Nolan rubbed the offended appendage but remained calm. "This is a peaceful boarding, not a battle."

"What was all that talk of freedom and war about? You ain't going to get what you want if you roll over and show your belly."

That Nolan somewhat agreed didn't help his mood. "Once all the colonies agree that armed conflict is the only way to solve our grievances with England, I'll be more than willing to act. For now, we keep the peace as much as we are able."

"You're a disgrace to your grandfather. I can tell you that." Wayland shook his head and stomped off. Nolan could only pray he intended to go below to avoid the British.

A rope ladder was tossed to the waterline, and Nolan stood with hands clasped behind his back while he submitted to several burly sailors heaving themselves over his ship's side. An instinct from his old life urged him to reach for his sword, but all he had strapped to his waist now was a sharp knife used for cutting rigging in emergencies. When he'd sailed with Bellamy, they'd never let another crew board their vessel. Now, regular seamen hauled their superior officer, a bloated, blue-coated lieutenant, onto the deck.

Lieutenant Greeley swung his jaundiced gaze in Nolan's direction, and Nolan knew this to be the first true test of his reformed nature. He would not order Greeley cut down. He took consolation in the fact that the marine officer, Devlin, had not joined this particular boarding party. Not that that was likely, since marines were only used for land missions.

Nolan mustered every last shred of self-control he had and met Greeley's hostile recognition with a placid gaze. More important than proving to himself how much he had changed, staying calm and conciliatory was good common sense. The British warship out-gunned them. A battle would be a massacre. Even still, a pirate would rather die than submit to this type of authority.

"Captain, is it?" Greeley buttoned his blue coat over the bulge in his middle and looked down his bulbous nose at Nolan—quite a feat, considering Nolan stood a head above him. Apparently that was all the acknowledgment Greeley thought he deserved. "Very well. Call your crew on deck. Let's see what you have."

"I'll see your press warrant, sir." Nolan almost convinced even himself with his bland tone that being ordered about didn't bother him.

"But of course, Captain." Lieutenant Greeley made a show of reaching in his pocket and gallantly handing over the papers. "Can you read, or shall I read them for you?"

"That won't be necessary." Nolan quickly scanned the document, then instructed Parker to assemble the crew.

Greeley spoke up. "I'll send my men to assist your crewman. Once our arrival is made known, sailors have a way of becoming scarce."

One particular member of his crew whom Nolan wished would hide appeared. He snatched the document from Nolan's hand. "Let me see that." Wayland stared hard at the press warrant with his good eye.

Nolan suspected the flowing script was unintelligible to Wayland, because Wayland's brown eye bobbed up and down instead of left to right.

"By what right be you stealing our crew? You pudding-eating lads ain't at war with Spain again? If so, I might be joining ya. Got a debt I'm owing to a Spaniard." Wayland leered at Lieutenant Greeley with his ice-blue eye.

Greeley stepped back. "What's the meaning of this, Captain?"

Nolan retrieved the press warrant from Wayland. "That's what we would like to know, Lieutenant." Since Wayland had raised the subject, Nolan might as well know if, indeed, the British had declared war on her rebellious colonies.

"You've no right to question the king's emissary, young man. You colonists need to learn your place. Too many fine English lads have died defending your land, and now it's time you contribute to our efforts."

Nolan lifted his gaze, pinning Greeley with a direct stare. "I thought we were all English. Are you saying otherwise? If that's the case, your warrant isn't valid. It only calls for the taking of English citizens."

"I'm in no mood to mince words with you, Captain." Greeley's face reddened.

Nolan stepped closer, towering over the lieutenant. If he could use his intellect to sail away without losing a man, it would be worth angering Greeley. Many of the men Nolan had known as a pirate had started their careers at sea as impressed sailors in the Royal Navy. The harsh discipline and endless hours of grueling work had prompted many to throw their fate in with the Brethren—when they could escape with their lives, that was.

The crew lined up on deck, and Nolan realized he

could not afford to lose a man among them. He reread the press warrant, looking for a way to outwit its authority. A clause stated the *Neptune* could only impress crew from ships returning to port, not ships leaving port. Nolan smiled, tasting success. The sound of a scuffle broke his concentration.

"This one was hiding in the galley, Lieutenant. He must be something special, because I can't see any other reason he'd think he'd be worth taking."

Nolan glanced over his shoulder. One of the British seamen dragged a puny boy on deck, who struggled between keeping on his rumpled hat and evading the tug of his captor. Whoever the boy was, he wasn't one of Nolan's crew members. Nolan directed a silent question to Parker, who shrugged.

All eyes turned to the struggling adolescent. When the British crewman released his captive, the boy straightened his clothes and yanked his mutilated tricorn down past his eyebrows.

Lieutenant Greeley sauntered toward the new arrival. "Who have we here?"

A stowaway. The words were on the tip of Nolan's tongue before he swallowed his response, recognizing the straight nose and soft mouth underneath the hat. Jewel's mouth, her lower lip ripe and full, haunted him in his waking dreams.

Lieutenant Greeley visibly examined Jewel. "What's your name, sailor?"

Thankfully, Jewel kept her head down. She coughed into her hand. "Joe, sir."

Lieutenant Greeley stepped back, covering his nose and mouth with a lace handkerchief he yanked from his sleeve. Disease ran rampant on sailing vessels and could wipe out an entire crew. Though Greeley's extreme reaction was a bit much. The man was probably something of a hypochondriac, which seemed to work to their advantage. To Nolan's relief, he appeared to have lost some of his initial interest.

"Why were you hiding?" he mumbled into his handkerchief.

Nolan moved between them. "He was afraid. Can't you see he's only a boy? He's my nephew."

Jewel's head jerked up. Her glance swung to Nolan, eyes slightly wide. Though she quickly realized that she'd given something away by her reaction to Nolan's words, the sweep of her lashes as she lowered her conspiratorial gaze caused more damage. The gesture was about the most feminine thing she could have done.

Before Nolan knew what Greeley intended, the lieutenant sidestepped Nolan and whisked off Jewel's hat. A torrent of coffee-colored hair spilled down her back.

"He's a she. Nephew, indeed! Your behavior is deplorable, Captain, but I expect nothing less from you uncivilized Colonials. No wonder you were having such fits that Devlin might snatch away your little bedwarmer."

"Take who you want and get off my ship." Nolan directed his heated words to Greeley, but his fierce stare centered on Jewel.

"It can't be soon enough, I assure you." The lieutenant strolled before Nolan's crew, examining each man as if he were buying a horse. Nolan was surprised he didn't look at their teeth.

Nolan finally pulled his gaze away from Jewel to look for an accomplice. She hadn't gotten onto the ship alone. Wayland shielded his eyes and studied the cloudless sky. Nolan didn't doubt he was the one. Parker's questioning stare captured Nolan's attention. His lieutenant's usual open admiration was clouded. Nolan shook his head, warning Parker not to ask for an explanation.

Greeley paused in front of Parker. "I'll take him."

Nolan stomped over. "No, you won't. He's my only officer."

"Officer? Is this a military vessel? Perhaps we should have a closer look at your cargo." Lieutenant Greeley smiled evilly.

"That won't be necessary." The last thing he needed was for Greeley to discover the only cargo they carried was ammunition. Not that Nolan wouldn't like to see the smirk disappear from the fat man's face when he discovered just how much firepower they had, but the British would still overpower them. "Take Mr. Tyrell if you must, but since he's second in command and it's obvious I'm shorthanded, I insist you replace him with a man of equal skill. Maybe yourself? Are you a second or third lieutenant, Greeley?"

The man caved in. "Very well, then. No need for that. We can't spare any of our lieutenants, and since you're so clever and want to trade, we'll just take some of your able-bodied men and replace them with our own."

Lieutenant Greeley picked ten hardy members of Nolan's crew whom he had earmarked for gunners. Greeley gave Wayland a wide birth, despite the man trailing his every move. Nolan spared another glance at Jewel. Her cheeks flushed and her eyes glittered as she watched. She looked to be enjoying everything.

He tamped down his annoyance. If it weren't for her untimely appearance, Nolan might have gained the upper hand with Greeley and not lost ten healthy crewmen. No doubt the men Greeley would trade would be lame or enfeebled.

After the entourage of British left the *Integrity* with Nolan's strongest crew members in tow, Nolan turned to Jewel, and for the first time in his life had to restrain himself from beating a woman. She caught his gaze and had the good sense to look at her feet. She jammed her hat back on her head.

"Mr. Tyrell, see to the transfer of men. I need to speak to my *nephew* in private."

Parker hesitated. He glanced at Jewel, then back to Nolan. The man was owed an explanation, but Nolan would be damned if he were going to give it.

His lieutenant nodded, his displeasure obvious. "Aye, Captain."

Nolan suppressed the urge to grab Jewel by the arm and yank her to his cabin. Instead, he steadily walked across the deck and stopped in front or her. She looked up with wide, innocent eyes.

"Follow me," he said, using a threatening tone he'd never normally use with a woman.

She visibly shrank and glanced at the faces around her, apparently for support. A low rumbling of disapproval vibrated from Nolan's crew. Nolan cursed under his breath. Were these good men worrying how he would treat a woman? He glanced at Wayland, who watched the interaction with amusement. Maybe the pirate would be better at handling Bellamy's daughter. The man would likely scare her, which she could use. Nolan certainly hadn't had much success with her. And he wasn't about to admit he didn't trust himself alone with the chit.

"Mr. Wayland, accompany our guest."

Nolan felt more than heard the collective sigh when he gave his command. What the hell did they think he was going to do to her? And how would the presence of an old pirate mitigate that? Never mind. Imagining that would do him no good. He stormed across the deck, not bothering to see whether Wayland or Jewel followed. God help them if they didn't.

Chapter Four

Nolan's angry stride had him at the companionway before Jewel's fear-tensed muscles could start working again. Never could she remember anyone being quite so angry with her, and the fact that she somewhat deserved his fury didn't help matters. His crisp blue jacket and polished boots belied the decidedly uncivilized promise of retribution she saw in his gaze. Nolan disappeared belowdeck without a backward glance, prompting Jewel to quickly follow.

Wayland's firm grip on the back of her jacket stopped her in mid-step. "Take your time, Joe."

"My name's not Joe, but I guess you already know that." Jewel took off her hat and ran her hand through her hair. His appearance no longer caused her to gasp and, at the moment, was almost welcoming. If he hadn't been kind enough to ask her where she was going when she'd become disoriented at Charles Town's huge wharf, she might never have found Nolan's ship. "We should follow him. No need to make him any angrier than he already is."

Wayland hooked his arm through hers. "I think the lad will appreciate a moment to collect his thoughts."

Instead of pulling away, Jewel welcomed his support. In reality, she wasn't nearly as ready to face Nolan as she confessed. "Are you angry with me for lying to you?"

The kind crinkling around his mismatched eyes soothed her, even accompanied by his broken-toothed smile. At least he was friendly.

"I knew you was a girl. I thought our captain could use a female on board to soften him up a bit. You can see I was right. He might not be so cranky if he had some womanly company."

"He wasn't too pleased to see me." Jewel understood the implications behind Wayland's words but didn't fear Nolan had any such inclinations. The man acted as if he had no human emotions beyond rage, and even the full-blown intensity of that had been a surprise. On his visit to the Quail and Queen, he'd treated her with a chilly respect that invited only distance.

Following Wayland, Jewel climbed down the ladder leading into the ship's shadowy hull. He waited at the bottom. "You know how to smooth a man's rough edges, don't you, lass?"

"As a matter of fact I do." No matter Nolan's justified anger at her deception, Jewel had the map. She'd do well not to forget that during their conversation.

Wayland grabbed her shoulders, directing her down the darkened corridor. "That's my girl. You give old Nolan hell."

Too soon, they stopped in front of a cabin door that Wayland opened without knocking. Nolan swung around like an animal poised for a fight, filling every inch of the tiny room with his bulk. Jewel froze in the doorway. Wayland shoved her inside the airless cabin, then followed, closing the door behind him. With his body blocking the exit, Jewel felt trapped.

"What in the hell are you doing on my ship?" Nolan's blue eyes burned.

Jewel resisted the urge to flee only because Wayland stood behind her. She forced herself to meet Nolan's gaze and reminded herself that he had come to her first. If he wanted the map, she came with it. "I'm sorry for the trouble with the British, but I'm here now." She stopped herself from saying *with the map*, not sure she could trust Wayland. "I think we should just forget about how I got on your ship and proceed with the arrangement we discussed at the tavern."

"I told you that was impossible," he snapped. He paused to tuck a strand of hair that had come loose from the tie behind his ear and took a deep breath. His eyes lost some of their fury, but Jewel still felt breathless. How much easier it would be if they were on the same side.

"Nothing's impossible, Nolan. You appeared in my life when I'd almost believed otherwise. I'll not return to Charles Town. There's nothing for me there." Jewel thought she saw compassion in Nolan's expressive eyes, and her stomach clenched as she braced herself for pity. She lifted her chin and squared her shoulders. "I'm not asking for special treatment. Just what's fair."

He leaned on the desk behind him, putting as much space between them as possible in the tight quarters. His fingers curled around the desk's wooden top.

"Jewel"—he said her name with more gentleness than she'd thought him capable of—"I do understand how hard it's been for you in Charles Town. I'll pay you for the map and I'll take you to Boston. You can start a new life."

"Working at the tavern's all I know. Let me have this adventure." Jewel glanced away, finding it impossible to hold his gaze. The cabin's tight space seemed to shrink. A sensation like the atmosphere before a thunderstorm forced the hair on her arms to prickle when she looked into Nolan's eyes.

He stared at her, unblinking. "No one will make you marry a man you don't want. I can promise you that."

For the briefest moment, his words left her too stunned to respond. Though he offered an option she was unwilling to take, not often had she received so much consideration. "It's not that simple. Women are expected to do things for their honor, their security. We don't have the same choices men do."

Nolan lifted his chin slightly, studying her. "You'll have choices. I'll see to that."

Jewel wanted to believe him, but she didn't see how he could change the past, give her a name and a family when she had none. Though he had championed her in the tavern, he couldn't always be at her side. Now was the time for her to champion herself.

Wayland rested his hand on her shoulder. She jumped, having forgotten anyone else was in the small cabin.

"Ye see, lad," Wayland said. "Ye owe it to the girl to help her make a new life, seeing as how ye . . ."

One glance told her why Wayland ended his sentence so abruptly. Cold fury showed in the gaze Nolan directed over her head.

Wayland didn't seem put off. Jewel heard a smug smile in his voice. ". . . Seeing how you both want the same thing: to find the treasure. And since the chit has the map, ye should help each other. I think Bellamy would have liked that."

Jewel turned abruptly, her surprise that Wayland knew she had the map obliterated by his second revelation. "You knew my father?"

Wayland nodded. "He was my best and oldest friend. A finer man there never was."

51

Nolan's voice chilled the warm exchange. "Since you two have become such fast friends, Wayland can help you find your way in Boston."

Wayland stepped in front of her. "Sorry, lad. I mean to help you find the treasure."

Nolan unfolded from his leaning position. His broad shoulders seemed to grow. "Sorry, old man—you disobeyed a direct order. I told you to leave the girl to me, and you went ahead and smuggled her on board."

"I'm not some helpless piece of cargo. I made my own decision to find my way aboard." Jewel glanced between Nolan and Wayland. Apparently she had a new source from which to discover what exactly had happened to her father.

"And found my ship moored at a remote anchorage and hid in the pantry all on your own?" While he spoke to Jewel, Nolan glared at Wayland.

"I'm very resourceful. You'll realize that once you agree to bring me along to find the treasure." Jewel had never liked to lie but she'd have to sharpen her skills at dodging the truth if she wanted to hold her own with these two men.

"There you go. Out of the mouth of babes," said Wayland.

"Get out." Nolan took a step toward him.

"I'm not a babe." Jewel held her ground. Nolan would have to go through her to get to Wayland. "I'm a grown woman."

"That's the problem." Nolan reached past her and held the door open for Wayland to leave.

The older man winked at her. "Remember what I told you," he whispered in her ear before he strode out the door.

Nolan slammed it loud enough to make Jewel jump. He turned his gaze on her and she couldn't remember what she was about, much less anything Wayland had said.

Nolan leaned against the closed door. "Where's the map?"

Jewel laid her hand on her chest. "Right here."

Nolan's gaze dropped briefly. He pushed away from the door and went to the desk. Confined by the small space, he somehow managed to neither touch nor look at her in the process. "I'm not going to try to physically take it from you, though I could."

Jewel wished she hadn't left her sword in her hiding place or she would dispute his claim. Harvey had taught her well. Still, she doubted she could run Nolan through any more than he would hold her down and take the map from her. As angry as he was, his threats never got past the scowling stage. "I don't think you would do something like that."

Nolan faced the desk. When he turned to her again, his jaw was clenched. "Don't tempt me. Even I don't know my own depths."

Jewel ignored the meaning behind his dark scowl, afraid she'd lose her nerve. At the moment, he looked as if he were capable of anything. "I was hoping we could make a deal."

Nolan cocked his head. "Are you good at making deals? What do you usually bargain with?"

His scrutiny made her uncomfortable. She felt naked before his gaze even in her male clothing. She resisted the urge to fold her arms across her chest. "You know, Nolan, there are many sea captains, but only one map."

"You would be the loser in that bargain, Jewel, I promise you. No one else can read the map—and if they could, what's to stop them from taking the treasure from you once they find it?"

She studied him for a moment, then discarded her knee-length jacket. "Do you think all men so low?"

Nolan's gaze flicked over her. "I know human nature."

Jewel plucked at the tie of her shirt. The way he watched her unlace the garment warned her Nolan battled his own human weaknesses, and to her surprise, one of them happened to be lust for her. The fact that they were alone settled on her for the first time, along with the awareness that the tiny room held a narrow bunk on the back wall along with a desk. The cabin served as Nolan's bedroom. She tugged another inch of lacing through its eyelets while she held his gaze.

"And what of you, Nolan? Is that what you intended when you demanded I hand over the map and let you walk out of my life?" She thought to unnerve him, to somehow gain an advantage, but the way he continued to stare warned he wasn't a man easily toyed with.

"I don't make promises I don't intend to keep."

"Neither do I." Before she undid the next layer of lacing, she turned and faced the door, keeping Nolan at her back. Though her breasts were bound and she could pluck the map without showing an inch of skin below her collarbone, Nolan's stare seemed to eat through cloth. Her hands shook even as she tried to convince herself being alone with him in his cabin meant nothing.

"Jewel. No! This won't be necessary."

She quickly refastened her shirt and turned to face him. "The map. You asked for it when you shut the door." She held the paper out to him.

Nolan stared at it as if she were holding a live frog. "You were getting the map?" He glanced back up at her, and she swore he blushed. He took it without touching her fingers.

"It's all I have to bargain with. Did you expect something else?" His reaction assured her he had, and that his desire for her had unnerved him. But as she stood there, trembling and out of breath, she wasn't sure if the knowledge would help her or, be a total disaster. Apparently she would not be able to slip past Nolan's defenses without breaching her own.

He leaned over the desk with his back to her. Jewel moved behind him to get a glimpse over his shoulder. He had the map unfolded on the desk, gently smoothing out the wrinkles with his tanned fingers. Jewel marveled at the gentleness with which his big hands caressed the crinkled paper. She wondered how he would touch a woman. She both feared and anticipated finding out.

When he glanced at her over his shoulder, his gaze searched her face. "Why did you just hand this to me? We haven't made any bargain. I could just take it, and that would be the end of it."

"You said you honored your promises." Jewel blinked at this sudden change. Whatever had passed between them was tamped down just as easily as his anger. She took a deep breath, knowing she wasn't nearly as efficient as he in hiding how she felt. She pursed her lips, fearing they had been wet and parted.

"Yes, but you don't know what that promise was. Jewel, you shouldn't trust me, or anyone. Please tell me, you haven't shown this to anyone else?"

"No, I haven't shown it to anyone else. I'm not stupid." Except when it came to him, apparently.

Nolan smiled at her before turning back to the map. "I can see that." He traced the first line of the text. "It's written in Latin, so I doubt it would do many people any good if you had."

It could have been ancient Persian for all she knew. It had never bothered her before; lots of women couldn't read. But the idea of admitting it to Nolan tightened her throat with embarrassment. She wanted to be viewed as Nolan's equal.

His gaze narrowed on the map. He shook his head as if he didn't like what he saw.

"What's wrong?"

He drew a line with his finger to the sketch of an island. "I thought my Latin lessons would show me what I missed before, but it still gives directions to Gardiner's Island. Bellamy and I, as well as half the colony of New York, have already dug there."

"You must have missed something." Jewel had gazed at as many maps as she could, trying to match the sketch. The small speck of Gardiner's Island, off the coast of New York, didn't resemble the drawing on this map.

"Maybe, or . . ." He paused, as if he meant to say something more but decided against it. "Or we dug in the wrong spot. Perhaps the directions will be clearer to me this time."

"I've been studying the map every night since my father left it with me. We'll find it." Though she couldn't read the words, she had stared at the picture so many times she knew she'd recognize the location of the treasure. Jewel raised her hand to lay it on Nolan's shoulder, then quickly thought better of it. She feared a simple comforting touch between them would not be so simple.

Nolan neatly folded the map and handed it back to her. "You aren't coming with me, Jewel."

She took the map from him. He pulled away before their fingers brushed. She said, "I don't understand. Why are you giving the map back to me?"

"Because my offer from the start was to give you your share of the treasure when I find it, and to see to your safety. That means Boston. My family is there, and they can find you an honorable situation. If you don't want marriage, there are upstanding widows in need of companions." He smoothed back the dark wisps of hair that refused to stay in the black silk bow at the back of his neck.

She stared at him, unable to believe what he was suggesting. "You didn't stay in Boston. Would either of the options you're giving me appeal to you?"

"I don't dictate what society sees as proper. I know life hasn't been easy for you, considering your circumstances." He looked away for a moment, and Jewel feared he assumed those circumstances were far more compromising than they had actually been.

She squared her shoulders, unable to tolerate pity from him of all people. "I have the map, Nolan, and with it, I plan to rise above my circumstances."

"I hope you see reason by the time we reach Boston. You can take my cabin for the voyage. Here's the key. Be sure to keep it locked at night." He dropped the brass key in her hand, again without physical contact.

She briefly wished to face his rage rather than his obvious dismissal. "I'm not giving you the map, and to get me to set foot on shore you'll have to drag me kicking and screaming."

"If that's your choice," he said. His calm demeanor only increased her anger and determination to make him see reason.

"None of this is my choice! You know damn well what I would choose." Her raised voice along with a curse tossed in for good measure didn't even cause him to blink.

"Well, Boston is all I'm offering. If you wish, we can still turn around and drop you off in Charles Town. You can decide while I see to the new men." Nolan picked up the red silk scarf the map had been wrapped in and slipped it into an inside pocket of his jacket.

"My scarf. I want it back. My father gave it to me." She didn't care about the stupid thing, but if he wanted it, she didn't want Nolan to have it.

He pulled the scarf out of his pocket. He rubbed it between his fingers. "Do you mind if I keep it?"

He wanted something of hers. She raised her eyebrows. Perhaps he wasn't as detached as he appeared. "By all means, keep it if it's important to you. Unlike you, I'm reasonable." She'd show him how to negotiate.

Nolan glanced up, his blue eyes cold and unreadable. "It belonged to my grandfather. It's one of the few things my father didn't get rid of. Between that and the map, I thought you wouldn't mind parting with the lesser of the two."

"Then you must understand how I feel parting with the only thing my father ever gave me." She folded her arms over her chest.

The dullness in his eyes sparked, and his answering nod was more curt than polite. "We'll talk later."

Then he left the cabin before he lost his temper, Jewel suspected. Perhaps if she could provoke his fury again, she'd discover a weak spot in the stone fortress he'd built around himself. Anything to penetrate his detached composure.

Jewel plopped down on the bed. Her teeth clanked together, jarred by its firmness. How did Nolan sleep here? She ran her fingers over the coarse woolen blanket covering the bunk. Obviously, he felt no need for softness in his life, not even the simple comfort of a decent bed. Though the bunk devoured a good portion of the cabin, she imagined Nolan's feet still hung over the edge.

She leaned her head back on the polished curve of the ship's hull. Nolan seemed just as determined to get rid of her as she was to stay. But he had his weaknesses or he would not have given her back the map. And like him, she'd learned a thing or two of human nature over the years. She'd be taking too much of a risk if she trusted another captain to help her find the treasure. Nolan Kenton was her only choice, and she'd do anything in her power to make him see that.

Chapter Five

Nolan followed the gaze of every man on board. Jewel's appearance on deck rattled his hard-won self-control. She had taken off her jacket, rolled up her sleeves and tied her shirt at her waist, exposing slim hips and a delectable rump in close-fitting men's breeches. Her arms were spread wide, with her palms and face turned toward the sun like some pagan worshipper. The wind caught her hair, creating a dark halo, and he corrected himself: *Jewel* was the goddess, and all the gawking men on board, himself included, were the worshippers.

Before he stomped across the deck and dragged her below—his first impulse—Nolan tried to slip back into the detached, rational man he'd been when he left her cabin. The man he'd convinced himself he'd become when he put aside his orderly life to retrieve his grandfather's cursed map. Unfortunately, maintaining a sober countenance didn't come as easily in Jewel's presence as it did in his parents' household. There, each hour of the day was scheduled with moral, bland activities. Even dinner, boiled beef, boiled potatoes and boiled beets, was served with a minimum of aggravating spice. Jewel presented Nolan a steady diet of volatile, spirit-harming emotions—guilt, anger and lust. If she had turned to face him in his cabin with her shirt open and her breasts bared, he would have been eternally lost.

According to his father, the good Lord had a way of sending what a person most needed to resist. He certainly was proving that by dumping Jewel in Nolan's lap.

Jewel dragged her fingers through her tousled hair, and Parker along with several other men gaped openly. Not that she was the most classically beautiful woman any of them had ever seen, but her unconsciously sultry appeal was impossible to escape. Her hair, a muted dark brown, caught the midday sun and smoldered with hints of fire. Her angular face was softened by full lips, which at the moment curled into a secretive smile. The freckles spattering her nose suddenly seemed exotic rather than innocent. And though Nolan was spared their effect at this distance, her unusual green eyes were hypnotic.

Apart from her physical appeal, it was the way she stood, arms splayed to the heavens; the way she'd confronted the soldiers in the tavern with unwarranted yet total confidence, that chipped away at his resolve. Jewel Sanderson had a passion for life yet to be tempered by reality. Which was why she had to be expelled from his ship. Nolan would not be the one to permanently cloud her bright gaze or strain her easy smiles. If being abandoned by her father and working in a tavern hadn't done that, he and his men would not. Though his crew were all good men, hand-picked for their honesty if not their seamanship, they were still men.

"Mr. Tyrell," Nolan finally shouted. Parker took several moments to respond, and when he finally did, it was with barely disguised irritation. "Take the new men and find them something to eat. It looks like the British starved them."

Parker nodded, then returned his gaze to Jewel. Hadn't he ever seen a woman before? Not one in men's clothing, Nolan would wager. "Mr. Tyrell, you have your orders," he warned.

Parker answered without looking at him. "Aye, Captain." He rounded up the sailors. As Nolan feared, they ranged from fifteen to sixty, most being on the extremes. He doubted even a month of good meals would put any meat on their bones.

Parker had to pass Jewel on his way to the companionway, but he didn't have to veer in her direction, then pause to bow flirtatiously. Normally, the man had the utmost respect for women, and the fact that he gawked at Jewel past a point considered polite proved how much of a problem Nolan had on his hands. Whether she had or had not ventured into bartering of the sexual kind, it bothered Nolan that Parker obviously thought she had. Yet who could blame the young lieutenant, Jewel wasn't ladylike. Her bold arrival on his ship proved that.

Nolan's advance encouraged Parker to move on, the new crew members in tow. Only the lads had the audacity to continue to gape at Jewel over their shoulders.

"What a beautiful day, Nolan!" she called. "I've never been on a ship before." Her eyes drifted shut while she continued to angle her face to the sun. She sighed deeply, sensuously. "I feel so free."

Nolan stood stiffly beside her with his arms folded over his chest. He remembered how he'd first felt on the deck of a ship. How free. That was an eternity ago, and some of his bitter lessons had soured his pleasure of the sea. He felt like he'd aged fifty years in her presence. "Jewel." Keep it formal, he reminded himself. "Miss Sanderson. As a passenger on my ship, I must ask that you abide by my rules. You should call me Captain Kenton."

Jewel saluted him, gave an insubordinate grin. "Aye-aye, Captain Kenton."

Nolan frowned until he felt a new wrinkle crease his brow. His intention was not to amuse her. "Secondly, I expect you to dress appropriately."

Jewel looked down at her clothes and, surprisingly, blushed. "Sorry, I guess I forgot my coat. The weather is so splendid. The wind smells of faraway places, not like on the shore, where it stinks of brine and rotting fish. I never imagined how wonderful it would be on a ship! How did you stay on land for so long?"

Nolan crushed the small surge of pleasure he felt at having his ship introduce her to the rapture of being under sail. "You forgot your *dress*. I can't have you parading around in men's clothing."

"But I have nothing else to wear." She tugged at the ends of the shirttail she'd tied around her waist, while Nolan tried not to notice that the action stretched the thin material against her breasts.

"Then you give me no choice. I must confine you to my cabin." He swallowed hard, trying not to choke on his words. They conjured up a flood of unwanted images, all of them involving Jewel and no clothing.

"That's not fair!" She let go of her shirt and balled her hands into fists, as if she longed to take a swing at him.

He willed her to, so he could respond by carrying her to his cabin without further argument. Unfortunately, the surge of desire warned Nolan he was in dangerous territory. He clasped his hands behind his back and didn't speak until he could confidently erase any hint of emotion from his voice. "What's not fair is your stowing away on my ship and causing my men to be pressed into service by the British."

She planted her fisted hands on her hips. The wind plastered her thin white shirt to her body, clearly outlining her small, firm breasts and hardened nipples. She'd most definitely done away with their binding. "That wasn't my fault. They were going to take your men anyway."

Nolan had trouble diverting his gaze, imagining he could see the reddish-pink circles at the tip of each breast. With extreme effort, he dragged his gaze back to Jewel's face. She folded her arms over her chest and looked at him as if he were a vile letch. He felt the need to say, "I'm mere flesh and bone like any other man. Your choice of clothes is a distraction my men don't need."

She glared at him. "Well, that's good to know. I was beginning to wonder—about you being flesh and bone rather than rock, that is. And as for the other, I'll wear my jacket from now on. You better get used to me, Nolan. If you want the map, I come with it. I don't think my going with you is too much to ask, considering what I'm bringing with me."

Nolan's control slipped. "You don't have the right to ask for anything. You stole on board my ship, knowing full well I didn't want you here. From here on out you will follow my orders without discussion like every other man on board this vessel. Now go below!"

She narrowed her gaze and lowered her voice. "You might be the master of this ship, *Captain* Kenton"—she sneered the title—"but you aren't the only captain in the Colonies interested in what I have to offer. Dump me in Boston and I'll find someone to take your place within the hour."

Nolan stuffed his hands in his pockets to keep from wringing her neck. The urge to tell her that she didn't have all the pieces to the puzzle, that she didn't have the book, almost overcame him just to dissolve her confident grin. Common sense and the fact that he wasn't sure how his father's book on the occult fit in stopped him. If she were a man, brute force would be past due to end this argument. "I'm sure you'd have no problem finding a man who could satisfy your needs and his own in the process. Is that what you want?"

She didn't flinch at his deliberate crudeness. In fact, she appeared more composed than he. "Apparently, that's what you want."

"I want the bloody map, and what happens to you after that is no concern of mine. Now go below." Nolan turned and strode to the railing, before he did something he might regret. He gripped the smooth, varnished wood with enough force to turn his knuckles white. The strong winds coming off the sea managed to cool his cheeks. He took several deep breaths. When he could again see the green of the ocean and the blue of the sky without the angry red film that had clouded his vision, he glanced over his shoulder. Jewel stood anchored in the spot in which he had left her. Her hands were on her hips and her feet were braced, daring him to drag her below.

He took several more deep breaths, then slowly walked back to where she stood. If she couldn't see that he teetered on the verge of snapping, he would no longer hold himself responsible for his actions. "Miss Sanderson, please go below."

She took a step back but held that new ground. Under the weight of his steady stare, her gaze finally faltered.

"I'm not giving you the map," she said almost under her breath. Then she turned abruptly and walked toward the hatchway, never giving him a backward glance.

He stood rooted to the deck. Damnation. He had been to sea for less than a month and already Jewel would force him to sink lower than he had ever wanted to go.

* * *

The brass handle turned without a catch. Nolan cursed silently. He'd told her to lock the damned door. Bloody hell, since meeting Jewel again he was swearing like a sailor and thinking like a pirate. Outwardly, he might still appear the decorous privateer captain, but inside he knew he was slipping back to his old ways. He had to get Jewel off his ship even if it meant using the pirate still lurking in his soul to do it.

He tucked the metal file he had brought to pick the lock in the waistband of his breeches. In the sleepy hours between midnight and dawn, he allowed himself to go without a coat, rolling up his shirtsleeves against the balmy southern nights. The gentle creak of the riggings blended with the faint sound of wind and wave. A calm night afloat could rock a grown man to sleep like a newborn baby. Surely it would lull one overconfident troublemaker into slumber.

Nolan hovered in the shadows at the entrance of the dark cabin until his vision adjusted. Moonlight filtered through the portholes like water poured from a pitcher, creating a blue-black halo around the bunk where Jewel slept. The night was exceptionally warm. Bedclothes lay tangled around her feet. To his relief, she was dressed in the same clothes she'd worn when he saw her last. Stealing the map from her was bad enough; he hadn't planned on playing the voyeur by gawking at her in the nude. But that didn't stop a small seed of unwanted disappointment from sprouting in the center of his chest. He tore his gaze from Jewel and headed for the desk.

She would have hidden the map someplace unusual. He knew enough about her to realize conventional wisdom eluded her. He turned away from the desk. With the excuse that it was only part of the task at hand, he stared down at Jewel. He kneeled and listened to her deep, relaxed breaths. He could not recall the last time he'd slept so peacefully.

Yes, he could. It must have been his fifteenth summer. He had been part of Bellamy's crew for almost a year. That was the point when the gilt wore off, revealing the jagged metal edges of the life he had chosen. That was the year Bellamy stopped cajoling him like a boy and started treating him like a man, and in doing so expected him to do manly things. Expected him to give up boyish lusts for treasure and adventure and to take up adult lusts for women, greed and glory. Adventure became synonymous with bloodshed, preferably someone else's.

That was also the year he'd lost his virginity to a Spanish whore on Tortuga—and his map to Bellamy Leggett. Bellamy had hoped Nolan would be so thrilled with the experience of losing himself in the warmth of a woman, he would be concerned with nothing else. For a while, Bellamy had thought right, but then Nolan had come up for air and realized he'd been betrayed. Trying to get the map back from Bellamy spawned their first battle. A few broken ribs, a black eye and a stab wound to the thigh later, Nolan understood his predicament.

Bellamy was stronger, wiser and a hell of a lot meaner than Nolan. The years dragged on, but nothing was ever the same. Not that he hadn't fornicated, drunk and looted his share during those years, but any pleasure he reaped was tainted by an aching guilt. Nolan knew the difference between right and wrong with the clarity of an adult rather than the besotted eyes of a child. His justification that the world was unfair because his father wanted him to be a clergyman rather than a sailor no longer held.

The point came when even Nolan could no longer deny the dark streak that curled inside him: a trait inherited from his grandfather, and one his father had tried to squash with everything from forced hours of solitary prayer to beatings. Finally, the ache of remorse grew so strong that Nolan would have cut out his own heart to banish it. Instead, he defeated his mentor and Jewel's father. And this woman had provoked the surge of self-righteous power that made that possible.

Nolan studied Jewel, surprised at how much younger she appeared in sleep. She'd stirred a longing in him those years ago, from the moment he and Bellamy had first walked into the Quail and Queen past the supper hour. The tavern catered to wealthy planters and merchants rather than cutthroats and thieves, but Bellamy always liked to rub elbows with his betters just to prove to himself and everyone else that there was no such thing. Jewel had taken their order, drawn to them without having to be called over, while the other barmaids and patrons stared warily. Even then, her eyes had glowed with the excitement of serving the two strangers. She'd laughed easily, and Nolan felt tongue-tied in her presence. Though he'd had vast experience with women at that point, never with one that couldn't be purchased.

Bellamy had enjoyed the encounter, had even encouraged Nolan to try to get her alone, but Nolan knew even then that he'd not taint anything he cared about in such a way. When Bellamy asked her to meet them later, Nolan had insisted they step outside. It was his first serious challenge to Bellamy's authority. That he'd discovered Jewel was Bellamy's daughter only increased his need to keep her from the life and man he knew. After everything, he didn't regret his choice—though she'd never understand.

With her dark lashes flush against her cheeks and her lips slightly parted in sleep, he found it momentarily difficult to remember her as anything other than a girl in dire need of protection. And despite the determined, headstrong woman he'd encountered today, he must see his mission through. The urge to touch her stretched to his fingertips, but he resisted. He was here for one reason only.

Taking the map from her was necessary to ensure her safety. She would try to find someone else to help her, and Nolan knew only too well the way most pirates treated women. They wouldn't bargain for her prizes. They would brutally take her and her map and her smiles. She wouldn't laugh so easily after that. He doubted she would laugh at all.

Nolan once had seen a member of Bellamy's crew brutally rape a women on the deck of a captured ship. Though he'd only been a little over fourteen, he'd tried to stop it, but a few of the others wanted their turn and easily overpowered him. Though Bellamy had been elsewhere at the time, at least he took his conquests below-deck. His claim to Nolan as protégé must have been what prevented the men from killing him. Later, after Bellamy let Nolan out of the barrel they'd stuffed him into, the woman had been nowhere to be found. Nolan never had the guts to ask what had happened to her, though of course he knew. They'd no doubt dumped her body overboard, whether she had succumbed to death yet or not.

Nothing like that would befall Jewel, and Nolan would do what he had to, honorable or not, to make certain of that.

She shifted, her face turning toward him. Nolan sat back on his heels, expecting her to wake. What would she do if she found him gawking at her? Probably smile at him with her confident grin, letting him know she had him right where she wanted him.

Her change in position revealed the sheathed sword at her side. Sleeping with a weapon didn't do a hell of a lot of good if one slept like a rock. Nolan had learned to sleep with a knife, but by then it was too late. Bellamy already had the map.

Nolan got to his knees. Since she slept with the blade, he'd wager the map was on her person or in the bed. Her pale, bare feet reflected the moonlight. Her slender ankles appeared dusted with pearls. Nolan forced his gaze away and ruled out boots as a hiding place. Guilt crept up on him. Pilfering the map from her was akin to kicking the cane from beneath an old man. If Bellamy had had a conscience, he might have felt the same way when he'd sent Nolan to gorge himself on Tortuga's decadence.

Jewel wouldn't understand any more than Nolan did, but that was just as well. Better to keep her at a distance. Nolan looked her over once more, not knowing where to start. He rubbed his palms against his cloth-covered thighs, wiping away the urge to touch her. With his thumb and index finger, he lifted the tail of her shirt, brushing her skin no more than a smithy would touch a burning piece of iron. He dipped his head to take a quick look underneath.

He swallowed hard. Her breasts were dark slopes, soft curves with hidden secrets. Slowly, he lowered the shirt, then remembered he'd forgotten to look for the map. He shook off the wave of lust tightening his loins. It was a natural response. He was a man in his prime and he hadn't had a woman in five years. God, had it been that long? No wonder Jewel made him crazy.

He glanced under her shirt again. This time he avoided the sight of her breasts and was rewarded by a hint of white cloth sticking out from her waistband. Was it a reward or a punishment? Being forced to unfasten her breeches to get the map would definitely be torture. He worked a worn button through its hole, then gingerly folded over the flap to reveal the map bound to her lower abdomen by a cloth wound around her hips. Even if he had the will to continue, which he realized he didn't, he couldn't pull the map out without waking her.

He sat back on his heels. This wasn't going to work. Of course, he could just physically take the map from her even if she did wake, but he didn't want to do that. Though sneaking into her room and stealing it while she slept wasn't all that much better.

Nolan leaned over Jewel to study her face. She smelled of fragrant soap that brought to mind white flowers. Magnolias. He remembered seeing the blooming trees in Charles Town. Their thickly sweet scent choked the air. He leaned closer. Breathed deeply. He could almost taste the sweet fragrance on her skin.

Nolan swiped his hand over his mouth. The desire to press his lips to her skin overcame him like a summer squall—dark, heavy and violent. Suddenly, his lust for the map paled in comparison. The salt, wind and fresh air had weathered his hard-won control over his baser instincts. He sat back on his heels, closed his eyes and forced himself back into the man he'd trained himself to be.

When he felt a brush against his cheek, he started violently, almost falling on his backside.

Jewel propped herself up on one elbow. Confusion clouded her eyes. "What's wrong?" That suspicion, or even fear, wasn't her first reaction proved she wasn't nearly as prepared to be the lone woman on a ship full of men as she thought. The flap of her breeches fell forward, finally gaining her attention. She touched the bindings with a frown. "I never suspected you would sink that low."

Nolan got off his knees. He should leave the cabin immediately, but the challenge and accusation in her eyes forced him to stay. She had no idea of the man she was dealing with, and at the moment neither did he. He sat on the side of the bed, forced her back down and braced his hands on either side of her. "I warned you:

70

even I don't know my limits." He bent his head and kissed her.

The first, soft brush of her lips against his brought a rush of forbidden pleasure that shoved away the small voice in the back of his head that railed against this.

She inhaled sharply. Probably from the same shock that pounded in Nolan's chest. He hovered above her, only touching her mouth with his, but that was enough. Her lips remained pliant and responsive to his gentle pressure. One taste, one brush of his tongue against her lips and he'd stop, leave the cabin. She met his second graze by pressing into him and brushing her tongue shyly with his. His body reacted with a surge of lust as strong as if she had taken him in the palm of her hand. He abruptly pushed off the bunk and surged to his feet. After he took a step back, he stared down at her, his heart pounding hard in reaction to the contact.

She gazed at him with luminous eyes and a wet mouth. He thought of Bellamy, promises he had made to himself, the impending revolution, anything to take his mind off continuing what he had began. Jewel remained uncharacteristically silent. Nolan warred between believing it was because she was too shocked by his actions and that she wanted him to continue. He took another step toward the door and away from convincing himself that a quick coupling would do them both good. He'd certainly feel better, at least in the short run, and perhaps afterward she'd give him the map and forget about finding another captain to take his place.

Nolan shook his head to dislodge his dangerous thoughts. Apparently, his struggle to be a changed man, the son his parents had wanted, a man society could tolerate, was far from complete. He reached the door and gripped the handle. "There are much more valuable things inside your breeches than the map. Next time I'll take it all."

He exited the room as quietly as he'd come. Outside the portal, Nolan paused to catch his breath like a man who had just escaped a fatal accident. Yes, he'd slipped off a precarious beam, but he'd caught himself. What twisted fate was in store for him with Jewel? Nolan dismissed the thought, fearing he already knew.

Chapter Six

Jewel chose the jade-green dress woven with a pattern of small white roses to wear for her meeting with Nolan. Opening the bundles Parker had delivered to her on their return from going ashore in Newport had been one of the happiest moments of her life. Never had she imagined possessing such finery. Even her fantasies of finding Captain Kent's treasure had not equaled the reality of running her hand over such silk brocade gowns. To see herself in Nolan's small shaving mirror she'd been forced to stand on the bunk, but even that glimpse assured her the gown's effect was transforming. Even her freckles appeared less glaring.

Of the two dresses, the green one was her favorite. She lingered outside the galley where Nolan waited, hating that the pleasure of the clothes would immediately be ruined by her and Nolan's biggest battle yet.

Even though she feared the gowns were purchased for the sole purpose of her imminent departure from the ship, she couldn't help but be thrilled with the quality and thoughtfulness of his purchases. No one had ever given her so lovely, or extravagant a gift. Or any gift, for that matter. She forced herself not to think about the kiss last night, or about whether the gowns were a token of atonement or something else altogether. Nolan suddenly deciding to make her his mistress because of a stolen kiss, even as heated as it had been, seemed unlikely. The idea that he was determined to leave her in Newport was not only more likely but preferable, because that would be easier to fight—and she wouldn't have to give up the gowns.

Nolan's continued silence unnerved her almost as much as his wary gaze. Hoping to keep their encounter on a light note for once, Jewel held out the ends of her skirts and twirled. When she faced him again, she felt her cheeks flush. "Thank you, Nolan. It's the nicest I've ever had."

"You had to wear something and I was in a hurry. Glad it fits." He stuffed a piece of bread in his mouth. "Please sit. We have something important to discuss."

She tried to sit on the long bench with detached grace. If she'd thought for a moment the kiss they'd shared swayed him to change his mind about sending her away, his gruff dismissal of her pleasure indicated otherwise. He continued to eat with hardly a glance her way. Keeping her expression placid grew more difficult. But she'd walked into this galley with her heart in her eyes and been thoroughly ignored—she wouldn't show her feelings again. She could be as cool and aloof as Nolan. She had to be.

"I'm listening," she said, raising her chin with a confidence she didn't feel. She'd hardly slept at all, and her restlessness had turned to full-blown agitation after Nolan's kiss. Her heart thudded all over again, and the fact that she had the map no longer gave her confidence. He'd proved he could take it any time he wanted—and after he'd sneaked in her cabin last night, she couldn't be sure he wouldn't.

He glanced up at her briefly, then returned to scrutinizing his stew.

Jewel touched the matching green ribbon she'd used to pull back her hair. She couldn't stand his silence a moment longer, refused to be as rude as he. "Thank you for the soap. Magnolias are my favorite. How did you know?"

He stopped chewing and stared a hole through her. "The seamstress picked it out. I had her collect all the things she thought a woman would need. I assume everything is satisfactory."

"Very." Her smile faltered. Did he somehow blame her for their kiss? Was he embarrassed? She stiffened at the thought. He always tried to put on a self-righteous air, and if that notion extended to kissing the likes of her, she'd make him say so.

"Good." Furiously, he ripped another chunk of bread from his loaf.

"Why are you so angry with me?"

His blue gaze burned. "I'm not angry."

Jewel couldn't take any more. When she tried to meet his gaze, he looked away. If he intended to send her off, he should be man enough to tell her and stop dragging this tortuous encounter out any longer.

Nervously, she toyed with a strand of hair that refused to stay in the bow at the nape of her neck. Nolan watched her with his head lowered. Jewel suddenly realized he wasn't ignoring her; he was unnerved.

She sighed, wanting to bridge the gap between them but not knowing how. Obviously, their magnetism was something beyond them both. Perhaps their mutual attraction was the reason he was so determined to send her away. She reached across the table to lay her hand on his.

"Don't," he said between clenched teeth.

Jewel folded her hands in her lap. She couldn't even look at him. "I'm leaving." She stood.

"Sit down, Jewel. I have something to tell you that I think you'll like."

She sat down, but doubted he had anything to say that would make up for his hostility. *He* had kissed *her*, yet he was treating her like a beggar on the streets, someone you'd go out of your way to avoid. "The only thing I will find agreeable is if you take me with you to find the treasure."

Nolan smiled, but without a hint of pleasure. "General Gage has declared martial law in Boston. The Continental Congress has named George Washington as head of the army. I've committed a portion of the treasure to them for a letter of marque when I return, and I plan to outfit several merchant ships for war. So you see, I don't have the luxury of waiting you out. I'm stuck with you. Now let's see the map."

To her utter horror, his detached words caused her throat to tighten. She forcibly swallowed the threat of tears. "If you find me so detestable why did you kiss me?"

Nolan made a face as if he had swallowed a bug. "Ah . . . what?"

"The kiss in your cabin—in the middle of the night. Don't act as if you don't remember. Why did you do it?" Her surge of anger swept away the hurt his words had originally engendered. How dare he try to snatch the moral high ground when he'd been the one to sneak in on her while she was sleeping to steal not only the map but a kiss?

Nolan rubbed the stubble on his cheeks. "I made a mistake." He looked at her as if he were bracing himself. "Do you understand the seriousness of the situation? This isn't a social outing, Jewel. Captain Kent's treasure is rumored to be worth close to one million pounds. As it is, the Continental Congress will have to borrow money from foreign powers to finance Washington's army. If I can find the treasure quickly, it would give them some funds to work with as well as a fleet of privateers to hit the British in their pocketbooks. So I'm taking you along because you have the map—no other reason. Be happy that you're coming and stay out of the way."

Jewel stood. Her motions were stiff, but they kept her from showing Nolan how she shook. He'd never said so much to her in a single sitting and, from now on she'd prefer his silent seething. Oh, how she regretted that she hadn't slapped him last night instead of discovering why women could so easily ruin themselves over men so obviously unsuitable.

She put her foot on the bench and hiked up her skirt enough to pluck the map from her garter. She threw it at him, aiming one of its pointed corners at his eye. "Here. This is what you want. Have it. Don't let me stand in your way. Oh, and just so we understand each other—*you* kissed *me!* So please stop acting as if I'm a threat to your virtue."

Nolan juggled to catch the piece of parchment. "Jewel . . ." He got up and came around the table.

She turned and strode to the door. With her escape in sight, she stopped. She wasn't going to flee like a child. He'd no longer dictate to her like the overbearing ogre he was proving to be. "We are partners. I expect to be treated as such. You'll consult me on your plans, and I want half of the treasure that doesn't go to the Continental Congress."

Nolan shook his head. The anger slipped from his gaze, and his tone held a note of apology. "*I* don't even get half."

She stood straighter. "Then I'll take the same share

as you." She whirled to leave, then turned back just as quickly. "Not everyone on board thinks I'm in the way."

Nolan's face darkened. "Stay away from my crew."

Jewel shrugged. "Fine. But how will you keep your crew away from me?" She turned and kicked the hook holding open the door, then slammed it behind her for good measure.

She climbed the steps to the upper deck two at a time, alternately stepping over and wadding up her pretty new gown in the process. She'd throw the damn thing in his face and go back to wearing her threadbare breeches.

Above, the pitch-black sky rolled with dark clouds that only let hints of a waning moon peek through sporadically. Even the stars seemed to vanish in the swirl of the turbulent sky.

Jewel leaned over the railing and stared at the ocean: that undulating murky, fathomless shadows. The waves lapped against the hull, while the rigging overhead moaned in mournful chorus, matching Jewel's mood. Perhaps her father commiserated with her from his watery grave. Apparently, her new life wouldn't be much different than her old. Nolan didn't want her any more than her mother or Harvey. For once, she simply wanted to find a place where she belonged. Some days, she was just tired of fighting for acceptance.

Nolan's dismissal carved a painful gouge in her heart. So many years had passed since she had actually tried to be anything other than a barmaid's illegitimate daughter, unwanted and in the way, and she'd forgotten how much the cruel judgment of others could hurt. When the map was her secret alone, it proved a source of strength, a magic talisman that would garner her instant acclaim when she deigned to tell the world of its existence. Nolan had proved that wasn't so.

A tentative touch on her shoulder had her quickly hiding her melancholy expression. She turned and discovered Wayland instead of Nolan, and that brought on a new wave of despair. She'd given him far too much credit just because he'd treated her fairly regarding the map, taken the time to buy her a few nice things and made her want him with the mere brush of his lips.

"What's the matter, little girl?"

"Nothing." She forced a weak smile, hoping he'd be polite enough to accept her blatant lie. "Nolan is going to let me stay. We'll all find the treasure together."

Wayland moved to lean on the railing. "Then why the long face?"

Jewel looked down at her dress, unable to find the pleasure it had given her earlier, or the strength for pretense. "Nolan thinks I'm in the way."

To her utter surprise, Wayland drew her into a gentle hug. "There, there, chit. He don't think that."

Jewel let him hold her for a moment before tactfully disengaging. His comforting gesture touched her, but he smelled like pickled fish and smoke. She straightened the folds of her dress, actually feeling a little better. "Nolan's only taking me along because I have the map. If not for that, he'd have nothing to do with me."

Wayland lifted her chin with a crooked finger. He read her eyes. "This is the first time you ever liked a fella, isn't it?"

Jewel shrugged, intending to deny it, but the lie wouldn't get past her lips. Not that she was swept away by Nolan's charm. Hardly. Unfortunately, he'd captured her attention in a way no other man ever had. "He has his brute appeal."

"Yep, he's a special one. And complicated. Let me tell you something about Nolan. Whatever he told you, you can bet he means the opposite."

Jewel studied Wayland's face for sincerity. The time she had spent in his company this past week had her believing the rumors that he was half crazy. She heard it whispered among the men that he had the French disease, which would account for his haggard appearance. The unhappy clouds writhed and let a stray moonbeam loose upon his glass eye, which glowed with blue life, but the rest of his face looked dead. Jewel stepped back, taking it all as a bad omen. "Thank you for the advice." She yawned loudly. "But it's getting late. . . ."

Wayland grabbed her arm. Jewel tugged, but he held tightly. "Listen to me, chit. I'm counting on you to set that boy straight. He doesn't know what he wants."

Jewel nodded her head in agreement, hoping he'd let her go. Fear crept up the back of her neck. She searched the deck, but the bow proved uncharacteristically deserted. No one could see her, and the low roar of the waves would likely swallow any scream.

"Nolan says one thing, but you and I both know he's thinking something different." Wayland also scoured the area with his good eye. Sheer panic set in, and Jewel tugged on her arm, but he continued to hold on with surprising strength. "He might say he isn't interested, but how does he look at ya? With fire. I've seen it. He burns for you."

Jewel stopped her struggle, her interest in Wayland's words swiftly overriding her fear. The old sailor let go of her arm, but she didn't run away as she'd planned. What he said made sense—or maybe it was just what she wanted to hear. "Everything I do seems to push him away. I wore the dress he brought me. I thought that was what he wanted, but it only seemed to make him angry."

"Pretty dresses are for boys like Parker. Nolan's a man. He's used to women who know what they're about. You can't be flaunting your goods, then pulling them back. You have to offer him what you got, plain and simple-like."

Jewel stiffened. "Just because I worked in a tavern doesn't mean I'm a whore."

"Well, I know that. If you were, we wouldn't be having this problem, would we? Trust me. If you want Nolan"—Wayland grabbed his crotch—"you have to take him by the ballocks. Then you'll have him." He finished his demonstration by winking. As if Jewel could have possibly misunderstood.

"I have to go." She turned away.

Wayland caught her by the upper arm before she could escape. "Never touched a man's cock before, have you?"

Jewel tried to yank free. "You have to ask?" She thought of slapping him with her other hand, but his mangled countenance probably wouldn't feel it.

Wayland held fast to her arm. "Calm yourself, chit. I see you're not quite your father's daughter after all. I thought you were made of stronger stuff."

She wrenched away with a hard jerk. "I'm made of strong stuff. I'm my mother's daughter, too. I've no intention of ending up with a swollen belly and no husband around when the child comes."

Wayland grinned. "Well now, you aren't as naive as all that, are you?"

Jewel was angry with Nolan and herself and, suddenly, her precious sire. She had been too busy mourning her fatherless state to fully understand the difficult position her mother had been in until now. Nor how much his abandoning her must have hurt. "No, I guess not. I just gave a show of kindness more credit than it deserved. So that's what Nolan wants, does he? Sex."

"I never said that. Well, not only that. Nolan isn't like your father, God rest his soul. Nolan wouldn't desert you if he got you with child—just the opposite. I'm only telling you how to get him where you want him. He desires you, all right. But he'll do what *he* wants until you have him stiff and hard in your hand . . . if you know what I mean."

She understood too well. With no one to protect her in the world, men thought her easy prey. She should have known what Nolan's hungry glances and stolen kiss really meant. Yet she'd thought he'd seen more in her than just the physical. Thought he'd discovered the woman who had the strength and desire to be more than what she'd been born to, who had the cunning to help find a long-buried treasure. "If you'll excuse me, I'm going to my cabin. I've had an exhausting day."

"Now, don't get your feathers ruffled. You're a pirate's get, and that's that. Don't be putting on airs. Nolan is a pirate, too, though he doesn't want to admit it. You two belong together, and I'm just trying to help."

Wayland's comments drifted over the roars of the sea and in her ears as she stomped back to her cabin. Nolan was no better than Latimer Payne. They both thought her desperate enough to take what they offered.

Once inside the cabin, she had the urge to tear off the dress Nolan had given her and throw it overboard. The reality of her position differed greatly from her adolescent dreams. Just because she held the map to a treasure didn't mean she'd gain acceptance or respect. She didn't know what she could gain.

She carefully unlaced the dress and hung it in the wardrobe. There was no way she was going to give in and deprive herself of the joy of nice clothing. And since Nolan had provided her with the means to be an unwanted female distraction, that was exactly what he was going to get.

Chapter Seven

They reached Gardiner's Island in less than a day and a half, record time. For Nolan, it was the longest voyage of his life. He had hurt Jewel, been a complete ogre, and she was making him pay. Their confrontation in the galley had not gone at all as he planned. He'd hoped to reach a chilly truce, but when she arrived in the gown, her eyes bright with pleasure, her sensuality hit him like a blow from one of her father's fists. He had hoped by dressing her like a female, his exaggerated fantasies would be shattered when he saw her as an ordinary woman. Too late, he realized his mistake. There was nothing ordinary about Jewel.

From a distance, Gardiner's Island appeared green and lush. Pines shot from its center. The gray crystalline sand soaked up the bright rays of springtime sun, beckoning them to come ashore. Even the large rocks peeking from the gentle surf, which could have easily splintered their skiff in a storm, gleamed innocuously: a far different picture from when Nolan and Bellamy had searched the island in the dead of winter, howling wind cutting through their clothing and bending even the tallest trees. Today, the island held the promise of hidden treasure.

Despite the sun's warmth beating on his back as he rowed one of the landing party's two launches, Nolan could still feel a sharp knife of cold rolling off the water. The chill had nothing to do with the just passed winter, but with one overconfident brat. Jewel's laughter danced across the water, abrading his eardrums like metal rubbing against metal. Nolan stopped himself short of wincing visibly. Parker, who rowed the skiff that carried Jewel, threw his head back in a laughing response to her tinkling giggles.

Wayland, who was Nolan's passenger, cocked his head at the other boat. "They sure are as tight as a virgin's thighs. She ain't given me the time of day since we left Newport."

Nolan yanked the oars harder than necessary, trying to relieve his frustration while propelling his boat farther away from Parker and Jewel. Avoiding her had been one thing; being shunned by her was another. Nolan didn't like it in the least, though he suspected he deserved it. Neither had his conversation with Parker regarding Jewel gone as planned. His lieutenant readily agreed that she deserved the utmost respect while aboard their vessel. Unfortunately, Nolan feared that a slight possessiveness had leaked into his voice while he was trying to warn Parker off, giving the completely wrong impression of her status on board his ship.

"I've set the parameters of our relationship, and she respects my authority as captain," he finally said to Wayland.

Another peal of feminine laughter sounded, crawling up Nolan's spine.

Wayland glanced to the skiff that Nolan managed to keep out of his own direct line of vision, then turned back to grin at him. "Aye, Captain." Apparently satisfied that he'd been thoroughly irritating, he turned around to face the island, a menacing figurehead sure to strike fear into any evil spirits.

Blessed silence accompanied only by the breathing of the crewman behind Nolan and oars efficiently slicing through water carried them the rest of the way to the island. Nolan was the first one up, and he waded through the icy water to drag the skiff to shore. Even the hottest day couldn't take the chill from the Atlantic. He longed to make his way back to the Caribbean's warmth. Maybe then he could be himself again, instead of two people battling for control. In the old days he wouldn't have had to handle Jewel with kid gloves when he longed to touch her, skin to skin. He shook his head to clear his thoughts: It was his desire he wanted to be rid of, not his restraint.

Nolan pulled the map out of his pocket and stared at the island, its green rolling hills just past the beach. Finally having the coveted parchment in his hands was tainted by the memory of how he'd got it. He wished he'd handled the whole encounter better. Jewel had been so forceful and stubborn up to that point, he hadn't expected his harsh words to hurt. He'd seen he'd failed, though she'd struggled valiantly to hide it.

His suspicions that her brash front hid more vulnerability than she'd like to admit were confirmed. And though it was true enough that he didn't want her around, a large part of his hostility sprang from his own unwanted desires. Last night, he'd restrained himself from seeking her out to apologize. He did have feelings for Jewel, feelings he dared not explore and that were getting harder to hide. That the attraction was mutual persuaded him it was better if they avoided each other.

Nolan forced himself to focus on the map. Captain Kent's treasure had been rumored to be hidden here on Gardiner's Island since Kent's execution over half a century earlier. Many had dug looking for it, including himself and Bellamy—all fruitlessly. Nolan had spent a good portion of last night paging through his father's book of the occult and comparing it to the map, but he couldn't find any new insight. He wasn't hopeful that today's outing would be fruitful, but they had to start somewhere.

He turned back to the beach in time to see Parker carry Jewel through the surf. "Mr. Tyrell, secure your skiff before you remove your passenger."

The man glanced over his shoulder. The third crewman was dragging the longboat to shore quite capably. "Aye, Captain." He looked down at Jewel and a smile broke across his face. He deposited her on dry land, then sprinted back to help the crewman drag the boat to shore.

Nolan could feel the corner of his mouth curl into a sneer. "Mr. Tyrell, may I have a word with you?" Nolan trudged to the far side of the beach, not bothering to address the rest of the crew for fear he'd see Jewel studying him with the knowledge that his request to speak to Parker had everything to do with her.

"Yes, Captain?" said Parker, only slightly winded from jogging across the beach after him.

"I thought we cleared up any confusion regarding Miss Sanderson."

"Confusion, Captain?" Parker returned Nolan's stern gaze without the slightest show of concern. The topic had already made Nolan start to sweat.

Dragging this conversation out would be worse than being blunt, he quickly decided. "I'm aware of the fact that you ran up some exorbitant tabs at a particular brothel . . ." Nolan began. He stopped when Parker looked away.

"I see my father enlightened you." Parker's neck distinctly flushed before he turned back. "I understand that

Jewel's not available on those terms. And, as you probably know, my tastes run toward older and more experienced women."

Nolan struggled with the urge to look away, himself. He really didn't want to know about Parker's sexual preferences, nor had he intended to make Parker feel uncomfortable about them. "As long as you perform your duties well, and you do, I'm not concerned with how you choose to spend your free time. I only brought this up because I want to protect Jewel."

Parker relaxed at that and stood a little straighter at the praise. "Thank you, Captain. And you don't need to worry. I know you've already staked your claim on Jewel."

"Our relationship is strictly..." Nolan began too abruptly and couldn't finish his sentence. He had no idea how his relationship with Jewel would be classified. "I have no claim on her," he finally said.

Parker and Nolan stared at each other for another long moment while Nolan tried to impart on his knowing lieutenant something he was having trouble convincing himself.

"That's all," he finally said, sure he'd again done more harm than good. "Make sure the crew gather all the supplies from the boats."

"Aye, Captain." Parker trudged off and Nolan resisted calling him back. He should just say that he did have a claim on Jewel and be done with it. Instead, he turned away and walked across the rocky beach alone.

"Wait!" Jewel called. Nolan paused but didn't turn. She'd not spoken to him since the incident in the galley, and he couldn't imagine that she would now. Her tug on his arm convinced him she had. "Let me see the map."

Ah, it was the map she wanted. He gave her a quick, dismissive perusal over his shoulder, trying not to notice that her floral dress was cut slightly lower than the green gown had been. "I'm familiar with Gardiner's Island. I'll hold the map."

She placed her fists on her corseted waist and again Nolan wondered why he'd thought it would be a good idea to put her in feminine clothing that showed off her curves. "Oh, really? Well, I believe your last excursion to this particular island left you empty-handed. Why not let someone with a fresh eye take a look?"

Nolan handed her the map, debating whether their silent battle of wills had been better than this. The tiny blue flowers and lace around her entirely-too-plunging neckline, he decided, made her look like a sweetmeat: feminine, soft and sugary to taste. Unfortunately, her pretty package in reality was bitter—at least for Nolan.

She turned, but not before Nolan caught her smirk of satisfaction at his obvious ogling. She waved to Parker. "Parker—"

Nolan grabbed her arm. "The map is only to be seen by the two of us. No one else."

"But Parker is your lieutenant. Don't you trust him?"

"It's better to trust no one. It's safer."

Jewel lifted her chin and studied him. "Trust no one. You must live a very sad life, Nolan, but I believe I understand." She yanked her arm away. "Much more than you think."

Her sheer stubbornness he'd grown accustomed to, but her touch of venom set him back.

She studied the map for a moment, then pointed west. "That way."

Nolan hung back. His intention had been to push her away, but he could certainly do without her condemnation. He was capable of berating himself on his own. When had he gone back to Bellamy's rules? Trust no one. Never turn your back. Those simple rules had worked for him in the past. He wasn't going to let a foolhardy woman force him to question himself.

Nolan caught up to Jewel, determined not to let her take over his expedition as she'd shouldered her way into his life. "The instructions say thirty paces." He took several long strides and focused on counting instead of the way the green island reflected in her eyes. He had not realized anger would make her so beautiful. He lost track of what he was doing and had to stop.

She came up behind him. "That's seven."

He continued pacing. Had he been mistaken when he'd seen the want in her gaze after he'd kissed her? Or maybe it was just pretense all along, another plot to get him where she wanted him. If only he could convince himself his own desires were as superficial. Nolan turned sharply right and started counting as the map instructed.

Jewel caught up to him, breathing hard. "This isn't right."

His conscience forced him to stop so she could catch her breath. "It's what the map says."

"No. I mean the hills aren't right. You should be passing through a valley. See?" She held the map up for his inspection.

"The drawing isn't supposed to be accurate," he said without a glance. "That's why he marks the paces to the spot."

Jewel cocked her head, apparently irritated. "Then why didn't you find the treasure before?"

Nolan took another stride and stopped. Was that twenty-two or twenty-three? "I didn't read Latin as well as I do now. Trust me, the drawing is meant to fool fools."

Jewel grabbed his arm. "Like me? Or maybe the Latin was meant to fool pompous know-it-alls who make assumptions about people without knowing anything about them!"

Nolan dropped all pretense of trying to retrace his

steps in his mind, and turned to face her. "What the hell are you talking about?"

She glared up at him with a hostility that was slightly surprising, deserved as it might be. "You play the gentleman when it suits you, but you're no different than other men I've come across." She folded the map, tucked it in her bodice, then determinedly strode off. Her words chilled Nolan; there were many incidents in his past that she could have named as examples to prove that he was infinitely worse than other men she'd run across. But she couldn't know that, could she?

Parker trudged up the hill, and Jewel stopped just short of embracing him. Instead, she conferred with him; Parker nodded, then both glanced in Nolan's direction. Were they conspiring? She had better not be discussing the map. No matter what she was doing, seeing her and Parker together irritated Nolan beyond his ability to fake civility. Though his conversation with his lieutenant had eased his mind somewhat, Jewel was purposely trying to create a rift in his crew. He had been wrong in assuming she hadn't inherited any of her father's personality; she knew how to find a man's weak spot and strike without mercy. Her ability to shed tears didn't change that.

He turned, stomping out the rest of the map's directions. He'd memorized them last night. Never again would he take a chance of losing them. He found the spot directed by the map with no sense that he'd done right. This wasn't where Bellamy and he had dug before; he knew that much. But the vague instructions on the map didn't give him much confidence.

Parker and Jewel approached ahead of two crewmen, with Wayland dragging along farther behind. It was as if she were the queen of the island, flanked by her entourage.

"Here." Nolan pointed to the spot where he'd paced.

At the top of a low hill, the place was fairly clear of large boulders and towering pines. A forest rose in the distance, and the beach to their backs created seclusion. The two crewmen took up their shovels and started to dig.

"This is so exciting," Jewel breathed. She contained herself from jumping up and down, but her breathtaking smile at every man in their party except for Nolan and Wayland vouched for her enthusiasm.

Nolan could feel himself snarl.

The two crewmen took off their shirts when the ground proved hard and unyielding. Nolan's plan had been to take shifts; he'd been expecting sand, but the men's slow pace changed his mind. He pushed away from the tree where he'd been leaning, intending to help.

"Let's explore the island. Parker, would you mind going with me?" Jewel asked.

Nolan took off his jacket. "The hell you will. Mr. Tyrell is on duty."

"I don't think she should go off alone, Captain," Parker said. He eyed Nolan, the first time he'd ever openly questioned him.

Jewel's glare told Nolan she wasn't about to respect his wishes. "We're doing nothing but watching them dig. And though you think otherwise, I'd like to see if that hill over there looks . . ." She stopped herself before she revealed anything about the map. "I don't see why it would hurt for us to look around a little more. At the rate these men are going, it could take another hour before they're deep enough to know if the treasure is there or not."

"Thank you for being so observant. I think we all should dig." Nolan bent down and grabbed a shovel. He flung it at Parker. "Start."

Nolan rolled up his sleeves. Parker followed his lead with only a weak shrug of apology to Jewel. Nolan grabbed another shovel and started digging a few yards from where the crewmen worked. Jewel plopped down under the canopy of a large elm. Wayland sauntered over and slid his back down the trunk of the same tree. Jewel scooted away, her face averted.

Nolan glanced between the two of them with sudden insight. The distance he had put between Jewel and himself wasn't enough to warrant her hatred. Wayland had caused this change in her. Nolan was certain of it. "Wayland, get over here and start digging."

"I'm not a digger, Captain. I'll leave that to you land men." The old pirate chuckled.

Nolan stomped over with a shovel in his hand. "Start digging or say hello to your new home."

Wayland shrugged, then pushed himself to his feet. Nolan couldn't stop himself from scowling. The pirate had told Jewel something about them—something about their tainted past perhaps—and it had turned her against them both.

A chill swept over his damp skin in spite of the hot day. If Wayland had revealed the truth about her father's death, Jewel would be more than a little angry. She'd be out for blood. His blood. Nolan rammed his shovel into the rocky earth with enough force to send a jolt up his arm. Maybe she was contemplating slitting his throat in the middle of the night. Not for the first time, he had doubts about who Jewel Sanderson was. What had she said about making assumptions about a person?

Nolan had the next three hours to ponder that question. His foul mood stopped anyone from commenting when the dirt became mud; then the mud, water. The sun sunk behind a clump of pines, taking with it every last bit of warmth left over from the fiercely hot day. That the treasure was not here grew more painfully obvious with the sucking sound of each mound of wet mud they removed.

Wayland leaned on his shovel. "Hey, Nolan, you didn't say nothing about me having to take a bath. I'm not due for another month."

The other men's chuckles were cut off. Nolan didn't say anything or even look their way, but irritation rolled off him in waves. His shovel entered the earth with such force, mud splashed the length of his pants and onto his white shirt.

"Maybe we should stop until tomorrow." Jewel stood at the edge of the pit, her hands clasped in front of her as if she were praying.

Nolan planted his shovel in the mud. "Or before we drown."

The men chuckled again under their breath. At least they still had senses of humor. Nolan should have stopped the futile search long ago, but he wasn't willing to admit failure in front of Jewel. The prick of jealousy that had started this day had festered into a roaring bad mood. Giving up empty-handed made him volatile. Especially since Jewel had suggested digging elsewhere.

"We're done here." When Nolan tried to climb out, his foot slipped on the hole's wet wall. Behind him he heard a slurping splash. One of the crew had fallen flat on his back. Parker and the other crewman trudged through the muck to help him. Nolan turned to find Jewel's pale hand looming before him.

"Let me help you out." She leaned into the hole, her feet braced and her arm outstretched.

A smile crept to Nolan's face. How easy it would be to yank her in. It would ruin her dress, but hell, he'd bought the damn thing. That same damn dress had his head spinning. Nolan lost his smirk. "I wouldn't want to ruin your pretty clothes, Miss Sanderson."

Jewel straightened, then turned abruptly. Her twirling skirt whipped across Nolan's cheek. She stomped to the other side of the pit where Parker and the other crewmen

helped their fallen comrade out. She didn't glance Nolan's way again.

"You need to work on your manners. You could piss
off an ugly whore." Wayland reached down to Nolan
from the side of the pit. He hadn't even noticed the old
man getting out. With no other help likely to come his
way, Nolan took the proffered hand. Wayland pulled
with surprising strength, helping Nolan get a foothold in
the mud.

"I'm not so desperate that I need to learn them from
you." Nolan brushed off his clothing, then stopped when
he just smeared the mud around.

"You could have fooled me." Wayland shrugged,
sauntering down the hill and disappearing into the night.

Jewel stood by the large elm, a safe distance from the
mud. Nolan went to the rescue of his crew. He reached
down and pulled Parker out first. "Mr. Tyrell, I'll leave
you in charge of rescuing our crewmen and refilling the
hole. I need to chart a new course. We're done here."

He picked up an armful of shovels and trudged in the
direction they'd come without a backward glance. Let
Parker get Jewel back to the ship. He was sure they both
preferred it that way.

The rustle of skirts forced him to glance to his side.
Jewel raised her gown off the ground, taking two strides
to his one to keep up. He didn't slow his pace. If she
had any sense, which he doubted, she'd not try to talk
to him until he'd had a bath and a large tankard of ale.

"You don't want to try again tomorrow?" she asked
hesitantly.

"No." He lengthened his stride, hoping she'd take the
hint.

"At least you gave it your best try. We know now the
treasure's not here."

Nolan stopped. "Which only leaves us the rest of the
world to search. Thank you, Jewel. I feel much better."

She blinked, and her tentative smile fell. "You don't have to be so nasty."

"Maybe I'm a bit testy because I'm covered in a layer of cold mud and had to spend the day watching you preen like a princess in your crisp party frock." A vein in Nolan's forehead started to pound. He sensed he was overreacting, but he'd been wrestling with his temper all day and no longer had the energy or will to continue.

Jewel returned his angry stare with fire. "What did you expect me to do? There were more than enough of you digging. I think you reached China."

"Just think, a whole continent of men you haven't yet captured in your web. I'm sure you'd love that." Nolan picked up his pace.

Jewel was right behind him. He had to admire her tenacity. His tone alone quelled men twice her size. "Has it ever occurred to you that a man might find me interesting for reasons other that what I have to offer beneath my skirts?"

Nolan stopped abruptly. Surely she jested. "Perhaps, but Parker's not one of them. Don't let that boyish face fool you. He'll have you on your back if you give him half a chance." He could tell her about Parker's sometime reputation for whoring, but he didn't want to reveal something his lieutenant wouldn't himself. Damn it. It made him angrier that she was coming between him and his only educated crewmember—even if the man had a weakness for easy and readily available sex.

Jewel paused, obviously considering. "I'm not sure that I believe you. Even so, Parker is my friend. And right now I need one."

Nolan shifted his armful of shovels, again thankful he couldn't get his hands on her. "Fine. But be careful. And don't tell him anything."

"Trust no one. I remember." She smirked as if he were a lunatic.

"That's right, Jewel. Your father taught me well when he stole that map. He was less trustworthy than anyone."

"I don't believe you. And Wayland was wrong—you're worse than my father ever was." Jewel turned and ran back toward Parker and the others.

Nolan watched her go, battling the impulse to drop the shovels and chase after her. In the end, he let her be swallowed by the falling night.

Finding out what Wayland had told her was his first priority. He needed to know what weapons the enemy held. With Jewel armed with information regarding her father and Parker's apparent interest, he could see another mutiny in his lifetime.

After a cold, saltwater bath and a change of clothes, Nolan found Wayland sitting against a railing, his feet atop a pile of rope. A new hat pulled low covered his eyes. In fact, he wore a new coat and trousers as well. The somber dark blue wool didn't match Wayland's usual macabre style.

Nolan instantly grew suspicious. "Where did you get the clothes, Wayland?"

The man didn't budge from his relaxed position. "Won 'em off a fella. No cheating." He shifted enough to fish something from his pocket, then held out his hand. The whiteness of dice shown against his palm in the weak light cast by the scattered stars and waning moon.

Nolan snatched them away. "I'd comment on your sense of fair play, except for the fact that I don't allow gambling on this ship." He took the ivory cubes instead of checking to see if they were loaded. The sharp jolt that urged him to roll them, just once, just to see if he still had the touch, had him tossing them over the railing and into the ocean. "Who did you win them from?"

Wayland crossed and uncrossed his legs until he

found a better lounging position. "Aw, that's a shame. You should have played me for them. Like the old days."

The way the old pirate steadily stared urged Nolan to look away for fear of revealing how the idea had briefly crossed his mind. Instead, he held Wayland's gaze.

"I'm only going to ask you one more time before you follow those dice. Who'd you win the clothes from?"

Wayland grinned, as if he found Nolan's increasing irritation endlessly amusing. "You'll find out soon enough. The boy was complaining he'd have to work in his birthday suit."

Nolan kicked the man's feet off the coiled rope with the heel of his boot. "Don't take, win or steal my crew's personal possessions. They're honest working men. They've earned every meager scrap they own."

Wayland quickly regained his balance. He rested his hands on his bent knees, as relaxed as ever. "I wouldn't have had to get me a new set of clothes if you hadn't ruined mine playing in the mud."

"Well, I'm sorry to have put you out." Nolan half-apologized, partially because it was true and partially because he had something more important on his mind. "Get up. I need to talk to you."

"Got a bug up your arse?"

"Something like that, or rather a rat on my ship. He's got one blue eye and one brown."

"Spit it out." Wayland slowly rose to his feet. Though he outweighed the man by at least three stone, Nolan struggled to resist the impulse to step back. Once, he would have thought himself a fool to face a seasoned pirate without a recently honed dagger in his fist.

But Nolan held his ground, and he was satisfied when Wayland kept a cool distance between them. A quick glance around the main deck showed the scattered glow of pipes being smoked by crew who had finished their shift. The off-tune wail of a fiddler in training cut through the rhythmic crash of the waves. Nolan gestured toward the bow with a crook of his head. "It's private. A matter between two old friends."

He let Wayland precede him, not entirely trusting of their shaky truce. Even if he could control the present, Nolan couldn't change the past—and that was his biggest obstacle. The longer he thought about it, the more worried he was by Wayland's potential to poison Jewel's mind. His need to play fair had left her in control of the map. Gardiner's Island had been a wild goose chase— one that Nolan imagined wouldn't be the last. The only real clue anyone had to point them in the right direction was the map. Though he'd been disappointed the directions hadn't been clear even with his knowledge of Latin, nor with the mysterious book on the occult, he'd found out everything he could about his grandfather's voyage these last five years. Following Kent's final passage, they would surely stumble onto the right path eventually—but he wouldn't even know it if he didn't hold the map, which meant he had to hold on to Jewel.

Even at anchor, a cold wind thick with mist blew across the deserted bow. Like their expedition to find the treasure, the day had taken a bitter turn.

Wayland stepped back. "Hell, I had to get wet to get the mud off me. I don't want to do it again."

Nolan grabbed his sleeve. "What did you tell Jewel?" Alone with the man, he no longer had the restraint to act even-tempered.

Wayland jerked his arm away. "Hands off, boy! This is the best short coat I've had in years."

"You told Jewel something about me and her father. What was it?"

Wayland tugged on the bottom of his jacket. "She just thought you'd leave her once you put a babe in her belly—like Bellamy left her mother. Don't worry. I told her you wouldn't."

Nolan stepped back as if Wayland had struck him. "Why would you two be having such a conversation in the first place? I've hardly even kissed her."

Wayland smiled, looking pleased with himself. "I didn't even know you'd done that. Well, good for you. I'm proud of ya."

"Don't be. That kiss was a mistake." Nolan hesitated. He was supposed to be getting information out of Wayland, not the other way around. "What else did you tell her?"

"To stop flirting with you."

"Thank God."

"Yep. I told her just to grab your rod. That's the way to a man's heart. Always works on me."

Nolan couldn't speak. He just stared at Wayland. Surely Jewel had enough sense not to listen. If she took Wayland's advice—God, it had been five years. If she touched him like that . . .

"No need to thank me."

Nolan surged toward Wayland. "I'm about to strangle you."

The pirate ducked out of his reach. "Don't blame me if she hasn't done it yet. I did my part, and you did everything you could to turn her against you."

Nolan paused; dancing around the slippery deck to catch Wayland had somewhat dissipated his immediate need to kill. "She prefers Parker."

Wayland laughed, apparently enjoying the fact that he'd driven Nolan to the verge of violence. "Can't say I blame her. Parker's a lucky man. Wish I had a pretty girl like that to stroke my—"

"Don't say it!" Nolan pinched the bridge of his nose. An image of Parker and Jewel popped into his head. "Jewel doesn't need any of your advice. She seems to be doing just fine where Parker's concerned."

"Don't think so. She seemed pretty surprised when I told her. But you know how young girls are. All flowers and cool kisses. You have to touch them right to turn them hot."

Nolan had begun to wonder. Jewel was a mix of paradoxes. She still had a romantic bent, despite her circumstances. Just as easily as she could challenge him with the unrelenting intensity of a man, she could be reduced to tears. Obviously she was much more vulnerable than she wanted anyone to know. "She didn't take you seriously, did she?"

"I guess Mr. Tyrell's going to find out instead of you."

"Why are you doing this?" Nolan rubbed his forehead with his palm. "I've never known you to do anything that isn't self-serving."

"Getting Parker a good time wasn't my idea. I was trying to steer Jewel toward *you*."

"So you're the matchmaking pirate now? Thank you, but I don't need or want your help."

"Fine, but you better get a woman quick. If you don't blow off more than just steam soon, I'm jumping ship. You ain't easy to be around these days."

"By all means, jump ship! But until you do, keep your advice to yourself."

Not that Nolan had any illusions he'd be so lucky. Any way he saw it, he had trouble on his hands. He couldn't afford to lose either Parker or Jewel to a misunderstanding fueled by Wayland's bad advice. They were all stuck together on a ship that grew smaller every day.

Chapter Eight

Jewel sat at Nolan's desk, smoothing out the map with careful strokes. Its familiar sight comforted her. On those long nights waiting for her father to toss pebbles up at her window so they could make their great escape, she'd studied the map, dreaming of the day they would discover its treasure.

The reality of the quest was sobering. Jewel wrapped her arms around herself in a comforting hug. Her cotton nightgown provided little protection against the night's chill. After such a warm day, the change in temperature was as disillusioning as her dreams.

She managed to tuck her feet under the billowing gown. Resting her chin on her knees, she stared at the map. If only Nolan wouldn't remind her at every turn that he didn't want her along, she might be able to salvage a small part of her fantasy. Seeing a world she'd only imagined, sailing across the open seas—it had all brought a wonderful rush, but Nolan seemed to go out of his way to dampen her spirits.

Unfortunately, his blatant hostility during the long

grueling day had done little to quell her feelings for him. Jewel finally realized why her mother believed men were dangerous creatures: You never knew which one would steal your heart. And once lost, there was no guarantee the one who claimed it would know its value. Her mother had learned that lesson the hard way. Now, after running away to change her fate, Jewel found herself in the same situation.

That Nolan refused to show anything for her but a slight contempt might have finally convinced her he wasn't worth the heartache, but then Nolan had revealed his vulnerability when they failed to find the treasure. He'd tried to hide it, but Jewel could see the hurt and bitter disappointment in every line of his body. She'd watched as he futilely pushed his shovel into the hard ground, his muscular shoulders and back straining against his white shirt. And his misery ruined any pleasure she gained by getting the upper hand.

Yes, he needed her, though he'd yet to admit it to himself. Her whole heart thumped with the idea. But when she'd offered him her hand at the side of the pit, her support, he'd refused.

Jewel turned the map, studying it from every angle. Maybe if she could find the treasure's true location, Nolan would let her through the stone wall he'd built around himself. It would give him a reason to trust her. Then, he wouldn't be so alone.

The answer to the map's riddle lay in the picture, no matter what Nolan said. Jewel had doubted herself at first because she couldn't read the words. Her obsession with the picture had only seemed to emphasize her ignorance, but Nolan didn't know where the treasure was any more than she did. If the words alone revealed the treasure's location, men would have found it long ago. Captain Kent hadn't wanted to make it that easy.

Jewel unhooked the brass lantern from the ceiling and

set it on the corner of the map. She had heard rumors of Captain Kent's treachery. He was a privateer who'd grown desperate enough to turn pirate. He'd attacked a ship flying British colors and killed even his own crew members who disagreed with the treasonous act. The man was Nolan's grandfather.

Did Nolan also hide a dark side? Jewel wondered. He was so stiff, if he actually laughed or smiled he might crack. Nolan Kenton made it his business to be the exact opposite of his grandfather. Even in the long-ago fight with her father, Nolan had honorable intentions. In fact, they'd earned him a knife in his chest and a few more years as a pirate.

Perhaps she placed too much importance on the small things Nolan had done for her, but when she decided to dismiss his kindness in the face of his continued hostility, it only left her with more questions than answers. He didn't have to stand up for her against the British officer at the Quail and Queen; she had been in no real danger of harm except for her pride. And despite bringing unwanted scrutiny onto himself, Nolan refused to let the men treat her with less respect than he thought she deserved.

Also, even though he dismissed the gowns he'd purchased for her as merely a necessity, Jewel couldn't believe the quality was an accident. Something with less lace and silk would have been more practical if that was Nolan's only purpose. No doubt the seamstress had swayed Nolan's purchases, because he couldn't possibly know the details a woman would need to complete her dress, down to matching ribbons for her hair, but he hadn't said no to even the most unnecessary luxury.

Nolan had put her comfort and needs above his own even in the surrender of his cabin, when he'd made it most clear he didn't want her aboard. Though the accommodations were small and cramped, she'd come to realize they were by far the nicest on the *Integrity*. Then, it would have been easy for him to remove Parker from his cabin, but Nolan hadn't done that. He took others' comforts into consideration before his own.

Though she'd be far better off taking Nolan's less-than-charming behavior at face value, she couldn't dismiss the man that lay beneath. He'd not denied his attraction for her, and she had a hard time letting it go at merely lust.

Jewel turned the map upside-down, hoping to make more sense of it than she could Nolan. When he wanted to hide his feelings from her, he went out of his way to act opposite. If Captain Kent wanted to hide his treasure, would he make the text a picture and the picture the text?

A hard pounding on the door made Jewel jump. She knocked into the lantern she'd set on the desk with her elbow. It tipped, but she righted it before it tumbled onto the map. Wax spilled from the candle inside, spattering her hand rather than the desk.

Jewel yelped, but steadied the lantern, and blew on her injured fingers. The door banged open, and Nolan was behind her before she had the chance to turn around. He reached around her to examine her hands.

"Are you hurt?"

"I'm fine." The slight sting in her fingers paled in comparison to her body's reaction to Nolan. She could feel his heat where his thighs and chest brushed her thin nightgown. And where he held her wrists with his hands seemed to come alive with a thousand new sensations, feelings she didn't even have names for.

As if he felt it, too, and found the strange contact as disturbing as Jewel found it pleasant, he pulled away abruptly. He stepped back, putting several inches between them. But his eyes proved just as intense as his touch. She glanced down at the plain white nightgown she wore. Long-sleeved and high-collared, the gown was less revealing than either of her dresses. Still, the way Nolan stared urged her to fold her arms over her chest, and heat crept up her cheeks.

He abruptly fixed his gaze to a spot over her shoulder. "Do you want to burn my ship down to the waterline?" He reached around her, grabbed the lantern and returned it to its hook. "Everything on a ship is designed for a purpose. I expect you to follow—"

"Lecture me later. I have something to show you." Jewel focused on the map, taking his lead in pretending nothing out of the ordinary had occurred. Her heart continued to race.

He backed to the door of the cabin and leaned against it. "First, there is something important we need to discuss."

Jewel grabbed his arm and guided him back to the desk. Instead of the fight she expected, he let her lead him. A quick glance at his face showed he watched her with a heavy gaze, but sleep looked like the last thing on his mind. Wayland had been right.

She rushed on before Nolan snapped himself out of his daze and began reprimanding her or insulting her or whatever he thought would best hide his interest. "Look at the map. Doesn't the picture look like words and the words look like a drawing of an island?"

Nolan glanced at the map. "I don't know. Jewel . . ." He sighed, apparently unable to continue with what he needed to say.

She turned her back on him and stared down at the map. To hear him talk of sending her home again was more than she thought she could stand. "Hand me something to draw with and I'll show you."

Nolan retrieved an ivory parchment much too fine for her purpose and a charcoal pencil. Before he changed his mind, she placed the paper over the map. "Bring that lantern closer. You can hold it to make sure I don't start a fire."

Nolan obliged, but Jewel could tell he only did so to humor her. The more he doubted her, the surer she was. Her steadiness surprised her as she traced the outline of the text. The obvious shape of an island that appeared on the paper even gave Jewel pause. "See?"

Nolan took the paper. At first he just skimmed the paper; then something caught his attention. He turned the paper sideways and upside down. Something flickered in his eyes, and she swore he paled; the stubble of his day's growth of beard appearing black in contrast. "It's nothing. Just a shape." He handed Jewel the paper, his gaze more shuttered than usual.

"You saw something. You recognized the place. I could tell by the look on your face." She shoved the paper back at him. Nolan could be stubborn, but to ignore the evidence just because it came from her was childish.

She held out her hand until Nolan took the sketch. He stared at it again, this time with real concentration. "It reminds me of a place I've been—but the island's not been charted. You won't find it on any map."

"Perfect! That's it. Don't you see? Where else would Captain Kent hide his treasure?" Nolan's frown only made her more desperate. "We have to look there."

"Jewel, it's probably nothing. I'm imagining I'm seeing something that isn't really there."

"Well, what about this picture?" Using her index finger, Jewel traced what she thought might be letters. They were drawings, but they reminded her more of the sharp angles of text rather than an actual picture. They were too stiff to be a poor attempt at creating landscape.

Nolan leaned closer. Finally, he nodded. "You might be right." He straightened, studied her a moment, then reached past and pulled a thin, leather-bound book from the top desk drawer. "I found this with my father's things after he died. I thought it might be a clue to reading the map. What do you think?"

Jewel took the book with reverence. Nolan had breached his trust-no-one motto for her. She flipped though the pages, then glanced up at him, hoping her sincere gaze showed how much his gesture meant to her. "I wish I could help, but I can't read." She'd not try to bluff her way through the first honest moment she and Nolan had shared.

He nodded, his eyes kind, but withheld further comment. Somehow, it seemed to be the right thing to do. Finally, he merely shrugged. "Being able to read certainly didn't do me much good today. Next time . . ." He paused, as if struggling for words. "Next time, I'll take your opinions into consideration. Maybe there is something here I'm missing."

"Thank you," she said, then returned her gaze to the pages. Nolan had taken her breath away when he was barely being civil. This new behavior was devastating. In the face of his admission of failure—something she suspected didn't come easily—combined with his surprising gesture of trust, her last resistance against the pull of her heart crumbled. To protect himself, or more likely her, Nolan ensured he was a difficult man to love—which only increased Jewel's determination to do so. She loved him.

She thumbed through the book, wishing she could find something to help them. Now that Nolan was giving her a chance, she wanted to succeed more than ever. The odd symbols and characters drew her attention, though she couldn't understand any of it. Obviously, the book was some sort of catalog of languages and symbols. A page that looked vaguely familiar caused her to pause. "What's this?"

Nolan glanced over her shoulder. "Let's see. Some

kind of ancient alphabet. Runes, the author calls them. He says . . ."

Jewel swung her attention back to the map. "These letters make up the picture," she blurted out before he could decipher the faded print.

Nolan leaned over, his broad chest brushing her gown. "Good God, you *have* discovered something."

The joy in his voice warmed her almost as much as his nearness. Proving herself worthy to be on this voyage pleased Jewel almost as much as finding the map's secret. At least some of her dream was coming true as she'd imagined.

Nolan stared at the map and shook his head in disbelief. "I have to get Wayland. We used to sail by some old Nordic charts. Only the old-timers could read them. He might be able to figure out what the map says before I can decipher the book."

Nolan strode to the door, but he hesitated with his hand on the brass handle. "Jewel. Good work." To her delight, she discovered he had dimples when he smiled. "I'll be right back." He disappeared.

He stuck his head back through the portal before she had the chance to recover, and shrugged off his jacket. "Here, put this on."

"I'm not cold." Since he had entered the room, the night's chill had been staved off by excitement—and something else altogether.

He tossed her the jacket anyway. "Put it on. Please."

A smile and a please? Jewel slipped the jacket on before he closed the door. She could hear her own heart beat in the vast emptiness left by his sudden departure. But he would be back—and what really lay at the heart of Nolan Kenton was the next mystery she was determined to uncover.

* * *

Nolan practically tripped over Wayland lurking in the companionway outside Jewel's cabin. Even though the man's nearness proved convenient, being spied upon annoyed Nolan. The fact that Wayland was the one doing the snooping created an even bigger problem. Wayland couldn't be trusted any more than the sight in his ice-blue eye.

Nolan dragged the ex-pirate from a shadowed corner beside the steps leading to the main deck. "What the hell are you doing down here?"

Wayland straightened his hat and jacket as if unjustly disturbed. "Can't a man get a bit of shut-eye? The galley's crowded, and I needed a place to get out of the wind. These old bones—"

"Forget it. I need you to look at something." Nolan turned back to the cabin's closed door. He'd not get an honest answer, so it wasn't worth pursuing.

Wayland paused before the cabin's threshold. "Nolan, I've done all I can for you. From here on out, you're on your own."

Nolan pushed open the portal, then stepped aside for Wayland to enter. "I said I'd only take you along if you followed orders. Now I'm ordering you to give me your opinion on something."

Wayland shrugged. "Whatever you want, boy. I don't know how Jewel's going to take to it. Never figured you to be one of those odd fellas who needed an audience."

Nolan was starting to worry about the man and his dirty mind. Maybe Wayland did have the pox, as all the crewmen thought.

Jewel looked up when they entered. She had the jacket on as he'd asked. He didn't like the idea of another man seeing her as he had. Her heavy cotton gown hid her curves well enough, but that only made it more necessary to look. Especially since he suspected she had on nothing underneath.

She approached them, her eyes glowing. "You found him. I can't wait to hear what he says. Oh, Nolan, I'm so excited."

Nolan smiled, really smiled for the first time in a long while. They were on the verge of finding the location of the treasure. Obviously, he had been mistaken when Jewel first showed him the tracing and he had believed for a heart-stopping moment it was the same island where he had marooned Jewel's father. Fate couldn't be that twisted. The only reason he'd imagined that island's shape traced on the page was too many sleepless nights thinking of little else. Remembering Bellamy standing alone on the deserted beach, yelling for them to come back as they sailed away—that still had the power to keep Nolan tossing and turning.

Wayland stepped between him and Jewel. He looked her over, then turned back to Nolan. "Jesus, boy. You do need help. You got it half right. You're supposed to take your clothes off, but she's not supposed to wear them. What were you doing with that whore on Tortuga, anyway—throwing dice?"

Jewel gazed at Nolan, her brow furrowed. "When were you on Tortuga?"

Nolan glared at Wayland, then turned to Jewel. "It was a long time ago. It doesn't matter anymore."

He'd been a saint during the five years he was in Boston. He wasn't going to feel guilty about an event that happened in his youth. Not even when Jewel turned those wet green eyes up at him. There could never be anything between them. If he kept reminding himself, maybe the rest of his anatomy would start to believe what his head already knew.

Wayland sighed with exaggerated exasperation. "I guess it's up to you, chit, like I said it would be. First off, get rid of that coat. And that gown." He grabbed a handful of white fabric. "This makes me think of me nana, and that's nothing to get a man's co—"

"That's enough," interrupted Nolan.

Jewel grabbed the fabric of her gown and yanked it from Wayland's grasp. She shoved past him. "Nolan, what's he talking about? I thought you said he could help us."

Wayland rubbed his chin. "This is worse than I thought. Have either one of you ever spent any time on a farm?"

Nolan put himself between them. "If I intended to seduce her, I wouldn't require your help," he snapped.

Wayland crossed his arms. "If you think you can do it; I'd like to see it!"

Jewel mimicked Wayland. "Me, too. All you've ever done was give me the sharp edge of your tongue. I'd like to see you woo a girl."

Nolan stared at her as if Wayland weren't in the room. "I said seduce, not woo. There's a difference, and I hope for your sake you know it." He didn't take his eyes off her. Obviously flustered, she stared at her feet. Her cheeks colored. He doubted if she had ever been properly kissed—except by him, of course. And that was nothing compared to the kiss he wanted to give her.

He blinked hard to clear his head. When he opened his eyes, he avoided glancing at Jewel. He squeezed past her to stand beside the desk. "Wayland, look at this map."

Wayland whistled once he caught sight of which map Nolan spoke. "So, this is it. Never thought I'd get a look. Bellamy kept the bugger stashed away once he snatched it from you."

"I think these words make the shape of the island, and the drawing hides something called runes." Jewel turned the map sideways and traced the letters with her finger.

Wayland scratched his head. "I'll be damned. It's runes, all right. Haven't seen nothing like this in a while.

111

Give me something to write with. This might take some time to figure out. If it gives the latitude and longitude, the numbers will have to be figured by the order of the alphabet."

Jewel handed him the sheet of paper with the tracing. "This is the outline of the island created by the words. Nolan thought he recognized it, but he's not sure."

Wayland glanced at Nolan briefly, a hard glint in his good eye. "Well, chit, you're in luck, because the only one on this ship who knows the waters where Captain Kent sailed better than Nolan is me."

Nolan's mouth went dry. The fact that Wayland, an uneducated pirate who no doubt couldn't read a newspaper, would know so much about ancient alphabets didn't surprise him. What had started the fierce pounding at his temples was the certainty that Wayland had already figured out which island they spoke of. He backed toward the door. Jewel glanced over her shoulder at him. She was happier than he'd ever seen her. He smiled back, despite the necessity of keeping his distance. He had never met a woman who could make him angry, make him crazy and make him smile all with a single glance. And what she did to his body in her chaste nightgown was best left unexplored. When Wayland confirmed Nolan's fears, Jewel wouldn't smile at him again.

"Hmm. If this is the island I'm thinking of, it's in the Caribbean. A stretch of sea that has nary a speck of land. That be the island you're thinking of, Nolan?" Wayland turned and stared, as always delivering up Nolan's darkest fears right on schedule.

Nolan rubbed his temple. "That's what I'm thinking."

"Damn, who would have thought—"

"Are you sure, Wayland? You need to be sure. I don't want your imagination swaying your judgment."

Jewel glanced at Wayland, then him. "I can't stand it! Tell me. Do you know where we can find the treasure?"

Wayland stood up. "Not sure, chit. I'm going to take these scratchings I made and study them. Wouldn't want to be wrong about a thing as important as this. I could use your help, Captain," he added to Nolan.

"I'll be along shortly. I have something to discuss with Jewel." Nolan's heart had stopped beating. Wayland had already located the island where they would find the treasure, and it was the same one that served as Bellamy Leggett's grave. Why else would the man call him Captain and be so serious?

"Don't go," Jewel called to Wayland. "Decipher the map here. I can't wait to know the location."

"I need to talk to you alone, Jewel," Nolan said. He picked up the book and handed it to Wayland. "This might help."

The old seaman glanced at the book's contents, then tossed it back to Nolan. "Don't trust no book. Neither did the Brethren. I'll be up half the night figuring this one out." He paused to wink at Jewel. "You did good, girl. Your papa would have been proud."

Actually, the irony of the situation would have killed Bellamy if he weren't already dead. Nolan's nemesis probably learned the truth—having been left to die on the island that held the very treasure he sought—when he went to hell. The man had likely sent Jewel as retribution.

Wayland shut the door behind him as he left. The cabin suddenly seemed to close in. The air grew heavy and thick. Jewel stared at her toes. Nolan did, too. She was barefoot. He could only imagine what lay beneath the hem brushing the top of her feet. He thought of finding Bellamy's skeleton on their quest for the treasure, and it sobered him considerably.

This was his opportunity to tell Jewel the truth. He should do it, and permanently banish her yearning

113

glances. "There's something I need to tell you. You're not going to like it."

Jewel sat on the bed, looking at Nolan with wide eyes. "You're not thinking of taking me to Boston again."

Nolan shook his head. "You discovered the map's secret. You deserve to go with us to find it. I won't try to deny you that any longer." Though he hadn't been wrong about the perils in bringing her on this voyage, and he was sure he'd regret it in the end.

Jewel brushed a strand of dark hair from her eyes and tucked it behind her ear. "Thank you. I appreciate that more than you know."

But he did know how much his words meant to her. The emotion showed in her clear green eyes. He held her gaze, unable to break away. What would it be like if fate had not put them at such odds? Bellamy was dead and his daughter was better off without him. Why should Nolan be forced to cause either of them any more pain because of a coldhearted bastard whose memory was best forgotten?

He shifted, forcing himself to look away. "You and Parker seem rather fond of each other." He hadn't decided to veer from his plan to finally tell Jewel the truth about her father's death until the words left his mouth. Once they had, he relaxed unexpectedly. His easy justification was that his original purpose tonight had been to cross the battle lines that had been drawn between them with a white flag. Telling her about her father wouldn't accomplish that.

Jewel shrugged, but a hint of guilt shadowed her averted gaze. "He's easy to get along with."

Meaning Nolan wasn't? He swallowed, not feeling as relieved as he had a moment ago. A part of him had eagerly anticipated her denial. She was so honest with her feelings, he'd half expected her to blurt out that she'd only been using Parker to make him jealous. He didn't want to believe there was a romance brewing between the two.

He cleared his throat and tried to sound fatherly. His stomach lurched at the idea. Definitely not fatherly; detached, then. "I'm only asking because I am concerned. I know you've had experience with men while working in the tavern—"

She held up her hand. "You can stop there."

Nolan felt his stony expression crumble, for tears filled her eyes. To her credit, she squared her shoulders, sniffed and stopped, but not before he knew he'd hurt her deeply. Why did he always have to be the villain when it came to Jewel?

"You're not the first man to assume me a whore," she said, the hard edge in her voice heartbreaking even to Nolan, who didn't think he had much of one.

"I didn't assume . . ." He let his words drift off when she shook her head, partly because he feared anything would sound crass and partly because he *had* suspected the worst of her.

"You did." Her sad smile pierced his heart. "So maybe now you see why I so desperately wanted to go with you to find the treasure. My choices were limited in Charles Town. It was marry a man I didn't love or be constantly at the mercy of men who think little of me."

Every instinct Nolan possessed surged at the idea of being Jewel's protector. He couldn't let himself succumb to the urge because it went hand in hand with a darker desire. He needed to leave the cabin immediately. "Good. Then you'll stay away from Parker."

Her eyes narrowed and, for a moment Jewel reminded him so much of her father that he felt at a disadvantage. "That's Parker's choice," she said.

Not if Nolan could help it. "Wayland told me about

your conversation regarding men. That's why I originally came to speak with you."

Jewel sat back on the bed. She turned her head and stared out the dark window. There was nothing to see in the inky night, but she obviously would rather look at nothing than him. "Well, was he right?"

"Wayland?" Nolan was no longer sure what he had hoped to accomplish. He feared no matter what he said, it would push her in a direction he didn't want her to go. Suddenly, Nolan wondered if he had ever had anything other than a superficial exchange with a woman.

Jewel nodded. "Don't make me ask you outright. Since you brought it up, just tell me. Was Wayland right?"

"If you wished to be bedded, you'd reach your goal in short order. Is that what you want, Jewel?"

She gazed at him with such intensity, he held his breath for a moment both fearing and hoping she would say yes.

"No." She looked down. "I want to be loved." Her voice was so quiet, Nolan had to strain to hear her words. She stared up at him again, transfixing him with her honesty. "Is that too much to ask? I don't know. I've never felt loved before. Have you, Nolan?"

He swallowed hard. He didn't have the courage to answer her. His parents had said they loved him, but he'd never felt it. He'd felt the sharp bite of a strap while his father beat him for every minor indiscretion. From impulsively lifting a single peach from a merchant's cart to bloodying the nose of a boy who'd taunted him in front of a girl he fancied, everything had required immediate and fierce punishment in order to save Nolan's wayward soul. His father always claimed the severity was out of love, and Nolan didn't doubt him; he'd just never experienced this emotion attached to the sentiment. "I'm sure your mother loved you . . . and your father."

"Maybe my mother did love me, but she was too bitter to ever show it. Love hurt her. My father hurt her. I can see that now. But my father—I always dreamed he would make it up to me. Now I've begun to doubt he was anything like I imagined."

Oh, he was never telling her his part in the fact she'd never know her father. A little white lie to appease his tremendous guilt at the moment wouldn't hurt anything. "Bellamy cared for you a great deal. He spoke of you often."

Jewel stood and walked toward Nolan until they were toe to toe. The desperate candor in her gaze held him immobile even when she laid her hands on his shoulder. "What about you? Could *you* love me?"

The lie that he found himself about to tell surprised him—not because he opted not to be honest with her in return, but that doubt played a part in his answer at all.

"No." He gently encircled her wrists and put her arms by her side. The shocked hurt that narrowed her pupils disturbed him more than he'd imagined. Never had he been confused about his relationships with women, and up to this point, even with Jewel, he'd assumed any feelings that plagued him had more to do with a healthy dose of lust than anything else. He should keep his mouth shut, his point made, but he found himself unable to tolerate the shadow he'd caused to settle on her features. "I don't believe in love, Jewel. I'm almost sure I'm incapable of the emotion."

She stepped back. "Don't you want a wife and children some day?"

"I suppose I do. But it will be a marriage of convenience, nothing more. I'll take a wife who will be financially and socially well connected."

Instead of sinking further into her obvious hurt, she

straightened. "I understand. Needless to say, I'm neither of those things. And besides, I see the way you look at me. Having any real feelings for a woman makes you uncomfortable. What are you so afraid of, Nolan?"

Himself, but he'd never tell her that. She had no idea how close to the brink he teetered, and if he fell, there would be no stopping his descent into carnality. He couldn't be the man he'd come to know too well while serving on a pirate crew. A man who could watch a woman be dragged away to be raped or a man gutted for merely saying the wrong thing, one who wouldn't lift a finger to stop either. A man who, when he found himself slightly troubled by what was going on around him, would merrily help himself to the captured ship's stockpile of rum. He refused to be that man again. He feared that if he stepped over the line he'd drawn with Jewel, he'd step over another, then another.

"If you insinuated yourself aboard my ship to find your true love, you've made a serious miscalculation," he gritted out. "I don't care what's between you and Mr. Tyrell, but it better not come to fruition until we've found the treasure and I've deposited you at the destination of your choice."

Jewel lifted her chin. "Once we do, then maybe I'll try Wayland's suggestion. Parker may enjoy it."

An image Nolan had earlier suppressed rose with stunning force. He reached for Jewel and pulled her firmly against him. He kissed her hard, all his pent up lust unfurling like a sail catching a fierce wind. She gasped, but he only took that as an invitation. His hand drifted down to cup her buttocks. Her soft curves felt so much better than his imagination. He tightened his grip as he maneuvered her against his growing erection. The contact flooded him with a wave of desire he knew he would soon be helpless to control.

His impulsive action obliterated the thought of Parker

permanently, but it brought more vivid images that disturbed Nolan more. Never had he needed a woman this urgently. He pulled his mouth away, realizing he gripped the back of her neck and that his other hand dug into her soft bottom. She panted for breath. Her fingers were curled in his shirt, and he was suddenly unsure if she had been trying to push him away or pull him closer. He struggled to take in air.

He gripped her shoulders and peeled her away from him. "That's what Wayland's advice will get you. I said I didn't love you. I never said I didn't want you. I hate to see you flirting with Parker, but only because I can't stand the idea of him taking you to bed when I want to. You're the only woman on this ship. It's a dangerous position for a naive girl."

"I'm a grown woman!"

"I know, and ripe for seduction. You ooze with longing—but women want love and men want sex. If you don't want to be hurt or follow in your mother's footsteps, you'll walk a careful path."

"But no matter how carefully I walk, I'll never reach you."

Nolan nodded. "I think we understand each other. If you get yourself with child, I'll set you on the first inhabited island we come to. No discussion."

She disengaged herself with a violent jerk. "I understand. And, of course, if I did wind up in the family way, it would be all my fault."

Nolan folded his arms over his chest to stop himself from touching her again. "I won't blame one of my men for taking bait that's dangled in front of them. I'd say right now you've got Parker practically hooked. Watch yourself, and I'll watch my men."

"Is that all, Captain?"

"Do we understand each other?"

She nodded stiffly. She took off his coat, as if it offended her, and flung it at him. "Please go."

Nolan turned to leave, not sure what he'd just accomplished. The kiss he had stolen burned to his toes. Jewel was angrier with him than she'd been when he entered. As for keeping her away from Parker, Nolan was sure he'd just driven her into the lieutenant's eager arms. And now, to top it off, they were going to the island where he had left her father to die. Bellamy must be laughing through his rotten teeth.

He stopped before he shut the door. "By the way . . ."

Jewel turned and glared at him.

"Good work tonight." The pillow left her hand before he finished his sentence. He jerked the door closed before it hit with a thud.

He found Wayland in the galley, looking more industrious than Nolan had ever seen. Not wanting to interrupt such a rare occurrence, he retrieved a key hidden in a loose panel and unlocked the pantry. Each crewman had a ration of watered-down rum. After his conversation with Jewel, Nolan had decided to take advantage of being the captain and increase his own share. He dipped two mugs in a barrel of grog. One he set in front of Wayland; the other he brought to his mouth, swallowing its contents in one long gulp.

Wayland glanced up briefly with a nod of gratitude. A map of the Caribbean was spread out before him, capturing his full attention. The spot Wayland had marked made Nolan take another long hard gulp. He needed it. He would have to face his ghosts after all.

Jewel was correct when she'd said he appeared to recognize the island well. He had drawn a similar outline in the middle of a vast empty ocean five years ago, then stuck the map in the bottom of a forgotten sea chest. His sketch might vary slightly from the map, but the island's one inlet, a jagged cove the shape of a broken heart, was immediately recognizable. The same inlet where they would be forced to land, and the same inlet where Nolan had ordered Bellamy marooned. Would Jewel recognize her father's skeleton?

"That's it, all right." Wayland interrupted Nolan's morose speculations. "The runes are as plain as day once you know what to look for. Gotta hand it to the chit."

Nolan refused to believe in such a wicked coincidence. "How can that be? You have to be mistaken."

Wayland laughed. "Sorry, lad. But it makes perfect sense to me. When Bellamy was captain, we must have taken that same course Captain Kent last sailed near twenty times, looking for the place he might stash his booty. Doesn't surprise me a bit you picked the same unmarked island your grandfather did to dump the demon dogging your heels."

Nolan shook his head. The truth in Wayland's logic showed him how foolish he'd been. He should have seen it for himself. He should have searched the island instead of taking Wayland's word that it was truly deserted. Maybe he would have found a clue. Maybe Bellamy had found the treasure after all, and they would have to pry his bony claws off a handful of gold coins.

He gulped the rest of his grog. "At least Captain Kent got to bury his demons on that island. Mine are still haunting me."

"Kent got hanged. That hidden treasure didn't buy his freedom like he hoped. All you've got chewing at you is one skinny chit whose father you killed. Sounds like you got the good end of that deal."

Nolan wondered, but he was ready to change the subject. "We'll need supplies. We'll stop at Nassau, then head straight for the island."

"What about Bellamy?"

Nolan sucked in air through his teeth. "I imagine he's good and dead by now."

Wayland shrugged. "Aye. But you're the one scared of ghosts. What are you going to tell Jewel?"

"Nothing." Taking her to the island where her father had been forced to take his own life or likely suffer a horrible death by dehydration was cruel. Sparing her from knowing whose carcass they tripped over seemed the least he could do.

Wayland rubbed his chin. "Don't want to drive her into Parker's arms outright, then? Just want to do it with your easy charm?"

Nolan feared he had already delivered her to Parker but didn't say so. "This has nothing to do with any feelings for Jewel. And I would appreciate you not giving her any more advice. You're only confusing her."

Wayland scoffed. "That girl's sharper than you or I. Even outdoes her sire, who was pretty damned crafty. She's the one what figured out the treasure's hiding place. We couldn't even find the island when we once bloody well stood on it."

"Perhaps, but she's still innocent when it comes to what goes on between men and women." Nolan stared into his empty grog cup and battled the urge for more. He realized he didn't know much more than Jewel about romantic entanglements.

Wayland waved his hand. "Hell, Parker will teach her all that. I imagine he'll be real gentle, too."

Nolan gripped his mug. "Are you purposely trying to drive me insane?"

Wayland's slow grin was his answer. Nolan wasn't sure why, but he suspected Wayland enjoyed seeing him lose control of himself—especially in drink and women, the two things that had made the pirate life tolerable, even sometimes enjoyable.

"How 'bout another drink, boy?" Wayland pushed his mug toward Nolan.

"Not that you care, but whatever you're up to is likely

to hurt Jewel much more than me." He snatched Wayland's mug, then wiped it out with a rag and returned it to its latched shelf.

The old pirate retrieved a silver flask from beneath his loose shirt and took a long draw. "If you ask me, you're the one who's done most of the hurting."

Damn him, Wayland was right. The hostility he'd used to disguise his attraction had done as much damage as any explicit instructions. And his fierce rejection might drive Jewel to a man she wasn't ready for. All she needed was some time to see him for who he was. Just a man.

A man who'd killed her father. Nolan cringed at the thought.

Wayland got up and stretched. "Going to get a bit of shut-eye. How 'bout you?"

Nolan gathered up the map and Wayland's notes. "I'm going to kick Mr. Tyrell out of his cabin."

"Suit yourself." Wayland shrugged, but Nolan could see the twinkle in his eye.

Chapter Nine

Jewel leaned on the *Integrity*'s rail and stared at the lights of Nassau. Nolan had already informed her that she wouldn't be going ashore tomorrow with the rest of the crew. She hadn't bothered arguing. Her easy agreement seemed to disappoint him. Not that she could tell much that went on behind the cool front Nolan Kenton presented her.

Behind her, a few sailors lounged on deck, smoking pipes that were only permissible when at anchor. Embers flared with each breath: the only sign that Jewel was not completely alone. Their presence was little comfort. Never had she felt so desolate.

She turned her face up to the sky and bathed in the wash of soft stars strewn like a luminous net across a dusky blue void. Caribbean nights proved as sultry as the days. Jewel had spent many an afternoon marveling at the azure sky that seeped into the turquoise ocean, painting everything in hot blue light. She longed to reach out and touch the clear water, to test Wayland's promise that the sea here was as warm as the constant winds.

Despite the fact that she had never learned to swim, she imagined she could ride the waves with the dolphins that followed the ship.

Yet recalling her joy at watching the sea creatures tag along behind them couldn't salve the sting of her last encounter with Nolan. Not even Parker could stir a smile from her. He had tried. And since he had been sent to shore with Wayland on a scouting expedition of Nassau, Jewel's mood had turned even more morose.

Nolan wanted news of the impending revolution as well as whether word had leaked that Captain Kent's grandson was again looking for the infamous treasure. If all went well—and in this case, no news was good news—Nolan's crew would have leave. If not, they'd sail on.

She turned her back on Nassau and searched the deck for Nolan. He cared for her, though obviously without the same intensity she felt for him. His aversion to love was clear. Every time she mentioned the word, he looked like he'd stepped on a jellyfish. He had charted the course of their relationship and decided it led nowhere he wanted to go. He relied on cold, hard facts. Feeling was something to struggle against. The very fact that he cared for Jewel worked against her.

Yes, she realized, Nolan forced himself to live by some standard that defied natural reason. He was strict about propriety, about control. Why else would he continue to wear his coat when the weather turned sweltering? Somewhere along the way, he had stopped trusting his heart and decided to live by a code alone. Getting through to him seemed impossible. He and Jewel each spoke a language the other didn't understand—and he didn't seem to want to learn the language of faith and love.

Jewel sucked in her breath and turned to face the ocean, letting the warm breeze relax the tightness in her chest. A surge of awareness rushed through her limbs as Nolan stepped on deck. She glanced in his direction, but he quickly averted his gaze, turned and headed away. The wall he used to shield himself had been rebuilt.

She leaned on the railing, no longer able to enjoy the night's beauty. God, she hated knowing there was no chance for them. She still longed for him. It scared her how thoroughly.

Wayland's head popped up over the side, right next to where Jewel was standing. He startled her out of her spiraling thoughts.

"Didn't you hear me, chit? I yelled at you to fetch a lantern. Parker almost slipped coming up the ladder."

"I did not," yelled Parker from over the side. "Get out of the way, old man, so I can get on board."

Wayland swung his leg over the rail. He seemed to have enjoyed himself in Nassau. His cheeks were flushed, and he looked absolutely jolly in the pirate garb they'd all donned to go ashore.

Parker, who followed up the ladder, appeared pale. His baggy canvas pants and striped shirt hardly disguised the starched young officer beneath. His clean hair looked far too neat, even with the red kerchief tied on his head. He even sported an earring.

As if he noticed Jewel's scrutiny, Parker yanked out the gold hoop and winced. She plainly saw red on his pale earlobe. "You're bleeding," she said. She reached out to examine his ear, but Parker pulled away.

"I'm fine. It was just bloody uncomfortable is all." He covered his ear with his palm.

Wayland laughed. "Thought we were going to have to get Parker here a wet nurse. Should have heard him mewl when I stuck his ear to get the hoop in."

Parker glared. "It was unnecessary."

Wayland winked. "As green as you look, we would have been picked for spies or redcoats."

"Your drinking certainly fooled anyone who doubted we were honest-to-God pirates."

Wayland playfully shoved Parker, sending him stumbling. " 'Honest to God?' That's it, Parker. We might get you swearing yet."

The lieutenant spun, his hands balled in fists, but Nolan approached before he could take a swing.

"What are you two doing back so soon?"

For the first time since Jewel knew him, Parker didn't snap to attention under Nolan's harsh gaze. "He's impossible. Completely unprofessional."

"Aw, he's just pissed because I asked Maria to let him suck on her tit. Don't know why he's so mad. She didn't mind at all, and she returned the favor by sucking on his—"

"Shut up." Parker's face reddened, except for his lips, which formed a thin white line. He jerked his head in Jewel's direction, but the gesture only confirmed Wayland's tale. "I was trying to see if she knew anything."

"Lieutenant Tyrell, I don't want to know what happened unless it pertains to our plans. What news do you have?" Nolan seemed to have no sympathy. No doubt he had experienced similar situations in his youth. Jewel could only imagine what it must have been like with a whole crew of Waylands and no one to keep order. No wonder it took a knife in his shoulder to keep him on her father's ship. All the same, Jewel felt sorry for Parker's embarrassment.

The man somehow found his dignity. He released his hurt ear and stood a little straighter. "We spotted some of the crew from the *Neptune*. It's down here. Greeley and some of the others who boarded us were milling about. I think they recognized us—or at least they recognized Wayland. He's pretty hard to miss."

Wayland clapped his hands, then rubbed them vigorously. "What do ya think, Nolan? Are you ready for a fight?"

Nolan shook his head. "We don't have a letter of marque, nor do we stand a chance against a man-of-war."

Wayland stepped forward. "Hell, I saw a load of me old mates at the Devil's Bounty. They'd be glad to fight with us."

Parker clasped his hands behind his back. "They do have our men, Captain. You said yourself the war is on. They've blockaded Boston Harbor. They're keeping us from our home. I don't think they should be allowed to keep our crewmen, too."

Nolan raised his eyebrows. "You're looking for a fight, Mr. Tyrell?"

"He wasn't keen on it at first, but after a few shots of kill-devil he came around." Wayland reached into his coat pocket and removed a bottle. "Here. Brought you some."

Nolan took the bottle and flung it over the side. "I'm not going to get drunk on bad rum and attack a British warship. Nor are we ever—and I mean *ever*—going to throw our lot in with a bunch of pirates who are as likely to slit our throats and take our ship as they are to help us."

Parker glanced at the deck, but the stern set of his jaw showed he wasn't happy. Wayland put his hands on his hips.

"If we're going to turn tail and run, we might as well put on skirts and start serving ale at the Devil's Bounty. Hell, I already saw a couple of mates eyeing Parker. His fast friendship with Maria broke their hearts."

Parker blushed again. He continued to look at his feet and didn't comment.

"We're not going to do that, either." Nolan didn't appear annoyed by Wayland's remark. In fact, he almost smiled. "We're going to be smart *and* we're going to get our men back. Parker, are you sober?"

"No, Captain." The red that tinged Parker's ears paled to translucent white. "I think I might be ill."

"I imagine you will. Go do it, then meet me in the navigation station. I've the design of a British man-of-war somewhere. Wayland, come with me. We have a mission to plan."

Nolan turned on his heel and strode to the companionway. Wayland followed in almost a skip.

Parker stumbled over to the side of the ship, and Jewel cringed when she heard him retch violently. Quietly, she stole away. She would have made sure he was all right, but she had more important things to do. This was her chance to be part of the adventure!

Nolan wasted no time. By eavesdropping and just standing around—no one seemed to take notice of her, anyway—Jewel learned the plan. And surprise was a key factor.

She went to her cabin to retrieve her weapons and change into her men's garb. If surprise was what Nolan wanted, surprise was what he would get. Jewel had no intention of staying in her cabin and playing the damsel in need of protection. She would help somehow. Harvey had taught her well how to use a sword, and she wanted to help, to pull her own weight. She had asked to come along, after all.

She recalled Nolan's face as he had spoken to his men. He had been lit up from within, growing more handsome with each word. Jewel had never seen him so passionate, and his crew hung on his every move. The few lanterns that hung from the riggings were extinguished, but the excitement in the air was apparent. As was the fact that, at this moment more than ever, this crew loved their captain.

No longer did Nolan hide behind a guise of formality. He was Captain Kenton, a natural leader. There were no rifts or struggles in his personality tonight. The ease and passion with which he planned their assault was inspiring.

The attack was based on an event Nolan had been involved in a few years ago called the Boston Tea Party. Jewel had heard of the uprising. Everyone had. And while the insurrection had shocked the world, Jewel was more surprised Nolan had taken part. She would have sworn him incapable now of stepping outside the limits of the law.

Tonight, Nolan's crew would be pirates instead of Indians. They would create a row, sneak on board the *Neptune* and get their men. It was common strategy to force recently impressed men to stay on board while the rest of the crew had leave. With any luck, this ship would be far away before the British discovered what had happened.

The men gathering on deck were too busy chattering and perfecting their disguises to notice her when she returned. Jewel straightened her scabbard, glad she wouldn't miss out on the excitement—even if it meant risking Nolan's wrath. At least, if she were caught, he'd be forced to confront her rather than continue to dismiss her with cool politeness.

Nolan arrived on deck in a crisp blue coat. Its brass buttons caught the light, making them glow in the semi-darkness. Jewel ducked behind a mast. If anyone noticed her, it would be him. But he seemed just as excited as everyone else. Jewel sneaked a peek around the mast, wondering if he intended to go with them. He was dressed even more formally than usual. If he had decided to stay on board the *Integrity*, it would ruin her plan to be available to help. He'd banish her to her cabin as soon as he saw her.

Wayland blocked Nolan's path to the center of the gathered men, examining him from head to toe. "I don't like it," he was saying. "You think polished boots are going to fool them lobsterbacks if they catch you on board their ship?"

Nolan brushed him aside. "Only the marines wear red coats. When they aren't in dress uniform, the officers wear plain blue coats. Trust me: They're not in full dress on a muggy night anchored in Nassau."

"I still think we should just swarm the ship. I don't like you going on board alone." Wayland stuck his hands in his pockets and glanced away.

Jewel leaned around the mast to get a better look. Her departure to change her clothes had been too soon; she must have missed part of the plan. And if she didn't know better, she would think Wayland was actually worried about Nolan's safety.

Nolan seemed set on his course of action. "You said yourself most of the *Neptune*'s crew is on leave. The guards left on board won't dare to question an officer, *if* they see me at all."

Parker stepped forward. "I've already passed out the clothing I secured on shore. We're ready to go, Captain." His eyes were red-rimmed, but some color had returned to his face. His haggard appearance finally succeeded in making his pirate garb look believable.

"Good work, Mr. Tyrell. You'll lead three boats full of men to the port side, and I'll take two empty skiffs with me starboard. Make sure some of your skiffs stay out of sight, but make a lot of noise. We don't want them to be sure how many launches are with you."

"You're not taking them skiffs by yourself. I'm going with you," Wayland said.

Nolan turned and shook his head. "Our decoy is a

rowdy pirates brawl. I think you should go with Parker and make sure everyone plays his part correctly."

Wayland smiled his famous gap-toothed grin. Jewel noticed the crew no longer cringed when he did. "Parker's a fast learner. He don't need me—do ya, boy?"

The lieutenant didn't answer.

"You're the one that's got me worried, Nolan," Wayland continued. "I'm thinking you're getting ahead of yourself, going at this alone. Not very fitting of a captain to put himself in so much danger. You got to keep that in mind."

Nolan paused. He studied Wayland. The uncharacteristic seriousness of the pirate's words chilled Jewel, too, despite the warm night and the wool vest and knee-length coat she wore over her breeches. She agreed that Nolan shouldn't go alone. The way things appeared, he definitely needed help. And she'd be damned if she were going to sit around and watch him commit suicide.

Nolan turned to Parker. "Mr. Tyrell, do you think you picked up enough expertise in being a drunken pirate to land the men in this without Mr. Wayland?"

Parker stood straighter, visibly composing himself. "Aye, Captain, I'm afraid I have."

Obviously struck by the absurdity of the situation, Nolan grinned. He turned away from the crew to hide his amusement, but Jewel's position allowed her to catch it. She found herself thinking there was hope yet for her and him.

He strode toward the longboats; forcing Jewel to retreat to the other side of the mast, then stared across the dark bay. A handful of ships dotted the harbor, lanterns fore and aft. Their target was more lit than the rest, and loomed twice as large. "Wayland, you're with me," he said.

"Aye, Captain." The old sailor went to untangle the lines that held the boats below.

Nolan halted him, a hand on his shoulder. "But before we set off, I'll have your promise not to follow me on board."

Nolan's back remained to Jewel, but she could see Wayland. The pirate's good eye widened as if in surprise. "I never thought of it, Captain."

"Good. Let the crew go first. We'll leave after they've gone." Nolan turned back to Parker. "Mr. Tyrell, find Jewel. I want to make sure she is suitably occupied before we start our little excursion."

Jewel bit her tongue to keep from swearing. When they couldn't find her below, Nolan would scour the deck. How could she help if she were confined to her quarters?

Wayland spoke up, gathering several ropes in his hands. "Saw the chit below. Locked herself in her cabin."

Nolan studied him suspiciously. Wayland shrugged. "I think she's pouting about something. Has been for the last few days. You know anything about it, Captain?"

"Parker, go check anyway." Nolan took the lines from Wayland's hands.

Parker looked paler than when he'd come back from shore. "What should I say?"

Wayland stroked his thin gray beard. "Don't you know a crying female makes a boy like Parker nervous?"

Parker stuffed his hands in his pockets. "I'm not nervous. I just don't want to upset her any more. She hasn't been happy lately."

Jewel didn't have to see Nolan's face to know he was losing patience. "All right, Wayland. Since you know so much about women, maybe *you* should go."

The pirate shrugged. "I already told you, I saw her below. I'm thinking you know more about what's ailing her than me, anyway. You should go."

Nolan leaned over the side of the ship. "Oh . . . we

don't have time to argue about it. Let's just get going. But if there's any trouble with Jewel, I'm holding you personally responsible."

Jewel let out her breath. She didn't like the idea that everyone thought she was sulking, but it was working to her advantage.

She kept to her hiding place until the crew who were playing pirates had swung over the railing and descended; then she peeked around the mast to find Nolan giving last-minute instructions to the remaining sailors. Wayland appeared to be gazing at the stars. She didn't stop to question her good luck. She crept to the railing and swung her leg over.

Trying to gain purchase on the bucking rope ladder while the ocean coughed and spat beneath her cooled Jewel's enthusiasm considerably. Once she got the hang of moving her feet and hands in unison, she quickened her descent. Below, a tiny shape bobbed in a black sea that reminded her of a giant beast's gaping jaws. She dared not look down again. In all her preparations for a life of adventure with her father, learning to swim had never occurred to her. As frightened as she was, the darkness below was a blessing. She aimed for the emptiest skiff. With any luck, everyone else would use the same process, no lantern, and would never see her huddled inside.

In the bow, she found a pile of ruffled shirts, velvet vests and jaunty tricorns, acquired on Nassau to disguise the rescued men. By the smell of them, Parker had snatched them from living, breathing pirates—drunken, sweaty pirates at that. Having no other choice, Jewel covered herself with the cast-offs and tried not to breathe too deeply. If she weren't stepped on when the pilot entered the boat, she just might go unnoticed.

It didn't take long until she heard the rope ladder

creak with someone's weight, and the skiff where Jewel hid rocked with renewed violence. The craft settled as its new occupant found his way to the center of the boat, miraculously missing Jewel. Not a pinprick of light crept past her cover of clothes, assuring her that the man didn't carry a lantern. Silence stretched for long minutes that seemed like hours until she heard the rope ladder creak again.

"I told you to grab a lantern," called Nolan from above.

"Don't want to alert the *Neptune* we're coming, do ya?" answered Wayland.

Jewel cursed under her breath. He was right next to her. She'd picked the worst possible boat.

Nolan stepped into his own skiff, and the wake from his movement rocked Wayland's boat again. "It would have been nice not to have to risk my neck before getting to the *Neptune*. It's dark as pitch out here."

Wayland shifted his weight. A spray of water tickled Jewel's back as the pirate used his oar to splash Nolan. "Bah. You crept around well enough in the dark when we was with Bellamy. I hate to see you going soft."

Another soft splash accompanied the feeling of forward movement. "Why do you insist on reminding me of things I'd rather forget?" Nolan asked. His voice sounded farther away. His boat and Wayland's had been untied, and they must be rowing to their destination.

Wayland chuckled. "You can run, lad, but you can't hide."

"Shut up. Voices carry over water," Nolan hissed.

For the rest of the trip, the only sound was oars gliding through the water. Both men were well practiced in rowing, because nary a splash gave away their progress. Jewel tried hard not to move a muscle, though a plume from a tricorn found its way to brush against her nose.

She pulled her sword closer to her body, hoping it didn't stick out of the clothing.

She wasn't quite sure what she would do once they arrived at their destination. All she knew was that she had to be there. She'd abandoned her old life on a whim, and if she wanted to be in charge of her new one, she had to continue to trust her instincts rather than meekly allow others to guide her course. And thus far, her hunches had proved correct—both in finding the map's secret and in going along on this expedition. It was madness for Nolan to try to rescue his crewmen alone.

Their pace slowed, and Jewel could no longer detect even the slightest swish of oars. Parker's voice carried over the water—at first faint, but growing ever stronger. "Aye, ya bloody . . . I know you got Sheila on board!" His words were slurred and faded in and out. The answering call from another ship was muffled. Then Jewel heard the roar of other voices. The crew of the *Integrity* was creating quite a distraction.

"You think you can make it up without falling?" Wayland asked Nolan in a loud whisper.

"I've climbed up an anchor cable before. When I get on board, I'll drop over a ladder the men can use to get down here. Move under it." Nolan sounded very close; Jewel assumed Wayland was holding his skiff.

"First ya say don't remind ya, and then you go and brag about your exploits," the old pirate said.

"*Shh.*" Nolan's wordless command ended their discussion.

"Like I said, he says one thing but wants the opposite," Wayland said. He spoke softly enough for only Jewel to hear. She stiffened, but when he said nothing more, she assumed he was talking to himself. A few muffled paddle strokes propelled them away from Nolan until their skiff clunked against something solid.

Jewel waited, not sure what to do next. Wayland

would see her unless he broke his promise to Nolan and followed him on board. Another sound, the distinctive clatter and creak of rope, signaled that a ladder had been unfurled from the *Neptune*. The skiff lurched as Wayland shifted to grab it.

"Looks like he made it," the old sailor said. "You would think he'd realize he's not as different from the man he was before. Thinks he's all polished brass and book learning now. Book learning can't climb up no anchor cable, and it sure won't keep a man warm at night."

Jewel never realized how much Wayland talked to himself. His one-sided conversation flayed her already raw nerves. As it was, she struggled with what she should do next.

"What do you think, Jewel?" Wayland asked.

She stuffed her fist in her mouth to keep from gasping. Did he imagine she was there, or did he know? He sounded so matter-of-fact, as if her presence was as ordinary as milk with tea.

"Come on, chit. You better get on with it," he said, his impatience clear.

Jewel sat up, the bundle of extra clothes falling from around her. "How did you know?"

Wayland perched on a bench in the middle of the boat, clutching a long oar he'd strung through the rope ladder to keep them in place. "You're as clear as that swill Nolan serves as grog. If he weren't smitten with you, he might see through you, too."

Jewel straightened her clothes and adjusted her scabbard. "Thanks for not giving me away."

Wayland nodded. He gestured to the rope ladder. "If you want to help, get on with it."

Jewel looked at the rope. "What am I supposed to do?"

Wayland shrugged. "How the hell should I know? I

got you here. You have to figure out the rest."

Jewel stood, almost falling at the boat's abrupt lurch. She caught her balance, grabbed the first rung and hauled herself out of the skiff. "I think Nolan needs me."

"I been saying that all along." Wayland put his hand on her rump and propelled her up. "Hope you know how to use that sword."

Jewel nodded, then continued up the ladder. The idea of using her sword in a real battle suddenly filled her with dread. Though she'd practiced with Harvey until her arm and shoulder ached, the idea of facing an armed opponent slowed her pace. Fear weakened her limbs. If Nolan's plan went right, she wouldn't have to test her skills against a trained soldier, but then he wouldn't need her help either. She didn't know why, but she felt her presence would change everything. Focusing on the fact that Nolan was alone, she swiftly pulled herself up the rest of the way.

She hauled herself over the railing and soundlessly slid to the deck. There she crouched and waited. Across the way, she could hear laughter and jeers from the *Neptune*'s crew, who appeared to be enjoying an exchange with Parker and his men.

She slunk into the shadows, watching the guards. Following Nolan would leave the rope ladder unguarded, and she didn't know her way around. She suddenly had second thoughts. What good was she doing Nolan hiding in the shadows?

Her struggle with indecision ended abruptly when she spotted a line of silhouettes creep across the deck in her direction. She pressed herself farther into her hiding place. Before she could do a thing to help, Nolan reached the rope ladder, followed by ten men. He signaled for them to start down. Keeping a constant vigil on the guards, he glanced periodically at the progress of his recently freed crew.

Jewel realized he was going to be furious when she revealed herself. He hadn't needed her after all, and she would be just one more person who had to get down the ladder before they could make their escape.

"Hey, you. Who goes there?" called a voice from the darkness.

The last of the escaping seamen paused on the top rung of the ladder. Nolan leaned over and pushed his head down, out of view.

"You're one of the new men," the unidentified voice continued. "Sorry mate—you know the newly pressed fellows can't go ashore. You wouldn't be thinking of jumping, would ya?"

Nolan glanced over the railing again, and, apparently satisfied the last man had reached the waiting skiff, freed the rope ladder. It dropped down over the side. Jewel held her breath to keep from stopping him. How the hell was she going to get down?

"Wouldn't think of jumping. Can't swim. I'm a land man you know," he responded.

Jewel wondered why Nolan didn't act the officer as he had planned and just tell the guard to go away. She tried not to panic, trusting he knew what he was doing.

The guard appeared and closed with Nolan. "Yeah, that's what they all say. It's a long way down." He leaned on the rail and looked over.

Before he had a chance to speak, Nolan hit him on the head with the butt of a pistol, then caught the guard and soundlessly laid him on the deck. In the process, he came nose to nose with Jewel.

"Bloody hell," he growled, low and menacing. He reached out and gripped her arm in a bone-crunching hold.

A shout from across the deck forced him to release her. "Hey, Martin, you see any . . ."

The voice trailed off. The second guard must have

spotted Nolan and his fallen comrade. The hiss of steel sounded as he drew his sword. Nolan did the same. Swords clanked as they joined battle. Nolan thrust again and again, making sure his opponent was too busy defending himself to call for reinforcements. The last fight she had witnessed with Nolan flashed through Jewel's mind. He'd been a clumsy youth that night he'd challenged her father in the sandy alley outside the Quail and Queen, and he'd been royally trounced. She prayed he'd sharpened his skill since. Judging from his opponent's frantic parries, he had.

Jewel slid against the side of the ship, staying crouched and hidden while she watched Nolan's fight. He pushed his foe toward the *Neptune*'s stern, away from her. He appeared to be winning effortlessly until suddenly he lurched to the left and his opponent slashed his arm. His hiss of pain carried across the deck.

Jewel leaped into action. The man Nolan had hit over the head had somewhat recovered, and he had crawled into the fray and grabbed Nolan's ankle. Crouching, Jewel tugged on the downed man's boots and tried to yank him away before he could cause any more trouble.

He kicked her off easily. She landed hard on her side but managed to scramble to her feet before he did. His wooziness from the earlier knock on the head gave her enough time to draw her sword. She stood motionless with it poised as Harvey had taught. Her heart swelled in her throat. She had never had a real fight before, and the rush of excitement mixed with fear made it hard to think. She struggled to remember Harvey's instructions.

Her opponent drew his sword without any such nervous hesitation—though not as swiftly as if he had not been recently injured. His sluggish movements might save her. He struck her blade with his, and it sent a rattle up her arm. She could hear swords clank violently nearby. Nolan's wound must have slowed him, because it sounded as if he was fighting for his life. Her own opponent's dulled reactions gave her time to compose herself. She loosened her grip, bent her knees and thrust, hoping to knock the sword from the clumsy, injured man.

His reflexes were rapidly improving, though, and he parried before she had a chance to formulate another move. Thankfully, information from her daily lessons came back to her instinctively. She met his thrust with one of her own. The battle was on. She used the sword as an extension of her body. The man stepped back and readjusted his stance, as if he had suddenly decided to take her seriously.

Jewel stopped thinking and let her training take over. Thrust right. Parry left. Look for the open spot.

She faked low. Her opponent followed her movement, and a target presented itself. She thrust hard. Her blade sank into the center of her opponent's chest. He staggered back, while Jewel prepared for his next attack. Even in the dark, she witnessed his expression of stunned surprise as he fell to his knees. Only then did she notice the red swatch that spread across his white vest. He still gripped his sword, but it hung loosely by his side.

She glanced down at her blood-coated blade. It suddenly occurred to her that she held a deadly weapon instead of the sawed-off broomstick she'd used to practice with Harvey. She dropped her sword and ran to the downed man. He had rolled onto his side, his legs sprawled awkwardly. He had stopped gasping, stopped breathing at all.

Jewel dropped to her knees and heaved him onto his back. She placed her hand on his soaked shirt, thinking she might stop the blood—take back what she had done. He stared without blinking. She slapped his cheek, hoping he was just stunned. A bloody imprint stained his tan cheek, but he didn't even blink. She angled his face so she could see his eyes, praying she'd find a sign of life. To her shock, he appeared her own age. Maybe even younger. As he stared—wide-eyed, mouth open in a desperate, last breath—he looked harmless. He could have been one of her customers at the Quail and Queen. He might have been one of her customers.

"No!" she whispered fiercely and shook him. "Wake up."

A strong arm snaked around her waist, then yanked her off her feet. She was dragged away from her victim before she knew what was happening. Even so, she couldn't react. Her world had tilted and everything looked different. She didn't know if she could stand, but Nolan didn't give her the chance to find out. He half-carried, half-dragged her to the railing.

She saw another fallen man. His eyes were shut and he wasn't moving. "Is he dead, too?" she whispered, and closed her eyes tightly. She couldn't bear to witness any more bloodshed. Her stomach already threatened to empty.

Nolan lifted her over the rail. "Can you swim?"

She opened her eyes. "No."

"Then hold on."

Before she had time to think what he meant, he had climbed over. He had one arm wrapped tightly around her waist. She realized what he was about to do only seconds before they were falling.

Thankfully she had not looked before they leapt, but the drop seemed like forever. She clutched at Nolan. They hit the water so hard, Jewel thought she might lose consciousness. She instinctively gasped for breath and got a lungfull of burning water. She lost her grip on Nolan, sure she wouldn't open her eyes again. Instead of sinking deeper, he held her tightly pressed against his chest. The urge to struggle, to get away from the pressure that gripped her lungs, forced her to try and shove him away. He only held her tighter, pinning her arms against her. Somehow they surged up above the waterline before Jewel had the chance to suck in any more water. She choked and sputtered, gasping for breath.

"Stop fighting me. I've got you," Nolan said.

She stopped thrashing at his rebuke, hardly aware that she'd been doing so. Too weak to do otherwise, she let Nolan guide her through the water until, without a word of warning, strong arms yanked her into the skiff. Her eyes burned from the saltwater, and her throat ached from swallowing the stuff. No wonder she had never had the urge to learn to swim. Who would want to? She was soaked from the inside out and completely numb. The men shoved her in the back of the boat, forcing her to sit in the bottom. She felt like a big fish being taken home for supper. A big, dead fish. Nothing would ever be right again. Her childhood dreams of adventure had turned into a nightmare that even Nolan couldn't wake her from.

Chapter Ten

"Cut the anchor line!" Nolan yelled as he hauled himself over the *Integrity*'s railing.

"We've almost got her raised, Cap'n."

Seven strong crew members leaned all their weight against the wooden arms of the capstan to raise the anchor from the ocean's depth. Their grunts of exertion revealed their understanding of the need for a quick departure. The newly rescued crewmen joined their mates, and the capstan practically spun on its axis.

"Good work, Mr. Lamont." Nolan raced to take the helm. "Raise the sails. Unfurl the main!" Thankfully, the tide was with them. One man was dead, another wounded. The British wouldn't take that lightly. They were in on the beginning of a rebellion, and Nolan loved it.

The fight had exhilarated him. He could still feel his heart racing. It had been a long while since he had done physical battle, and even longer since battle had moved him. His last years with Bellamy had been numbing. He had seen so much bloodshed, and his skill had grown to the point where he had lost all fear. Worse, he'd been fighting for things he'd stopped believing in. He'd been fighting for monetary gain.

Nolan spun the wheel hard to the right, readying the *Integrity* to fly from the harbor once the main sail was unfurled. Tonight's battle had been different. This truly had been about freedom and a man's choice of how he would live his life, not a young boy's wayward wish for glory and adventure.

The wind caught the ship's sails, and the *Integrity* was thrust forward, racing off to their next destination. For Nolan, it was almost ecstasy. Almost.

His thoughts turned to Jewel. God, but she had surprised him. At first her presence on the *Neptune* had sent cold fear running down his spine, but then there was no time to think at all. Jewel had matched her opponent thrust for thrust. And she had bloody well saved his life. With the cut on his arm, he couldn't have defended himself against two men. He realized, with only a slight tinge of horror, that he was glad she'd killed her opponent. During the battle, Nolan had almost forfeited his own fight with his constant glances her way.

He looked down at his wound for the first time, finding his wet sleeve colored with blood and a healthy dose of red dotting the puddle of seawater at his feet. Once they were safely out to sea, there would be time to attend to it.

They cleared the harbor. As they did, Nolan let up on the helm and pointed the *Integrity* on a steady course, running with the wind astern. He told himself: Jewel had had no other choice but to aim for her victim's heart. She couldn't risk a flesh wound. Her opponent had outweighed her by almost double. He would have killed her if he had gotten his hands on her. Death was her only option, and Nolan was glad she'd had the courage to take it.

He steadied the wheel against a fierce wind. Waves had begun to crawl over the deck in regular intervals. A storm was brewing. Nolan checked the sky to find the stars being crowded out by roiling clouds shot through with charcoal gray. Hurricane season had hardly begun, but he was well acquainted with the unpredictability of the sea. He wouldn't be surprised with anything thrown his way. After tonight's triumph, he felt as if he could conquer anything.

A huge swell broke over the deck. He was already soaked, so Nolan took little notice when the foam washed over his ruined boots. At least it wiped away the traces of blood from his arm. Ignoring the growing throb in his wound, he ordered the main topsail reefed against the growing howl of wind.

Parker rushed forward, out of breath. "Something's wrong with Jewel. She's sick."

Nolan raised an eyebrow, but he didn't take his gaze off the churning sea. "Seasickness?" He hadn't noticed Jewel to be affected before, but the ocean had definitely turned wicked as they'd veered away from the shelter of the Bahamas. Or was it . . .

Nolan could have kicked himself. How could he have forgotten how Jewel would feel after killing a man? She'd fought so well, it hadn't occurred to him she had never killed before.

He had been like her once, and he remembered the first time he ran a man through. He'd been so exhilarated from fear and victory, he hadn't thought of the life he had taken until he closed his eyes to sleep. Then, the restless night had been spent unwillingly recalling the features of the dead man.

He'd been burly and twice Nolan's age. The fight had broken out in a tavern after a late night of drinking and whoring. Nolan had been too young to do much of either, but he'd had no choice but to join in the fray or he wouldn't have left the tavern alive. The man had engaged him, no doubt expecting an easy kill to warm up his sword arm. Desperation had made Nolan quick, and he'd stuck the man in the gut before his opponent ever took a proper jab. The man had died with shocked surprise on his face. His eyes had stared at Nolan all night. If he tried, Nolan could still remember. Over the years, he'd learned never to try.

"Take the helm. I'll see to her. Is she in her cabin?" he asked.

Parker relaxed visibly. Obviously he found steering a ship into a storm a preferable task to dealing with a hysterical woman. "She's hanging over the railing. You can't miss her. Wayland's with her."

Nolan heard Jewel before he saw her. Her sobs drifted over the roar of the waves, and he braced himself against the tumble of emotions she evoked. Empathy, compassion and a protectiveness laced with a possessiveness he recognized as all too dangerous: all collided and surged in chorus with the storm. He didn't want anyone else to be with Jewel but him.

Despite the warning that urged him to stay clear of her, Nolan quickened his pace. Wayland had his arm around Jewel, keeping her from tumbling off the ship in the event of a large swell. She had her head hung over the side and didn't see him approach.

He gestured with a nod of his head for Wayland to go. For once, the man eagerly obeyed.

Nolan wrapped his arm around Jewel's stomach, bracing her backside against him so he could massage her shoulders with his other hand. She instantly stiffened at the intimacy.

"It's all right. I know you're hurting. I should have been here sooner," he said in a soothing tone he hadn't even known he possessed.

She relaxed against him, and Nolan bit back a groan.

She felt so good. But it hadn't been his intent to take advantage, just to comfort her. And he'd be damned if he would give in to how she felt.

"Harvey never taught me to wound my opponents, just to kill them," she said suddenly. "I think he thought I was just having fun and would never get into a real swordfight," she added between sniffles.

"I think he taught you well. You had no choice. In a real fight, you can't aim to wound when your opponent is aiming to kill."

"But *you* didn't kill . . ." Her words trailed off. He heard her ragged breaths and understood she was struggling not to cry.

"I probably should have. Dead men can't tell tales, nor can they find you later."

Jewel shivered. "I can't think like that."

He pulled her more snugly against him, wrapping her in his arms to warm her with his body. "It's the only way, if you live by the sword. Your father taught me that."

Her slight tremble warned him that she had given in to her tears. The silent sobs were worse than any loud, hair-raising ones. Why was he saying this? He was supposed to be comforting her, not sharing his feelings. "It was a hard lesson to learn for me, too, Jewel, but learning it kept me alive. I'm glad you did what you did, or we could have been the ones left lying on the *Neptune*'s deck."

"I wish I had died."

Nolan squeezed her tight. "Don't say that!" She remained motionless in his arms. He turned her to face him, squeezing her arms. "Don't ever say that again."

She hung her head, avoiding his gaze. "I feel so wretched. I was a fool to sneak onto your ship in the first place."

And in that moment, Nolan realized the extent to

which his life had changed because she had. If she hadn't forced her way into his life, he would have likely spent years chasing a false trail. She'd seen something he never would have. She was a kind, smart, beautiful woman. And though he tried to convince himself those were the only reasons he experienced such a tremendous sense of loss at her words of woe, he couldn't.

He lifted Jewel's chin, forcing her to gaze up at him. "You saved my life," was all he felt safe revealing. A tremendous surge of emotion savagely swamped him, leaving him as off balance as his ship riding the storm. "You need to sleep. You'll feel better in the morning."

"I don't think I'll ever feel better." She leaned her forehead on his chest.

He rubbed his hands up and down her arms. The brisk wind had chilled her wet clothing. Her shirt felt like a sheet of ice. He kissed the top of her head, pulling her into him. A drop of rain fell on his cheek. He lifted his head before he became lost in the embrace. Luckily, none of the crew paid any attention. They were too busy reacting to the storm.

He gently set Jewel away from him. She stared up at him, her eyes wet and full of a sorrow he'd do anything to erase. He wiped away a tear rolling down her cheek. A raindrop quickly replaced it.

"Don't cry. It will be all right. Go to your cabin and get some rest."

Jewel clutched his sleeve. Nolan winced and pulled his arm away.

"You're hurt." She eased out of his embrace. "I'd forgotten. Let me see."

His arm didn't bother him, but it would if she tended it. She needed to rest. He wanted to see her back in good spirits. A compromise quickly came to mind. "I have a young surgeon on board, and he can use the practice.

As soon as I know you're in your cabin trying to get some sleep, I'll have him tend to it."

She gazed at him for a moment, seeming to struggle with something. "Nolan, I don't want to be alone."

"I know, sweetheart." He understood. But he couldn't watch over her with the storm on their tail. He struggled to choose one of his men who could stay with her until she fell asleep. Someone he could trust with her. Wayland came to mind, but only because Jewel would find him unattractive. He couldn't blame her; Wayland wasn't exactly cuddly. He swallowed his jealousy. Jewel was too important not to swallow it. "Would you like Parker to keep you company?"

"No. I want *you*." She dragged her thumb across the hollow of his cheek. The touch, combined with the words he took secret, selfish pleasure in hearing proved as erotic as anything he'd ever had said to him.

"I have to have my arm tended, and see to the ship. I'll check on you after that. But you have to promise to change into dry clothing and try to get some sleep." Nolan knew he shouldn't be making such an offer, but he could deny her nothing at that moment.

"I promise—if you promise you won't forget about me."

Nolan took a deep breath. "I couldn't forget about you even if I tried."

Jewel gazed up, obviously trying to see through him. Hiding his feelings from her was growing increasingly difficult. He cared more than he wanted to, but now was not the time to withhold the one thing he could give her: his honest compassion. He kissed her knuckles. "Go, before I change my mind and send Wayland in my place."

His teasing succeeded in getting Jewel to smile. She took a step back, holding his gaze, then turned and hurried belowdeck.

The Pirate's Jewel

The patter of rain increased to a steady pour as Nolan went to check on Parker's progress; then he visited the surgeon. When he was done, he'd send Jewel grog spiked with Wayland's special brew. A hot meal would be better, but they couldn't light a fire with the unsteady sea. With any luck, the combination of an empty stomach and strong spirits would knock her out before he did something they'd both regret.

The sea's violent thrashing surrendered to the sky's dominance as the dark clouds unleashed their fury. A steady pounding on the deck above assured Nolan the weather had not changed since he had retired to his temporary cabin. Despite the needle dipping in and out of his arm, he relaxed. "Aren't you through yet? I should have let Mr. Blake stitch me after all."

Wayland poked him extra hard with the next pass of the needle. "Aye, but you didn't let that young puppy do it. Ya came to old Wayland. And not a bloody moment too soon. I hate sewing up a festering wound." He made an overexaggerated sound of disgust.

Nolan glanced down. Though they sat huddled together on the small bunk, he had avoided watching Wayland's progress. "It hasn't had time to fester. And I came to you because I thought you could get it done fast." And because Blake was a pup. Nolan would rather his young surgeon practice on someone else. He didn't want another jagged scar, but he'd keep that to himself.

Wayland picked up a bottle and offered it to him. When he refused, the old pirate poured the fiery liquid down Nolan's arm. Nolan jumped and cursed. "What's in that? Gunpowder?"

Wayland chuckled. "No, no 'Blow-me-down' tonight."

Thank God for that. The last time he partook of "Blow-me-down"—a Madagascar favorite among pirates; a concoction mixed with gunpowder for an added kick—Nolan had woken up naked under a table at one of Bellamy's favorite taverns, two whole days unaccounted for. "Is that what you gave to Jewel? I hope it didn't make her sick."

Wayland's brows narrowed, and he focused on sewing Nolan's wound. The grizzled old pirate's uncharacteristic silence made Nolan long for his usual bizarre words of lunatic wisdom. Wayland pulled the stitching tight. "The lass looked awful pale. She was asking for you. Wanted to see you something fierce. Said you were coming later."

The silence had been better after all. Another forceful jab of the needle made Nolan clench his jaw. A fine sheen of sweat broke out over his skin. He was beginning to feel like a pincushion, and he had no doubt that was what Wayland intended.

"You got no business using the chit like this, Nolan. Bellamy wouldn't like it." Wayland squeezed the wound. Blood seeped out from between the stitches. "Puss. Told you it was festering."

Nolan jerked his arm away, the curved needle dangling from the thread that crisscrossed his biceps. He would have finished the job himself, but stitching wounds had always made him queasier than delivering them. "Bellamy never did a damn thing for his daughter. The only time he ever saw her was to use her. The only reason he gave her that map was to keep me with him. He'd thought to keep me in line by putting his innocent child in danger."

Wayland poured more rum over the wound. Nolan sucked air through his teeth. He grabbed the bottle out of Wayland's hands and took a long swallow. The liquid hit his empty stomach like an ember bursting into flame.

Wayland took back the bottle and set it on the small table near the bunk. "Don't know nothing about that.

But I know Jewel ain't no child now. All I know is, she saved your life and now she's paying the price. I don't like to see women doing men's work."

Nolan stood. "I didn't ask her to kill that man. Or to come along"

Wayland remained where he was. "Sit down. I'm not done."

Nolan eased back down, but only so Wayland could finish stitching. He didn't need the pirate to tell him how to handle Jewel. He knew he owed her his life—but that wasn't why he wanted to comfort her, to take care of her. It was more than that.

Wayland patted his wound with a white cloth. Nolan looked down at his clenched fists. He forced himself to relax so the man could continue. "I thought you were pushing us together."

Wayland poured rum on the cloth, then wiped off the needle. "Maybe I changed my mind since I got to know her. It ain't right for you to be after her like a rutting sea lion. You being the man who killed her father and all."

Nolan forced himself not to move. Having an argument with a man who was sewing your flesh together put you at a disadvantage. He kept his voice low and controlled. "I'm not after her. And taking Bellamy out of her life was one of the best things I could have done. However"—Nolan ground out the rest through clenched teeth—"I . . . didn't . . . *kill* . . . Bellamy."

Wayland's next jab with the needle felt as if it had been fired from a cannon. "All right. Well, Jewel ain't no whore. That's all I'm saying."

"I know that!" And he'd not explain himself further. Nolan had come to realize during their conversation regarding Wayland's advice that Jewel had some misguided ideas of love attached to their mutual physical attraction. He'd not hurt her by taking advantage of that.

She'd had enough illusions shattered for one lifetime. Unfortunately, she needed someone to comfort her right now, and he wanted to be the one to do it.

Jewel was his now. He owed her. He might deny it to Wayland, but he did feel responsible for Bellamy's death. And if he'd been reluctant to shoulder any responsibility for Jewel before, the fact that she'd saved his life changed it. Not only did he owe it to her to help her through her grief tonight, he *had* to do it. He would give her what he'd never had, and maybe she could put her brush with brutality behind her instead of carrying it around for the rest of her life.

It was funny: how different they were, yet how often their lives had taken similar turns. Not for the first time, Nolan had the unsettling sensation that his and Jewel's destinies were entwined. Bellamy had been only a thread, not the whole cloth.

Wayland cut the end of the thread with a dagger he pulled from his belt. "You're done." He stood and headed for the door with one last warning: "Don't be hauling any buckets with that arm tonight. You've already lost too much blood."

Odd, Nolan's blood surged at the idea of what he *would* be doing for the rest of the night.

Chapter Eleven

Jewel reached for the pewter mug resting on the desk wedged against the bunk and forced a sip past her lips. After struggling to swallow, she groaned. Wayland's tincture tasted worse than it smelled. The wretched mixture scalded her tongue and urged her to spit it out. Yet she badly wanted to sleep, and Wayland had promised the brew would do the trick. She would have rather drunk the pools of stale ale that formed under the taps at the Quail and Queen.

What a fool she had been to ever sneak on board Nolan's ship. Or to fall in love with him.

He had broken his promise. He wasn't coming. Though she shouldn't be surprised, considering the state of their relationship, she had somehow convinced herself he'd put aside his restraint in light of her misery. Never before had he seemed less guarded than when comforting her on deck. Perhaps her desire and need for him had overshadowed her judgment. She'd revealed herself miserably to him, and perhaps he'd merely said what he must to calm her down and encourage her to go below.

As usual, she'd been another problem someone had to solve.

She held her nose and forced down a large swallow of grog. Her face screwed up almost painfully in her effort to keep the vile concoction down. Knowing drinking it all would be impossible, she set the mug back on the desk, blew out the lantern and stretched out on the bed, hoping that what she had forced down would be enough to make her drowsy. Unblinking, she stared into the darkness.

The rain beat steadily on the deck above. Occasionally, she could hear the men shuffling, but mostly she heard the rain. She dared not close her eyes lest she see him: her murdered foe. Just a boy. Why had she ever asked Harvey to teach her to fight? Better yet, why had her father ever come into her life at all, spurring her to ask to learn? In light of her current situation, her life at the Quail and Queen had been almost blissful. Right now, she'd give anything to be home, in her own bed.

Jewel thrashed to one side, then the other. Everything seemed lost. Even her desire to believe in the good— some good—of Bellamy Leggett. Killing was what he had done on a regular basis. Certainly the ships he had attacked didn't always give up without a fight. Why had the wrongness of such a life never occurred to her before?

The door to the cabin clicked quietly before its handle slowly turned. Jewel sat up abruptly, clutching the sheets to her chin. Even in the dark, she knew the tall, broadshouldered shadow that crept into the cabin. It silently closed the door, then leaned back on it.

"Nolan," she whispered.

He hesitated. "I thought you might be asleep."

She shook her head. A burning built behind her eyes, but she didn't think she had any more tears to shed. "I couldn't . . ." She swallowed her words, unwilling to ex-press the horror of what she felt. She balled the sheets in her hands.

He sat on the bed, and his weight dipped the tick covering. She slid into his arms. "It's all right. I'm here now," he said. He seemed truly sympathetic, smoothing his hand down her back while pulling her against him.

Jewel meant to slip her arms around him, but his sharp intake of breath stopped her. She tried to pull away, to see his wound, but he held her to him. "Your arm. Let me see," she said.

His palms moved over her back in soothing circles, erasing everything but her desire to lean more deeply into him. "It's been taken care of. All's well."

She braced her hands on his chest, careful not to graze his arm again, then slid her hands down his ribs and around his waist. His inhalation of breath sounded deeper, huskier than before. With her cheek pressed against his chest, she gorged on his scent. He smelled of rum and heat, spice and wind. She closed her eyes, relieved to find only the image of Nolan invading her mind. Her limbs grew heavy and hot, while her thoughts seemed to float above her. She leaned into Nolan, the only thing grounding her, and briefly wondered if Wayland's concoction had finally started to take effect.

"I didn't think you would come," she whispered.

Nolan didn't say anything, just held her tighter. With his free hand, he brushed the length of her unbound hair.

"Mmm, soft. I knew it would be," he murmured.

His voice reverberated over the rain and the thump of his heart. The thick timbre of his words stirred Jewel's senses with the same intensity as his physical nearness. Time slowed to the hazy density of a dream. She didn't know if they sat entwined for minutes or forever. Wrapped in Nolan's arms, feeling the beats of his heart as if it were her own was all there ever was, all she ever wanted there to be. He leaned down and kissed the top of her head. Without thinking, she turned her face up to his, offering him her mouth. Her pulse counted out the moments he hesitated, first searching her face, then staring at her with trancelike fascination. Then, slowly, as if he was pulled to her by a will that wasn't his own, he pressed his mouth to hers.

Jewel had been kissed before, some stolen kisses, some invited, but this was like none of those. The heat from Nolan's mouth flooded her senses, bringing on a shocking hunger for more. She parted her lips slightly. He brought his hands to her head, holding her in place while he moved his mouth over hers, tasting her in slow, languishing nips. She heard his breathing quicken, a low groan in the back of his throat, before he pulled her closer and slipped his tongue into her mouth.

He took control of her body and mind with that powerful, demanding kiss. The sheer force of his desire held her in place, waiting for his next command. When he slipped his hands down her back and guided her to sit between his parted thighs, she eagerly did as he directed. The heat from his body scorched her, but she leaned closer to the flame. Her nipples strained against the cotton of her gown and she pressed into his hard chest, bringing herself to an even more fevered pitch. Her action brought a groan from him as he tore his mouth from hers to slide wet kisses down the curve of her neck. She let her head fall back, giving him access to her tender skin.

His fumbling with the buttons of her nightdress captured her attention. She brushed his hands away and opened the garment to her navel. That she wanted him to kiss her breasts, touch her wherever he desired, was a given. Only the knowledge that she burned for him even lower, would let him go as far as he intended, sent out a shiver of warning to her brain.

Nolan parted the gown, dragging it off her shoulders

until he exposed her to the waist. He stared briefly, before tasting her in a trail of liquid fire. As his kisses dipped lower, she ached with anticipation. She felt her heart race as she had heard his do earlier. The same blind urgency surged through her, and she arched her back to get closer to him. He kissed his way down to her breast and took her nipple into his mouth without hesitation. That wet heat weakened her with its unfathomable pleasure. She clutched his shoulders to stay upright, her head seeming too heavy to be held up by her neck.

His hands found the flesh of her backside, and she discovered her descent into ecstasy had just begun. He pressed her against the hard ridge between his legs and she knew exactly what that meant—even if she'd never been truly told. An answering heat surged through her. The awkward position hindered Jewel's movement, so she managed to shift her weight to bring her knee to the outside of his thigh. Instinctively, she rubbed her moist sex fully against him, the unexpected intensity of that pleasure forcing her to gasp. In that moment, she knew why a woman could so easily succumb to a man's will. Driven by lust so consuming she could do nothing but follow its lead, Jewel longed for Nolan to take full possession of her body.

As if he sensed her total surrender, he efficiently rolled her onto her back. He settled between her thighs before she could orient herself to the new position. He thrust his tongue into her mouth and ground his fierce arousal into her desire's wet center. Even with the buffer of their clothes, the shock of the contact, so much more intense with him in control, forced her to gasp for breath; but he was there, too, invading her mouth with his tongue, his taste. Her rapid heartbeat warned her she might faint if they didn't slow down, but even breathing was less necessary than getting closer to Nolan.

He pressed again with his hips, creating a subtle

rhythm her body instinctively recognized. She undulated beneath him. The arching of her pelvis sent lightning streaks crackling through her nerves. A rumble of thunder sounded, and she wasn't sure if it was in her own head or outside. She slipped her hand beneath his hair to cup the back of his neck, deepening the kiss in an attempt to blur their edges. A desperate ache grew that only increased with each slight twist of his hips.

His hand followed the curve of her thigh, bunching her nightgown to her waist. Another warning sounded at his breach of the last of her defenses, but the heaviness of his cloth covered legs brushing against her bare ones banished any hope of intervention. The worn leather of his boots and the wool of his breeches caressed her skin. Each new sensation shot ripples of pleasure across her. The need to touch his skin urged her to yank his shirt free. She caressed his back, all of him soft and hard at the same time. The muscles under his skin bunched and jumped in response to her grazing explorations.

Abruptly, he pulled away from her touch and sat up. She braced herself on her elbows to watch him fumble with the buttons on his breeches. She shivered with the realization of what he was about to do. She remembered the desperate pants and deep grunts she'd heard from a couple she'd stumbled upon in the storeroom at the Quail and Queen. Another cool shiver snaked across her hot skin. Her mind cleared somewhat, though her body still vibrated with need. A woman's fear reared its rational voice, urging her to stop before it was too late.

She wasn't sure if Nolan read her thoughts, or if he saw her slight shaking in the dark. He froze, staring down at her without blinking. Before she could speak, he braced his hands on the bunk, then swung off her.

Jewel sat up and gathered the remnants of her nightgown. Nolan moved to the farthest corner of the small cabin, keeping his back to her.

"Nolan?" She pulled her knees against her body and clutched together her open gown.

He paced the length of the room like a howling wind caught in the masts. "Forgive me, Jewel." His raw voice shook with an intensity she hadn't heard before.

She sagged with relief against the wall. Then she realized he was angry with her. Tension rolled off him and onto her like waves pounding a ship.

He strode to the desk and fumbled to light a lantern. In its flickering glow, his eyes looked wild and dangerous. Strands of hair hung over his shoulders where they had escaped their ribbon. His shirt was untucked, and a corner of his breeches hung open. He turned his fiery gaze on Jewel, raked her with it.

She involuntarily slunk back. Nolan wasn't angry; he was furious. She clutched her gown until her knuckles turned white. With her other hand she rubbed her swollen lips, still wet from his kisses. She must appear frightful. Her body still quivered from his touch. Just thinking of it caused her an involuntary shudder. She lowered her gaze, suddenly feeling ashamed, though she was sure she had done nothing wrong.

"Did I hurt you? Tell me if I did," he demanded.

"No. You didn't hurt me." She raised her gaze and saw his fists were clenched. He seemed on the verge of strangling someone, and since she was the only one in the vicinity, she feared it would be her.

"Then I scared you." He lowered his head and pushed his fingers through his tangled hair. His ribbon came loose, but she doubted he noticed as it fluttered to the floor. "I don't know what happened. Good God, I'm sorry."

Jewel didn't know what to say. What had she done to cause this change in him? She was too embarrassed to ask, but obviously she had committed a serious mistake. With all the bawdy talk she'd overheard at the Quail and Queen about what went on between a man and a woman, she hadn't realized there was something a woman could do to offend a man enough to dim his lust. Quite the opposite, in fact. The patrons at the Quail and Queen always seemed raring to go, encouraged by almost anything.

"You didn't scare me," she said, unable to bear the silence. Nolan's reaction must have something to do with a particular aversion to her.

He glanced up again, taking in her appearance with a quick sweep of his eyes. He shook his head, as if what he saw completely disgusted him. "I need to go."

Jewel scooted to the end of the bunk, ready to block the door. The very idea of him abandoning her was unbearable. It would be worse than before he came. She swallowed her pride and found her voice. "Nolan," she pleaded, "tell me what I've done. I swear it wasn't intentional."

He paused at the door but didn't turn to look at her. "It wasn't you, sweetheart. Go to sleep. You'll feel better in the morning."

"Don't go. You promised." She got up from the bed and walked toward him. "Tell me what I've done to offend you."

"Nothing," he ground out with such violence that she found it impossible to believe him. He took another deep breath, then turned to face her. His scowl appeared as fierce as she'd ever seen it. "I can't stay. I'll make love to you if I stay."

Jewel laughed, releasing a tight ball of tension. "That's what I want." Once the words were spoken, she realized that only the joining of their bodies had any hope of curing the intense longing she'd developed for

Nolan over these past weeks—and she feared even that might not be enough.

Nolan splayed his hands against the solid wood of the door as if holding back an awaiting army. His chest heaved with each breath. "You're vulnerable right now. You don't know what you want."

She reached for him, placed her palms firmly on his chest. "I want *you*." She fanned her hands, exploring the hard muscles in his chest, the shape of his ribs. His reaction encouraged her. His eyelids grew heavier as he stared down, mesmerized by the movement of her hands. It was as if his whole being were connected to the point where they touched. Just the warmth of him, the feel of his solid body, brought back the comfort and pleasure they had shared a moment ago. Jewel forgot her earlier twinge of fear in her desperation to return to the mind-lessness of their mutual lust. To do that, she'd use every instinct, every rumor and every innuendo she had ever heard to take him with her.

She veered her exploration lower. She dipped her hands underneath his shirt and around his loose waist-band. No matter his words, nothing had cooled in him. His skin was as hot as it had been before, maybe even hotter. Stretched taut over his hipbones, it sent sparks through her caressing fingertips and pulsed heat through her body.

He leaned his head against the door, and she sensed his resistance melting. She slid her hand lower. The coarse hair curling just below the smoothness of his taut belly gave her pause, but only briefly. She slipped her fingers through those crisp curls, marveling at how different they felt. Nolan's breath encouraged her in heavy gusts against her hair.

Her fascination lured her on, not courage. Wayland's suggestion had seemed insulting only a few days earlier; now it seemed a natural continuation of their first kiss.

Jewel's fingertips found the source of his fierce heat, and a mere brush caused Nolan to jolt. He kept his hands at his sides, but he appeared anything but relaxed. Jewel glanced at his face. His head tilted back and his eyes remained tightly closed. She measured the length of his sex with her palm, then used her fingertips to slide back up. Hot liquid formed at its tip. She rubbed her palm across the swollen head and let the moisture coat her hand. Her heartbeat pounded in her throat. A damp, consuming heat pooled between her legs.

She wrapped her fingers around him, knowing without knowing that touching him this way was right; then she tightened her grip. She closed her eyes and moved her hand up, then down, following a rhythm as instinctive as breathing. She ached, longing to match the movements with her hips.

She couldn't reach his lips, so she lifted his shirt with her free hand and kissed the center of his chest. She turned her head to the right and found his nipple. She flicked her tongue across it, teasing him with her mouth as he had her.

He grabbed her wrist that disappeared down the front of his breeches. He squeezed so tightly, she gasped at the pressure.

"Stop. Please, Jewel," he gritted out between his teeth.

She gazed at his face, taken aback by the dazed glow in his eyes. Though his features strained as if he were in pain, she could tell he didn't want her to stop—far from it. A small smile tugged at her lips. Wayland was right. She stroked Nolan again and wasn't surprised when he loosened his grip on her wrist, almost guiding her movements: a subtle coaxing to change her rhythm and concentrate her touch. His head fell back again. He bit his lip and his brows drew together.

"Lay with me," she whispered.

With those three simple words, he came into motion.

He lifted her in his arms, carried her to the bunk and deposited her with more urgency than gentleness. He fell down on his knees between her thighs. Without encouragement, her nightdress conveniently worked its way up to her waist. In the soft glow of the lantern, she felt horribly exposed. At least when she had touched him, she couldn't see her hand wrapped around him; could only feel him.

He dipped his head between her spread legs, and then the heat of his mouth was on her. Licking her. She arched into his kiss, not sure if she were trying to get away or maneuver closer. It was all too shocking. "Nolan," she panted. The tip of his tongue found a spot she hadn't even known existed, and she relinquished her battle to speak. Sensation created a pressure deep inside her that was both delicious and unbearable.

Nolan brushed his hand along the inside of her thigh, and Jewel realized her every sense had been heightened. He eased a single finger inside her, and she couldn't stop the shameless press of her hips against his mouth. Her body took over, denying any restraint she'd ever had. She was all sense and hunger. "Nolan?" she whispered, slightly panicked at how thoroughly he controlled her with his hands and mouth. He didn't answer.

She closed her eyes, writhing at the sweet torment. He slipped his finger from her body, then pressed forward again with two. This time, it was with an urgency and rhythm that signaled his control was slipping. Her body responded in kind to his abandon. Each movement of his hand brought a wave of pleasure greater than before, but painfully less satisfying.

"How does it feel, sweetheart? Torture me and I'll always pay you back tenfold," he said.

She felt his breath on her cheek and opened her eyes. He gazed at her face with such intensity she couldn't speak. Before she could even think to answer him or ask what he planned next, he covered her mouth with his. His lips were wet with her taste. Mingled with his own unique flavor, the combination drugged Jewel. With the last of her inhibitions ripped free, she moaned into his mouth.

He reached between them, and the tip of him nudged her wider. With slow rocking motions, he pummeled through her untried body's resistance—all the while distracting her with his tongue. She wanted him. Her body ached for him, but there was still a small part of her that had the consciousness to fear what would come next. She kissed him more fiercely, reaching out to caress his invading tongue with her own, hiding her sudden bout of nerves.

"Jewel . . . You're so sweet and . . . so . . ."—he rose to his elbows and dropped his head, watching their joining—"tight." The moan that followed assured he found the revelation to his liking.

She herself was aching for more of him. Already slick from his kisses and with each tiny rock of his hips, she grew warmer and wetter. She wanted to thrust, to end the waiting, but she stilled herself. She brought her knees up higher, giving him better access to her body.

He liked that, too; she could tell because he made a breathless sound deep in his throat. The patter of rain and his heavy breathing filled the cabin, and still he gently rocked, his movements too shallow to reach her building ache. She writhed underneath him, to no avail. Finally, she reached up and wrapped her hand in his dark hair and urged him on.

He thrust deep, deeper than she thought possible, and his warmth filled her. She sucked in her breath and pushed against his chest. His weight hovered over her, solid as stone. Every muscle in his body poised and tensed. The place where they were joined throbbed. The pain of his invasion eased, but Jewel still felt too full, too stretched.

He dipped his head and nuzzled her ear, his tongue delving into the hollows. She tried to move her head away, but he went deeper, purposely tickling her. Her giggles were rewarded with his low chuckle. When he began a slow suckling of her earlobe, her body began to throb in a different way. In the place where they came together, they shared one pulse. Though she never lost the intense sensation of having his length buried deeply inside her body, he remained motionless. Every so often he shuddered, soft and involuntary. Her body responded by clenching, adjusting to his invasion with a sweep of pleasure. Ready for more, she arched her hips. All the gentle sensation that had deserted her on his forceful entry flooded back in a torrent.

"Are you ready?" he whispered in her ear.

She wasn't sure what was next, but her body yearned to find out. "Yes."

He moved: Out on a long fluid stroke and fast back, burying himself in her so thoroughly she gasped. He paused, then eased out with slow deliberateness, wringing every last ounce of pleasure from the motion. Again, with the same controlled ease, he entered her, making sure she felt every inch of him sliding into her. He repeated the languid torture, adding a twist to his hips.

"Come for me. Show me how much you want me," he whispered next to her ear. His breath was a hot and damp caress of its own, though his words alone had no meaning. He put his hand between them and touched the concentrated tangle of nerves he had awakened with his tongue. His thrusts slowed to the earlier rocking. He moved over her, arching his body until he rubbed the pleasure point he had touched with his fingers.

"Is this it? Is this what you like?" He dropped his mouth to her neck and kissed its length to nuzzle the hollow there before returning to her ear. "Yes. I feel you clenching around me. You're close."

She didn't feel close. Her skin itched with a need for more. She thrust against him anxiously. His small movements were making her ache grow, not easing it.

As if he sensed her agitation, he moved his hips in a circular motion, bringing her to the brink of insanity. His slight change in angle forced a gasp. And then . . . every muscle in her body contracted and released. She moaned with her violent undoing.

He paused only until she caught her breath, then rose above her, deepening and quickening his strokes in a way that forced his jaw to tense. The abandon that surged through him proved fierce and all-consuming, because he abruptly surged into her with a low groan. His hair hung over his face until he threw his head back, thrusting deeper when she was sure he was buried as far as he could go. A breathless moan ripped from his throat. His violent jerks eased, and he collapsed to his side. He wrapped his arms around her and rolled her with him, maintaining the connection.

They lay nose to nose, both struggling to catch their breath. He traced the side of her face with his fingertip, brushing a lock of sweat-dampened hair from her cheek. She grabbed his hand and kissed the tips of his fingers. Their joined hands fell between them. Nolan's eyes shone with emotion. She knew hers did as well. Neither could deny the love that simmered between them.

His eyelids lowered, as if he couldn't keep them open another moment. She snuggled against him, fitting into every contour and nook of his hard-planed body. His wet skin adhered to hers, letting her experience the relaxing of his breath, the slowing of his heart as if she were the one drifting off to sleep. His body slipped from hers, but his heat stayed with a sticky warmth between her legs. He invaded every one of her senses as thoroughly as he had just taken her body. She closed her eyes in perfect bliss. Nothing could harm her as long as she was consumed by Nolan. She belonged to Nolan and he to her. Everything would be all right after all.

Chapter Twelve

Nolan lay with Jewel in the crook of his arm and stared at the beams forming the deck above them. Things between them couldn't have taken a more treacherous bend. Had she said lay with me or *stay* with me?

It didn't matter. Even if she had offered an invitation, he was still a fiend for taking it. How easily his resolve had fallen in shreds. It disgusted him. Of course, he could argue that she'd been more than willing; tempting him beyond endurance, in fact. And he might have allowed himself a moment's reprieve if not for the fact that she'd been vulnerable, scared and alone, and he was an animal, a rutting animal. He'd said he would be damned if he didn't hold himself to not taking advantage of her, and damned he would be. Having a wife whom he lusted after but who hated him should do it.

There was no question he had to marry Jewel. If he'd doubted she was a virgin, the slight trace of blood on her thighs when he took her the second time proved it beyond a doubt. He cringed, remembering his desire the second time. She had been sleeping, for God's sake!

He'd awoken after passing out like a drunk, a drunk besotted with lust. When he had rolled over and found her there, it all came flooding back to him—her incredible tightness as he pushed past her barriers to bury himself inside her. Not an ounce of shame or even regret could quell the carnal demands of his body. His ravenous hunger had taken control of the situation before his sleepy brain could protest. He had licked the smooth contours of her ear until she looked up at him with sleep-filled eyes, the most trusting eyes he had ever seen. She'd wrapped her arms around him and opened herself. He'd rolled onto her, was inside and moving before he fully realized what he was doing.

Why hadn't he sent Parker here in his place? He'd had a raging erection before he even walked into the room. Though no doubt a part of him knew better—the part above his waist—he'd convinced himself he was the master of his baser instincts. There was no question now who was master. If only Jewel hadn't been so willing, he might have escaped with both their honors intact. The way she had touched him . . . Would she have touched Parker like that?

Nolan flexed his arm, instinctively pulling her flush with his body. The thought was unbearable. Not for a moment did he believe Jewel would be in Parker's arms right now if the lieutenant had come in his place. Jewel had all too clearly revealed her romantic bent. She thought she loved him. And damn him for liking it. He'd used her misplaced devotion to his advantage better than Bellamy ever could have. But he would be punished for it.

Yet, he could atone. He could do the right thing by Jewel, get off this hedonistic path for the rest of his life. While he'd veered off course in his quest for self-control and honor, he had the opportunity to correct it before it was too late. In fact, marrying Jewel would not only make up for the fact that he'd taken her virginity, it might ease some of his guilt where her father was concerned. He could provide a better life for Jewel than Bellamy ever would have.

His justifications served him so well, he almost relaxed and enjoyed the sensation of Jewel nestled against him. Then he recalled that she would have to know about his involvement in her father's death. Not telling her would be a deception he couldn't live with. It would be as bad to marry her under false pretenses as not marrying her at all. Of course, he had to ensure that she married him, so it might be best to wait until after the wedding. That was when his punishment would start. Would she keep him from her bed? More than likely, and it was as good as he deserved.

Nolan let his hand drift over Jewel's hip, past the dip of her waist, then cupped her breast. Lust. Desire. Selfishness. Reverting back to his true colors happened faster than he'd ever imagined it could. In the back of his mind, he'd given himself a good year before he would find himself holed up, feasting hard in some den of debauchery. He had fooled his father and friends for a while, but deep down Nolan had always known he was pretending. His heart was dark and wild. His passions ruled him. Tonight had proved that in every way. He had loved the battle aboard the *Neptune*. The moment he'd drawn his sword, exhilaration surged through him like a long-lost friend. Even the letting of his own blood had made him feel more alive. And to finish his night with carnality, he'd sniffed out the woman plaguing his dreams and rutted until he was sore.

Damn, but he was already hard again. He gritted his teeth against the urge to press into Jewel's backside. This would be his hell. He would probably spend the rest of his life with an insatiable erection and a wife who hated him. And it would be just.

The Pirate's Jewel

* * *

A hesitant knock caused Jewel to lose her grip on the roll of hair she had coaxed into a reasonable imitation of a chignon. The limp strands cascaded around her shoulders in a dark sheet, refusing to show even the slightest wave for her efforts. She turned away from the mirror, immediately forgetting her struggle with her painfully straight hair. Her desire to appear transformed was nothing compared to her need to see Nolan.

Parker's presence on the other side of the door erased her grin. "Oh, it's you."

Parker laughed in spite of the dismal greeting. "Well, good morning to you too, Miss Sanderson."

Jewel's cheeks burned. She hadn't meant to be short with Parker. In fact, seeing him after what she had done last night conjured a surge of guilt. She had used Parker unfairly in her quest to win Nolan's heart. "I'm sorry. I just expected . . . someone else." It had just occurred to her that her relationship with Nolan should be kept a secret. She knew what they shared went deeper than an illicit fling, but what would others think?

Parker winked. "I know who you expected."

Jewel could feel the heat of her earlier embarrassment creep down into her chest. Suddenly, she couldn't meet his gaze.

Parker had the grace to clear his throat. "And that somebody wants to see you on deck. You'd better make an appearance before he takes any more of his bad temper out on the crew."

Jewel frowned. She felt absolutely blissful today. Her whole life had fallen into place. She'd thought Nolan would experience the same sense of rightness. An uneasy twinge sprouted in the center of her happiness like a weed, ruining the rosy view.

Parker gently touched her arm. "Don't worry. He'll lighten up once he sees you. He always does."

173

She latched on to Parker's suggestion. Nolan's foul mood might be due to the fact that he was as nervous as she over the change in their relationship. They just needed to see each other to be reassured. She forced a smile, but a seed of doubt held on in the pit of her stomach. "Give me a minute to braid my hair. I wanted to put it up, but it's hopeless. I've spent the better part of an hour trying to make it stay pinned."

"You need to twist it."

Jewel turned away from the mirror to glance at him. "What do you know about arranging a woman's hair?"

He looked her straight in the eye, but she could have sworn she saw a hint of red around his collar. "Um . . . my sister taught me."

She struggled to contain a grin, but Parker surely knew she didn't believe him. Still, he'd been so accepting about what happened between her and Nolan last night, she was more than willing not to question him on his exploits—no matter how surprising they appeared to be. "Could you fix mine?"

"I'd be honored." He followed her to the mirror without the least bit of hesitation, then gathered the loose strands. "We need to brush it out first."

She reached around him to grab a brush from the desk. "I did, but it tangled while I was trying to put it up."

Parker pulled the brush through her hair, working out the tangles with practiced strokes. The gentle tug of bristles across her scalp encouraged Jewel to relax. She let her eyes drift shut, and imagined Nolan's surprise when he saw her hair up instead of in the simple braid she usually wore. Hopefully, the more sophisticated style would help her face him with confidence. Why she needed confidence to face the man to whom she'd pledged her love, in action if not words, was a matter she didn't want to think about too carefully.

She glanced past her lashes to watch Parker's blue eyes narrow in concentration as he twisted and gathered her hair in his large, rough hands. "Parker, I'm sorry if I misused our friendship," she said.

He grinned, but he didn't take his gaze from her hair. "That's what I like about you, Jewel. Right to the point."

She smiled, meeting his laughing eyes in the mirror. "You're not angry?"

"I'm relieved. You were putting me in a terrible position. I was waiting for Captain Kenton to order me flogged at any moment." With a quick twist of his hands, he swept her hair up in a perfect chignon. "How's that?"

Jewel gasped. The artful sweep made her narrow face graceful. It even distracted from the freckles dusting her nose by accentuating her pale neck. "How did you do that? I've been struggling all morning."

He winked at her. "Lots of practice."

"You knew I was only trying to make Nolan jealous? Why did you go along with it?" She held up her palm so Parker could pluck pins from her hand.

He answered, "When you're on a ship full of men and the only girl on board—and a pretty one at that—is flirting with you, you don't care why. Even if it means demotion to cook."

"I like you, Parker." Their easy banter relaxed her. "But it's coming to my attention that you're not the gentleman I thought you were. I don't think your sister taught you how to do this."

"I *know* she didn't," a new voice said. Jewel and Parker both turned to find Nolan standing in the doorway with a scowl that could melt the sun.

They glanced at each other, then back to Nolan. His stare skewered Parker. Without a word, the lieutenant returned the pins he still held to Jewel's palm. She grabbed her chignon so he could swiftly make his exit.

Nolan blocked the man's escape. "Just because I need

you to be a stand-in for me doesn't mean you have any other rights to my wife."

Parker nodded. "Aye, Captain."

Nolan continued to stare as if he could wilt Parker with his gaze alone. After a moment, he stepped aside and Parker quickly left the room.

Nolan slammed the door, then turned his scorching gaze on Jewel. "You *like* him? Trying out some of your new skills? The tactics you used on me last night would work on any man, I assure you."

With jerky movements, she stuck the remaining pins in her hair. Her trembling fingers made the simple task exceedingly difficult. Surely she'd misunderstood him. "I didn't use any tactics, Nolan. I just wanted to . . . touch you. I thought you wanted the same."

"I did, and now I must pay the price. I'm willing to take responsibility for my actions—and, by God, you will, too!" He strode over to her with such determination, she stepped back. Before she knew what he meant, he plucked a hairpin and then another from her unfinished coiffure.

"Ouch." She slapped his hand away. "You're hurting me. Leave it alone."

He grabbed her by the shoulders, his grip tight enough to force her to stare up into his penetrating eyes. "I won't have another man touching what is mine."

She relaxed and leaned toward him. He was jealous and unsure of where their relationship stood after last night. He probably felt as awkward as she with their newfound intimacy. And he'd misunderstood what she'd meant about Parker. "He was only arranging my hair, Nolan." With her fingertips, she touched his cheek, then his lips.

He let go of her as if he could no longer stand the contact, but the fierce lines around his mouth softened. He gently removed the rest of her hairpins, obviously taking great pains not to pull her hair again. "He was just 'arranging your hair' like I was just 'trying to comfort you' last night."

Jewel forced herself to relax, though he pulled his fingers through her hair and obliterated any signs of Parker's neat creation. "You *did* comfort me."

Nolan smiled, but it was tight and cynical. "No, sweetheart—I *fucked* you." He picked up a ribbon from the table. With a hand on her shoulder, he turned her so he could tie it. She glanced sideways in the mirror. He'd missed whole chunks of hair in his haphazard efforts, but she dared not say a word about it.

"How can you be so crude? I love you, Nolan."

She watched him in the mirror. Every line in his face tightened at her words. She wanted to close her eyes against what she couldn't bear to see: He didn't share her feelings, not in the least.

Before she could think of something to say in the awful silence, he rested his hands on her shoulders and slowly turned her to face him. His expression was no longer angry, but grave. "I hope that's true, Jewel . . . because I've arranged for us to be married this afternoon."

"Married?" Her excitement rushed up like a fountain, obliterating what had just passed between them. What he had said to Parker upon entering the room came back to her. "How? Who will marry us?"

He dropped his hands, removing any hint of emotion from his face. "I will perform the ceremony. Parker will stand in for me as groom."

Jewel lunged to hug him. That was why he'd spoken to her so harshly. He had wanted to ask her to marry him and was infuriated to find another man—Parker, of all people—with his hands in her hair. She realized how it must have looked. She kissed the small space above Nolan's tightly tied neckcloth, planning on proving her

177

devotion to him. "I'll make you the best wife."

"That won't be necessary."

Jewel glanced up to find him stiff and unmoving. He didn't even return her embrace. She pulled away, but continued to grip his arms. The vacant look in his eyes gave her the impression that, if she let go, he would be lost to her forever. "What is it? Is it Parker? We're merely friends."

Nolan stepped away. "I wish he were the problem. It's me, I'm afraid. There is something you must know before we marry."

Jewel wrapped her arms around her to stave off the chills creeping up her spine. The sensation of losing Nolan grew stronger. Whatever it was, she didn't want to know. "It doesn't matter."

"I'm afraid it does. It's about your father and our relationship. It changed drastically after our visit to you."

She squelched the desire to defend herself. It was unfair of Nolan to hold the past against her. "Are you angry because I let my father hurt you? I didn't know what he was going to do. I was only a little girl."

Nolan sighed and rubbed his shoulder. "No. I don't want you to feel responsible. I'm going about this all wrong. Sit." He gestured to the bed with his upturned palm.

She sat hesitantly, feeling as fragile as glass. He rubbed his bottom lip with his index finger, while looking through her. Perhaps she had turned as transparent as the oval window at her back. The man who had lain with her, adored her on this very bed, didn't appear to recognize her—nor she him.

"I killed your father," he blurted, his words delivered like a blow.

Jewel could only blink. Her hands grew numb. "I don't understand," was all she could mumble. But she feared she did understand.

All those years ago, when her father had given her the map for safekeeping, she'd hardly thought about Nolan. He'd been the enemy, the reason she wasn't able to leave with them to find the map. When he'd walked into the Quail and Queen five years later, she no longer saw the shaggy boy who had challenged her father in desperation to leave his crew, but a gentleman in buff breeches and blue coat who came to her rescue. Of course, she had suspected briefly that Nolan had done in her father, but she had easily convinced herself otherwise. What she'd felt upon seeing him . . . And Nolan was here; a living, breathing childhood fantasy come to life, while her father had abandoned her just as he had her mother.

His features remained stony even as her expression must have shown the frantic direction of her thoughts. He perched on the desk's edge, unmoving, revealing nothing of his feelings. "I was a member of Bellamy's crew. An involuntary member, if you remember. I led a mutiny. I won; Bellamy lost. He was sentenced to death, and I became captain in his place."

His tone was sickeningly icy. He acted as if he were speaking about the position of the sun rather than the death of a man Jewel had never really known but who had still been her father. Had Nolan any remorse? He certainly hinted at none. Nolan knew how many childish dreams she'd vested in her father—probably unfounded, true, but that didn't make his desertion any less painful or Nolan's words any less cruel. Why had he decided to tell her this gruesome tale now?

"Who sentenced him to death?" she asked, fearing she knew the answer but still hoping to whisk away the black dusk settling over what she'd thought would be the start of a bright new life.

"I did." Nolan straightened, then came to stand in front of her. "Do you want to be married in that?"

She glanced down at her dress: the green one, the one she'd thought was Nolan's favorite. It no longer held any pleasure for her. She didn't want to be married in it. She hated it. When she glanced up at his cold, blue eyes, the same chill swept over her skin. "I need some time . . . to think."

He folded his arms in front of him. "No. Time to think would definitely be a mistake. We'll be married within the hour. That should be long enough for you to compose yourself." He turned and strode to the door.

Jewel jumped to her feet, her fists clenched. Fury she didn't even know she possessed welled inside her. The man who faced her was not the same who had shared her bed last night—and if he were, he'd played a merry game at her expense. "No, I don't need time to think. I'm not marrying you. I don't even know who you are."

He stood stiff, daring her with his gaze to strike him. "You know exactly who I am. I'm the same man who fought your father for his freedom in an alley behind the Quail and Queen. I lost that time. Later, I won. I didn't do it to hurt you. Just the opposite, but I don't expect you to understand. If you recall, I tried to keep my distance from you from the start."

She turned away from the indignant curl of his lip and tight line of his jaw. Hitting him became the furthest thing from her mind. She couldn't even dare to look at the remote stranger who had replaced the man she had mistakenly thought she loved. "Well, what were you thinking when you came to get the map from me?" She wanted to ask him what he was thinking last night when he'd made love to his victim's daughter, but his crude summation of the event had already told her.

"I was retrieving my property. The map belonged to me. It always did." His bitter tone warned her that his stance hadn't softened in the least. In fact, he was becoming angrier.

Jewel thought of the young British guard she had killed. Having to face his mother or sister would easily tear her in two. If he had a child—and she prayed he was too young—the guilt would be suffocating. The very idea that she might have forced some little boy or girl to endure the loneliness and want she had, crippled her with remorse. A man who could do such a thing, then deliver the news with such cold detachment, couldn't be the Nolan she thought she knew. He must have some explanation. He must. "How could you face me?"

"I didn't invite you on board my ship. You stowed away and continued to insinuate yourself into my life when I wanted nothing to do with you. Now you're stuck."

Again, the truth clawed at her sense of righteous betrayal. She had forced him to see her as a woman when he was bent on ignoring her. Her desperation to have him at all costs had included taking the advice of a disreputable old pirate whose only experience with women undoubtedly came from prostitutes. "I didn't know. You didn't tell me the truth. If I had known—"

"Nobody else gets the truth, Jewel. Why should you? You wanted me to be some kind of hero, but I'm just a man. You played on my needs and I played on your vulnerability. We used each other, and now we have to pay for our mistakes."

She backed away from him. He'd bedded her knowing he had murdered her father. He'd thought about it.

A flush crept across Nolan's face, and a vein in his neck indicated his rapid pulse. "You will marry me," he said. His voice was frighteningly calm in contrast to his appearance. "And believe me, I don't like it any more than you do."

"I won't marry you. You're a killer!" That he obviously didn't care for her in the least made last night all the more vile.

"So are you." His fists were clenched.

She shrank from his accusation. A sob tore from her throat, and she turned away, hating her weakness. "Get out. Leave me alone. I don't want anything to do with you ever again."

He stalked up behind her, and she felt his breath on her neck. After a pause, he said, "I'm sorry I said that. It's not true. You were defending yourself and me." He placed a soft hand on her shoulder, and she jerked away. His voice grew harsh again. "Don't be a little girl, Jewel. I can't 'leave you alone.' You could be carrying my child. I won't abandon my child as Bellamy did his."

Jewel turned, this time, provoked enough to strike him. "You have no right to put yourself above my father."

Nolan didn't move a muscle. He almost looked to be anticipating a blow. "Fine. I'll never speak of him again. But *my* child won't be born a bastard. And if you would stop being so bloody selfish, you would realize why we must marry. Today!"

"You didn't marry your other whores. Why bother with me?"

His smile was a strained, half-mad grin. He spoke words she didn't expect. "They didn't make me want to explode from their sweet fingers. With them, I was able to control myself better."

She felt the blood drain from her face. She turned away, unable to look into his smirking features any longer, but he grabbed her arm and forced her to face him. His smile faded. "I know you're not a whore. I took your virginity, and I know I have to suffer the consequences of what I did. Think of the child you might be carrying and you'll see there are no other choices. And think of your own rep—"

She pulled away from him, and he let go without the least resistance. He was right. Her mother's shame came back to her in waves. And even more powerfully, her own shame. She wouldn't risk laying the burden of her foolishness on a child she might be carrying—not if she didn't have to. She should be grateful to Nolan for offering marriage. Unfortunately, her hurt didn't allow her to be. "How do I know you won't leave us if we become too much trouble?"

"Never," he swore. "Once we're married, I'll never desert you. I'm committed to the revolution, and I plan to fight, but I'll give you my name and my financial support. You and our children will be provided for always." He fell silent, waiting for her answer. Abruptly, he shoved his hands into his pockets. He smiled without humor. "And who knows, perhaps that's good. With the war on, there's a chance my ship will be lost at sea."

Jewel raised her chin. Over the years she'd learned to hold her head up even if her heart was breaking. "Well, at least there's something to hope for."

Nolan's smile faded. "I'll expect you on deck within the hour, prepared to become my wife." He turned and headed for the door. When he paused, Jewel jerked her head up. Why did he still linger in the room? They'd both already said more than either wanted to hear. She forced the hurt on her face into a mask of indifference. She was sure she failed miserably, but a life with Nolan would surely give her many chances to practice.

"As my wife, you belong to me. I won't stand for another man trespassing on what is mine. Be forewarned—unless you want another death on your conscience."

The moment Nolan shut the door, she snatched the discarded brush from the desk, ready to attack the tangles he'd created in her hair. Instead, she reared back her arm to hurl it, fantasizing the brush was a dagger and the door was Nolan's broad-shouldered back. The door swung open, and she quickly clutched the brush to her chest.

"I want your hair down. I never want to see it up again," Nolan commanded.

Jewel let the brush tumble to the deck with the rest of her wistful dreams. All her childhood fantasies had abruptly come to an end.

Chapter Thirteen

Nolan studied the stiff couple standing before him, who looked almost as miserable as he felt. Parker stared at his feet. Considering the man was standing in as the groom, his efforts to avoid eye contact with the bride were valiant. But Parker needn't have tried so hard. Jewel's gaze drifted out over the sea. Deep sadness pulled at the corners of her eyes, betraying her broken heart. Maybe she was contemplating her options.

Nolan wouldn't be too surprised if she chose to jump rather than marry him. Unshed tears created a crystal film over her green eyes. In her misery, those eyes shone like jewels, truly befitting the name Bellamy had requested for his daughter. Nolan wished he didn't remember that particular anecdote at this particular moment.

Stray tendrils of hair he had missed in his rough efforts to pull it back whipped across her cheeks and blew into Jewel's eyes. She didn't bother to brush them from her face. Her unhappiness seemed to consume her. No doubt she hated him as much as he hated himself. Nolan stared up at the sky and winced. How dare the sun shine today?

He glanced at Wayland, who stood on Jewel's right. The man had insisted on standing in for her father. When Bellamy Leggett's name had been mentioned, Jewel turned a chalky shade of white. Nolan was sure he'd done the same, and had hastily agreed to Wayland's request. More than enough ugly things had been said in anger for one day.

Wayland rested his hand on the long dagger in his waistband. "Are you sure this is official?" he asked.

Nolan returned his glare. "It is. You have my word of honor."

Wayland made a noise in the back of his throat. "A little late for that, isn't it, lad?" he said under his breath.

Nolan took a step toward him. He had an image of strangling the stringy bastard's neck, and it felt too good not to follow through. He needed a release from his tension, and Wayland was overdue for a good thrashing.

Jewel stepped between them. She held up a crumpled bouquet of herbs. In the other hand, she clutched a red silk scarf. "Let's get this over with. Please."

Nolan returned to his place. Wayland rearranged his knife as if itching to use it. Nolan would have loved to give him the chance, but he owed it to Jewel to make this painful charade quick. He glanced back to her. The dried herbs she clutched smelled of onions and salted pork. "Where did you get that?"

"The galley. Actually, Wayland found it for me. He thought I should have a bouquet." She glanced at the old pirate and smiled weakly.

Nolan narrowed his gaze. It seemed even Wayland had managed to work his way back into her good graces. He gestured to the red scarf she clutched in her other hand. "No. That."

"You left it in my cabin. I wanted to have it with me.

Something borrowed." She shrugged and studied her feet.

Nolan had carried the bit of silk since the moment she had snatched it from her bodice and handed it to him with the map. It must have dropped from his pocket when he had hastily peeled off his clothes last night. The cloth was a symbol of his desire for a woman he had dared not touch. For Jewel, the scarf was a reminder of her father. The idea chilled Nolan, the link of his downfall and Bellamy's.

He cleared his throat. Jewel's knuckles had gone bloodless, clutching the dried herbs whose brittle leaves crumbled to the deck. This was one of the worst moments in four people's lives and it was all his fault.

Parker shifted again, as if the deck had grown unbearably hot under his feet. Not only did he probably fear Nolan would cut him down at any moment; he'd barely escaped matrimony to a very religious and dour young woman himself before they'd set sail—his father's plan to settle him down. Nolan had stepped in and offered to take him as a crewman, and no doubt Parker was remembering the close call.

Jewel stood stiffly straight as she stared into the distance. Wayland showed his rotten teeth like a mangy mutt ready to pounce. Nolan didn't have to see himself to know he appeared the scowling vulture, looming over them all. He likened himself to his father at the pulpit preaching fire and brimstone. Only Nolan was the difficult path, not the salvation at the end.

He couldn't even blame Bellamy for this miserable gathering. Nolan had done it all to himself. Telling Jewel about his awful part in her father's death had been the right thing to do, but it should have been sooner. And he could have been kinder. His curt delivery of the facts had been more to punish himself than her. When he'd begun to tell her how meeting her had changed him, had made him realize he must defeat Bellamy not only for himself but to protect her from his ever revealing she held the map, she'd blamed herself. He realized then that it would be like trying to make her take responsibility for a decision that belonged solely to him. Nor did he want her to know that her father would put her in jeopardy for his own selfish purpose.

After seeing her with Parker in such easy camaraderie, something he and Jewel could never share, he'd been a little crazy, a little desperate for her not to hate him. He'd perhaps feared he'd sway her to his side with some manipulation of the truth—or worse, a request for her mercy, something he didn't deserve. Of course, he needn't have worried. There was never a good, safe way to tell your future bride that you'd killed her father.

Nolan gritted his teeth. They all waited for him to start, but no one said a word. Despite the misery he was causing, he didn't regret a thing. He wanted to marry Jewel. And that thought unleashed something in Nolan. Something he no longer had to fight. Had he been making things too difficult for himself?

He felt his tight features soften as he rested his gaze on her. The sun shone on her dark chestnut hair, igniting the red streaks obtained from her time in the tropics, tempting him to touch her. She was so beautiful and ethereal. He ached to be a real groom, if only she would let him. He would be a devoted husband and a good father. If she gave him the chance, he would make everything up to her: the past, her lonely childhood, the hardships she had suffered and especially his harsh words of that morning. She'd never want for anything again.

A sharp jab in Nolan's side jarred him from his thoughts. He glanced down to find the tip of Wayland's curved cutlass pressing against his ribs. The pirate snarled, exposing more gum than teeth. "Get on with it. I won't have you changing your mind."

Nolan's gaze returned to Jewel. She stared back at him anxiously. Was she hoping he would back out? He would have to disappoint her. It was too late for either of them to change their mind. With his palm on the flat of Wayland's blade, Nolan pushed it away. His own guilt kept him from speaking to the old man harshly. A father would have done no less—unless, of course, it was Jewel's father. Bellamy would have simply given Nolan a matching scar on his other shoulder.

He cleared his throat. "We are gathered here to-day . . ." The sound of Wayland replacing his cutlass hissed in Nolan's ears as he forced the dry words from his lips.

He rushed through the ceremony, cutting out any unnecessary phrases. He got to the part where he had to ask Jewel if she would take him as her husband. He wanted to skip it, but he knew the marriage wouldn't be legal if he did. "Will you, Jewel Sanderson, take Nolan Kenton to be your wedded husband?"

"Prudence," she whispered.

Nolan turned his head to hear better. Having her repeat her words, especially if it were a public rejection, burned his cheeks. "I didn't catch that."

"My middle name is Prudence. It was my maternal grandmother's name. I want you to say it."

Nolan couldn't help but grin, surprised and relieved. "Prudence?"

To his delight, Jewel returned the smile, tentative though it was. "Not very appropriate. Good thing my mother let my father pick my first name." Her grin faded with the mention of Bellamy, and so did Nolan's short-lived bubble of hope.

Wayland crossed his arms over his chest. "The time

for you two to get acquainted already raised anchor. Get on with it."

Nolan took a deep breath, then turned to Jewel, meeting her gaze. He would have to look into her eyes as he repeated the question. He prayed his voice wouldn't shake. "Will you, Jewel Prudence Sanderson, take Nolan William Kenton to be your lawfully wedded husband?"

She held his gaze, as if trying to see the depths of his soul. "I will."

He sighed in relief. He didn't want to press his luck by forcing her to repeat a lengthy list of vows, so he turned to Parker. The lieutenant's hands were clasped in front of him while he studied the billowing sails above his head. "Will you, Nolan William Kenton, take Jewel Prudence Sanderson to be your lawfully wedded wife?"

Parker continued to stare into oblivion, as if he weren't part of the proceedings. Not that Nolan could blame him; the man was too smart to do anything else. Nolan whistled shrilly. Parker snapped to attention.

Nolan didn't bother repeating the question. "Say, 'I will.' "

Parker nodded. "I will."

With a sigh of relief, Nolan looked down at the lines he had scribbled on a piece of paper and ran through the rest of the ceremony. "I now pronounce you man and—"

"Hold on there, lad. I don't see no ring," interrupted Wayland.

Nolan hadn't even thought of that. He looked down at his hands, knowing he didn't wear jewelry but not sure what to do. "I don't have one. I'll buy it later."

"I heard that one before." Wayland pulled a ring Nolan hadn't noticed from his pinky. He tossed it over. "This'll do."

Nolan caught the ring. When he opened his hand to look at it, the deck of the ship might as well have lurched beneath him. The sensation of falling forced him to adjust his stance. The plain gold ring had two initials on its face: WK. William Kent. It was Nolan's grandfather's ring. The last time Nolan had seen it, the ring had been on Bellamy's finger. Bellamy had stolen it from Nolan along with the map. He hadn't gotten it back before he'd marooned the old bastard.

Nolan glanced to Wayland for an explanation.

Wayland raised an eyebrow. "You made your bed, now it's time to lie in it. So to speak."

Nolan closed his eyes and composed himself. His sense of doom threatened to throw him to the deck a second time. If he opened his eyes and saw Bellamy's ghost hovering over the ceremony, he wouldn't have been any more taken aback. But Wayland was right. It was too late to turn back now.

He opened his eyes and saw only Jewel, and he felt his strength returning. Gently, he took her left hand and slipped the ring on her finger. It was too big, but she made a fist to keep it from sliding off. When she wrapped her fingers around his grandfather's ring, Nolan had cause to hope. Maybe things had come full circle and his marriage to Jewel would right some eternal wrong.

He cleared his throat. "I now pronounce you man and wife. You may kiss the bride." Nolan jerked his head up as he realized what he had just said.

Parker held up his hands as if at knife point and took a giant step backward. Jewel stared at her feet. Nolan moved forward, afraid she wouldn't let him kiss her. He touched her shoulders and she glanced up. Before she could pull away, if that was her intent, Nolan lowered his head and captured her lips. The contact seared him with a flood of erotic memories. He forced his mouth to remain soft and yielding. After five years of celibacy, last night's encounter had only whet his appetite.

Unexpectedly, she grazed the tip of his tongue with

her own. He pulled away abruptly, the shy caress as powerful as a stroke of his cock. He loosened his tight grip on her shoulders and slowed his breathing. He didn't want his crew to see how effortlessly she controlled him. A touch of her tongue had him burning for her.

She lowered her eyes at his withdrawal. He could sense her hurt at his curt response, and he vowed to later show her how he felt. This was to be a real marriage, one that would be consummated. And he looked forward to consummating it.

Jewel plopped down on the hard bunk. Blue evening crept through the portholes. The lone lantern that had guided her through the ship did little to brighten the cabin or her mood. If only Nolan would explain the events that surrounded her father's death, perhaps she could reconcile the fact that she was about to bed his killer. What had happened? Had her father and Nolan fought and he'd won? Had the crew thrown Bellamy overboard or hanged him from the main mast?

Jewel covered her face with her palms to stop the images that churned in her mind. Nolan was her husband now, and she longed to trust him. He said there had been a mutiny. Everything she knew about Nolan told her he was a fair man, if harsh. Though he had bedded her while keeping such an awful secret, he had married her promptly afterward. She knew from other, less fortunate, women's experiences that men didn't always take that kind of responsibility for their casual pleasures. Yet right or wrong, noble or devious, Nolan was the man responsible for her father's death.

If she still didn't want him so badly, her guilt might not have been so awful. But every time Jewel thought of the ache in her belly created by the sight of Nolan, she was reminded of her father's death. She stood and carefully turned down the coverlet. She smoothed out the wrinkles and fluffed the pillow. Her wifely duty required she give herself to her husband. Her body craved the union, though her mind screamed out betrayal.

Before her wedding, she had furiously scrubbed the pink blotch staining the bed. The sight of the blood galled her. It had been spilled between them, hers and her father's. Had Nolan run her father through like she had that young British sailor? Had he stared into her father's shocked face as he removed the blade? Had he thought of that moment when he had rolled off Jewel, her virgin's blood smearing him?

She shook her head. Of course he hadn't. She was being morbid. She tugged at the laces of her dress and slipped into her nightgown. The warmth of the Caribbean had dried the garment after she washed it with the sheets. The smell of wind enveloped her, and her thoughts returned to Nolan.

He had been drinking. Though their wedding celebration had been meant to be a tame affair, every man on board got an extra mug of grog at the end of his shift—which had led to a new round of toasts with the sounding of the bells. Wayland had poured Nolan's drinks from a special bottle while everyone else drank from the cask. At four bells, the signal for the late watch, Nolan's eyes were glassy. His hungry stares were so blatant, they'd caused Jewel to blush more than once. She'd barely got a drop of grog down her own constricted throat and retreated here to her cabin at the earliest opportunity.

She buttoned her nightgown to her throat. A quick glance in the mirror showed her tangled hair and drawn complexion reflected the harrowing events of the day. She tore the ribbon from her hair. This really was her fault. From the moment she'd sneaked on the ship to the fateful touch of her fingers on Nolan's . . .

Her face burned with shame. Would her father have come back for her if Nolan hadn't taken his life? She would never know. She glanced at her reflection again. In a hasty, impulsive movement, she twisted her hair into a chignon as Parker had taught her, and secured it with the scattered pins from that morning.

A hesitant knock sounded at the door. Jewel opened it before she lost her nerve. Nolan leaned against the frame for support. She touched her upswept hair and stepped back for him to enter. A tilt of her chin exposed her neck and jaw. She dared him to comment on her hair. He needed to know he wasn't going to dictate her actions. She had been too shocked this morning to argue. Now, her taut nerves ached for an opportunity to rail at him. "Do you like my hair?"

He leaned against the door jamb instead of entering. "You look beautiful." His words sounded torn from his throat. He stared around as if he didn't recognize the room. His hesitancy was as unsettling as the loud tick of a clock in a quiet room. She didn't know what she expected—maybe that he would fall on her and ravage her like the savage he had hinted himself to be. But she had never known that kind of treatment from Nolan. She had been trying to convince herself otherwise to lessen her own guilt, but he hadn't ravaged her. He didn't have to.

She glanced up, irritated by her own longings. "Are you staying or not?"

He stepped into the room, closed the door behind him, then leaned against it. She inched toward the narrow bed, putting space between them. Sitting down, she drew her legs up under her gown. Even her exposed feet seemed too provocative in light of his scrutiny. Last night had been so simple. Right now, the idea of their making love seemed awkward and unnatural. They were truly strangers. Her heart beat rapidly in her chest. She

rubbed her shoulders and shivered with anticipation—
and just a little fear.

"I won't hurt you. You should know that." He pushed
himself away from the door and stalked toward her.

She glanced up, unable to ignore the way his dark
blue breeches strained with an unmistakable bulge. It
seemed to swell further under her attention. She swallowed hard and closed her eyes.

The tick shifted as he sat next to her. He kissed the
exposed skin on the back of her neck. She shivered.
Putting her hair up had been a mistake. Her impulsiveness would be the death of her yet.

He used his tongue and mouth to plunder vulnerable
skin. Jewel's breath quickened. He rested a hand on her
knee, and slowly it slid across the cotton gown to the
apex of her thighs. Jewel watched with fascination as he
cupped her. His palm was hot through the cotton, and
the added layer sparked an already combustible tension.
Almost against her will, she arched into his touch, the
pleasure too great to resist.

To Jewel's surprise, Nolan rose from the bed instead
of pushing his advantage. "This time I won't take you
half clothed." His words were gentle, but the way he
yanked out of his coat showed impatience. His shirt
quickly followed. He held her gaze, obviously enjoying
her fascination with his body. She had never seen him
bare-chested. It was well muscled, with dark hair spread-
ing in an inverted triangle. One thing marred his
masculine perfection: a bunched scar above his left nipple. How he must have hated her father for that!

Jewel's gaze jerked up to Nolan's face. He moved to
the edge of the bed, wearing only his loosened breeches.
He picked up her icy hands and massaged them. "What
is it? You're too pale."

Jewel tried to pull her hands away. No matter how
strong her body's desire, her father's memory wouldn't

let her forget what Nolan had done. "You *know* what's wrong."

He dropped her hands like hot coals. Getting up, he stomped the short length of the cabin before turning around with his hands on his hips. "We've already been through this."

Jewel willed herself not to cry in the face of his anger. "We didn't go through it. You abruptly told me you killed my father, then forced me into marriage."

"You agreed to be my wife, and I expect you to honor your vows. I won't have you cowering from me."

Jewel stood, her shoulders squared. "I'm not cowering. I'm confused. I'm upset."

He kept his back to her and ran his fingers through his hair. "I can't change the past, Jewel."

"I'm not asking you to."

"Then what are you asking?" He turned so abruptly, and with such violence, all her courage sank into her knees.

"I don't know." And she didn't. What could he possibly do or say to make the situation better?

His hard gaze softened, as if he knew the impossible divide he would have to cross to reach her. "I . . . Let me make you my wife. Give it a chance."

She nodded, her throat tight with desperation. Despite everything, the idea that their marriage would end before it began frightened her.

He stepped toward her and reached for the buttons of her nightdress. She stood stiffly as he undid them, and willed her mind to relax. Her skin tingled where his warm fingers brushed it. Even the whisper of air where he opened her gown felt like a caress. He glided his hands back over the material still covering her breasts, using the soft cotton to tease her nipples. When his slow trek reached the neck of the gown, he gripped the edges of the collar, forcing her to tilt her neck at the pressure.

His mouth came down on hers in a slow, gentle caress. He tasted her in sips. Small wet kisses persuaded her lips to part. He dipped his tongue into her mouth and she let him invade her, overwhelm her senses. She closed her eyes tightly, pushing away thoughts of her father. Nolan was her husband. Bellamy Leggett was a vague memory who had never really earned her loyalty.

Nolan let go of her gown and grabbed her passive arms, and he draped them around his neck. She let him maneuver her like a rag doll. She focused on his touch. The warmth of his skin. She let the spicy smell of him envelop her while the last traces of thought surrendered to sensation and then, abruptly, he was gone.

Her eyes fluttered open at the cold air that caressed her instead of heat from Nolan's hands and lips. He held her at arm's length, and the space between them loomed as deep and wide as any ocean. His gaze narrowed in the first signs that his anger was returning. "I don't want to do this by myself."

She placed her hands on his bare chest and felt the rapid thud of his heart. The ache of lust had begun, a slow burning at the apex of her thighs. Nolan's eyes drifted shut and he inhaled deeply, apparently satisfied with her wordless response. He gently rested his hands on the curves of her hips, but he remained motionless, allowing her the luxury of exploring him.

Jewel replaced her fingers with her mouth. She loved this man. He was here. He was real. He was all she would ever have, and she had to make things work between them. Maybe if she let her body guide her, her mind would follow. She stood on tiptoe, moving her lips over the puckered scar put there by her father.

Nolan jerked back. "Don't," he whispered fiercely.

The fire in his blue gaze warned her that all his patience had left him. He set her away, grasped her nightgown and pulled it over her head before she could protest. She covered her breasts with her hands. Without her long straight hair unbound and covering her, she felt exposed.

She could feel Nolan's gaze on her, searching her, touching her. He grabbed her wrists and guided them down by her sides. "I like your hair up after all."

He bent down and scooped her into his arms, depositing her on the bed. Jewel tried not to shiver, tried not to think of the scar that marred his perfect body or his fierce words when she'd come too close to what lurked beneath their union. Apparently unaffected by what had just happened, he yanked off his boots and just as swiftly discarded his breeches.

If she had any doubt of his intention to consummate their marriage, his body betrayed him: his arousal was thick and much larger than she remembered. She blushed to think of the way she had caressed him. He seemed less intimidating when she had been the aggressor. With no help from her whatsoever, he was ready to take her. She felt as if her participation didn't really matter at all. Her mind started churning again. Nolan was a dangerous man when he was determined, something her father had found out too late.

Nolan fell on her without the slightest indication that he realized her sudden panic or even cared. She put out her hands to keep him from crushing her. He scooped her to him, oblivious of her protest. When his head came down, she turned her face away, exposing her neck. He took full advantage of the move and nuzzled her nape with openmouthed kisses. His hand captured her breast, his fingers closing around her nipple. She flinched at the abrupt pressure, and he instantly lightened his caress.

"Sorry," he mumbled into her neck.

She shoved at his shoulders. "Nolan. Please stop."

He braced his arms, lifting his weight so he could gaze down at her. "I'm going too fast?" The fire cooled in his eyes as he continued to study her face. "I'm sorry, Jewel. I'll slow down."

He shifted again, and she took the opportunity to slide from beneath him. She braced herself against the ship's hull and hugged her knees to her chest as a barrier between them. "This is harder than I thought it would be."

He brushed his loose hair from his face. He looked as if he had just been abruptly wakened from a deep sleep. "Because I rushed you. After last night, I thought you would be more . . . willing."

Jewel massaged her forehead, an ache growing behind her eyes. "Not that you've said anything to encourage my feelings. And last night was before you told me you killed my father. Is that so strange?"

His compassionate gaze hardened. "What happened had nothing to do with you."

The indignant anger in his voice stirred her own. How dare he sound so wronged? "You knew I was waiting for him to come back and get me. You took that away."

Nolan squared his shoulders, and she could see the muscles in his neck bunch with tension. "Bellamy never was coming back for you. The man you're imagining never existed."

Jewel closed her eyes against his words, knowing they were true—but that didn't change the fact that Bellamy Leggett was her father, and that she'd never found out the kind of man he was for herself. Nolan had stolen that from her. And worse, he seemed unrepentant of the hurt he had caused.

He got off the bed. "I was honest with you. I told you about Bellamy because I wanted to make the best of a bad situation. You agreed to marry me, and now you act like a petulant child."

Jewel scrambled up, clutching the sheet to cover her body. "A petulant child? A bad situation?" She paused, shocked. "Is that all I am to you, a bad situation?"

Nolan yanked on his pants. He was still fully aroused, and Jewel thought she saw his jaw jump as he fastened the last button at his waist. "It started off like that. But . . . I want to make this work. Why can't we just pretend the past never happened?"

Jewel tugged at his arm as he tried to pull on his shirt. "Because I'm hurt. Why can't you understand that?"

"Don't you think I'm hurt? No. I can't argue with you any more. There are things I should be doing on deck. We're going to put into port tomorrow." He reached down and picked up her nightgown, tossed it to her. "Get some sleep. It's been a long day."

"Don't walk out on me. Let's talk about this."

"You don't want to talk. You just want to condemn me," he snapped.

"Because you won't tell me what happened! Explain things to me, so I can understand. Maybe it was all just a misunderstanding, an accident."

Nolan held Jewel's gaze. The slow shake of his head reflected the finality in his fathomless blue eyes. "It wasn't an accident. I'm not going to tell you about it, because you don't need to know." He raked his hands through his hair. "You can't even touch me any more because of what I told you. Do you think I'm going to give you more details?"

Jewel glanced down at her curling toes, unable to take the look of rejection in his eyes. She had lost her father, and now she was losing Nolan. The broken quality in his voice told her she had pushed him too far. She glanced up. She wanted to go to him and wipe away the hurt she saw in his eyes, but she couldn't; she had too much hurt lingering in her own heart. "Well, are you sorry you did it? Are you at least sorry you killed my father?"

Nolan's face became a mask. "No." He turned and walked out the door.

*   *   *

Nolan let the breeze cool his heated body. His loose shirt billowed against him, even its light fabric teasing his charged body. He cursed himself for rushing Jewel; he had lost his head. But she was his bride. His wife. It was his right to lose himself in her body, and he had been drunk with the knowledge.

He had conveniently pushed aside the rift between them in anticipation of gorging himself on her flesh. But she hadn't forgotten. She wouldn't. She couldn't stand his touch, and it ripped a hole through his heart more efficiently than Bellamy's blade could ever do. Jewel's father had won, and the stolen ring on his daughter's finger gloated in victory.

Nolan stared off across the water. Would Bellamy Leggett ever die?

Chapter Fourteen

Seeing Wayland sitting on the companionway, his feet resting on the ladder's top rung, Nolan stopped short before he reached for the ladder leading abovedeck. He glanced around, looking for a way to avoid him. Ever since they had stopped for supplies on St. Martin, the old pirate had been watching his every move. No doubt Wayland was up to no good, but Nolan had too much on his mind to care.

He'd been avoiding Jewel, sleeping in a hammock on deck. Not that he'd been an inattentive husband. He'd gone out of his way to try to make sure her meals were better than usual. When Wayland had inadvertently caught a lobster one night, he'd had it prepared especially for Jewel. Though he had dined with her, eating the usual fare of salted meat and biscuit stew, she'd been sullen, eventually admitting she was menstruating.

Which meant she wasn't pregnant. There was less of a need to continue with this miserable ordeal that was their marriage, only Jewel's lost virtue. The wedding had yet to be recorded anywhere except in Nolan's log. It would be just as easy to dissolve the private union as not. Yet that knowledge only alerted Nolan of how much Jewel had come to mean to him. He wanted to make things right with his wife—and before they found any treasure and she decided she wanted out. Getting her with child was the surest way.

Wayland leaned his head between his knees to yell down at him, distracting Nolan from thoughts of bedding Jewel. "Are you coming up?"

There was no escape. "Are you moving?" he responded.

"Actually, Captain, I've been meaning to have a word with you, and this seems like as good a time as any."

Nolan grabbed the ladder. He would force his way through even if he had to step on Wayland. "I'm busy."

The old pirate scrambled out of his path. Once Nolan set foot on the main deck, he made long strides to the quarterdeck. The sun beat through the thin cotton of his shirt, sending a trickle of sweat down between his shoulderblades. Fat cumulus clouds hung suspended in the sky, unruffled by even the slightest breeze, warning that the fierce heat had no intention of abating.

Wayland stayed on Nolan's heels, unaffected by Nolan's desire to be rid of him or the oppressive temperature that silenced even the ship's caged hens.

"Got something to talk about, and I don't think ya want the whole crew hearing."

Nolan stopped abruptly. There were several things Wayland knew that he would rather forget. And several more he didn't want anyone else to know. "What is it? Be quick. I want to see if the island's been spotted yet."

"That's just what I wanted to speak to you about. That and your wife—or lack of one, you might say."

Nolan's eyes narrowed. "What do you mean?"

Wayland smiled. "Ya make the perfect pirate captain with those dark brows and your wicked scowl."

Nolan had stopped fooling himself he had any will-power left where Jewel was concerned. His present situation proved that. "Tell me what you know about my wife."

"Nothing about the girl. You're the problem. Not many females warm up to a husband who would rather sleep with his crew than his wife."

"You don't know anything about it." Nolan shaded his eyes and studied the progress of a crewman who'd climbed into the rigging to free a tangled line. The man quickly completed the task, and the sail coughed, then inhaled enough wind to fill its belly. Nolan glanced back at Wayland.

Sometime over the last months, the old salt's weathered visage and mismatched eyes had again become familiar, almost comforting. Not that, even back when Nolan was a lad on Bellamy's ship, Wayland could have ever been called anything close to a guardian; it was just that Nolan knew he could always come to Wayland and ask for the brutal truth. Even after Bellamy had stolen his map and assured Nolan it was for his own good, Wayland had told him he'd just been duped. If only Nolan had had the insight to ask whether Bellamy's friendship could be relied upon, he had no doubt Wayland would have steered him true. "Jewel can't forgive me for killing her father, and—"

Wayland cocked his head and studied Nolan. "I don't believe that. That girl's too much in love with you to think straight. It's you who won't forgive yourself."

Nolan swallowed, hard. "I wish that were true. But I'm glad I ended Bellamy's reign of terror. My only regret is that I didn't do it sooner."

"That's what I mean. You're not guilty 'cause you did Bellamy in. You feel bad because you're glad about it. All that Bible-schooling your father gave you doesn't work in the life we lead. You're judging yourself by a preacher's standards. Well, a preacher wouldn't have survived a day on Bellamy Leggett's ship."

Nolan almost laughed, but his humor quickly soured. "You're wrong about that. Bellamy would have taken great pleasure in ruining such a man's soul."

"That's what you think Bellamy did to you, eh? I don't believe it. You're too strong for that. You did what you wanted and blame Bellamy for leading you there."

Nolan's smile faded. "I never wanted to end up like him."

"You didn't. But you ain't no choirboy, either. Accept that about yourself, and get on with it. You're decent enough. Bed your wife. Make things right before it's too late."

" 'Decent enough' coming from you makes me fear I'm in worse shape than I thought. And as far as my wife is concerned . . . I don't intend to rape her."

Wayland cleared his throat and spit on the deck. "Enough of that talk, lad. Don't think I don't remember the fights you and Bellamy got in over the treatment of our women passengers. You wouldn't hurt any woman, I know. But you don't have to. Sweet Jesus, why do you think just because you got a little fire in your veins that you're the devil himself? Just show her you're interested. Show her that fire."

Nolan crossed his arms over his chest. As much as he longed to believe Wayland, he couldn't trust the man any more than he could his own lust-clouded thoughts. Especially not on the subject of bedding his wife. They were both bad seeds, he and Wayland. Although, maybe Wayland was worse. "I don't need moralizing from you. What do you mean, before it's too late?"

Wayland poked him hard in the chest. "You better set things right with your woman afore we get to the island. There are ghosts there, and they're liable to haunt you more than Jewel."

Nolan ignored what would have been a physical challenge from any other man. How did Wayland know so much about his marriage? He knew things Nolan hadn't even admitted to himself.

Nolan forced himself to ask his next question with a trace of mockery, though he secretly hoped for a real answer. "And how do you suggest to make things right with a woman who abhors my touch? My mere presence makes her think of her dead father."

"Bah. That's in your head."

Nolan raked his fingers through his hair. "Believe me, it's not." Whenever he was around Jewel, rational thought escaped him. A more aggressive and demanding part of his anatomy took over, driving him to be all the things he hated. His passions ruled. But still he saw her fear, her loathing.

"Make your wife yours, lad. Don't let Bellamy come between you. Stop looking for Jewel to forgive you for something you had to do. Force her hand. Take her guilt away."

Nolan shook his head. "I don't understand."

Wayland put his hands on his hips. "Be ruthless. You got it in you. Seduce her. Be firm with her. Just do what you have to do. And don't let her take on the guilt for something she had nothing to do with. Of course she feels bad about lying with her father's killer. She's a softhearted woman with way too much love and forgiveness."

Nolan stared at the deck. "You're right. I don't deserve her."

"At last we agree on something. You don't deserve her—not the way you're acting now, so you better start being a better man. It's obvious the chit loves you, though why is a mystery to me. We both know Bellamy was a rotten father. He'll only hurt the girl more if you give him the chance. You, on the other hand are her husband. And you could be a good one. Give her what she wants—a man who loves her. She wants to love you. Let her. Be man enough to take on the guilt, and love her till she's too senseless to even think of the no-good father who deserted her."

Nolan's head reeled with Wayland's words. He had been wanting Jewel's absolution. The realization left him feeling small and selfish. It wasn't Jewel's responsibility to absolve him from the guilt that still crept up on him every time he thought of what he had done to Bellamy.

Yet Wayland's advice sounded too good to be true. And since it was coming from Wayland, it probably was. In the past, Wayland had always championed Bellamy. Suspicion clouded Nolan's burst of hope. "Don't let Bellamy do more harm to his daughter? What happened to not speaking ill of the dead?"

Wayland grinned. "A sudden interest in the living."

Nolan didn't ask for any more information. He didn't care. The old pirate had helped him open his eyes, no matter his motives. At his first opportunity Nolan would make Jewel his wife in reality. He would no longer expect her to come to him without doubts; he would kiss away those doubts. He would no longer expect her to turn against her childhood image of a man who didn't exist; he would give her one that did.

Nolan felt he'd just been released from a gibbet. "Climb up to the crow's nest with me and let's see if our course is right," he said to Wayland. He started walking in the direction of the main mast.

The bustle of excited shouts reached them before they found their destination. Nolan quickened his pace to discover the cause for excitement. He hadn't expected to find the island just yet, but there were some narrow straits that could point them in the right direction.

Parker had climbed a quarter of the way up the mast.

He held on to a step and leaned out. A spyglass was fixed to his eye, and he focused on something left of the horizon.

"What is it Mr. Tyrell?" Nolan called.

Parker lowered the glass. "I hoped the watchman was wrong. It's a ship. Take a look yourself."

Parker tossed down the telescope. Nolan caught it in one hand and brought it to his eye. The ship was a sloop, faster than the *Integrity* but surely not as well armed. He didn't see any reason for concern. Even if it were British, he doubted it would be bold enough to attack. Nolan scanned the length of the vessel. His gaze stopped at the black and white flag flying on her stern.

Pirates!

Chapter Fifteen

As the hours passed, the pirate ship's approach went from a slow creep on the horizon to the speed of a dolphin slicing through the water. Sunset was upon them. The other vessel would be at their side before the turquoise sea extinguished the sun's last fiery rays. Nolan rubbed his bristled chin. His beard itched, but his gruff appearance would help his plan. He prayed he wouldn't see the approach of a third ship in the distance. He could handle one. Two might defeat him, and he couldn't be defeated.

The *Integrity* kept her course. Out-running the other ship was a futile effort. And one didn't have to be a former pirate to know how angry pirates became when forced to chase or a fight. Total submission was always expected, for it was received most of the time. Once the pirates showed their standard, captains surrendered in hopes of better treatment. Nolan had firsthand experience with pirates' "leniency." He wouldn't take the risk.

Jewel had wandered onto the deck earlier in the day, and Nolan had sent her below with a brisk command.

He couldn't risk her being spotted. The last thing he wanted was for the pirates to know he had a woman on board. With Wayland at his side, Nolan hoped to convince their pursuers he had gone on the account, returned to his former life. Bellamy had had quite a reputation in the brethren of pirates. Nolan had shared in those exploits, even had a few of his own.

Though pirates weren't as keen on brotherhood as on getting what they could with the least amount of effort, Nolan might be able to avoid a fight with the lure of joining efforts to pick off other merchant vessels—a proposal he would never keep. But more than likely, if the other ship thought him a fierce foe, their day would be won without a shot, and that would keep other sea rovers from thinking them easy prey. Nolan planned to prove himself fiercer than any pirate past or present.

He discarded his blue coat and opened his white shirt to the middle of his chest. With the sleeves turned up to his elbow, his hair falling around his shoulders, he fit the image the other ship expected. A large gold earring the size of a child's wrist, one Wayland had stashed, completed the facade. Even better would have been procuring a jeweled cross or something equally decadent; such obvious greed for plunder was a highly admired trait among pirates. The hole in Nolan's lobe had grown closed, but he'd reopened it with a little encouragement. He only wished he had a Jolly Roger to raise.

While back in Boston, the idea of ever flying under the black flag again had been unthinkable. But nothing had gone as he had planned since leaving. At this point, he was open to anything. He'd avoid a battle if he could . . . yet he had no qualms about blowing the other ship out of the water, if it came to that. Nothing would be too drastic to keep Jewel from falling into the approaching ship's hands. If he doubted his resolve for a moment, which he didn't, he could summon female screams from his past that still haunted him.

He waited, letting the on coming pirates decide their own fate, with a sinking suspicion about their presence. The white skull with crossed swords underneath, emblazoned against a black background, was unremarkable. Several pirates flew such varying versions of the skull-and-crossbones.

He glanced at Wayland again. The pirate swore he had nothing to do with the ship on their tail, but he had been acting strange ever since St. Martin. Had the man set a trap in order to steal the map? Did that make sense?

The decks were cleared for an attack, though Nolan made sure no visible signs gave away their readiness. Their guns were loaded, but the gunports remained closed. The other vessel would think them at a disadvantage, unless they already knew who they were. Which was Nolan's biggest fear.

Nolan glanced at Wayland. "Do you recognize them?"

"Not the vessel. But that don't mean anything. Never knew a pirate not to abandon either a ship or a whore if a better one came along." The pirate kept his gaze on the swiftly approaching sloop.

Its single mast appeared slightly crooked as the ship bobbed and dipped a little drunkenly. If this was the best vessel the pirates could capture, Nolan could stop worrying. He handed Wayland the telescope. "Take a look at their captain."

Wayland scanned the other ship's deck. "What do you know? It's an old friend of yours."

Nolan turned abruptly. His nagging premonition became dread. "What? Who do you see?"

"Look for yourself." Wayland returned the spyglass. "Surprised you didn't recognize him. That's Handsome Jack Casper. We had a run in or two with him on Tortuga."

"What happened to his nose?" Once Wayland said the name, Nolan's gaze was drawn to a man standing in the center of the deck.

Wayland laughed. "That's why he's called Handsome Jack instead of Smiling Jack these days."

Jack Casper was pointing and giving orders. His hair had turned from brown to gray, and a significant part of his nose was missing. He wore a permanent sneer. Nolan readjusted the glass and looked again. He wasn't sneering. Part of his lip had been cut away as well. "I'm glad I got out of this business in one piece."

"You get a little more courage with every part you lose. That's worth more to a man than a pretty face."

Nolan glanced at Wayland's scarred visage. Nolan never put much value on his own good looks, but he'd take a pretty face over the alternative. He didn't need courage today. He was a trapped man with something very important to defend. Therefore, he was dangerous. "Should we kill Handsome Jack outright, or should we hear what he has to say first?"

Wayland shrugged. "Just 'cause he answers to Handsome Jack don't mean he lost the sense of humor that got him his former nickname. Also, kill him outright and you're liable to bring the Brethren down on our heads."

"I don't remember there being such kinship in the pirate folds. The Brethren had a relationship more like Cain and Abel, as I recall."

Wayland laughed. "An apt description. Still, kill him and the others might be alerted we have something of value. I think it's better to deal with Jack—tell him we're looking for plunder like himself, and send him on his way."

Nolan stiffened. "And what of Jewel? What if things go wrong? My crew—"

"Nothing will happen to the chit. I'll see to that."

"You won't have to, because I'll blow them out of

the water if something goes wrong. I'll kill them all, myself." Nolan knew with certainty he would carry out the threat. He had been suppressing the violence he was capable of for too long. If his dark nature could keep Jewel safe, he would give it full rein.

Parker rushed forward with a brass horn in his hand. "The other vessel summoned us," he said. "They want us to send a boat over with you on board. They asked for Nolan Kent."

Nolan had been so involved in his thoughts, he hadn't heard. They'd asked for Nolan Kent—his notorious grandfather's name—instead of Kenton. They knew exactly who he was, and probably that he carried the famous map on board. Not a pirate alive hadn't dug for his grandfather's treasure at least once. To have the map, men would take risks beyond reason. Bellamy had kept the desperate and foolhardy at bay with his larger-than-life reputation. For the first time since Nolan had dispatched his former mentor, he wished to have Bellamy by his side. He stared at Wayland again, accusation undoubtedly showing in his eyes.

Wayland's brown eye narrowed. "I told you, I don't know anything about this."

Nolan grabbed the horn and strode to the railing. "You come over here, Casper."

"You're inviting those villains on board?" Parker asked.

"They're getting out the grappling hooks," said Wayland.

"Parker, are the swivel cannons loaded with chain shot?"

The lieutenant hesitated, as if caught off guard. "Yes, Captain."

"Good. Have the gunners aim them for Casper's main mast." Then Nolan shouted a warning to the other ship without the horn: "The first grappling hook that lands on my vessel brings down your mast."

Nolan could feel himself changing. He felt more and more as if his current dress fit the man inside better than a stiff coat and brass buttons. He adjusted the sword slung low on his hip. He was ready for a fight. "Does Jewel know to stay below?"

Wayland nodded. "I knew you had it in you, Nolan. This is the man you should be. Tough. Commanding. Merci—"

"Open the gun ports." Nolan gave the command to no one in particular, but he heard his words echoed through the ship, followed by the creak of wood as ports slammed open and cannon rolled out.

"If you surrender now, we'll spare your crew," came a shout from the other deck.

Nolan knew a bluff when he heard it. He had feared a battle with Jewel on board, but now he would take the risk. A show of weakness would never work. He had the upper hand and he needed to keep it. "Get over here, Casper, before I blow you out of the water."

"I heard you turned land lover, Nolan. Guess I was wrong. Buy me a drink?" Jack yelled. He might have lost the ⸏ame "Smiling" but good humor still rang in his voice.

"You've got five minutes to have your longboat in the water with you on it," called Nolan. He handed Parker the speaking horn, then folded his arms over his chest. Negotiations were over.

Handsome Jack complied in half the time. Almost immediately he was on the *Integrity*'s deck with his hand extended and, despite his mangled visage, what would have been a smile on his face.

Nolan stood, feet apart, ignoring the show of friendship. He no longer was playing a part. He had come home, and the knowledge chilled at the same time it comforted him. He no longer had to struggle against his dark side, fighting something he couldn't control. Though the thin appearance and bent frame might have made another man dismiss him as a threat, Nolan watched Jack's hands. The pirate was known to keep a dagger or two stuffed in his boots, and his accuracy was legendary.

Handsome Jack didn't take offense at Nolan's unwelcoming stance. Instead, the old captain cocked his head and studied him from head to toe. "I knew Bellamy's days was numbered as cock of the walk once he took you on board. You've done your grandpa proud."

Nolan didn't shift his feet or flinch as he once would have done when compared to his infamous grandfather. He could no longer deny the truth, no longer wanted to. His hand rested on the hilt of his sword, and he met Jack's gaze with a stare. "State your business."

Handsome Jack rubbed his thin belly. "How 'bout a bite to eat or maybe a drink? Not much to ask between old friends, is it?"

"How 'bout I let you keep the rest of your nose?"

Jack raised his eyebrows and turned to Wayland. "He's gotten mean as Blackbeard hisself. What's got into him?"

Wayland stepped forward. "He's not one to turn the other cheek—but then, you said you heard about Bellamy. You threatened us, and we want to know why."

"Can't a fella make a living anymore? It's been lean years. I saw you sneaking around St. Martin, Wayland. When I followed you back to your ship, I saw Nolan here. Thought maybe you needed a ship to join ya."

Nolan glanced at Wayland. If Jack had followed him without his knowledge, the old pirate must be losing his edge. He raised an eyebrow in question and Wayland looked away. Nolan smirked, glad to finally have unnerved him.

"Your crew looks like they've been hit by scurvy more than once," he said to Jack.

The pirate laughed. "Not scurvy, just a little too much rum. We can still fight, though. What do you say?"

Nolan looked Jack over. He had never been much of a pirate. He loved the good life. His takes ranged far and few between because he stayed drunk every chance he got. His raids were motivated to fund his lascivious habits. Jack had always had a cup for Nolan and a smile. He'd had one for everyone. Against his better judgment, Nolan let his sense of fair play have one last stand. "Come below, Casper. We'll feed you and then you're on your way."

"You're a good lad, Nolan. I always said so, didn't I, Wayland?" Jack eagerly followed him.

"Ah, who could understand you when you were in your cups most of the time," Wayland grumbled.

They entered the galley, and Nolan sent a cask of undiluted rum over to the other ship as an added incentive to keep the peace. Drunk pirates were worthless. Jack and his men didn't look too threatening, but Nolan wasn't taking any chances. Jack eyed the keg hungrily. Nolan filled a tin cup, and handed it to him. With the threat of battle over, Nolan ordered the cook to light the fires. Everyone could use a hot meal.

Jack and a few of his men who had come aboard to join in the festivities sat at the galley's long table with Wayland, exchanging raucous stories. Nolan recognized men he'd known in his youth, a few that hadn't been much older than he. The glass and brass lantern that lazily swung above their heads cast evil shadows across their gaunt faces. Jack wasn't the only one who'd not fared well over the years. Not a man at the table didn't have a visible scar or a missing digit to boast of their exploits. Skin the color and texture of old leather stretched across their hollow faces, making it hard to put an accurate age to any of them.

Nolan stood by the wall, refusing to relax his guard. Jack and his crew appeared harmless enough, more eager for drink than a fight. Even so, Nolan couldn't shake the chill of dread brought on by once again being surrounded by a band of pirates: men who could slap you on the back one minute and slit your throat the next. Though he had invited them on board to prove his swagger was backed up by a heavily gunned ship, he'd be glad when the show was over.

Handsome Jack slipped his hand into the tattered coat he wore without a shirt. Nolan tensed and moved away from the wall. Though all the men had been thoroughly searched, Nolan knew not to take anything for granted. Jack held up a deck of cards. "Don't pounce on me, you're liable to break something. These old bones aren't what they used to be. Just thought a friendly game could make my visit worthwhile."

Nolan leaned back against the wall. "I don't gamble."

Jack returned the cards to the inside pocket of his jacket. "I can see that."

Crockery bowls were filled and passed to the visitors, but Jack only toyed with his stew, preferring the grog. After several glasses of the watered-down brew, his hands stopped shaking. He said, "That was something, the way you brought down Bellamy Leggett. There was no love lost between us, that's for sure, but still, it was a shock to know he'd been done in by the lad he treated like his own son."

Nolan shifted slightly. He continued his relaxed facade but was ready to spring at any moment. "He treated me like his slave."

Jack shrugged. "Yeah? My own father treated me worse than that. Sold me to a merchant when I was barely old enough to buckle me shoes." He took another long swallow of grog. "I still think I see old Bellamy sometimes."

Wayland stared into his cup. "You've probably started to see things. They say that's what happens when the rum starts to kill you."

Jack lifted his cup in a toast. "Well, if anyone should know, it'd be you."

Wayland's scathing rebuttal was lost as Nolan drifted away from the conversation. The word would be out soon enough that he was on the account. The tightrope he had been walking since the mutiny had snapped, and instead of hurling to earth, Nolan felt he had caught the wind and finally would be able to soar. His loyalties had not changed. He still believed in freedom, for his country and himself. He had killed Bellamy because he had to. He would kill again in the coming months, but this time for a just cause, not money. No longer would he let his father's sense of morality stand in the way of what he wanted or needed. That included his relationship with his wife. Pirates plundered. Nolan closed his eyes and imagined his next visit with Jewel.

He heard her voice, followed by a muffled scream. He opened his eyes, jerking away from the wall. Hearing her shriek in terror was not part of his fantasy. "Keep an eye on them," he called to Wayland as he rushed from the galley.

He leaped up the steps leading to the deck. Night had settled in a thick black blanket. He listened but didn't hear any more noise. The scream had come from up above; he was sure of it. "Parker," Nolan called out.

"Over here. He has Jewel," the lieutenant yelled from the stern.

Nolan ran while drawing his sword. He spotted Jewel pushed up against the railing. A man he didn't recognize stood beside her, not much bigger than Jewel but holding her tightly. In a few more steps, Nolan saw the glint of the knife against her throat. He slowed to a more cautious approach.

Parker held a pistol trained on the couple.

The man tightened his grip on Jewel at Nolan's approach. Her sharp intake of breath sounded in Nolan's ears like a cannon blast. A dark trickle of blood slid down her white neck.

"Back off, mates, or I'll slit her throat. That's a promise." The sailor scooted sideways with Jewel. Parker followed with the barrel of his pistol.

"Mr. Tyrell, put that away," Nolan ordered, his voice surprisingly calm. He put his own sword away.

Parker grudgingly lowered the pistol, but his stance warned he was primed to pounce empty-handed—which didn't do anything to relax the man who held Jewel.

Nolan moved forward with slow, careful steps. He heard footsteps coming up behind him, but he didn't turn around. Someone carried a lantern. When the ring of light reached Jewel, the fear it illuminated on her face tore at Nolan's ability to be rational. The man holding her was going to die for this.

"What the hell are you doing, Marcus?" called Handsome Jack.

"She's mine, Jack. I won't be sharing her. Tell them to back off unless they want to see her slit in two," said the pirate holding Jewel.

Nolan sensed Jewel searching out his gaze, but he avoided glancing at her directly. He didn't want to take his eyes off her captor for a minute. After only one glimpse at her face, Nolan knew that if he focused on the terror clouding her eyes, he wouldn't be able to do what he must.

Handsome Jack stepped beside Nolan, his hands raised in surrender. "Did you get the map at least?"

Wayland pointed at Jack accusingly. "You bloody bastard. That's what you wanted the whole time."

"I-I forgot about the map," called Jewel's captor.

Nolan recognized the first signs of panic. It made the man more dangerous, but it also weakened his resolve.

Jack turned to Nolan. "I got a deal that will make everyone happy. We'll trade the map for the girl."

Nolan had already committed a crucial mistake by showing these bastards the slightest consideration. He wouldn't repeat it. "I told you, I don't gamble."

"I ain't giving up this girl. They'll kill me if I do, Jack. That dark-haired one's got cold eyes."

Jack smiled. The effect was frightening. "It won't be a gamble, just a fair trade between friends. We'll give you back your lady friend, and you give us your grandpa's map. I know you got it. Don't think a dried-up old buzzard like Wayland would be with you for any other reason."

Nolan returned Jack's smile. "No deals. But I'll make you a promise, Casper. If you don't get your crewman to release the girl, I'll slaughter every member of your crew. Starting with you."

Jack nodded, then bent to retrieve something from his boot. Nolan reached for his sword. The other man stopped and winked. With slow, careful movements, he pulled a thin dagger from a slit in his boots—apparently a hiding place Nolan's crew hadn't been thorough enough to find. Nolan held his breath, then nodded.

"I know you're a man of your word, Nolan, so I guess that leaves me no . . . *choice*." Jack swiveled on the balls of his feet and flung his knife at the pirate who held Jewel. A howl of pain tore from his throat as Marcus clutched a handle that quivered from his left eye. Jewel stumbled forward. Her captor fell to his knees, his screams worse for their horror and pleas for help.

Nolan reached for Jewel and yanked her against him. She trembled in his arms, so he pressed her tighter. He kissed the top of her head and whispered soothing words in her ear, despite the onlookers that would surely note his weakness. "Glad you haven't lost your aim, Jack," he said when he was able to find his voice. Even his best efforts didn't stop the telling emotion from making his words raspy.

Handsome Jack massaged a wrist. "Well, maybe a little. I was aiming for his throat."

Jewel pushed out of Nolan's embrace. "You knew! You knew he was going to do that. Why didn't you just give him the map?" she gasped.

Nolan tried to pull her back into his arms. "Calm down, sweetheart. You're safe now." He needed to hold her to calm his own racing heart. He had seen Jack throw before, even lost a small fortune in betting against his accuracy. Letting Jack take down his own crewmember had caused Nolan to risk more than Jewel's life. He'd risked his own. If he had made a mistake and Jewel died, it would have killed him.

She struggled against him, but he held on to her arm, keeping her from bolting.

Wayland slapped Jack on the back, saying to Jewel, "Don't fret, chit. A knife in the eye did the trick as well as a cut to the neck. 'Course, it might not be fatal."

Jack walked to his crewman. "This one will be."

Marcus rolled on the deck. "Jack, Jack. Where are you? Am I going to die, Jack?"

Jack signaled to Wayland. "Help me with him, will ya?"

Wayland knelt beside the injured man and looked at Jack. "You want me to take the knife out?"

"Nah. I'm afraid the eye will come with it." He glanced at Wayland. "No offense, but I can't stomach that. Just help me pick him up." He put his hands under Marcus's shoulder and tilted him up.

"Jack. Are you there, Jack? Am I going to die, Jack?"

"Afraid so, Marcus." Jack reached behind him and removed a larger dagger from the lining of his jacket. Nolan was going to have a talk with his crew about search procedures as soon as possible. Jack dragged the knife across Marcus's neck, silencing his cries. "Let's toss him. Ready? One, two, three." He and Wayland lifted Marcus's lifeless form and tossed him over the side. After a few seconds, a splash broke the silence.

Jewel turned her face into Nolan's chest, sobbing. Nolan stroked her hair. Night disguised the blood spilled on the deck. The large pool appeared as harmless as water. To spare Jewel, he'd have a crewman scrub it away before morning. Nolan felt nothing but cold satisfaction at the grisly scene.

Jack turned back to Nolan. "Are we settled?"

"Settled? I think not. You try to steal from me while I was feeding your mangy crew?" Nolan held Jewel tighter. He shouldn't let the other man see how much she meant to him, but he couldn't let her go. Thinking how close he'd come to losing her sped his heart to an unsteady beat. "We are far from settled, Jack."

Jewel wrenched free. "Is this all you care about? Your precious map. I was almost killed! Why didn't you just let them kill me?"

Jack spoke up. "Because he woulda killed me, too. Messing with a man's woman is a serious offense."

Jewel turned to Jack. "I'm not his 'woman.' I'm his—"

Nolan grabbed her arm and jerked, hard. "Quiet. You've caused enough trouble for one night." His grip tightened until he could feel the bone beneath her skin. He didn't doubt he was bruising her.

Jack wanted the map, not unlike a hundred other pirates who knew of Captain Kent's legend. Bellamy's fierce reputation had kept the treasure hunters at bay while he lived. Nolan's growing reputation would have to do the same. Having his Achilles heel exposed was a risk he couldn't take. It was fine if they thought he was smitten with his latest whore. He didn't want word to spread that he had a deeper, more permanent bond with the woman on his ship.

Jewel closed her mouth, but the look she gave him told him how much he'd hurt her. He shoved her behind him, keeping a tight grip on her wrist.

"You're in luck, Jack. You saved my woman's life, and seeing as she's a fresh piece, I'm quite grateful. So I'm going to let you live."

Jack smiled. "I knew you was a good lad."

Nolan returned his smile. "You and your crew can take refuge in your longboats while we burn your ship to the waterline."

"Come on, Nolan. Let me make you another deal."

"No, deals, Jack. I'm giving you your life. That's more than you deserve."

Jack shrugged. "Could we have a little libation for our journey? It's a long way to shore."

"All you want."

Jack smiled. "Ah, you *are* a good lad, Nolan."

"But that's not the message I want you to give to the Brethren. Make it clear that Nolan Kent is following in his grandfather's footsteps. Anyone else who has any ideas about getting the map won't get off as lucky as you."

Jack bowed. "My pleasure, Captain Kent."

Nolan grinned, satisfied that it held enough of the sinister to convince anyone he was a bloodthirsty villain. "Parker, set them in the water and clear out anything of value from their ship."

As Jack and his crew were herded onto the rope ladder, Nolan let Jewel yank her wrist free of his grasp. "Why didn't you tell that man I'm your wife?"

Nolan shrugged. "Because you're not."

223

Jewel stepped back as if he had threatened her with his fist. "You lied to me? That wedding wasn't legal? You just planned on using me to get what you wanted!"

Nolan raked his fingers though his hair. He snagged the forgotten gold earring. He would keep it. It suited his change of plans. "We both know I haven't gotten what I want. But that's going to change."

Jewel backed away from him, eyeing him warily. "You have your precious map. What else could you want?"

Nolan grabbed her wrist and pulled her to him. "You. In reality as well as in name."

He bent his knees, forcing Jewel over his shoulder. She braced her hands on his back and lifted her upper body, trying to force him to put her down. "I-I won't be treated like this."

Nolan didn't release her, even when she started to kick. "It's your choice, sweetheart. You're not my wife *yet*, but you will be. We can do it the easy way or the hard way, but by daybreak this marriage will be consummated."

Chapter Sixteen

Jewel backed into the farthest corner of the cabin the moment Nolan set her on her feet. He had risked her life for his precious map: she wouldn't just docilely bend to his will now that he had the whim to toss up her skirts. With his hair wild, dark stubble covering his chin and a gold hoop glinting wickedly against his tanned neck, the Nolan she knew had disappeared. She should be terrified, but her heart raced and traitorous desire tightened her belly.

Nolan leaned against the bolted door, watching. "Come here."

Jewel shook her head. "Who are you?"

Nolan grinned. His teeth looked white and ferocious against the black of his beard. "I'm the man you want. I'm the man you've wanted since we first met." He spread his arms wide. "And I'm all yours."

He stalked toward her. The intensity in his blue eyes effected her with the same physical sensation of a finger drawn down her spine. He hadn't looked at her like that since before their wedding. "I was only a child when we first met."

He yanked his loose shirt over his head, then dropped it to the floor. "A little girl with dreamy eyes. You wanted someone to rescue you, and I did."

Jewel scoffed and put her hands on her hips. The flood of ire eased her desire, which was battling for control. "Hardly. I wanted to escape being forced to marry a man I didn't love."

She wished she could take back her words the moment they left her lips. Oh, yes, she had escaped one unpleasant fate only to land in an ironically opposite predicament. Instead of living a life with someone she didn't love, she'd be forever pining over a man who didn't love her. Jewel raised her chin, not wanting Nolan to witness the shadows that must have danced across her gaze at her own thoughts. "And you certainly didn't rescue me. I had to sneak on your ship, in case you've forgotten."

Nolan stopped when they were toe to toe. Jewel held her breath, afraid he would touch her and even more afraid that he wouldn't. The stare he leveled on her certainly didn't hint at indifference. Though Jewel had come to understand that lust and love were entirely two different things, at the moment it didn't seem to matter. The pull of Nolan's heated gaze weakened her knees to the consistency of warmed honey.

Jewel's back hit something solid, and she found herself pinned in the narrow space between the bunk and the curve of the hull. Nolan braced his forearms on either side of her, trapping her, then bent his head to whisper in her ear, "I haven't forgotten anything." His breath was the only thing that touched her. "I haven't forgotten the way you looked at me when I walked into the tavern that second time. You were a woman then. A woman hungry for adventure . . . and for a man."

Jewel turned her face away from his; she couldn't look into his eyes and lie. "That's not true." She sneaked a quick peek at him. His expression betrayed nothing beyond desire. "Well, only a part of it's true. I wanted to escape Charles Town—see the world, the way my father promised."

Nolan smiled. "And you wanted me, too. Maybe you didn't understand it. But you did want me." He touched his tongue to the vulnerable side of her neck, which she had foolishly exposed to him. "Say you did."

She turned her head abruptly, sending hair across the spot he'd been teasing, and glared at him. "I won't say it. I wasn't looking for a husband. That was my mother's idea."

He pressed his hips against hers. His body was fully ready to carry out the promise in his smoldering gaze. "I don't want you to say you wanted any man. I want you to say you wanted me." He smelled her hair. "You belong to me and I to you. I fought it, but I won't any more."

Jewel forced herself to stare into his gaze and not lean into the hard planes of his body. If his words were spoken with even a hint of tenderness, she might toss aside her doubt and give in to the tension that had begun to gnaw at her belly. He left no question that he wanted her in this moment; but what came after that still frightened her. She was afraid to even suspect that his feelings might go deeper than he'd ever admitted. Words were easily given, but actions were truth. "Yet you'd risk losing me for the sake of that map."

Nolan slipped his hands around her waist, pulling her snugly against the hard proof of his determination to bed her. "Never." He kissed her neck and then her earlobe. "It was the only way. They would have taken you for sure once they had what they wanted. And I would have thrown that knife myself, but my hands shook too badly."

He rubbed himself in slow, lazy circles around the apex of her thighs. Jewel leaned her head back and closed her eyes. She had missed him so. "I want to believe you, but . . ."

Nolan took her hand and guided it between their bodies. Heat radiated through his clothing. Jewel closed her fingers around him before she could stop herself. Her heartbeat quickened with the pulse beneath her fingertips.

Nolan's breath came out a husky sigh. "Then, believe this: I haven't forgotten what it feels like to be inside you. Believe what there is between us, because it is real. I'm your husband, Jewel. This is right."

Jewel pulled her hand away, bringing it to his chest to push him off. "It's not that simple."

He gripped her wrists. "Yes, it is," he ground out between his teeth. He put her arms around his neck, then pulled her to him roughly. "I don't expect you to forgive me for what happened. I know you can't. But I still want you as my wife."

She stared at his face, trying to understand the change in him. He moved his hands up from her waist to massage her back. He kept up the subtle pressure, forcing her against him. Of their own will, her fingers wrapped themselves in his hair.

"I know what I am now. I took you, and I'm keeping you. You're my wife." His hands cupped her face. "Accept that and accept me."

He held her still while he lowered his mouth to hers. No part of her mind or body had any strength to resist. His lips were soft and coaxing, even gentle. The kiss displayed nothing of the hunger he had shown when he entered the room. She leaned into him, returned his kiss.

He forcefully slid his tongue into her mouth. She clung to him, hungrily accepting his invasion.

His hands drifted to her bottom. He cupped her and pulled her to him. Liquid heat dampened her thighs at the contact, forcing her to arch against him, the urge to be rid of the layers of their clothing unbearable. A low growl in the back of his throat set off another wave of lust that sent pulses straight to her sex.

He didn't press his advantage, but seemed to linger with the slow, torturous kisses he trailed to the hollow beneath her chin. "That's it. Melt for me, sweetheart. I'm going to make everything up to you the only way I know how."

He reached for the lacings of her gown. He peeled away her clothes, kissing each section of exposed skin as it was revealed. He got to his knees to untie the waistband of her skirt. She stiffened and stilled his hands by placing her own over them. He gazed up at her, his eyelids heavy and his gaze glazed. "Let me undress you. I want to see you. All of you."

She blushed but nodded, the intensity of his request too powerful to refuse. It felt strange to have him on his knees before her, worshipping her. She touched his hair. Strange, but intoxicatingly wonderful. With a sudden realization, she knew she would let this man do anything he wanted to her body, just so she could be close to him.

He placed a feather-light kiss on her navel. "I want to see your smooth belly swell with my seed. Then there'll be no chance of you leaving me."

She brushed back his hair and tried to relax while he slid her skirts over her hips. "Oh, Nolan—I won't leave you. I never even thought of it." She almost told him again that she loved him but swallowed the words before they were out. Their union was still too precarious. She wasn't ready for any more illusions to be shattered if he didn't respond favorably to her confession.

He swirled his tongue inside her belly button. "Prove it to me. Let me be your husband. Let me consummate our marriage."

She laughed. "Do I have a choice?"

He lightly nipped the sensitive skin covering her hip-bone. "Absolutely. You have to want it, too. As much as I do."

He kissed the curls at the apex of her thighs and she tried to pull away. His hands cupping her bottom held her firmly in place. He gave her another quick kiss and lifted his head. "Don't pull away from me."

His palms roamed over the curve of her bottom, then dipped into the vee at the top of her thighs. Despite her commitment to retain an ounce of modesty, he coaxed her thighs slightly apart. A draw of his tongue across the overly sensitized flesh he managed to expose forced a gasp from Jewel that sounded deceptively like a breathless moan.

"Your scent tells me you like this. Spread your legs for me. Let us both have what we want."

The sight of him kneeling before her, his face so close to her most private part, flooded her with a heady mix of anticipation and shock. "Shouldn't we get in bed?"

He slid his palms around her thighs, gently nudging them wider. "Why?"

She was forced to move or fall. "I thought you wanted my consent."

He dipped his head and licked her. Heat rushed to the points his tongue touched. He chuckled, deep in his throat. "You're so wet, you're screaming 'yes,' sweet-heart."

Jewel tried to pull back, but he held her thighs firmly. "Then stop."

"We *want* you wet." He lifted his head only long enough to say those words. When he touched her again, he used his mouth and his tongue, devouring her in an openmouthed kiss that threatened to buckle her knees. He dipped his tongue inside her, and she cried out.

"Nolan," she pleaded, in serious danger of collapsing.

To her relief, he slid his hands and mouth up her body. But with his withdrawal, her body throbbed in protest. She felt as if she had swallowed her heart and it beat thickly between her parted legs. She tried to find the courage to beg him to kiss her there again. He stopped at her breast. She forced herself to breathe evenly, to get hold of her racing desire, but it was impossible as he forged ahead undaunted. He suckled one nipple and then the other, so thoroughly she thought her knees did buckle. When she wavered, he steadied her with a firm arm wrapped around the small of her back.

He guided her to the bunk. "Tell me what you want me to do now, Jewel."

She felt too weak to even put up a token struggle. She was wet, warm and aching for him. All her sensations centered between her legs. If he didn't hurry, she would be begging him.

He stood over the bed, the cocky grin on his face warning her that her want showed too plainly. "Tell me. *Say* it."

Her eyelids were heavy, and she had no desire to argue over his confident expression. He had her right where he wanted her and they both knew it. She let her gaze slide down to his erection. He had shucked off his pants and boots. She swore he visibly swelled while she gazed at him. She glanced back up at his face and saw he had lost his satisfied smirk. She smiled and stretched, arching back off the bed. The look on his face gave her all the courage she needed. She touched her wet center, shocked by the heat radiating from her body. "Kiss me here again."

She lifted her knees and he rewarded her cooperation by kissing the inside of her thigh. His hot breath was as heady as his kiss. He maneuvered himself so he lay half on the bunk while he knelt on the deck. "Do you want me to make you scream?" He yanked her to him a bit roughly. He spread her thighs, and she closed her eyes, readying herself for the wash of sensation that would make thinking impossible. He traced her opening with a single teasing finger. "Do you?"

She squirmed, but he held her still. His gaze questioned her.

"No. Not yet." She laid her head back and relaxed, giving in to the attention her body craved. "When did you get so . . . difficult?"

He kissed the inside of her thigh. His thumb found the center of her pleasure and she bit her lip to keep from moaning. "Since I stopped trying to deny what I want." He used his tongue to lick closer to where his hand caressed her, and a tremble raced through her limbs, tightening her already hard nipples. She would let him do anything he wanted from here on. Her knees dropped to the sides of their own accord.

He chuckled, probably at her wanton abandon, and straightened her leg with his free hand. He lifted his head and nuzzled the back of her knee. All the while, he kept a finger moving inside her and his thumb circling the center of her desire. "I love the taste of you. The feel. I want to be inside you."

His husky voice played on her nerves as thoroughly as his hand and his mouth. The muscles in her thigh started to contract, and she knew she was spiraling quickly to a place where she would have no control. The way he touched her, the way he leaned between her spread legs left her so vulnerable. She feared she would crumble before he ever got inside her. "Please, Nolan."

"Please what?"

Her hips bucked to the rhythm of his finger. Her gaze fell back behind her eyelids. "Make love to me."

He continued his assault while nuzzling up and down the inside of her thigh. "I am."

"No. You know what I want."

"Tell me." He shifted his weight.

The hard tip of him nudged against her opening and she came apart. Her body convulsed against his finger. He nipped at her leg and held her while she writhed. When her contractions slowed, he withdrew his hand.

She could barely catch her breath to protest when he nudged his shoulder under her other leg. He pulled her down and entered her in a hard, deep thrust. "Is this what you want?"

She felt the tension build again before it was fully released. His urgency flooded her with another wave of desire. His hands gripped her waist, pulling her down with each of his thrusts. She felt herself tumble toward ecstasy again when he suddenly stopped. He held himself buried deep inside her. She could feel his involuntary pulses. She opened her eyes, seeing a line of sweat trail down his taut neck, and the firm set of his jaw. He teetered on the brink of release.

He moved to kiss her mouth, covering her completely with his body. The kiss was a gentle peck, nothing like the driving urgency to which he had just put an untimely halt. She closed her eyes and undulated her hips. He held her firmly to him, stilling her movements. "Look at me."

She opened her eyes. His blue gaze devoured her with its intensity. "You belong to me now—under the law of man and God, you belong to me. Say it."

She licked her lips. "I belong to you." She reached up and touched his cheek. Her finger drifted to trace his lips. His tongue touched the tip of her finger, urging it into his mouth. He sucked the digit, sending shivers all the way down to the point where they connected.

He closed his eyes and moved again, slow and deep. Her passion built swiftly and, after a few thorough strokes, her body clenched around him. She clung to his shoulders to keep from being sucked under by the pleasure wracking her.

He thrust deeply once more and stiffened. He buried his head in her shoulder and moaned something unintelligible into her neck. She held him as he tensed in her arms. She kissed his ear and imagined he told her he loved her. After he had exhausted himself, he collapsed against her. He must have kept some of his weight on his arms, because the pressure felt more comfortable than crushing. She snuggled closer to him, wrapping her arms around him.

He rolled over to his side, taking her with him. He returned her embrace, hugging her tightly. At that moment, she felt closer to him than when their bodies had been linked together. He gradually eased his grip, but they clung to each other.

Nolan kissed her ear and smoothed her hair. "Now, you're truly my wife and no one can ever tear us apart."

Jewel watched Nolan from across the deck. Nothing had been resolved between them, but everything had changed. Even his appearance. He always wore his hair loose now, and he no longer bothered with his stern blue jacket. He fit every image of the lustful adventurer she had dreamed of as a girl—all the way down to his black knee-length boots and the gold hoop catching the light at his ear. His one concession to civilization was his clean-shaven face, and that only because his beard left her cheeks and less visible parts of her anatomy raw.

She sighed, enjoying watching his powerful movements as he gave orders to his crew. They were truly man and wife. Nolan had proven that at every opportunity. She stifled a yawn. If she wanted to survive another long, sensuous night, she needed a nap. Despite their unresolved past, she wanted to survive. She wanted a long life with her husband.

"Not getting enough sleep, chit?" drawled Wayland.

She glanced to find the old pirate lurking behind her. His advice had gotten her into this mess in the first place . . . and she had never even thanked him. She gave him a mischievous wink. "I'm sleeping just fine, thank you very much."

Wayland closed the distance between them. "Then it must be your husband that's making you look so frazzled."

To her surprise, she smiled instead of blushed. "Perhaps. And what have you to say for yourself? Were you put off by soap and water at an early age?"

His good eye widened. "Gotten a little bite, have we? I guess you had to, to keep that one in line." He nodded his head toward Nolan.

Jewel tugged on his sleeve. "I'm just teasing you."

"I know better, but I can take your abuse. At least you're smiling at me again."

Jewel shrugged and strolled along the deck. "Things haven't been easy. I didn't like the way you suggested Nolan and I get together, but I guess it worked."

Wayland followed but stopped her with a gentle touch on the arm before they'd gone far. The serious frown he wore gave her pause to turn and give him her full attention. "You're happy, then?"

Jewel's reassuring smile faltered under his intense scrutiny. "Don't look so glum about it. I thought that was what your devious mind wanted all along."

Wayland covered his heart with his palm as if gravely offended. "Devious? Has Nolan been planting the wrong ideas about old Wayland?"

Jewel looked down at the deck, suddenly finding the way her hem brushed the top of her brown leather shoes fascinating. Nolan had suggested a lot of things, but none of them regarded Wayland. She glanced at him from the corner of her eye. "I've gotten smarter is all. You knew a lot more about my father and Nolan than you led on. You pushed us together when Nolan tried to keep his distance."

Wayland glanced out across the sea in an obvious attempt to avoid her gaze. For a moment, Jewel thought he was truly ashamed. That couldn't be, though, because it went against everything she knew about him. He was an opportunist, pure and simple. She really had gotten smarter. People rarely seemed to be what they presented themselves as. How wrong had she been about her own father?

"Wayland, why did Nolan kill my father?" The question that continued to plague her left her lips before she knew she meant to ask it.

Wayland jerked his head up. Jewel winced at her own impulsiveness. Suddenly, she feared hearing the truth, and had the urge to recall her request.

Wayland stuck his hands in his pockets. "He didn't, really."

Jewel blinked, stunned by his answer. She grabbed Wayland's arm and turned him toward her. "Say that again."

"It's like this: Nolan didn't want to kill Bellamy, he just wanted out of his crew." Wayland stared over Jewel's head, not looking her in the eye.

She pulled on his sleeve, trying to force him to meet her gaze. "I already know that. I overheard their argument."

Wayland turned his face to her. His cold blue eye stared in her direction while his brown one drifted over her shoulder. "You probably seen the scar, too. It almost killed him. He got an awful infection. That's why it didn't heal up proper. I did everything I knew for that boy."

Jewel's heart tumbled over itself at the idea of losing Nolan. They were talking about her father's actual death, but the real torture came from the idea of losing Nolan before she'd even found him. "Go on. Get to the part about how Nolan didn't really kill my father."

Wayland shifted. He paused, appearing to choose his words carefully. "It was mutiny. That's all. Nolan made no bones about the fact that he didn't want Bellamy as his captain. True enough, he was ready to leave before Bellamy put a knife in him, but after Nolan healed up, he wasn't the same. The boy bided his time, and when Bellamy started chasing ships for women and rum over the ones with booty . . . well, some of the others got disgruntled. They sided with Nolan."

"So the whole crew mutinied against my father?"

"Almost all. I stuck by his side for a while, but he'd been drunk going on a fortnight, and I just couldn't see losing my own hide because he was a bleeding idiot."

Jewel swallowed hard. Though she had expected her sire's character was less than sterling, no one had ever been so blunt about his shortcomings. "My father was an idiot?"

Wayland slapped his leg. "I didn't mean that. It was just my memories talking. Your father was a savvy one—but the life he chose started eating at him. He kept trying to drink more, fight more and womanize more all to make his unhappiness go away when all he really wanted was you."

Her old wound ached at Wayland's words. "Did he tell you that? Did he talk about me?"

Wayland brought his brown gaze to rest on her face. "No, chit. He didn't. Bellamy wasn't what you would call a kind man. He didn't do right by you, and I don't know if he ever would have. I do know he was empty inside."

Jewel shook her head. If Wayland was trying to make

her feel sorry for her father, he was going about it the wrong way. She didn't have a father, and the hard work her mother had endured to raise her had taken the woman from Jewel also. She rubbed her temples. "So you're saying the crew killed my father, not Nolan."

Wayland sketched an invisible circle on the deck with his toe. "Nolan gave the order to kill Bellamy. But he did it in a decent way when the crew wanted to rip him limb from limb, slow and tortuous. They wanted to make a sport out of it and wager to see how long it took him to die—and that's no exaggeration. An unhappy crew of pirates is something you don't want to reckon with."

"So Nolan had no choice?" If Jewel could believe that, her problems would be solved. She could bury the past once and for all.

Wayland glanced over her shoulder again. She followed his gaze to where Nolan had climbed up the main mast with his spyglass. "Nolan sparked the crew's grumbling. No one had the ballocks to stand up to Bellamy 'cept him. He took those cutthroats in hand and they followed. Would still be following him if he hadn't decided to go honest. He's back where he belongs now."

Jewel watched Nolan jump to the deck, then scan the area until he caught sight of her. Even from a distance, she could feel the intensity, the possessiveness of his gaze. He didn't wave to acknowledge her. He didn't have to. He smiled at her briefly, then turned to give orders to a crew member. Jewel faced Wayland again. "How did my father die?"

Wayland's mouth became tight. "You don't need to know that."

Jewel knew Nolan wasn't a cold-blooded killer. If he were, he wouldn't have let Jack and the rest of his crew go free. "Do you think Nolan did the right thing?"

Wayland scoffed. "What does that have to do with anything? Right or wrong don't come into our kind of life. And it sure didn't keep me to my ripe old age."

"But you said he didn't want to kill my father. He did what he had to do."

"That don't make it right. But if that's what you're looking for, I guess Nolan would be your man. He's got that useless sense of good and bad more than most."

Jewel smiled. "And you don't?"

Wayland gave her a lopsided grin, which was much more pleasant than his toothless smile. "I just might be learning in spite of myself."

She tilted her head and laughed. "Been around Nolan too long, huh?"

"Nope, been around you."

Jewel narrowed her gaze, trying to surmise if he was teasing her. He glanced away, immediately hiding the rare show of sincerity. "Don't listen to me. I've had way too much kill-devil in my day. I just wish Bellamy could have gotten to know you like I do. You would have given him a treat, you would have." Wayland started to walk off.

Jewel smiled, the closest thing to contentment she'd ever experienced in regard to her father. "You think I could have had the same effect on him as I've had on you?" she called out.

He turned and walked backward for a few paces. "I certainly hope so."

Chapter Seventeen

They reached the island shortly before dawn. The inkling of dread he'd thought he would experience the moment they slipped into the welcoming arms of the sheltered cove didn't plague Nolan in the least. In fact, a certainty that the journey he'd begun at fourteen would soon come to its culmination, banished the last of his doubts.

Nolan and Parker lowered the longboats in the hazy blue light. No one wanted to wait for daybreak. They were all too excited. If the rumors were true, there was enough treasure for everyone—and more importantly, enough to finance a war. At least a good portion of it.

Nolan paused to feel the soft breeze caress his tired face. The island's tropic scent drifted over the stale smell of sea and brine, always a welcome event. During the long passage here, Nolan had grown to trust his fledgling crew. In the months they had been together, they had all grown, especially Nolan himself. Finally he was his own man. Answering only to himself—not Bellamy, not to his father and certainly not to a ghost.

He took Jewel's hand, kissed her knuckles. A firm grip on her arm in the event she slipped, he helped to establish a foot on the rope ladder's first rung, then held the lantern while she climbed steadily down. Parker waited below to settle her into the skiff. He wrapped his hands around her slight waist, supporting her transfer into the rocking boat. She glanced up at Nolan, and he smiled to reassure her. Jealousy no longer flashed its fangs at the slightest cause. The fear that he'd lose her to another man had stopped creeping into his thoughts, at least when it came to Parker.

Nolan's smile faded as Jewel looked toward the island. He wasn't going to lose her to anyone, he told himself. He followed her gaze. The island was blanketed in shadows, the perfect home for a ghost.

"You told her you love her yet?"

Nolan turned abruptly to find Wayland breathing down his neck. "Haven't you learned not to sneak up on people?"

"I've been standing here the whole time. You haven't told her, have you?"

"Get in the boat if you want to go."

"You can't take her for granted. You got to tell the girl how you feel. Women need more than a rough tumble to know their man loves them." Wayland wedged himself between his captain and the rope ladder.

Nolan took a whiff of the pirate and snapped his head back. "How much have you had to drink?"

Wayland pushed him away. "I always smell like rum, and I'm damn proud of it. It's a good tonic for the skin."

Nolan raised the lantern. "You don't shave. No one can see your face."

"I can see yours well enough, and it's got me wondering why you're staring at the island like something is waiting there to eat you alive."

Nolan glanced at the island's dark shape and tensed.

Despite his earlier optimism, a bad feeling seeped around him like a graveyard mist. "You know why. Get in the boat and let's get this over with."

Wayland shrugged. "All right, but you don't sound like a man going to find a king's ransom."

No? Nolan followed Wayland down the ladder. As soon as he had the treasure on board and they sailed away from this place, he'd shriek with happiness. He settled in the boat and took Jewel's hand, letting the other men row.

Maybe he *should* tell Jewel he loved her. He had never thought of it, because he didn't know that he did. He definitely lusted after her, but love . . . He wasn't sure the feeling existed. The only love he had known had been for his parents. The sensation had been cloying and repressive, always leaving him with more guilt than pleasure. He didn't feel that way about Jewel. A little obsessive maybe, and there was guilt when he caused her to be unhappy. The tightness in his chest when he looked at her could be described as cloying, but . . . no. It wasn't the same. Men weren't expected to natter on about things like love. He had married her. That was enough.

He lifted his head, and his heart stopped as the ghost came into view. Nolan shifted, sitting up straighter. No one else must have seen it, because they all still appeared half-asleep. He focused his gaze. A man dressed in tattered rags stood on the edge of the beach, waving his arms over his head in a desperate attempt to gain their attention. Nolan's stomach lurched.

My God, was he going mad? If anyone could accomplish making him so, it would certainly be Bellamy Leggett—dead or alive.

Parker glanced at Nolan, his oars raised from the water. "There's someone on the beach."

Jewel peered around the men blocking her view.

Nolan's gaze shot to Wayland, who looked not the least bit surprised. Then, with the force of an unexpected blow from Bellamy's solid fist, Nolan knew. He almost wished he had been going mad. Bellamy had topped himself in deception and manipulation. Nolan had been his pawn from the very beginning. "Son of a—"

Jewel squeezed his fingers. He turned and glared at her. For the briefest, heart-stopping moment, he thought she had been part of her father's diabolical plan. Her bewildered expression told him his suspicions were unfounded. They had used her even more cruelly than they had him, which only added to Nolan's murderous fury.

He pinned Wayland with a look that would have shoved him out of the boat if that had been possible. "This isn't over. Far from it. It's just begun."

Wayland appeared neither offended nor smug. Instead, he shrugged in detached resignation. "Tell that to him."

"To who?" Jewel asked. "Do you know that man on the beach?"

The shore's sudden approach saved Nolan from answering her question. Both he and Parker jumped out, having anxiously removed their boots the moment they entered the boat. They dragged the skiff to the beach.

Bellamy Leggett stumbled in their direction. His clothing hung in tatters, but his pride and joy, his thick golden hair, had been recently brushed and hung past his shoulders. Gray streaks had begun to dull its sheen. The face that had terrorized Nolan's dreams was clean-shaven, giving Nolan hope that either Bellamy had gotten dumber or himself, smarter.

"Nolan, is that you? I knew you would come back for me. I knew you wouldn't forsake me."

Parker paused to stare. Nolan fought the urge to applaud at Bellamy's performance. He heard the gasp from the boat and realized Jewel had recognized her father.

Nolan held himself in check, stiffly waiting for her reaction. He would let Bellamy make this game's first
move.

Jewel climbed out of the boat. She trudged through
the sand, oblivious to the surf soaking the hem of her
gown. Bellamy stumbled toward her, blinking furiously,
as if trying to clear tears from his eyes. From where
Nolan stood, the man's eyes were as dry as the sand
itself.

He opened his arms to her. "It can't be. I must be
having the visions again. A man's mind goes when he's
spent so much time alone. Deserted. Forgotten. Left to
fend for himself. Is that you, Jewel?"

She nodded, but didn't move closer to his waiting
arms. She turned her gaze to Nolan. Confusion clouded
her usually bright eyes. Nolan knew his violent stare
provided no answers, and she returned her focus to her
father. "I thought you were dead."

Bellamy dropped his head into his palms, hiding his
face. His shoulders rounded. "I thought I was, too," he
said brokenly, through his fingers. Jewel rushed to him,
then slung an arm around his shaking shoulders.

Nolan glared in their direction. He was doomed. He
must have been a fool to think he could get rid of Bellamy Leggett so easily. He really wouldn't have minded
if Bellamy had survived the "little inconvenience" he
had put him through. Hell, deep down he had expected
it. It was why he hadn't killed him outright. The guilt
that had plagued him over the years had sprung from
the fact that Bellamy had never proven his survival, so
Nolan had thought him dead. Well, this little episode
was certainly accounting for lost time. Bellamy still
reigned as master, and Nolan remained his lowly pupil.

Jewel wrapped her arms around Bellamy, stroked his
hair. "It's all right. You'll be safe with us now." She

glanced over her shoulder to glare at Nolan. "Won't he, Nolan?"

Nolan shifted and crossed his arms over his chest. He was absolutely furious and wanted to tell them both he was having Bellamy strung up on the tallest palm tree on the island. "It doesn't look like he's been doing too badly for himself."

Jewel's gasp of disbelief was audible. Bellamy lifted his gaze to smirk at Nolan over the top of her head. The man's murky green eyes, less like his daughter's than Nolan remembered, sparkled with triumph and a deep, soulful satisfaction. He kept his mouth closed, though, letting his daughter fight his battle. Nolan couldn't have had a more dangerous opponent, and the bastard knew it.

"Look at his rags," Jewel said. She grasped Bellamy's hand in a gentle yet chillingly obvious show of support. "How did you get here?"

Bellamy stared at his feet in a display Nolan had never before witnessed. Nolan braced himself. Bellamy probably had to lower his face to hide his smile as he delivered Nolan's death blow. "*He* left me here five long years ago. Left me here with nothing."

Another gasp, this one laced with a sob. Jewel's hand flew to her mouth, and for a moment she looked as if she were going to be physically ill. Nolan stepped toward her, not thinking, just wanting to be there if she needed him. She held up her hand to stop him. When he did, she took a step back. A step closer to her father. "Why?"

Nolan knew exactly what she meant. Why had he left her father alone on this island? His jaw ached from clenching it. The horror etched on her features and the tone in which she asked told him she already knew the answer.

Unable to leave a nail in Nolan's coffin unhammered,

Bellamy spoke for him. "He left me to die a slow, horrible death. That's what they do to you when you get too weak to defend yourself. Worse, when it's the boy you raised to a man."

Tears welled in Jewel's eyes. "How could you be so cruel?"

That was it. Nolan couldn't hold his tongue any longer. He stomped over to Bellamy. "Cruel, my ass. Look at him." He reached out and pinched a handful of fat in Bellamy's midsection. "Coconuts have agreed with you. You've gained at least two stone since I saw you last."

Bellamy pushed Nolan's hand away. "I've been resourceful. The hope of seeing my little girl one more time sustained me."

They both glanced in Jewel's direction. She stood stiff, wiping the tears that fell on her cheeks with jerky swats of her hand. To Nolan, she appeared about to break, and he knew she wouldn't let him comfort her. He turned back to Bellamy. "I know you've been off this bloody island, you bastard." He shoved Bellamy hard, sending him back into the soft sand, then pouncing on him before he had the chance to get up.

The power with which Bellamy threw him off proved Nolan's speculation. Bellamy was still as strong as he'd ever been. He hadn't been wasting away on this island for five years.

Nolan hung on. They rolled in the sand, each trying to gain the upper hand. It was the only thing that had felt right since they'd anchored in the crescent-shaped harbor. He should have jumped Bellamy the moment he saw him.

Bellamy rubbed a handful of sand in Nolan's eyes. Nolan blindly reached out and grabbed a fistful of the man's long hair and tried to pull it from his scalp.

Jewel's scream finally broke through Nolan's rage.

She was hoarse and sobbing. He loosened his hold on Bellamy. A powerful blow to his chin sent his head burrowing into the soft white sand.

He must have lost consciousness for the briefest of seconds. When he woke, he realized it was nothing but a dream. Jewel stroked his face, urging him to wake when he wanted nothing more than to stay in bed with her all morning. Funny; Jewel never woke before he did. Nolan tried to blink. His head ached and his eyes felt like someone had rubbed broken glass into them. He felt as if he had been on a week-long bender. But he hadn't done that since he was in his teens and was part of Bellamy's . . .

Nolan tried to sit up, but Jewel held him down. He could have pushed through her resistance, but he liked the turn of events now that he remembered what the events were.

"You don't act like a man who's dying!" accused Jewel.

Nolan hoped she was talking to Bellamy, and he struggled against a grin. It wouldn't hurt to keep his eyes closed a little longer.

"Nolan, can you hear me? Are you all right?" She caressed his face again. Nolan turned his head into her touch.

"He's fine. Look how he's snuggling up to you like a suckling kitten."

Nolan forced his eyes open. That was Bellamy's voice, and it sounded far too close. He blinked hard, rubbing the sand from his eyes with his fists. Bellamy was leaning over him. Nolan sat up this time, despite Jewel's protest. He got to his feet, but let her help him just to keep her close.

Bellamy put his hands on his hips. He barreled his chest in one of the cocky poses Nolan remembered all too well. The man was so damn proud he had bested

Nolan, he forgot his role as weakened castaway.

Nolan rubbed his chin. "That was quite a punch."

Bellamy shrugged. "While you've been playing schoolboy, I've been . . ." He glanced at Jewel, then Nolan. "I've been living off the land like a man. Surviving just so I could see my girl one more time."

Jewel's grip on Nolan's arm tightened. "And what was your excuse before that? You never took the time to see me before, so why would you change your mind?"

"I didn't have the chance to. I swear it. I was going to come back for you," her father blurted.

Jewel stared at him, her jaw tight. She didn't appear to believe him.

Bellamy nodded, as if agreeing with her disbelief. "I don't blame you for doubting me." He sighed theatrically. "The truth is, I've been forced to do a lot of thinking since I've been here by myself. Never knowing if each day would be my last made me realize all the things I missed. And you're what I missed the most, Jewel. I missed seeing my baby girl become a woman."

"Son of a bitch," Nolan growled through clenched teeth.

Jewel let go of his sleeve, and she rushed to embrace her father, who caught and held her. Nolan balled his hands into fists. He wanted to pry them apart. He had never felt like such an outsider.

Jewel finally broke the embrace. "So much has happened. I don't know if I can forgive you for leaving me. I know now you never were who I thought you were. I don't even know you."

"I'm here now, Jewel. You can get to know me." Bellamy brushed a stray hair from her eyes just like a real father might.

The man sounded so sincere, it made Nolan nervous. Jewel stepped away from him. "I need some time to think." She glanced at Nolan, and he knew she felt deceived and wronged by him as much as by her father.

He had to say something, take control of the situation any way he could. "Nothing has changed, Jewel. I marooned Bellamy because that is the usual way of punishing a crewmember who breaks the rules."

Wayland stepped forward. Nolan had to admire him for not greeting Bellamy as if seeing his long-lost friend for the first time. Surely these two had communicated and planned this, but Wayland had hung back with the rest of the stunned crew, watching the drama play out. "Nolan's right, Jewel. Bellamy hisself ordered it for crewmen who disobeyed him."

Bellamy glared at Wayland, as if he couldn't believe what he was hearing. "But I was the captain!"

"That's right. A pirate captain. That makes it even more important to follow the rules every man on board swears to follow," Wayland argued. He stopped when he reached Jewel's side, then squeezed her shoulder. Nolan was surprised she didn't turn away, but seemed to gravitate toward the old dog. "I know it don't seem right to you, chit. But that's the way it's done."

Bellamy glanced at the two. He swaggered forward, as if he had nothing to lose and everything to gain. "No harm done. You came back for me. Didn't you, Nolan?"

Nolan crossed his arms over his chest. "No."

"He came back for the treasure," said Jewel. Her voice held a touch of accusation Nolan didn't like.

Bellamy looked too incredulous to be believed. "The treasure? Not Captain Kent's treasure?"

No one answered. Bellamy's little game was wearing thin on everyone, especially his daughter. Why was he putting her through this? Nolan knew the answer to his question: Torturing her was the surest way to get to Nolan, and Bellamy knew it.

"All's well that ends well. Just give me half and we'll call it even." Bellamy smiled. "I'll forgive you, and maybe my little girl can forgive you, too . . . someday."

"We're all sharing the treasure." Jewel glanced at Nolan. It didn't look as if she was in the mood to do much forgiving anytime soon.

Since Bellamy was alive, Nolan didn't see he had anything to be forgiven for. "She's not your little girl. She's my wife. And she *is* my wife, Bellamy. Legally, morally and physically. But I'm sure you already know that."

Bellamy raised his eyebrows. "How could I?"

Nolan prowled toward him, ready to spring. "The same way you got fat, shaved and made it back to this island before we got here. You knew what we were up to the entire time. And I've a damn good idea who was helping you."

Jewel put her hands to her ears. "Just stop it. Both of you."

Nolan briefly glanced at her but was unwilling to take his gaze from Bellamy for any extended period of time.

Jewel stomped her foot in the soft sand. "I'm sick of your bickering. There's enough treasure to go around."

"No, there isn't. Not for him," Nolan said. "I'm not going to finance him so he can terrorize and plunder anyone else who crosses his path. He's a menace, and needs to either be in jail, marooned or dead."

"You little brat. You had to get the whole crew behind ya to beat me, didn't ya? This time I'm taking more than your little map, boy. I'm taking your crew, your treasure and my daughter."

Nolan reached for Bellamy. Bellamy's frayed shirt ripped in his grasp. The foiled momentum sent Nolan off kilter for only a second, but Bellamy's reflexes were fast and he swung at Nolan's head, forcing him to fall forward onto his knees to avoid the blow. Not a beat passed before Nolan leaped to his feet and whipped around to face Bellamy head on, fists clenched.

"Stop it!" yelled Jewel. "Kill each other if you want, but don't pretend it's over me." She turned and ran across the beach.

Chapter Eighteen

Jewel ran until her lungs burned. When she slowed, catching her breath in painful gulps, she found herself in the center of a lush jungle. She pushed a thorny vine away from her face. The foliage was so thick, leaves had stuck in her hair and clothes. She welcomed the feeling of being swallowed by the jungle's density. The tall trees formed a canopy, blocking out the sun's violent heat, surrounding her in a cool green fog. She rested against one of the larger trunks, then slid down to its base to sit on a soft patch of dirt. Being completely alone on this island didn't seem so bad.

She leaned her head on her knees. This should be one of the happiest days of her life. She had a husband she adored and had been reunited with a father who said everything she had always longed to hear. Her marriage would no longer be shadowed by her father's ghost. Instead, it would be threatened by a living, breathing man who seemed bent on ruining it.

With awful clarity, she realized how wrong she had been about her father. Her childish fantasies had grown too strong to be dispelled easily. Bellamy Leggett in all his glory was the only one strong enough to banish his own myth. But he still was her father. She couldn't stuff him in a trunk like a toy she'd outgrown. With her eyes open, she could forge a relationship with the real man. It would not be the one of her dreams, but it would be better because it was real. Now, if she could only get her husband to keep from trying to kill him.

With her breathing returned to normal, she tried to order her thoughts. Running off like a child would solve nothing. She had come too far to let either man go.

She got up and brushed off her skirt. She wasn't ready to face them yet. Not only did she have to forge a relationship with her father, she had to untangle the one she had with her husband. Without Bellamy's death hanging over their heads, there was still uncharted water in her hasty marriage.

Nolan was adamant about wanting her for his wife. His physical display of affection couldn't be disputed, but he had yet to even hint at the fact that he loved her. Everything else that lay ahead, as well as behind, remained draped more in mystery than clarity. She continued to walk deeper into the interior of the island, heading up a slight incline. An orchestra of birds sounding overhead helped to lighten her mood. She glanced up, mesmerized by the light spilling through the leaves.

Her heart scared her. She wasn't sure it could be trusted. She had spent a lifetime believing in a man, her father, who she realized was undeserving of her loyalty. What if her judgment of Nolan was no better? After all, he had been a pirate like her father. He had been seduced by visions of glory and wealth. Perhaps her mother had had the same romantic illusions about her father as Jewel had with Nolan—until the adventure ended with a baby and no husband to stand by her side.

She had no reason to believe Nolan would be so uncaring, but if they didn't discover the treasure here, it might prolong her finding out. Their adventure wouldn't have to end. There would be more time to gain confidence in her marriage.

The sound of running water hurried Jewel's pace. Exploring the island lifted her mood in a surge of independence. She had spent too much of her time waiting to be rescued or led.

It was strange that she suddenly dreaded finding the treasure. She didn't know what she had ever hoped to gain. The wealth seemed more likely to lead to the loss of the man she loved rather than any happiness.

The sound of water grew louder. This was no ordinary stream. Jewel pushed aside branches and ignored the twigs that tore at her hair in her haste to reach her destination. A small clearing welcomed her. A slight spray dampened her skin, and she blinked in awe at the sheer beauty of an enormous waterfall. Light refracted off the cascading water, creating a rainbow. A steep black cliff set off crystalline falls. Lush ferns surrounded a deep pond at the base. She moved to the edge. The water churned the pool, creating a fathomless bottom and a surface of black, undulating glass.

The pristine scene tempted her to strip off her clothes and dive into its open arms. She kneeled to scoop up a handful of water. Wading in wasn't an option. The pool appeared to descend into the other side of the world.

Surrounded by the dense heat of the jungle, the chilled water begged to be entered. Most of the water she tried to capture spilled through her cupped fingers, but she touched her tongue to the little she could keep. Fresh. It had been forever since she had bathed in fresh water. She leaned over and washed her face, reminding herself she couldn't get in no matter how much she wanted.

She stilled. An urge to fall into these cool depths compelled her with such force that she hopped to her feet and stepped back. She had the sensation of someone watching her, guiding here to this spot just to see what she would do. The air around her hummed with intensity like a forest enchanted by witchcraft from the tales she'd heard as a child. Everything beckoned even as it repelled her.

She glanced up at the waterfall again. Its shape reminded her of something she had seen before. One of the runes on the map! The rune resembled the waterfall, all the way down to the two tree trunks trapped by rock near the top. With calm, sure sight, Jewel knew she had found Captain Kent's treasure.

Their angry voices carried across the beach. Jewel paused at its edge, still partially hidden by dense foliage, wondering if they even realized she'd been gone.

"This is going nowhere. Get the swords or shut up," barked Wayland.

"That's fine with me. I've been waiting five years to teach this pup a lesson," Bellamy shouted back.

Jewel stepped onto the beach. She could see Bellamy and Nolan facing each other, with Wayland in the middle. Bellamy paced back and forth, while Nolan held his ground. The rest of the crew hung back, looking indecisive.

Nolan glanced in her direction. Jewel's heart lodged in her throat. He *had* noticed. He had to have, or everything they had was a lie.

He turned back to Bellamy. "I'm not going to fight you, old man. I'm here to get the treasure and then I'm leaving without you."

Bellamy spotted Jewel from the corner of his eye. He didn't turn to acknowledge her presence any further than that. "And without my daughter. Isn't that right, Jewel?"

It infuriated her that he would be pompous enough to

think he could use her so easily. He had in the past, but no more. "I haven't made up my mind."

Her words finally snagged Nolan's full attention. Her husband turned, his gaze fiery. An instant later, he hid all emotion behind a scowl—a scowl the likes of which she hadn't seen since their wedding day.

Bellamy seemed satisfied with her answer, because his smile was unmistakably triumphant. "Don't worry, girl, I won't let this son of a whore leave without paying for dishonoring my daughter."

Nolan gritted his teeth. "I'm responsible for her welfare, not you."

Bellamy put his hands on his hips. "Ha! I don't for one minute believe that wedding is legal. It was just a dirty trick to get my girl to be your strumpet without a fuss."

Nolan took a step forward. Wayland put a hand on his and Bellamy's chests, keeping them an arm's length apart. "Don't tell me it weren't legal. I was there."

Bellamy threw his head back and laughed, purposely tossing his long mane of hair. "I never thought you would succumb to his altar-boy trickery. He's just as self-serving as the rest of us. He just pretends to be righteous to get his way."

Jewel trudged across the thick white sand to meet Nolan, all the while begging him with her gaze to deny her father's taunt. "You said it was legal. Are we married or not?"

He gripped her shoulders, stared down into her face. His intensity tempted her to believe everything he said. "It's legal. Don't doubt that."

Bellamy yanked them apart. Jewel stumbled back. "Don't touch her. It ain't legal. You're a privateer without a letter of marque, and that makes you a pirate. Wayland told me. Captain or no, you ain't got the authority to marry a couple of bilge rats."

Nolan lunged for Bellamy. Both Jewel and Wayland reached them at the same time. Wayland restrained Bellamy, and Nolan backed off on his own as Jewel touched his arm. He wrapped her in his embrace, pulled her against him.

Wayland kept a firm grip on Bellamy's shoulder. "Settle it with swords, 'cause words ain't getting either of you anywhere. But first let's find the treasure. That way, we can all divvy up both your shares after you two kill each other."

Jewel wanted to pull away from Nolan. Her mind reeled with the knowledge she mightn't really be married. How was she going to save a marriage that didn't even exist? Had Nolan intentionally deceived her, or had he believed they were wed?

She tried to wiggle from Nolan's arms, but his grip was unmovable. He held her too tightly, like a possession he feared would be ripped away. His devotion might have given her hope for them if she didn't fear he was purposely antagonizing her father. She braced her hand on his chest, trying to keep her balance. This seemed to reassure him, because he eased up slightly.

Nolan's gaze flayed Bellamy. "I'll get my letter of marque from the colonies soon enough, and the first thing I'll do is make my marriage official. And if that doesn't please you, I'll marry her again, anywhere, anyplace."

"Fine," Bellamy spat back. "But until then, take your hands off her."

The man rushed forward, leaving Wayland with the rest of his tattered shirt. Nolan shoved Jewel behind him, but she didn't plan on staying there. She dashed in front of Nolan, her hands out to ward off her father. "Stop it! Both of you. If you two would stop arguing for a few seconds, I could tell you what I found."

The words left her mouth before she'd realized what

she intended to say. That she had temporarily forgotten such an important fact the moment she returned to the beach and found Nolan and Bellamy still at odds warned her that the treasure wouldn't accomplish what she had always hoped. Riches alone wouldn't buy her the acceptance she craved; neither did finding it mean what she'd thought it would.

Both Bellamy and Nolan, along with the entire crew, paused to stare. Everyone seemed as relieved at the break in the hostilities as she.

She let her arms fall to her side. "The treasure. I found the treasure."

Nolan's eyes widened. "Where is it?" His excitement was obvious in his posture and suddenly bright features. Perhaps only she heard the bitter tone in her voice.

"It's under a waterfall. Come on, I'll show you." She turned and headed back toward the jungle.

Bellamy's voice halted her. "Hold on one second. You two ain't going traipsing in the jungle for a little fling. I've never seen any waterfall, and how in the hell do you know that's where the treasure is?"

"If you knew your daughter better, you'd realize she has a sense about these things. She discovered the treasure was on this island. This tiny island. The very place you called home for the last five years," Nolan sneered.

Bellamy abruptly froze and gave him a tight-jawed glare. Jewel might have been foolish where her father was concerned, but she wasn't stupid. She knew what his uncharacteristic lapse into silence meant. He didn't know about the waterfall because he hadn't been on the island all this time. But the lie didn't mean much; she still wanted to believe the best of him. She almost laughed out loud at her tenacious desire to still believe he hadn't come back for her because he'd been stranded on this island. A door closed in her heart, and she realized all the false faith she'd had in Bellamy Leggett was vanishing forever.

She stepped forward and tugged Nolan's sleeve. If she could distract them, perhaps the situation could be defused. She had no intention of continuing the argument about Bellamy's location for the last five years. "Maybe I'm wrong about the treasure. But the waterfall is real enough."

Bellamy waved his hand, dismissing her completely. "What if it is? It's too bleeding hot to go stomping around this hellish place. Let's see the map and use *it* to find the treasure, instead of listening to this slip of a girl."

Jewel's newly acquired insight into her father's less-than-loving character didn't stop his total disregard from wounding her. Her grip on Nolan involuntarily tightened.

Nolan slipped his palm under her hair and rested it on the back of her neck: something Jewel took as not only a protective gesture, but one of unconditional support. "You'll never lay hands on the map again, or anything else that belongs to me," he said.

Wayland went out of his way to shove past Bellamy and join ranks with Jewel and Nolan. "The map's got its own secret language, you idiot. The chit's the one who figured it out. If she says it's at some waterfall, then I'll gladly follow her. When you had the map, you couldn't even find your arse." He turned and winked his brown eye at Jewel, then offered her his arm when he reached her. She took it.

Nolan tightened his grip for only an instant before he let her head toward the jungle with Wayland. He continued to face Bellamy, and Jewel realized he wouldn't turn his back on her father.

When they reached the end of the beach, she heard someone trudging up behind them. "I would have figured the bloody thing out eventually. Having a crew full of sots like you didn't help my thinking any," Bellamy muttered as he reached their side.

Jewel glanced over her shoulder to find the rest of the crew following, with Nolan at the rear. She relaxed, realizing she had staved off bloodshed between her husband and her father for the moment. But Nolan wasn't her husband.

She would have stumbled if Wayland hadn't tightened his grip. She looked over her shoulder again, searching for Nolan. His gaze was already on her, and he gestured with a slight nod of his head. She'd given up her hold on the tarnished image of her father, but she'd never give up on Nolan.

After several agonizing minutes, much longer than Jewel thought it humanly possible to hold your breath, Nolan broke the water's surface. Jewel kneeled by the side of the pool, panting as hard as he because she'd been unable to take a breath while he remained underwater. She reached for him.

He swam to the bank with a few efficient strokes. "Get back. I don't want you falling in. It's deep."

Jewel did as he asked, feeling rejected by his harsh words rather than reassured by his care for her safety. He hadn't spoken or gotten near her since they'd left the beach.

With his palms braced on the bank, Nolan pulled himself from the pond. Droplets rippled down his heavily muscled shoulders and chest. He had stripped down to his breeches. It seemed like years since Jewel had last touched him, instead of only this morning. After today's events, she wondered if she would ever get to hold him again. He seemed so powerful, coming up from the depths of the black pool like a myth. And just as illusive.

Parker moved to the pool's bank. He had paced the

side while Nolan remained underwater. He wanted to go down as well. "Did you find anything?"

Nolan opened his hand, palm up. Mud dribbled from his fingers. He shook the contents until more muck slithered down his wrist and several solid things clinked. Gold peeked through the black silt. Both Parker and Jewel leaned in to get a better look.

"What's he got?" Bellamy stood, wiping dirt from his breeches. Even at his age, his slightest movement flexed well-toned muscles. The extra padding around his waist only served to make him appear more solid.

Jewel reached for a coin. She had the sudden desire to hide it from her father's view. That he hadn't been wasting away on the island was as apparent as the fact that he couldn't be trusted.

Bellamy plucked it from her fingers. He bit it, then spit out the mud. "It's gold, all right."

Wayland crowded behind her. "Is that all?"

Nolan held up his hand, offering Wayland the rest of the coins. "Can't tell. It's too dark to see. You have to feel with your hands."

Bellamy slapped Nolan on the shoulder. "Guess you better develop some gills—aye, boy?"

Nolan glared a warning, and Bellamy removed his hand.

Jewel didn't like the idea of Nolan going back down there. Her father's obvious pleasure at the prospect scared her even more. "Why would your grandfather dump his treasure at the bottom of a pond, anyway? How was he going to get it if we can't?"

Nolan pushed past the circle of men surrounding the pond. He shook the excess water from his long hair, then stepped in a ray of sunlight piercing the jungle roof and turned to face them again. "He was desperate. Pirates don't usually bury their treasure. They're too busy spending it."

"Why did he?" Jewel could see the gooseflesh on Nolan's shoulders. She walked toward him but stopped short. She wanted to rub her hands along his arms, warming him. The distance in his eyes held her back.

"He hoped to use the treasure as leverage. He wanted a pardon. I figure the coins and whatever else is down there were in wooden crates or bags. The current from the waterfall broke it up over the years. Seventy years ago the treasure would have been a lot easier to retrieve."

Jewel wrapped her arms around herself, feeling cool from the shade and the mist from the falls. "They give pardons to pirates?"

Bellamy swaggered forward. "Nay, lass. Captain Kent started out as a privateer, but once he got a taste of the good life in Tortuga, he turned pure pirate. Same as what happened to Nolan, here. Did he ever tell you about Tortuga?"

Jewel stiffened. "I believe he mentioned that's where you stole his map."

Bellamy laughed. "You got spunk, I'll give you that, girlie. Did he happen to tell you what he was doing when I secured his map for safekeeping?"

Wayland moved between them. "Kent was hanged 'cause some fancy aristocrat got greedy. He hadn't gone on the account. They say he had passes from the vessels he plundered proving he only attacked the ones sanctioned by his letter of marque."

Jewel shook her head. "I don't understand."

Nolan folded his arms over his bare chest. "Bellamy wants you to know that I was entertaining a woman of questionable virtue on Tortuga, and I'm not quite sure what point Wayland is making."

Wayland pointed at Nolan. "Your grandfather was unfairly hanged, is what I'm saying. He turned himself in after hiding his treasure. He gave the High Admiralty in

New York his passes, proving his innocence, but they shipped him off to London to be hanged just the same."

Nolan shifted. "How do you know this?"

Bellamy waved his hand in dismissal. "It's just a rumor. You know how sea dogs like to talk."

"It ain't no rumor. I met someone who was locked up in Newgate with your grandfather. My friend got deported to Barbados, and Captain Kent got hanged when he should have been set free. The bloody lord that sponsored him just wanted his treasure."

Jewel touched her chin. "Can they still do that? Hang a privateer to get his treasure?"

Nolan grinned. "That's why we're fighting a war. A monarch can do anything he wants. Old George is through using us to fatten his coffers."

Jewel found it hard to breathe. "But will you be killed?"

Bellamy settled under a palm tree. "He ain't no privateer. He's a pirate. Always has been and always will be. He's just like his grandpa."

Nolan moved out of the sunlight to stand at the edge of the pond. "For once you're right, Bellamy, and I'll take the comparison as a compliment."

Parker kneeled beside Nolan at the water's edge. "Do you want me to go down, Captain?"

Jewel came up behind them. Things had definitely changed in their relationship. She could sense it. Nolan had relaxed with his crew, and now they loved him as much as respected him. He commanded with easy self-assurance, no longer holding himself rigid, as if he were about to come apart at any moment. And Parker had changed as well. He no longer bothered to tie back his hair, and its sun-bleached tangle brushed the tops of his tanned shoulders. The dark stubble on his face, several shades darker than his hair, added a few years along with newly defined muscles that ran the length of his lanky body.

Nolan stood. "You'd better save your breath for tomorrow, Parker. It's getting late, and we'll need to spend the rest of the afternoon rigging something to haul the treasure up. We can't do it by hand."

"Baskets? We'll need something that lets the water pass," the lieutenant suggested.

"Excellent idea. You and I and the other strong swimmers will take the baskets underwater and fill them with sediment from the bottom, and the rest of you will pull them to the surface." Nolan turned to face the group. "The waterfall can hold you under if you get disoriented. It could be dangerous. All the divers will be volunteers."

Bellamy leaned his head back on the palm tree with his eyes closed. "Good thing we have a big strong captain to lead us."

Nolan strolled over to him. "You'll be the only forced diver. You're a strong swimmer, but you've never been the type to volunteer for hard work."

Bellamy opened his eyes. "Not when I have a young lad around fool enough to do it for me."

Nolan shrugged. "The only problem with that is when the young fool gets old enough to shove you off your throne."

Bellamy winked. "We'll see about that, boy."

Jewel shivered. She didn't like the gleam in her father's eye. He had given in to Nolan's taunt too easily. Nolan strode back over to study the pool. She wished her father had refused to dive with them tomorrow. His easy agreement had to be a ruse.

Nolan glanced at her as he passed, and he grinned. It was the first time he had smiled since they had landed on the island. "Lets get back to the ship and get to work on Captain Kent's revenge. The British killed him for this treasure, so it's our duty to get it back and use it to blow them out of the water."

Nolan's crewmen cheered. Jewel tried to smile in an attempt to hide the fact that a lump of dread had settled in her throat. She prayed Captain Kent's grandson fared better than the luckless man himself.

Chapter Nineteen

Nolan lay on his bunk, letting the damp night breeze cool his naked body. He rested his head on his curled forearm and counted the grooves between each beam of the deck above. Today, he had found his fortune but lost his heart. With that thought, his mood plummeted even further.

Even the revelation that his notorious grandfather wasn't the villain of legend, and that Nolan's father had portrayed him to be, couldn't dislodge his bleak state of mind. The fact that he wasn't the spawn of some evil and depraved man only confirmed what Nolan already suspected: He and he alone had steered the disastrous course his relationship with Jewel had taken.

True enough that fate had thrown in some fairly serious obstacles, but Nolan had used those to build a fortress of misunderstanding and distrust. From the moment he withheld what had really happened to her father when he'd gone to retrieve the map, to the time he saw Bellamy Leggett on the beach and could only think of proving to his former mentor who was the better man, Nolan had locked Jewel out.

It hadn't occurred to him that the better man might take his wife's feelings into consideration and try not to strangle her father no matter how much he deserved it. That was, until Nolan lay alone on his empty bunk. Jewel's scent surrounded him, hardening his body with a surge of lust tainted by fierce longing.

He should have insisted Jewel come back to his ship. If he had, Bellamy and he would have come to blows. Again. They were both looking for any opportunity to act on the hatred between them. Nolan wanted to punch Bellamy right in his smirking mouth, and he could feel the same desire rolling off Bellamy in waves. To avoid an all-out war, Nolan had no choice but to concede to Bellamy's insistence that his daughter stay on the beach with him rather than return to the *Integrity*.

Arguing with Bellamy wouldn't help his relationship with Jewel. They had been fighting over her like two dogs over the same bone. Each tug tore her love apart. If Nolan weren't careful, there would be nothing left.

His hatred for Bellamy had nothing to do with Jewel, anyway. She had to understand that. He couldn't pretend Bellamy had changed just because he was her father. Bellamy had been dangerous before Nolan disbanded his crew. Nolan intended to make sure Bellamy didn't get the chance to take up where he had left off. Financing his next sailing venture would be just as if Nolan wielded an evil sword himself. He couldn't let Bellamy loose in the world with a share of this treasure.

Nolan lay his curled fist against his forehead. In keeping her father in his place, Nolan could lose Jewel permanently. She would never understand why her father could not share in the vast fortune. It was apparent she was beginning to see Bellamy's true nature, but her generous heart would never wish the man or anyone to be treated unfairly. The guilt of leaving Bellamy alone on the island would kill her. And that's exactly what Nolan intended. Bellamy could find his own way off. He had before. Let his whole plan explode in his face.

The bastard had succeeded, though. Bellamy's treachery would steal a part of Nolan that had become more precious to him than the bloody treasure. He didn't even want the damn thing. Look what it had done for his grandfather—or worse, his father, who had lived his life in pious repentance, hoping to erase the murderous taint from the family name.

Nolan's father had seen Kent's lust for adventure and associated it with his own son, squashed it unmercifully, unfairly comparing a mischievous boy with the most infamous pirate in the Caribbean. Worse, his grandfather had been unfairly punished. Nolan realized now that what his father had feared, had taught him to hate in himself—a hunger for life and all it offered—didn't have to be evil or all-consuming. Tempered with a desire to do right by the world, such passions would help build a nation and even make a good and loving husband. He would be so, if Jewel would give him the chance.

Unfortunately, he still had to keep his focus on the treasure. Nolan wanted the riches for the revolution, and he would use every penny of it on ships and weapons. He would probably have his letter of marque by the time he returned to the colonies—but by then it could be too late for he and Jewel.

He truly had believed his marriage legal under the law and God. His word was as good as any document or stamp. He prided himself on that. He had vowed to take Jewel for his wife, to cherish her and protect her. That was enough for him. Yet the look on Jewel's face when Bellamy pointed out the flaw in his reasoning told him it wasn't enough for her. Bellamy was right, of course, and that knowledge gave Nolan one more reason for murder.

He turned onto his side and punched his pillow. A thin stream of light shone beneath his door. He froze. When no sound accompanied the intruder, Nolan carefully reached for the pistol he had already loaded. His sword was also close enough to grab in a hurry. With Bellamy nearby, Nolan had prepared for anything.

The intruder tried the door's handle. It didn't turn. Nolan had locked it, knowing he wouldn't be able to sleep otherwise. Sneak attacks were Bellamy's specialty. Nolan moved off the bed in silence.

A soft rap sounded. Definitely not aggressive. The knock was almost hesitant. "Nolan?"

He leaped for the door, turned the key and yanked it open before she changed her mind. "Jewel, what are you doing here?"

Her eyes widened. "I had to see you." She dropped her gaze, and a grin crept across her face. "I guess I got my wish and then some."

He pulled her into the room and locked the door. It wasn't that he didn't trust her, but he wouldn't put it past her father to trick her into doing something she hadn't intended. "Does Bellamy know you're here?" Not waiting for her answer, he turned to pull on his breeches. He didn't want to have to face Bellamy stark naked if he didn't have to.

"Wait! Don't."

Nolan glanced at her over his shoulder. His muscles tensed at the urgency in her voice. A blush spread across the bridge of her nose and down her neck.

She took a deep breath, the kind needed for courage, and stepped toward him. "I want to see you. All of you. And, no, my father doesn't know I'm here."

Nolan let his breeches fall to the floor. He straightened, turning to face her, letting her gaze at him in the light of the lantern she had carried into the room. Her words altered his mood instantly. Forget Bellamy. Nolan's heart thumped in his chest, and there was only one thing on his mind. He spread his hands slightly. "Take your fill."

She found a hook on which to hang her lantern, then moved near enough to put her palms on his chest; but left enough distance so she could gaze at his body. Nolan's blood quickened. For every second that passed, there was more of him to see.

"I missed you." She trailed her hands over his arms.

Nolan wanted her with an urgency that had nothing to do with logic, but some last stronghold of reason warred with him. Her loyalty could no longer be divided. She had to choose him. He forced himself to keep his head. "Why did you stay on the island?"

She dropped her hands to her sides. "Oh, I had a choice, did I? You and my father argue over me like I'm not even there. It sounded like you two agreed I would stay on the beach."

Nolan didn't move. She was fully dressed and angry. He was naked with an erection. Some men might decide it was time to put on some clothes, save a little face. Nolan hoped if he didn't move she would start touching him again. "But you're here now. Aren't you?"

She crossed her arms over her chest and tilted her chin. "I didn't like the way you two decided my fate. After my father fell asleep, I woke Parker and had him row me out to the ship."

Nolan smiled. He didn't want to argue with her after all. That was the last thing he wanted. His body was definitely winning the battle over reason. "Good thing I left some men to guard you."

Her tight features relaxed. "I thought they were guarding the treasure."

"You mean more to me than that treasure."

"Is that true?" The moist sheen that brightened the hopeful expression in her eyes tugged at his heart. That she doubted how much he cared for her, loved her, squeezed his throat until he feared his own eyes might water.

He glanced down, more comfortable with another form of his affection for her. "I think that's obvious."

He didn't reach for her. She had to come to him. The way she looked up at him with her head tilted, lips parted, clearly invited his attention, but he forced his arms to remain by his sides.

Her gaze slid down him, stopping at his arousal. Nolan could feel the rush of his own blood expanding his erection with a mindless urgency that stomped out all other thoughts. He closed his eyes.

When she pressed her hands on his chest, he willed himself not to move. His patience was paying off. The tension between them today had reminded him of their wedding night, and he had no intention of repeating his previous mistakes. This was her seduction, though they both knew she'd had him the moment she entered the cabin. Still, he'd let her set the pace.

She let her palms graze the contours of his abdomen before moving lower. "Are we truly not married?"

Once her destination became clear, Nolan found it harder to follow the drift of her conversation. Every muscle tensed in anticipation of the drift of her hands. She brushed her thumbs across the hollow near his hips, and Nolan bit back a moan. He swallowed, not sure if he would have a voice to speak. "To me we are. I'll marry you again if you want."

She somehow avoided the very demanding part of him that craved her touch so much he pulsated, and smoothed her hands over his thighs. "That means we're not married. I'm not sure the first time wasn't a mistake."

He opened his eyes. Her answer crept rudely into his daze of pleasurable sensation. What he saw almost made him forget why he'd opened his eyes in the first place. She had dropped to her knees. Her palms had slipped to the back of his thighs, continuing on their downward exploration. Her mouth hovered intoxicatingly close to paradise.

"Why . . . mistake?" he asked.

She glanced up at him and grinned. Her confident expression told him she knew what she was doing to him. "I want you to love me more than you hate my father."

Nolan exhaled loudly, which sounded a little like an anguished gasp. He should just tell her what she wanted to hear. Unfortunately, he didn't behave that way, not even under this kind of torment. His hatred for Bellamy was a living thing. It had been growing for years. Just thinking of it made lust's strangling grip loosen. "Let me love you. I'll show you."

"That's not what I mean." She gently guided his hips forward. Using only the tip of her tongue, she touched him.

This time he did gasp. Strong desire streaked from his sex, gripping him even tighter than before. His breath came in short gulps. There was no point in rational thought. His center became the feel of her warm wet tongue. "Marry me. I'll make you happy."

"Killing my father won't make me happy." She took him in her mouth. Nolan had the brief thought that someone had told her to do this to him, but who that might be was not something he wanted to think about at the moment.

He leaned his head back and closed his eyes. His knees felt weak, but he didn't want her to stop. Not for anything. He forced himself to hold still, not to thrust.

He didn't want to scare her. "I won't," he said, not sure if his breathless words were intelligible.

She gripped him at the base with a firm hand while her mouth and tongue applied maddening attention to the head of his sex. Apparently experimenting, she alternated between sucking then licking the length of him, drawing a wet line on its sensitive underside. Oh, someone *had* instructed her, Nolan thought briefly, and it had better just have been verbally.

"Not enough, Nolan."

"No?" He agreed. It wasn't enough. Not near enough. He buried his fingers in her hair. The urge to thrust compelled him beyond control, so he slightly rubbed his aching cock against her soft cheek and into her hair. The sensation gripped him like a fist and he did it only one more time, pulling away with the realization he could find release this way in the breadth of a heartbeat.

She kissed his hipbone, apparently aware of how close to the brink he was, backing off the torment. And just when he thought he could form a semirational thought, she blew on his burning skin, still wet from her thorough attentions. The new sensation took him to another level of insanity. "No more fighting. Make peace with my father so we can stay married."

The need to have her mouth on him again blurred the edges of his vision. His eyes were hard to keep open, except when they lazily focused on her mouth so close to his engorged sex. He had to say or do something to encourage her to do that to him again, just for a minute, just one more time. He tugged her hair gently to guide her back. She didn't budge. He stopped before using any force. "No more fighting . . . with Bellamy. Yes?"

With exaggerated slowness, she wrapped her fingers around the base of his erection and guided him into her mouth. Nolan let his head fall back. He glanced down, watching her sweet lips work to please him. A rush of lust so strong poured over him he had to fight to control it. He hissed and jerked away.

She looked up at him. "Did I hurt you?"

He leaned down and pulled her up. "More than you know."

He stepped back, landing on the bed with her on top of him. Getting inside her immediately was his only thought. He arranged her legs so she straddled him. Even before he slipped his hands under her dress, he knew she wore nothing under it.

He moved his hands up her thighs, caressing her bottom. His tide of urgency subsided enough to be manageable until she rocked against his hard flesh, still slick from her mouth. She caught on fast. Too fast. He was wet enough to ease their coupling, but he wanted her to be closer to his level of arousal. Once he entered her, he wouldn't last long.

He sat up, forcing her onto her back. He pushed her skirts around her waist. Without any coy warning, he nudged her legs apart and licked her with the flat of his tongue.

She gasped when his lips touched her in an openmouthed kiss. She was already wet and tasted like pure sex. He tightened his grip on her thighs, pulling her closer. The soft sound of pleasure that slipped from her throat sent an erotic shiver across the tight skin of his cock.

He gripped her buttocks in his palms, raising her hips, pinning her as he focused his assault on the center of her passion. She cried out loud enough for the crew to hear, but he didn't care.

With her feet braced on the bed, she angled her hips, straining to get closer to him. He slipped a finger inside her, matching the rhythm of her movements. She contracted around him, and he jerked in response. She teetered on the brink of release, and he needed to be deep inside her when she shattered.

He covered her, but she pushed on his shoulders, stopping him. His mind struggled for an explanation. His braced arms supported his weight, so he knew he wasn't crushing her.

She stared at him under heavy eyelids. "I want it to be like before."

"What do you mean?"

She lowered her gaze. It amazed him that she could still be shy after what she had done to him with her mouth. "I want to be on top."

He smiled. "Please, be my guest."

He moved off her so she could sit up. Watching her unlace her dress added a drugging dimension to his raging lust. He wanted to help her, but his hands shook. If he wanted to let her have her way, he had to use all his will to hold back. He sat on his heels, his erection burning against his stomach.

She slipped out of her gown and smiled at him. It was a sly smirk that terrified and excited. "Lie back."

He did as she commanded. When she crawled on top, he immediately reached to position her. She grabbed his wrists and pushed them to his sides. "Don't touch me until I say. Don't even move."

Nolan swallowed hard, hoping he could comply. She guided him into her slowly, not taking him all the way. He could barely tame the urge to thrust. She backed off way too soon. He curled his hands in the bedclothes to keep from pulling her down.

She braced her hands on his chest, her head back, her long hair brushing his thighs, her eyelids heavy with desire. God, but she was enjoying this. Her movements were like a hypnotizing dance, and the beat of the music was his own heart. He closed his eyes, unable to watch. She moved up and down, taking no more than half of him, circling her hips, pleasuring herself and torturing him. He wanted to climax. Needed to.

"Jewel. Please," he managed between wracking grips of pleasure that made it hard to breathe.

"All right. You can touch me." She guided his hands to her breasts. "Here," she purred. He watched her through half-closed eyes. He massaged her breasts, gently pinching her nipples.

She undulated her hips, and the movement seemed to please her, but for him it was just a new form of torture because she still hadn't taken him all the way. He increased the pressure on her engorged nipples and arched his hips, unable to restrain himself. Finally, a moan slipped past her lips and she slid all the way down his length. There was no way he could stop his hips from arching against her sweet descent. Her muscles squeezed him from the inside while her soft bottom caressed him from the outside. He couldn't take it anymore.

He grabbed her hips, pulling her hard against him as he thrust upward. She convulsed instantly. Her contractions milked his last shred of resistance. He arched back, almost coming off the bed with the force of his release.

Jewel collapsed against his chest, their bodies still joined. After he regained his strength, he rubbed light circles across her back. He hadn't lost her after all.

He kissed the top of her head and tried to recall what he had promised to get him here. Memory flooded back, and his exhausted muscles tensed all over again, but not in a way that promised another round of blissful release. Unaware that his peaceful reprieve had been snatched away by the tentacles of reality, Jewel nuzzled her cheek against his chest. Nolan brushed back her hair and tried to breathe while he convinced himself that a truce with Bellamy would be worth it if it brought him more moments like this.

Not fighting with Bellamy would be an unnatural act. He would have to be a saint. But better a saint than a priest. Now, all he had to do was to keep from getting killed while he walked on water.

Chapter Twenty

Jewel held up a ring topped with a fat green stone, angling it so the sun pouring through the clearing created by the waterfall could shine through. The square-cut emerald sparkled with life as it captured the sun and breathed from within. The ring was the most spectacular item they had recovered yet. At least, Jewel thought so. The others seemed just as impressed with the growing pile of gold coins the divers had retrieved from the pool's dark bottom. Kent's treasure equaled if not exceeded its rumored valve.

"It matches your eyes. If it were up to me, I'd see you kept it for yourself."

Without glancing at her father, Jewel tossed the ring in a basket with the rest of the jewelry. Brooches, pearl necklaces and a ruby- and onyx-encrusted cross filled the container to overflowing. Parker had excitedly named the precious stones for her. Jewel had never seen such riches, not even in her dreams. None were as fine as the ring, but she would rather wear the tail of a firefly around her finger than inherit her father's greed. "The treasure's for everyone to share evenly."

Bellamy leaned against the tall palm that shaded Jewel while she sifted through the muck brought up from the pond's bottom. "Bah—since when shouldn't a woman have a pretty bauble?"

Jewel glanced at her father. "When it belongs to someone else. The Continental Congress gets their share and then the crew divides the rest." She touched the gold signet ring, her wedding ring, that hung around her neck on a cord she'd snatched from a corset. "I have all the jewelry I need."

Bellamy nodded his head toward the ring. "He took that from me afore he left me here."

Jewel stared down at the ring as if it would somehow spring to life and bite her on the nose. She pulled it over her head and examined it. In the turmoil of her marriage, the ring, which belonged to Wayland anyway, hadn't seemed important.

There were initials engraved on the front. She'd noticed them before but assumed they belonged to some nameless victim of Wayland's. In her musing, the ring had been won in a game of dice, nothing more.

"WK," he said, without actually seeing the letters she herself wouldn't have been able to name. She could tell by her father's steady stare that those initials should have significance.

When she still didn't respond, he finally said, "William Kent."

"You stole it from Nolan in the first place." She narrowed her gaze, but her father only smirked at her show of anger.

"Aye, but he stole something more valuable from me, don't you know."

Jewel returned to her work. She assumed he meant

279

her, and she had no intention of discussing it further. Last night with Nolan had settled everything ... she hoped. His promise to leave her father alone had been coerced, but she felt justified. Even the fact that her special instruction had come from Wayland—with lots of blushing on both their parts—didn't make her regret the extreme measure she'd taken to win Nolan's promise. She had to save her marriage as well as her father's life. Not that Bellamy deserved her protection, but unfortunately he was still her father. She couldn't turn her back on him no matter how much she desired.

She stuck her hands in the basket of pond muck and dumped two fistfuls into a smaller basket. She poured water from a bucket to wash away the worst of the silt, then sifted through what was left.

Her plan to seduce Nolan had been born of desperation. Bellamy had driven a wedge between them, and Jewel would have resorted to anything to return them to the harmony they'd experienced before their arrival on this island. Perhaps the way she coerced his promise to find peace with her father had been wrong. Nolan had always given of himself so easily when they were intimate, if not in other aspects of their relationship. Last night had exceeded her expectations. She felt her power over him, and she reveled in it. His reaction to her bold advances aroused her more than she had ever imagined. For a brief moment in time, she had controlled their relationship. She had the forceful Captain Nolan Kent moaning her name and begging her for—

"Does that pretty blush staining your cheeks have anything to do with Nolan agreeing to let me have a share of his grandpa's precious treasure?"

Jewel glanced up. She had forgotten her father still leaned against the tree. Her cheeks burned, and she had to drop her gaze. "Hadn't you better get back to work,

Bellamy? The others have brought up twice as many loads as you."

"Bellamy, is it? Have you forgotten I'm your father? Nolan hasn't, I can assure you."

Jewel glared at him again. She felt the rise of emotion welling up inside her, but this time it was different. Her hurt had turned to anger—righteous anger directed at the father who abandoned her. "You were never a father to me, so why should I honor you with more than you deserve? I told Nolan to leave you alone. That's all I owe you. It's more than you've ever done for me."

Bellamy smirked. "Aye, lass. And you two will live the rest of your lives in wedded bliss without your old sire around to spoil your happiness."

His sarcastic tone undermined her belief that she had settled anything between her and Nolan, but she wasn't about to let Bellamy know it. The one thing she had learned about her father was that he found the littlest tear in a person's armor and drove his sword home. "Nolan gave you what you wanted. You have no reason to torment us further."

Bellamy folded his arms over his chest, either feigning his relaxed stance or truly not giving a bloody damn about the trouble he caused. "I could see the muscle working in Nolan's jaw when he told me he would give me an equal share of the treasure."

Jewel picked up the basket and shook it harder than necessary. Mud-encrusted coins flew over the side. She picked them up and dumped them back in the basket. If she ignored Bellamy long enough, maybe he would go away.

"It's eating at him, you know—knowing I'll be getting a share of Kent's treasure. Over the years a feeling like that festers in your gut."

Jewel plunked two more muddy handfuls into the strainer. Mud spattered her cheek. She wiped it away, realizing she had forgotten to take out the coins she had just cleaned. "Why don't you leave me alone?"

"Because I'm your father." Bellamy stepped away from the tree, his smirk gone. "There are a hell of a lot of women in this world, and it's not right that Nolan had to go and pick my child."

Jewel threw down her basket and got to her feet. "You deserted me. The way I see it, you don't have any right to claim me."

Bellamy beat his fist against his chest. "You're my blood. As the years pass, Nolan's going to be looking into my green eyes, not yours. That's what he'll be thinking, I promise you. And he's going to think about how much he hates me and the sacrifices he made for you, and then where will you be?"

"What's between us has nothing to do with you!" How many times had Nolan told her that? But she hadn't believed it then and she wasn't at all sure she believed it now.

"Nolan's always been popular with the ladies. He could have had an heiress, a lady of standing, at the very least a wealthy widow. Some folks don't know about his grandfather, and those that do think Nolan's holier-than-thou father atoned for the family sins." Bellamy looked her up and down. "So tell me, why would he pick a scrawny, illegitimate tavern wench as his bride?"

Jewel couldn't breathe. Her vision blurred. She glanced around her for something to throw. The bucket of mud-encrusted coins appeared in the corner of her gaze. She turned and scooped out a fistful of wet mud and threw it in his face. The slurpy thwack that sounded as the muck found its target brought her back to reality. He stood there for a moment, black slime dripping down his face and splattered across his chest, appearing just as shocked as she.

With slow, precise movements, as if he had been dining on tea and crumpets with royalty, he wiped the mud from his eyes and then the rest of his face. "You see my point."

Jewel's chest heaved with her spent anger. She had no answer to his painfully valid observation, and the silence that hung between them confirmed it.

"It's only a matter of time before he gets tired of his revenge against me and comes to resent you. There's no happy ending in that for you, Jewel. I see the way you look at him. It's plain you're besotted. He's only using you to get at me. He doesn't feel the same."

Jewel rubbed her temples with the backs of her dirty hands, shutting him out. But her own thoughts echoed his hateful words. "Stop it. He's not like you."

"No. I know Nolan better than anyone. I watched him grow to a man. He's *not* like me. He's worse. He may believe he truly cares for you, but it's me that eats at his vitals. I'm what's driving him, and he'll want to fight that hatred but won't be able to."

Jewel glanced at the pond, searching for Nolan. Parker sat at the side, catching his breath. Nolan must be under the water. Six men, Bellamy included, had taken turns swimming to the bottom. They shoveled silt into a large basket, then tugged on a rope to have the crew above pull it to the surface. Jewel had been left in charge of sifting through what they found. It was exhausting work. As much as she wanted reassurance from Nolan, she didn't want to distract him.

She just had to believe he would tell her father differently. It would surely lead to blows between them, but at least it would prove . . . Jewel let the rest of her thought trail off. She glanced back at her father.

Bellamy must have seen the confusion and doubt clouding her features. "He hates me more than he could ever love you. And you're feeding that hatred by being my daughter."

Jewel dropped to her knees and frantically sifted through more mud. "Parker looks exhausted. I think it's your turn to go down with Nolan."

Bellamy smiled to himself, and it chilled her blood. "As a matter of fact," he said, "it is."

He strolled away from her, taking what was left of her heart.

A rapid explosion of bubbles broke the pond's dark surface. Jewel glanced to Wayland. "What's that mean?"

"It means they'll be up in a minute. Stop that pacing, chit. You're wearing me out," Wayland answered without opening his eyes. He lay flat on the ground with his arms folded over his chest, his shirt balled under his head for a pillow. He was even scrawnier than he appeared in clothing, but he must have strength in that wiry form because he had pulled up the heavy baskets of silt and coins since early that morning. She had never seen him work so hard. Obviously, gold motivated him.

Jewel paced the pool's length again. The ripples from the erupting bubbles drifted toward her in lazy abandon. Even the water's surface had started to look gilded in the setting sun. She had seen enough gold for one day. It would be dark soon. Nolan had no reason to go down one last time. Nor Bellamy to volunteer to accompany him.

Most of the crew had left to haul the treasure back to the beach. All the men were exhausted, and even the lure of wealth had lost its appeal in favor of much-needed rest. "Parker, would you dive down and check on them?"

Parker lifted his head from the arm he used as a pillow, his long body curled under the shade of a bowed palm tree. From the slow way he opened his eyes, Jewel could tell he had fallen asleep. "Pull on the rope. He'll yank back."

The men who went down tied ropes around their waists to ensure they could pull themselves to the surface in the event they became disoriented. Exhaustion set in long before they had retrieved half of the treasure, but sheer excitement drove them on. They had continued working until more silt then gold was brought to the surface.

Jewel picked up a bundle of ropes. One end was tied to a tree, the other either to a man's waist or a basket. Only three ropes led underneath the water. One must be tied to Bellamy, one to Nolan and the third to the basket they had taken with them.

Jewel neared the water with all three ropes in her hand. Suddenly, one of the ropes went taut. Bellamy broke the surface of the water, gasping for breath. Jewel dropped the rope attached to him before Bellamy could get a breath. She started gathering the excess of the other two. "Where's Nolan?"

Bellamy swam to the side. "There's been an accident. Nothing I could do."

Her frantic yanking dragged one of the ropes across the sandy bank, frayed and dripping water. The end had been cut with a knife. "You did this!"

Bellamy pulled himself out of the pond. "Had to. He got tangled in his line."

"Why did you come up without him?" Jewel strode toward the pond's edge. She sucked in as much air as she could take in her lungs. A hand on the back of her dress stopped her from jumping into the deep water.

"I thought you couldn't swim," Bellamy growled.

Wayland leaped to his feet. "She can't."

Jewel tried to wrench free of her father's hold. "I have to find Nolan."

Parker shook off his sleepy haze and rushed to the pool. "Don't let her go. I'll go down."

Before he reached the edge, Nolan exploded like a

cannonball from the pond's depths. He choked and gasped for air. Jewel reached out to him, but Bellamy still held the back of her dress. Parker leaned over the side and helped pull Nolan out.

Once on solid ground, he braced himself on his hands and knees. He coughed up so much water, Jewel feared he would still drown even though he was on dry land. His face was red and he couldn't catch his breath.

Before she could break away from her father, Nolan's choking eased and his raging gasps subsided. With his head still hung between his shoulders, he took several shuddering deep breaths. After a long moment, he turned and glared at Jewel. The hatred in his gaze stopped her heart. No. Not at her. She started to breathe again and followed his gaze. He poured all that venom and fury at the man who stood by her shoulder, her father.

Bellamy backed away. "Just a little joke, Nolan. I wanted to see if you could still get untied if you were forced to walk the plank. Remember how I used to drop you overboard with your hands bound and bet on how long it would take you to surface?"

Nolan got to his feet. "You were trying to kill me, you bastard."

Bellamy continued his retreat. "If I wanted to kill you, you'd be dead by now."

Nolan took two steps toward Bellamy, then broke into a run. Bellamy didn't even have a chance to brace before Nolan dove at his knees, sending him onto his backside. He tried to kick Nolan's head before either could recover from the momentum of the fall. Nolan managed to duck while clawing Bellamy in his attempt to get a better grip. The two men rolled on the ground, Bellamy squirming to get away and Nolan hanging on like a bulldog.

Jewel ran toward them. "Stop this!" Nolan was surely going to kill her father this time.

Wayland rushed forward to help her, but Parker hung

back. "Let them go. They need to settle this."

Jewel bent down, tugging at Nolan's arm. Parker's words echoed in her head with a finality she could no longer deny. Despite all efforts, the only way the feud between Bellamy and Nolan would ever be settled was with one of their deaths. The proof of her father's words was chilling. Her meddling had only furthered the bad blood between them.

Wayland stood above the men, randomly grabbing an arm or a hunk of hair, only to be shaken off. "It's like putting your hand in a hornets' nest," he said, answering the plea in her gaze.

Nolan had gotten his hands around Bellamy's throat and wouldn't let go. Bellamy's face rapidly changed from red to purple. But instead of trying to pry off Nolan's grip, Bellamy squirmed underneath him, his hands nowhere in sight. It looked as if he wasn't even trying to defend himself.

Jewel tugged at Nolan's arms. "Help me," she called to Wayland.

She darted a quick glance around Nolan's shoulder to see if Bellamy was still conscious. He was, and his arm reared back to plunge a knife into Nolan's neck. There was no time for her to even scream.

She grabbed Bellamy's wrist, desperate to stop the force of the blow. "No!" She succeeded in misdirecting Bellamy's aim. The knife glanced off her shoulder. A rush of fear and instinct forced her to gasp, then she jerked away.

Nolan must have realized what had happened, because he wrestled the knife from Bellamy and threw it into the water.

Jewel got to her feet and was surprised when she swayed. Anger and shock competed for dominance. Either way, she was ready to give up on both her father and her husband. When she touched her fingers to her wound, they came away red. It didn't hurt so much as feel very cold. She stared at her hand, not believing what she saw. With the realization that she'd been truly hurt, Jewel started to shiver. Her knees buckled, but Nolan was already at her side, guiding her to the ground. "How bad?"

"I don't know." She didn't feel much of anything. Maybe she was going to die. Nolan pulled aside the sliced cloth of her gown. Jewel turned her face away, just in case it was particularly awful. If she were mortally wounded, she didn't think she wanted to know. She waited for the pain. It came when Nolan started probing the wound. She sucked air through her teeth, but willed herself not to cry.

Bellamy leaned over Nolan's shoulder. "It's just a flesh wound."

Nolan turned around and slugged him in the mouth.

Wayland squatted in front of Jewel, blocking her view. With great effort, she pushed herself up on her elbows to peer around him to see if the brawl had started again. The cursing and yelling told her it had.

"You could have killed her. You bastard!"

Bellamy tried to best Nolan in volume. "If you would have let go instead of trying to strangle me, I wouldn't have had to pull my knife in the first place."

"You stabbed her. You stabbed your own daughter. That's a new low for you, Bellamy." Nolan's voice shook with menace. Though not as boisterous as his adversary, he sounded angrier, more dangerous.

Jewel strained to see over Wayland's shoulder. Only the tops of Nolan and Bellamy's heads as they circled each other reached her line of vision. Neither man had a weapon, but Jewel feared they were mad enough to kill each other with their bare hands.

Bellamy turned his head and spat. Jewel could easily imagine the blood-tinged spittle that stained the sand and provoked another foul curse from her father. "Letting you live to lie with my daughter one more night would be a new low. That's why it's not going to happen." Bellamy's lunge for Nolan was a blur in the corner of her eye, but Nolan's grunt assured her he'd hit his mark. Jewel's neck ached and she let her head fall back onto the rolled cloth someone had thoughtfully placed beneath her. Wayland blocked her view completely. Even with her eyes closed, she knew her father and husband were rolling on the ground like two schoolboys. Two schoolboys bent on killing each other.

Wayland touched her chin, forcing her to look at him. "It's a shallow wound. Your pretty dress got the worst of it. Don't even need stitches."

Jewel blinked, clearing the tears from her vision. "Make them stop."

Wayland nodded and stood. The compassion in his tired gaze shook her with a new wave of sorrow. He knew better than she how hopeless was her request. Jewel propped herself on her elbows and watched Wayland stride toward the two men locked in mortal combat and kick them apart. "Can't you two stop long enough to see that Jewel's wound is tended to?"

Miraculously, they let go of each other and got to their feet. Wayland braced his hands on the hipbones that jutted above the waistline of his baggy breeches. "I'm sick of seeing you two chasing each other's tails like bleeding mongrels. Let's finish this thing right."

Both men nodded, their chests heaving. They each looked as if they had just been awakened from a disturbing dream. All three approached her. Jewel hadn't realized Parker had taken her hand and cradled her head until Nolan growled something at him. Parker quickly moved aside so Nolan could take his place. He clasped her hand, but instead of comforting her, his slick skin

289

radiated heated anger. The pulse at the base of his thumb raced with erratic agitation.

Wayland pulled a silver flask out from his trousers. He knelt in front of her and lifted her skirt. He paused, a pink tinge creeping across his tobacco-colored skin. For the second time in their acquaintance, she'd made Wayland blush, a reaction she'd not thought possible from the grizzled pirate.

He lowered his gaze. "I figured you wore those petticoat things. They're made of soft cotton, so it won't scratch your skin so much. Make a fine bandage."

Jewel smiled. "I do. Go ahead." Now that she'd found Wayland's soft spot, she couldn't let the moment pass without getting him back for the thousand times he'd caused her to blush—even if her shoulder had gone from icy numb to burning hot. "I didn't realize you were so familiar with a lady's unmentionables."

Bellamy squatted, studying her wound. "Most of the women Wayland knows would be insulted if you were to call them ladies. They don't wear anything but a light skirt that's easy to toss over their heads."

Jewel refused to acknowledge her father. Instead, she watched Nolan, fearing her father's nearness would cause them to come to blows again. Nolan stared straight ahead, his gaze unfocused. Though he still gripped her hand tighter than necessary, she understood his mind was not on her. She could see the muscle working in his jaw and feel the fury rolling off him like white heat.

Asking him not to fight with her father had been a mistake. A mere day of pent-up anger had left him more volatile than she'd ever seen him. A lifetime would eat him alive and pervert any love he felt for Jewel into hate. Her father had been right, damn him.

Wayland poured the contents of his flask onto the bunched cloth from her petticoat and pressed it to her wound. She drew a sharp breath between her teeth. The fire in her shoulder exploded into a thousand tiny sparks hot enough to sear her flesh. She exhaled on a sob.

Wayland wiped away the excess blood and examined the wound once more. "It's a puny thing. Bled more than it's worth. Don't even need a bandage. The fresh air will heal it faster than anything." He pulled out a small knife and cut away the fabric that surrounded the wound. "There." He handed her the flask. "Clean it at night and in the morning. In a couple of days you'll have forgotten it altogether."

Jewel twisted to examine the wound herself. The sun had disappeared completely. In the light blue twilight, the wound looked little more than a thick scratch.

Wayland resheathed the knife, then stood. He looked at Bellamy and Nolan. "Now, let's settle things between you two, so the rest of us can have long and healthy lives."

Nolan's wet grip tugged from Jewel's and he got to his feet. Jewel let him go without a fight. She really had no choice. Though he hadn't strayed from her side, he might as well have been an ocean away. She pushed herself to a sitting position, still feeling too unsteady to stand—whether from the wound or the drift of the conversation, she couldn't say.

He faced Bellamy, his stance that of a broad-shouldered avenging shadow in the growing darkness. "Tonight, on the beach. We'll light torches and the crew can stand witness."

Bellamy folded his arms over his barrel chest, looking way too happy with the turn of events. "Don't sound too fair to me. As I remember, last time you also had a crew on your side."

"I'll relinquish command of the crew to Mr. Tyrell right now." Nolan glanced at Parker.

The lieutenant straightened from the palm trunk where he'd been leaning. "Is that really necessary? How far are you two actually going take this feud of yours?"

"Nope," said Bellamy. "If I win, I get the crew and the ship just like what you stole from me."

Nolan squared his shoulders, narrowing his gaze. "My crew wouldn't serve under you even if you delivered them my head on a platter."

Parker strode to stand between them. "No one is putting anyone's head on a platter." He glanced at Jewel. "Do you think she wants to hear this?" he asked Nolan.

Jewel closed her eyes and hugged her knees to her chest. The image of Nolan's words had already turned her stomach; it was too late for him to take them back as Parker urged.

"I have to finish this once and for all. No matter the outcome. The way things are right now isn't healthy—especially for Jewel. I think that's obvious." She heard Nolan's voice, felt his gaze rest on her, but she refused to acknowledge him. Did he actually expect her to agree?

Wayland joined them. "Save it for when you got your sword in your hand." He turned to Bellamy. "Nolan earned the respect of your crew while you lost it. He doesn't have to order his crew to follow you. This fight is between you two and nothing more."

"Fine." Bellamy's smile shone in the dark. "The sooner the better."

"I'm not going to be a part of this." Parker's voice rose a few notches.

"Afraid of a little bloodshed, boy?" Bellamy laughed. "Some fierce crew you got here, Nolan."

Parker swung his gaze toward Jewel's father. "You deserved a lashing for trying to drown Nolan—or better yet, he should haul you in and let them hang you in Charles Town. From what I've heard, you no doubt have a price on your head." He turned to Nolan. "Fighting the British for our freedom is one thing, but, Nolan, why would you waste your skill and time proving something to this common criminal? I say, lock him in irons and let the authorities deal with him."

"Parker, no. They'll hang him." Jewel struggled to her feet. She didn't like the idea of Nolan and her father having another swordfight, but neither did she like Parker's idea.

"I'd like to see Nolan try to throw me in chains. Who's going to help him—you, puppy?" Bellamy sneered at Parker.

Parker held the man's gaze for a moment before he glanced away, apparently choosing to ignore the taunt. Though, he didn't definitively back down either. He squared a shoulder that had gotten noticeably broader since the start of the journey.

Nolan broke the tension between them. "Jewel's right. I won't turn Bellamy in as a pirate. I'd have to turn myself in right along with him. We'll settle this by the rules of the Brethren. A fight to the death."

Even Parker seemed too stunned to have an answer for that. If no one would speak up to stop this lunacy, neither would Jewel. She felt Nolan's gaze on her again and forced herself to meet his eyes. The first scattering of stars dotted the sky, pulsing in glee while the man she loved stared at her without the slightest hint of a smile. His expression mirrored the bleakness that sank through her limbs, numbing even the wound in her shoulder. "I have to do this."

She forced herself not to blink or glance away. "I know."

He turned back to the other men. "The rules are—there are no rules. Agreed?"

Bellamy pointed at Parker. "Tell pretty boy over here that the crew is not to get involved. Even after I've stuck so many holes in you you'll be spewing blood like a fountain."

Parker's voice sounded lower than normal. He'd recovered from his shock with a new surge of anger. "I won't interfere. I won't be around to see it." He strode past them and into the jungle.

"Lads today have no respect for their elders," mumbled Bellamy.

"Are we agreed?" asked Wayland.

"Agreed," said her father and husband in unison.

Jewel closed her eyes to block out the sight of her father and Nolan staring at each other with such undisguised hatred. She would lose one of them. As desperately as she loved Nolan, she couldn't wish her own father to die. She also knew Nolan would rather die in a fair fight than live the rest of his life forcing himself to be civil to a man he despised with his whole being. Either way, Jewel would lose. "Agreed," she whispered to no one in particular.

Chapter Twenty-one

Nolan paced the perimeter of light created by the torches, while they waited for a crewman to bring the swords from the ship. Ordinary cutlasses wouldn't do for this occasion. Nolan had two beautiful, well-balanced swords crafted from Damascus steel hoarded from his days with Bellamy. The gold hilts each sported two rubies and a large emerald, but that wasn't why Nolan kept them when he had renounced every other ill-gotten item he had acquired in his youth as a pirate. He had convinced himself the weapons represented a perfection in craftsmanship that he valued above their monetary worth. But the truth was, he had saved them for this moment. The swords were perfectly matched. Neither he nor Bellamy would have any advantage in weaponry.

He stole a glance at Bellamy, who looked peaceful and calm as he lounged in the shadows of the night. The older man saved his strength. He would need it.

Nolan fed on his anger, not wanting to sit and calm down. All he needed was to close his eyes and see the blood staining Jewel's dress, and endless, hot strength spewed up within him. He glanced around the men crowded on the beach. That Jewel was not among the crew saved them both the emotional turmoil sending her away would surely cause, a distraction he couldn't afford. After this was all over, he would find a way to convince her to still love him. And if he didn't win, it wouldn't matter.

Though Parker was barely speaking to him and certainly not taking his orders, the man agreed to watch out for Jewel during the fight. He didn't say it, but it was understood his care would extend beyond that as well if need be. Not that Nolan still believed a romance budded between them, but Parker was a good man with three sisters and a mother. He knew what women needed better than most. Also, though his sexual preferences ranged on the edge of deviant, Parker was an honest man. That he was so adamantly against what Nolan was about to prove might mean he was a better one.

Though Nolan believed in the revolution, would fight for the patriots the best he could, his longing to have another chance at Bellamy was greater than his commitment to that cause. Not even the promise of the treasure waiting in his ship could persuade him otherwise.

Nolan had never beaten Bellamy in a fight. True enough, Nolan had had the crew behind him during the mutiny, and the fact that Bellamy had been on a month-long bender rendered him easy to overpower. At the moment, Laggett appeared more sober and alert than Nolan had ever seen him. But neither was Nolan still a boy. He was a man, with a man's anger. He had waited years for this. Fear of death or love for a woman could not stop the inevitable. His hatred for Bellamy had been building for too long.

Nolan turned at the sound of someone trudging across

the beach. The crewman lumbered under the weight of the large box encasing his swords. The man fell to his knees when he reached the center of the circle of light. Nolan strode toward him. The sand's density, which left the other man panting, didn't slow Nolan's pace. Nothing would.

Nolan flipped up the case's lid. He lifted one of the heavy swords with the same effort it would normally take to lift a bamboo reed. He turned toward the nearest torch, letting the jewels in the hilt come alive and the blade's steel wink in deadly contrast.

Bellamy remained lounging under a palm tree where the jungle encroached on the long stretch of beach, his face hidden in the shadows. Nolan strode forward and, without warning, tossed a sword to him by the hilt. Bellamy caught it with a minimum of motion. His actions were swift and sure, like a diver cleaving a still pond without a ripple. Either his relaxed pose was feigned, or Bellamy's reflexes hadn't lost their sharpness over the years. If anything, they had quickened. Then again, Bellamy didn't drink near as much as he used to.

Nolan turned to retrieve his own sword. The first shiver of fear penetrated the heat of his anger. He wrapped his fingers around the cool hilt. His determination quelled his fear. He had no choice in this. Never again would he let Bellamy manipulate him. Nolan's time had come, and he planned on proving it to Bellamy—even if he had to kill the man to do so.

Quickly, Nolan composed himself and turned to face Bellamy. His stance had changed to that of a seasoned warrior. He gingerly tested the edge of his sword with his fingertip, then raised his weapon and slashed through a small tree. The sapling tumbled in two neat pieces on the sand. Bellamy nodded in satisfaction.

Wayland moved to the center of the light cast by the

torches, signaling to Bellamy and Nolan to step forward. The crew's unusual silence added to the confrontation's seriousness. No yells of encouragement or heckling penetrated the heavy tension. This was no friendly tussle. This was a fight to the death, and everyone knew it.

Wayland stood between Bellamy and Nolan. "I want you two to shed everything but your breeches. I don't want no extra weapons sneaking into this. This fight's going to be a fair one."

Nolan kept his gaze on Bellamy while he shrugged out of his shirt. Bellamy glanced at the scar on Nolan's chest. Nolan stiffened.

Bellamy smirked. "Didn't learn your lesson the last time we fought over my girl, did ya, boy?"

Nolan yanked off his boots. His anger made his motions stiff and the simple task difficult. "She isn't your girl anymore. She's my wife. Nor am I a boy. Your daughter can verify that."

Apparently, Nolan's words finally nicked Bellamy's composure. His jaw clenched, and he buried the tip of his sword in the sand. He stripped off his shirt in angry movements that matched Nolan's. "She's going to be a widow, is what she's going to be." The handle of a knife stuck from Bellamy's breeches. He pulled it from his waistband and dropped it to the ground. "Even if you win you're going to lose, Nolan."

Barefoot and bare-chested, Nolan picked up his sword and backed away. He knew Bellamy was right, but the man he thought himself to be, the man he needed to be, wouldn't rest until he proved Bellamy couldn't beat him. "That won't stop me from drawing your blood."

Bellamy retrieved his sword from the sand. He held it in front of him, as if expecting Nolan to attack at any minute.

"Wait." Wayland stepped between them. The rest of

the crew kept their distance. Wayland strode toward Bellamy. "Lift your arms."

Bellamy did as instructed. He lifted the sword above his head effortlessly. Nolan felt that twinge of fear return. He wouldn't put it past Bellamy to have signed a pact with the devil. How else could he have remained so strong after all these years? And in one piece. Most pirates had been hacked away like Wayland and Handsome Jack. It was a testament to Bellamy's strength and cunning, his looks. Nolan gripped the handle of his sword. The scar on his chest itched with memories of their last battle.

Wayland circled Bellamy, searching him with his gaze. Shaking his head, he pulled something from the back of the ex pirate-captain's breeches. He tossed the pistol to the ground. Hands on hips, he faced Bellamy. "You got anything else hidden, or do you want me to go fumbling around your Jolly Roger?"

Bellamy glanced at Wayland and smirked. "Sorry to disappoint you, but that's it."

Wayland stalked away, grumbling under his breath. Bellamy called to his back, "Hey. Aren't you going to search our boy, Nolan?"

"He's too honest for his own good. That's why you two are fighting." Wayland turned to face them. "Have at it, lads. Kill each other."

Nolan held his sword in front of him with both hands. His initial impulse was to rush Bellamy and take the first swing. He denied his desire, opting for a more strategic attack. He waited for an opening. He forced all his raw anger back in on itself. He would have his chance.

Bellamy grinned and winked, apparently amused when Nolan held his ground. It was obvious he had expected a wild, emotional attack as well. "Learned something have you, boy?" He started to circle.

Nolan followed Bellamy's movements, keeping his opponent in front of him. Ignoring Bellamy's confident grin, he focused on the man's blade. He wouldn't let Bellamy taunt him. He was no longer an adolescent with more temper than sense.

"Bet Jewel's glad you're not rushing ahead of yourself, anymore. Remember that whore on Tortuga you liked so much? What was her name?"

Bellamy continued to circle wide and Nolan followed, with tighter, more concentrated steps. He studied every twitch of Bellamy's taut muscles. Bellamy's cajoling bounced off Nolan's icy concentration. The first slip or opening, Nolan would be there.

"Rosalinda. Aye, that was her name. She used to come to me after you had worn yourself out on her. She needed a real man to satisfy her after your boorish fumbling. We used to laugh about it, we did."

Nolan smiled. Not because of anything Bellamy said. He heard the words but didn't quite process their meaning. Bellamy's wide circles were tiring him. The powdery sand could wear a man out quickly. No doubt Bellamy knew that, but he was waiting for Nolan to lose his temper and attack with uncontrolled ferocity. And why not? Bellamy's strategy had always worked in the past.

Not this time.

"Yep, wonder what my girl thinks about Nolan the Noble in bed. 'Course, she doesn't know better. Not to worry. Once I do you in, she'll have her pick of young bucks. Probably a different one every night." Bellamy lunged.

Nolan was ready, his stance solid. When Bellamy's blow came, Nolan put all his strength into parrying. He got his blade under Bellamy's and used his knees and arms to propel the weapon into the air. He pulled back his sword and jabbed at Bellamy's ribs. Bellamy fell back into the sand before the blade found its mark. He tried to scoot away, but Nolan charged him. He straddled Bellamy's prone body and Bellamy abandoned his backward crawl. With both hands, Nolan brought his sword straight up, positioning it to hammer down into the center of Bellamy's chest.

Bellamy stared up at him with a mixture of shock and terror in his eyes. Nolan was glad Jewel wasn't here. It would hurt her deeply to see her father like this. The thought sobered him like a dunk in icy water.

He froze, with his sword still poised to strike. No matter what he said, Jewel wouldn't forgive him for killing her father. He was her husband. He could physically force her to stay with him, he frantically reasoned. She had no one else.

He slowly lowered his sword, something stronger than rage or even rational thought controlling his actions. He loved Jewel too much to hurt her like this. He let his right hand drop behind him, burying the sword's tip in the sand. Still holding on to the hilt, he offered his other hand to Bellamy.

Bellamy's gaze veered from Nolan's lowered sword, then back to Nolan himself. His expression hardened and Nolan had the impression that Bellamy felt cheated. He made no move to take Nolan's offered hand. Another realization shook Nolan. After everything Bellamy had put him through, he couldn't kill him. Bellamy had taught him with a cruel hand, but he'd made Nolan the man he was today. Bellamy had fathered the woman he loved. If not for Bellamy, he would never have found Jewel, and Nolan suddenly knew he could bear anything but losing her—even Bellamy Leggett.

"Lovely display, but you can drop the sword, Captain Kenton." A chorus of muskets being readied followed the vaguely familiar voice.

Nolan swung his gaze to see a red-coated marine flanked by two dozen soldiers already assembled in firing formation. And to a man they had their muskets trained on Nolan and his crew.

Jewel threw a rock into the reflection of the moon. In the surface of the pond, the night sky looked like a huge pearl surrounded by a thousand diamonds all lying in a bed of black satin. Not much of a hiding place for a fortune. If she hadn't found the treasure, either Bellamy or Nolan would have. Still, she wished she had the extra time. Wished things were the way they were before. She threw another rock and cursed the rippling pearl and diamonds. The real treasure had been just as fragile.

It was no treasure at all, but a glittering pile of metal that brought nothing but heartache to its possessors. Look at Captain Kent. The first Captain Kent. He'd lost his life because of the treasure. Jewel would lose her heart and soul.

The treasure started it all, and would end it as well. It was what had brought Nolan and Bellamy together in the first place, and them to her. Their first jaunt to the Quail and Queen had nothing to do with her father's desire to visit his forgotten daughter, nor had Nolan's second visit been a gallant gesture to rescue her from an arranged marriage. And just to ensure she understood her lowly status in the order of things, the treasure jealously claimed her suitor. Jewel would be left with nothing but a cold fistful of metal.

Jewel dragged her finger through the water, disrupting her first memory of Bellamy and Nolan together. They had fought that night. The same night she had first seen her father. How had she ever thought she could change either one of them?

She didn't have to use her imagination to know what

was happening on the beach. They had played out a similar argument before her very eyes, long ago. The thought stopped her heart. She choked on a sob as she tried to draw breath that wouldn't come. Unbidden, the first fight between her father and Nolan played out in front of her closed eyes with a clarity she'd been unable to retrieve until this moment. She saw the blade pierce Nolan, and she could feel the pain herself.

"No!" Her eyes flew open and she sprang to her feet. Her father had cheated that time. Nolan hadn't wanted to hurt him, but her father had attacked him when his guard was down. She couldn't let it happen like that again.

A strong arm wrapped around her midsection the moment she trod upon the worn trail that led back to the beach. The sudden cessation of her flight pulled her back against her captor, and they both temporarily lost their balance.

"I can't let you do that, Jewel." Parker managed to keep them both on their feet.

Jewel jabbed an elbow in his ribs—not as hard as she could, but a subtle yet serious entreaty for him to let her go. "I have to stop the fight."

To his credit, he neither grunted nor loosened his hold. "Nolan doesn't want you there. Let it go."

"My father's going to cheat. Please." She soon lost her breath struggling against his unyielding grip. "Please. I have a bad feeling."

"I'm letting you go now, so don't run. I'll only have to chase you and it's dark as hell out here. I don't want either of us to break our necks." He slowly eased his hold.

She turned to face him. The fact that he wasn't at the beach either made the situation more desperate. He appeared to be the only one who had retained his common sense during this ordeal. "We have to get to the beach—my father's going to cheat like he did before."

"I think Nolan knows that," Parker said, apparently resigned.

"But Nolan could be *killed*." She raised her voice, trying to break through his acceptance of something she couldn't.

"Wayland says he won't let that happen." Parker shrugged. "At least that's what he said when I asked him to help me talk some sense into Nolan."

"And you believe Wayland? I have to get to the beach." Jewel turned and started in that direction, not expecting Parker to try to physically stop her again if she kept an even pace. As she hoped, he fell in beside her.

"I don't believe any of this. I can't believe my old schoolmaster is fighting to the death with a known pirate. Joining with Nolan to find a treasure seemed a grand idea back in Boston, but now I don't know. I'd hate it if something happened to Nolan, and serving under your father scares me just as much."

"Nolan was your schoolmaster? I didn't know that." Jewel quickened her pace. Speaking of normal things helped to slow her heartbeat while it seemed to distract Parker from stopping her.

"I wasn't the best student, I have to admit, but I liked going to my classes because I got to be around Nolan. There were rumors about him, though he thought he was fooling everyone. No one ever said it to his face, but his father's whole congregation knew the Kentons were descended from Captain Kent. That's why he had such a big following, I think."

A yellow haze, the glow from the lanterns, hovered over the tops of the foliage that separated them from the beach. Parker sidestepped her and blocked her way. "You can't go on the beach."

"Parker—"

He stopped her with a raised hand. "I'll see what's going on first and then, if it's all right, you can insist they stop. All right?"

Jewel studied his serious features. He'd not been aboard the *Neptune*, and she doubted he could handle the sight of death and bloodshed any better than she. He was just an ex-schoolboy.

"All right. But I'll be right behind you. I'll stay in the brush until you say it's all right—but Parker, if it's the worst . . ." She swallowed, unable to say if Nolan had been mortally wounded, or even her father for that matter. "If it's the worst, I want to be there."

He nodded, then turned and headed for the light. The jungle's dark green foliage writhed in black shadows from the flickering torches. Tonight seemed excessively warm, and a thin stream of sweat wound its way down between her shoulder blades. She'd left her hair undone, too distracted to wrestle it into a braid, and strands adhered to her cheeks and neck.

A metallic sound that didn't seem like the clink of swords reached them first. Jewel's premonition of doom grew stronger. Unaware that something wasn't right, Parker pushed forward with a determined stride. She grabbed the back of his breeches, the only thing he was wearing besides boots, to stop him.

"Wait," she whispered fiercely. He glanced behind her, his tan face worried. His nod confirmed that he sensed it, too. Together, crouched behind a tropical plant's enormous leaves, they waited and listened.

"Where's the girl? I would so love to catch up," said a voice she didn't recognize as one from the crew, but sounded vaguely familiar. It had an aristocratic edge, with the crisp pronunciation of someone recently emigrated from England.

"How would I know? Back in Charles Town, I would

imagine." Nolan didn't sound at all like himself. Something was horribly wrong. And then Jewel knew. The British voice belonged to Devlin, the marine officer who had propositioned her at the Quail and Queen. The man attached to the same ship that boarded Nolan's vessel to impress his men, and the one where they'd rescued those same men. She'd killed one of their crewmen. My God, had they come for her?

She leaned forward to peek past the leaves, but Parker pulled her fiercely back, landing her on her backside. He shook his head, panic in his eyes. She cupped both hands around one eye like a telescope, silently signaling that she only intended to look. Apparently he understood, because he nodded.

Once she moved into position, Parker crowded behind her to get a glimpse from the same opening she created in the foliage. It was worse than she'd imagined. Surrounded by soldiers with muskets at the ready, Nolan and Bellamy stood together, chains around both their wrists that led down to their ankles. The rest of the crew, including Wayland, had been herded together in a group, and were circled by a similar number of red-coated men. Devlin, the officer from the tavern, lorded over them all. He'd discarded his wig, and his light brown hair slipped from the tie at the back of his neck, but he still had the privileged bearing that made him easy to recognize.

"Come now, Captain—"

"I'm the captain. You'll be addressing me if you have any questions," interrupted Bellamy.

Nolan didn't show any reaction; no one did, except for Devlin, who raised an eyebrow, obviously skeptical.

"Very well, Captain. Your crewmember here is not only mutinous, but a liar as well. We picked up Jack Casper in dire need of rescuing. He and his mates were crammed together in a leaky skiff, three sheets to the wind. Since we were already on your tail, he pointed us in the right direction. He also mentioned you two had a falling out over a female passenger with dark hair and an unusual shade of green eyes."

The marine officer delivered his speech to Nolan, only providing Bellamy one or two dismissive glances. "So, where's the girl?"

Both Nolan and Bellamy remained silent. They had their backs to her, but Jewel imagined the defiant expression that played on their features.

Devlin shrugged, as if it didn't matter. "I'll find her, you know. It's a small island. And you don't have to worry that I intend to do her harm. That is the last thing on my mind. Since her protectors will soon be indisposed, my inquiries are for her safety as well as my curiosity. But on to the business at hand . . ."

Devlin swung his gaze to the other crewmen. He trudged through the sand in his heavy boots. He wore a red coat that reached his knees and a white vest of similar length. His dexterity and stamina were surprising, considering the heat and consistency of the powdery beach. Before Jewel realized what she was doing, she sized the man up for a fight.

After a casual perusal of the *Integrity*'s crewmembers, he turned back to Nolan. "So, where's the boy?"

Again, no one spoke.

"Captain or Captain?" Devlin prompted. "The boy who killed our officer on watch. The other wounded man described you"—he nodded to Nolan—"and a slight youth who had incredible skill with the sword. We'll want to single him out, of course. Not that you all won't most likely meet the same fate. But that's for the Lord High Admiral to decide. My job is simply to deliver you."

"And our fate is . . . ?" asked Nolan.

"Hanging. They hang pirates, or didn't you know?"

said Devlin with the same polite, condescending tone he'd used to Jewel at the Quail and Queen.

Bellamy laughed. "Captain Kenton here ain't no pirate, or didn't *you* know? He's a privateer."

Devlin strode toward Nolan and examined him. "Who issued you a letter of marque?"

Nolan stiffened somewhat, and Jewel knew he was doomed. She thought of his grandfather and realized that, despite all Nolan's efforts, he had fallen into the trap he'd been trying to dodge since he started on this journey.

"I plan to obtain one from the Continental Congress."

Devlin nodded, unfazed by his answer. "Ah, treason, then. That simplifies things. Looks as if I'll be delivering you to Newgate instead."

Jewel fumbled for Parker's hand and gripped it. Parker squeezed hers in return, his palm hot and thick with sweat. He knew as well as she how dire was the situation. Nolan should have scoffed at Bellamy and claimed to be a pirate. At least then there would have been hope. Nolan had committed no crimes of piracy, so at his trial they'd have no evidence with which to convict him. But with treason, Jewel knew he had no chance.

The royal courts in Charles Town had no qualms in convicting citizens of the crime for merely speaking out against the crown's representatives. Sneaking aboard a man-of-war and rescuing his impressed crew, then admitting to being at war with his mother country would result in immediate and swift punishment.

"Corporal, let's first take our two captains to the *Neptune*'s brig. A snake's no harm without its head." He turned and gazed out to sea. "I imagine our men have dispensed with the crew left on Captain Kenton's ship. With these torches on the beach, I can't make out whether there are three lanterns on the bow or not. For now, we'll keep the rest of the crew on shore while I search for the boy—and for our lovely female friend."

The men relegated to handling Bellamy and Nolan gave a shove to start them moving. Jewel tapped Parker on the shoulder, then melted deeper into the dense foliage. When they reached the base of a palm, where the green canopy above their heads was so thick she could no longer see the torches on the beach, she stopped.

Even in the dark, she could sense Parker's panic, hear the heaviness of his breathing. "I have to hide you," he said.

She paused a moment, that being the last thing she intended. "No, we need to let Devlin find me."

"Are you insane?" he hissed.

"Parker, we have to rescue Nolan. He'll know what to do. Can you use a sword?"

"No, I can't. Not well, anyway. And even if I could, we don't have one."

Jewel's heart sank at the realization. They didn't have any weapons. Lifting a sword against another human being was the last thing she'd ever hoped to do again, but do it she would, and gladly now. That her plans had been dashed, she felt punched by Parker's initial panic. All the *Integrity*'s weapons, at least the ones they had on the island, were piled on the beach, confiscated by the soldiers. Only two or three crewman remained on watch aboard the ship. Even if they had prior warning, the British would overtake any escape easily. The torches on the beach, combined with the spectacle created by Nolan and her father, ensured that no one noticed whether there was another ship docked in the wide harbor.

At this point, Parker and she had absolutely nothing to their advantage, except perhaps the marine commander's obvious interest in her. When he revealed he'd thought a boy killed his crewmate, she'd been confused until she remembered she had been dressed in men's clothing, her long braid tucked in her jacket. Apparently, the officer wanted to continue his quest for her company that had begun in the tavern. Fortunately for him, Jewel was in a position in which she had nothing to lose.

Chapter Twenty-two

Handsome Jack Casper lounged on the deck of the *Neptune*, his head bowed between his bent knees. Nolan's glare alone should have wounded the mangled pirate. Not for the first time since Devlin mentioned how he'd obtained his information about Jewel, Nolan wished he'd sliced Casper down when he had the chance. All his worrying about teetering a fine line between piracy and privateering had been fruitless. He fell grossly short on both counts. He'd failed as a privateer *and* as a pirate. Most of all, he'd failed Jewel. What would happen to her now made him literally sick every time he thought of it.

The heat, pain and desperation behind his worries must have been powerful enough to reach across the deck to Casper, because suddenly the man lifted his head. His eyes widened when he spotted Bellamy. He stood on shaky feet and swayed in their direction. Apparently the British had been showing their gratitude for Jack's cooperation with his favorite victual: rum.

"Bellamy Leggett! I knew you were too mean to die.

How you doin', Nolan? Good to see you again, lad."
Jack sounded as amiable as he had two weeks earlier,
when Nolan last saw him.

The corporal and his men paused at Jack's approach,
apparently to enjoy the spectacle that would surely follow.

Nolan didn't have the will to disappoint them. "Jack
Casper, you worthless son of a whore, I'm going to get
out of here and slice away the other half of your face."

Jack tried to assimilate this information with a few
rapid blinks and a tilt of his head. Soon, he seemed to
give up and turned back to Bellamy. "Hey, I want more
for this one. Bellamy Leggett's got twice the price on
his head than Nolan."

The corporal chuckled with a hint of affection. "Never
heard of 'em, Handsome. Go have yourself another
drink."

Jack narrowed his gaze on the soldier. "Bellamy Leggett. He's one of the last grand pirates to terrorize the
Caribbean. I'm going to want triple what you paid me
for this one," he repeated.

"This old codger? Sure, Handsome Jack. Don't you
worry. We'll give you five more bottles of rum," said
one of the guards.

Bellamy stiffened beside Nolan. Jack, on the other
hand, seemed happy with the agreement, because he
grinned from ear to ear—literally. "Good to see you
again, mate. Let's share a grog." Jack threw himself at
Nolan. With his hands shackled in front of him, Nolan
had to take the impact with his body. He braced his
knees, intending to send Jack across the deck with a
heave of his chest and tell him he wasn't his mate.
But . . .

"I didn't tell them 'bout the treasure. We'll even up
later. Don't worry, I'll get you out of here," Jack whispered in his ear.

A soldier pulled Jack off Nolan, and the corporal shoved them both forward. "He'll have to have a grog with you another time, Jack. He's got a previous engagement with the brig."

The marines' enjoyment of Jack seemed to prevent them from noticing anything but the absurdity of the exchange. Nolan's glance at Jack, who now draped his arm around the shoulder of the man leading him away, gave no clue as to whether Jack's promise was drunken nonsense or an attempt to strike a bargain.

The desperate question plagued Nolan through the difficult trek to the ship's belly. And that he was considering Handsome Jack's words as a viable means of escape proved how truly hopeless the situation was. They tossed him and Bellamy into a small hold that smelled of urine and blood and closed the door, leaving them in total darkness.

"Jack said he'd rescue us if I gave him part of the treasure," Nolan said the minute he heard the booted footsteps fade.

"Old codger? That boy must have just got out of swaddling clothes not to never have heard of me. His superiors should know about this. Let he and I cross steel and we'll see who's the old codger."

Nolan brought his hands up to rub his temples, but his chains stopped him short. "Jack didn't exactly say it like that, but he said he didn't tell them about the treasure." With the pounding in his head and the beating of his own frantic pulse, he couldn't even hear Bellamy breathe. "We have to get out of here," he said, a note of panic creeping in his voice. "I don't want them to get their hands on Jewel."

Besides the fact that he wasn't at all sure if Devlin was the type of man to resort to rape or not, he feared that if they had her on board, the man Nolan wounded would recognize her and realize there was no boy. Then she'd be in the same trouble as they, on her way to the gallows.

"Then, why the bloody hell did you let them capture us to begin with? We shouldn't have surrendered without a fight. I didn't teach you that." Bellamy's voice cut through the darkness.

"They had their muskets trained on us. Half my men weren't even armed." That he should have posted a watch, should have done many things differently, was of no help at the moment.

"Bah, if they were pirates—"

Nolan cut him off. "They're not," he said, realizing too late he wasn't much of a pirate himself. Instead of an honest crew, he should have picked men with a few more notches on their swords. "So, what are we going to do? Do you think Casper will help us escape?"

Before Bellamy could answer, a key was thrust in the lock and the door swung open. Even the soft light of a lantern temporarily blinded Nolan after being immersed in total darkness.

"Yes, it's you all right." He instantly recognized Greeley's voice, but it sounded a little weaker, a little less pompous. "Is this the man who engaged you?"

Nolan's vision adjusted, and he made out Greeley's haggard appearance. The man wore his heavy dark blue coat, but his neckcloth was loose above his sallow features. Beads of sweat dotted his face and pooled in the dark circles under his eyes.

His interest in Greeley and the other man rattled Nolan's chains, and Greeley shrank back. A sailor dressed in the identifying striped shirt and canvas breeches of the English navy stepped forward, shakily pointing a musket at him. Nolan realized that all the marines, the only men aboard trained to fight hand to hand, must have been dispatched to shore. Not only that, Greeley had all the signs of fever. Being locked on a ship where crewmen had started to succumb to tropical sickness would normally be a disaster. To Nolan, it was a sign of hope.

Another man, who looked in worse health than Greeley, peeked around the sailor with the musket. "That dark-haired one is the man. But the other was a boy. I told you. That one ain't him."

"We've seen enough," he heard Greeley say before the door was immediately slammed and locked, thrusting them back into total darkness.

"They seem to be undermanned. If we can get out of here, we might have a chance of escape." Nolan yanked on his shackles until his wrist burned.

"I've got more than a chance. I'm going to gut that fellow who called me an old codger." Bellamy shifted, clinking his chains.

"And how do you intend to do that?" Nolan tried to keep his mind focused, but thoughts of Jewel on the island, pursued by a detachment of British marines, kept sneaking into his mind and seizing him with panic.

"Sit down, Nolan, and save your strength." Bellamy paused for a moment. "Why didn't you kill me on the beach?"

Nolan shuffled his way to the portal and tried the handle. He knew it would be locked, but he wanted to check the latch's strength. "Because I love your daughter."

The brass handle didn't seem all that sturdy; perhaps if he wrapped the chain attached to his feet around it, he could pull with his body weight and do some damage.

"Stop fiddling with that, Nolan. Even if you get out, you're still shackled. You actually love the girl? But she's my child. How can you forget that?"

Nolan fell against the door with his shoulder. The portal coughed with promise. "She's nothing like you." He stopped his testing of the varnished wood. "Why did you claim to be the captain?"

"Knew they'd separate the captain. Was hoping you

315

could rally your men and rescue me." Bellamy paused, but Nolan could tell he wanted to say something more. "I didn't know you loved her. I might not have tried to drown you if I knew that. Thought you were just using her to get back at me. Does she know?"

Nolan leaned his back against the door and tried to think. "Of course, she . . . I don't know. I guess I haven't been the best husband." The thought that he'd be whisked away to England, then hanged without ever seeing Jewel again, almost broke him. He turned and gave the door another hard shove with his shoulder. This time, he thought he heard the wood splinter.

"Get away from the door. We don't want them to know that we're hell bent on escaping just yet. Let them think they have us where they want us."

Nolan laughed, but its desperate hoarseness worried him. "They do have us where they want us."

"You know, you're going to make a much better husband than you ever would a pirate. The first time, when you didn't let the crew do me in, but left me on the island to die, I let it go, thinking you were young and I had been a father figure to you."

Nolan's dry laugh was genuine this time.

"Let me finish. You have to look your enemies in the eye when you do them in. But it's obvious you'll never understand that one. Then, when the error of your ways shows up in your life, you not only give me a second chance, you don't kill me when you should have."

"Because it would have hurt my wife."

"Couldn't even go find the bloody treasure until your old sire gave you permission by dying a natural death. Thought you'd be at it again before five bloody years. Didn't think you could stand the pious life *that* long." Bellamy snorted. "Thought you'd see the error of your ways and come back for me, begging to join my crew again to save you from dying of boredom."

"And what if I had come back? You wouldn't have been there. What have you been doing for the last five years besides getting fat?" Though arguing with Bellamy wouldn't help their cause, it was relieving some of Nolan's tension.

There was a long silence, and he began to think Bellamy wouldn't answer. Perhaps the comment about his weight had been uncalled for.

"I suppose the mutiny unnerved me a bit." Bellamy's words were slow and obviously reluctant. "Went on a bit of a bender, bad even for me. Wayland got tired of me and went to watch the girl, so as not to lose the map. Think he got a bit too attached, though. He thinks he's her father."

"So I've noticed." All Wayland's meddling with regard to Jewel would be worth it if what Bellamy said were true. Wayland would be just as anxious as Nolan to see Jewel safe, and he might have the means to do something about it. Though Parker was with her, the man didn't have the experience to begin to know what to do. "So, you sobered up when you heard that I was out for the treasure again?"

The chains clinked accompaniment to the sound of Bellamy slapping his belly. "Yep, and I'm better than ever, if I do say so myself. I might be out of practice, but I still almost got you."

Nolan refrained from pointing out that he'd relieved Bellamy of his sword in short order. Bellamy's delusions shattered his earlier confidence that his old mentor's ability to get out of any scrape would hold true. Fear and panic tightened his nerves all over again. He slid to the floor and hung his head. "Do you think Jack will help us? You know him better than I do." That Jack Casper was his only hope at the moment only spiraled Nolan's mood lower.

"Casper's a pirate. He'll play whatever hand is the

best bet. Luckily for us, we got the better pot. He's got to know the British will make him stand trial just like us."

Nolan stood, unable to remain still. Bellamy was right. "I've never known you to be so patient. Or rational."

"Learned it waiting for you, Nolan."

Jewel saw the light cast and heard the men's rumbling long before they approached her and Parker's hiding place. "They're coming. How do I look?"

"Terrible. I hate this idea. Jewel, I'm going to have to insist that we think of something else." Parker had done a lot of insisting, but Jewel hadn't heeded one of his urgings.

She ran her fingers through her tangled hair once more, then tugged at the lacy trim of her chemise. She'd discarded her favorite green gown—it was ruined from her father's knife anyway—not only for effect but practicality. If she did get her hands on a sword, she'd be hindered by her heavy skirts and tight lacings. Her thin chemise and petticoat provided much more maneuverability—not to mention that it showed the bloody scratch that appeared nastier than it was. "If you won't bruise me, then at least help rip my underskirt."

Parker folded his arms over his bare chest and refused to budge. "I won't go along with it. It's too dangerous. Those men are more likely to rape you than want to help you."

She turned back to the trail to check the soldiers' progress. "That's why we have to make sure we approach them when Devlin's with them. You're going to help me, Parker, and this is what we are going to do, so get ready."

She heard him shuffling behind her. If she turned around and confronted him again, she feared she'd be swayed by his argument. Her heart surged in her throat and pounded out the utter desperation of her plan with each beat—but with no weapons, they had little other choice.

A group of red-coated soldiers came ambling down the path. They were still too far to show if Devlin was in the lead. The men stuck to the path, only periodically sticking their bayonets into the brush.

"How do you get that yellow fever, again?" she heard someone say.

"Bad smells, I think."

"All right, men. Enough of that. It's not bad smells. This is my second tour in the West Indies and everything smells slightly putrid. It's due to the heat and damp, not disease."

Jewel recognized Devlin's voice. The soldiers fell silent, but she could tell they weren't convinced. If things went wrong, she'd have to be sure and pretend that she had the disease. Charles Town had been plagued by yellow fever for several summers in a row, so she had plenty of experience with the symptoms.

She sucked up her courage and stepped out into their path. All the men stumbled to a stop. She had planned to dramatically throw herself at their feet, but when faced with a large group of armed men who stared at her as if she might be some sort of apparition, it stole her nerve. All she could do was blink.

Devlin pushed through the group. "Are you hurt, girl?"

She nodded, her throat tight with fear. She was sure she looked absolutely terrified. She was.

He took in her appearance, studying her from head to toe and then back again. She wasn't quite sure if what he saw horrified him or excited him, but either way he appeared moved. Damn Parker for not leaving a bruise on her arm as she'd asked.

Devlin swept off his coat and draped it over her shoulders. "Did they take you against your will?"

She wasn't sure who *they* were, but she nodded yes anyway. The "mysterious boy" was who she planned to have called her attacker. "He dragged me into the jungle with him when you came."

"Who? There's another man with you?" Devlin's head shot up, and he glanced over the top of the bushes. His soldiers came to attention as well, raising their muskets.

"He's young. Not more than fifteen, but he . . . he overpowered me. He's very good with a sword." She lowered her eyelids. Hopefully, she wasn't leading them on too obviously, but she really didn't have the time or the nerve for subtlety.

"Excellent. Where is he?" Devlin appeared absolutely convinced.

"He ran behind the waterfall. There's a cave. He tried to drag me with him, but I got away." Jewel didn't have to pretend to be breathless. Tension did it for her.

"Where's the waterfall?"

"Down the path. You can't miss it."

Devlin brushed a tangled lock from her face. "Thank you, love. You'll be safe now. Shall you wait here while—"

"No." She grabbed his sleeve. "Please don't leave me."

"Of course. Johnson, you stay with the lady."

"I want *you*," she stood on her toes to whisper near his ear. She glanced at the man who Devlin had spoken to as if he had pointed ears and a spiked tail. "I don't know him, and I've been through so much. I'm afraid to be left alone with another strange man."

He glanced back at the gaggle of soldiers, who didn't even sniff for fear they might miss a word of the conversation. "Corporal Caffy, take the men and follow the path. I'll be along shortly.

"Is the man armed, love?" he asked Jewel, so kindly she was starting to feel a twinge of guilt for what was about to befall him.

"Only with a sword."

"Excellent. Wait for me by the waterfall, Caffy. Keep the men at the ready, and we'll take the chap on my orders."

The sergeant nodded, but gave Jewel a very unkind look as he passed. The other men merely smirked, apparently proud or envious of their commanding officer.

Devlin took a torch from the last man, then waited until they had disappeared down the winding path before he faced her again. "You have nothing to fear from me or my men. I know how to treat women." He gently brushed aside the coat he'd draped over her shoulders and caressed the back of his hand over the swell of her breast, exposed by her low-cut chemise. He saw the cut on her shoulder and blanched visibly. "He'll be punished for this, I promise you."

Jewel sneaked a quick glance at the brush while Devlin recovered from his shock and redirected his attention to her cleavage. The plan was for her to lure him into the brush, and for Parker to sneak up behind him. Though they were still on the path, now seemed as good a time as any for an ambush. As squeamish as Parker was over this plan, she worried that he'd not figure that out.

"What's going to happen to me?" she asked, not sure exactly what to do.

"Keeping a mistress aboard ship is not uncommon for an officer. My cabin is small, but I assure you, your situation will vastly improve. And you'll not be without means when my tour is done here. You have a lovely mouth. Have you been told that before?" He traced a thumb over her lower lip.

"Would you like to go into the brush?" she asked.

Parker apparently didn't understand that the plans had changed, so she had better go to him.

Devlin laughed. "You have been mistreated. I won't handle you so crudely. I can wait until we return to my cabin. I need to find my men. You'll be safe waiting here. You have my word. . . . I don't even know your name."

Before she could answer, Parker slipped onto the path. He appeared terrified, completely unsure of himself, but he had the rope they'd recovered, their only weapon, stretched taut. He slipped up behind Devlin. Jewel brushed her hand over the officer's chest to keep him distracted.

Despite his claimed hatred for this task, Parker brought the rope over Devlin's head and yanked it around his neck with dexterity and enthusiasm. Devlin struggled a bit, thankfully didn't scream, then rapidly turned red to purple before his eyes rolled back in his head.

"That's enough," yelled Jewel when Devlin collapsed, yet Parker didn't show signs of easing his hold. The officer wouldn't be any good to them dead.

The lieutenant finally eased his hold, panting as if he'd been the one deprived of air. "God, I hope he's not dead," he said.

Jewel drew the sword from the scabbard slung across Devlin's shoulder, then searched him for any more weapons. A hand with surprising strength grabbed her wrist and squeezed. Devlin glared at her with red-rimmed, furious eyes.

"Again, Parker. Now!" Jewel whispered fiercely. The urge to scream the command was hard to resist.

Parker tightened the rope still around their victim's neck until Devlin ceased his struggles. Jewel stood, took the officer's sword and pressed its tip against his chest.

Parker released his stranglehold before Devlin passed out again.

"So that you understand I know how to use this, I'm the boy you're looking for." She pressed the point of Devlin's sleek sword against his chest until the tip pierced his shirt, nicking his skin and forming a distinct circle of blood. "But I don't intend to kill you unless I have to."

He held her gaze, not flinching at the abuse but nodding his understanding.

"Tie him," she instructed Parker. "Cooperate, and he won't have to strangle you again," she said to Devlin. This time, he didn't bother to nod, but neither did the officer resist when Parker rolled him over to tie his hands behind his back.

Jewel spotted the forgotten torch that had dropped into the moist soil that formed the trail. A small flame sputtered but had found no other purchase in the verdant surroundings. She returned her gaze to Devlin. Parker helped him struggle to his feet. The marine officer's coloring had returned to normal, but he chose to remain silent. The red burn around his neck stood out clearly in the weak starlight that filtered through the jungle's canopy.

"Yell for your men and we'll gut you, then disappear into the jungle," Jewel warned with a calmness that surprised her.

Again, her captive merely nodded.

Jewel stepped out of the path and motioned for the men to proceed her, her sword at the ready. Who looked more unhappy was a toss up between Devlin and Parker. Of course, she couldn't see herself and didn't doubt she appeared as haggard. With her sword positioned in the center of Devlin's back, they marched to the beach.

"You'll tell your men to drop their weapons and free

our crewmen," she said—not that she didn't think he already knew what they had in mind.

"They'll not," he croaked, then stopped.

Now she knew why he'd been so complacent. He couldn't speak. Parker must be stronger than she thought, or more likely his terror had caused him to use more pressure than necessary. Thank God they hadn't killed him. She dared not glance at Parker to share her fears. They both were drawing courage from places they didn't know existed. When she'd followed Nolan on board the *Neptune*, she'd not known what she'd merrily thrown herself into. Though she'd been grateful that she'd saved Nolan's life, she'd have taken back killing the young man if she could. Now, sooner than she could ever have imagined, she'd be forced to do the same thing. But nothing was too drastic to rescue her husband.

"They'll not lay down their weapons for me, so you might as well run me through," Devlin whispered in a brittle voice that was painful to hear. "They'll shoot you on the spot," he said in barely a whisper. He panted and swallowed afterward, the effort obviously costing him dearly.

"I believe they will trade you for our crewmen. We're willing to stake our lives on it. We have nothing to lose." Jewel finally glanced at Parker, and his determined gaze proved her words to be true for him as well. "And if a single shot is fired, you'll perish with us."

The lights from the torches still on the beach shone just before they heard the roll and crash of waves. They pushed Devlin through the foliage. His voice would do no good in reassuring his men all was well, so Jewel didn't bother suggesting he do so.

The soldiers left to guard the remaining crew didn't appear immediately concerned when the three of them walked onto the beach; they glanced in their direction without raising their muskets. Jewel spared a moment to find Wayland's gaze, and his grin, which exposed every rotten tooth he still had in his mouth, gave her a tremendous surge of confidence.

"Drop your weapons or we'll run him through," boomed Parker in a voice deeper than Jewel had ever heard him use. Though she held the sword, she was grateful for his intervention. The soldiers would doubt her threat, and she had no desire to prove herself to be more than she appeared unless she absolutely had to.

The men looked to Devlin but didn't immediately comply. Their commanding officer didn't speak, whether because the sound of his voice would give more credence to his captors' cause or because of a sincere sense of self-preservation, Jewel couldn't guess. Perhaps it was the look on his face, something she couldn't see since she remained at his back, the tip of her sword unrelenting, but the first soldier laid down his weapon and the rest followed.

The *Integrity*'s crew sat huddled together on the beach, their hands tied in front of them. The moment the last British soldier laid his weapon in the soft sand, Wayland jumped to his feet, and his bindings fell to the sand. They were already cut. He brandished a wicked-looking dagger and picked up a musket from the sand.

"You did it, chit! Knew you could. Now, let's go get our captain."

Chapter Twenty-three

A key rattled in the door, and Nolan sprang from his slump against the curved hull of his prison. He'd not sunk to the floor as Bellamy had, but the complete darkness, lack of air and time to do little else except contemplate his life had made him light-headed. If this was his chance to escape, he wanted to be ready. He took a deep, cleansing breath, though that didn't help much, considering it consisted of stagnant air from a disease-laden ship.

Only dim light from a distant hatch reached them. Their visitor didn't carry a lantern.

"All right, boys—before I let you out of here, we'll be talking our terms."

"We're listening, Casper." Bellamy spoke somewhere beside Nolan, his presence only a vague shape. Nolan hadn't even heard him rise. "We know you're not much better off than us. They're going to hang you sooner or later."

"Glad you see the spot I was in, Bellamy. And I'd like to say I'm glad you're not dead." Handsome Jack kept his voice lowered, but he didn't bother to step into their makeshift cell. He must not trust them any more than they did him. "How 'bout you, Nolan—you willing to let bygones be bygones?"

He wasn't, but he sure as hell wasn't going to mention it right now. "You help us, Jack, and I'll show you in coin how forgiving I am."

"I was hoping you'd say that, Kenton." Jack slipped into the small hold and shut the door behind him, plunging them all into total darkness. "Me and my crew have been biding our time. Looks like tonight's our best chance to take this rat trap."

A rattling of chains sounded next to Nolan, followed by a metallic scraping noise. Bellamy had something with which he was trying to pick the lock of his shackles.

"I don't want to take the ship. I just want to get to shore and Jewel," said Nolan, the hair on the back of his neck suddenly standing on end at having to cast his fortunes in with these two.

Nolan heard Bellamy's chains fall to the deck. Before he could fully comprehend what that meant, Bellamy gripped his shoulder. "Hold your hands up. We have to take the ship. They'll catch us otherwise."

"I can outrun them." Nolan held his hands in the air while Bellamy poked his wrist a few times with a metal object, finally fitting it in the lock and releasing him from his shackles. He placed the key in Nolan's hand, and Nolan attacked the metal bands on his ankles.

"What do you know, Jack?" Bellamy asked, as if Nolan hadn't spoken at all.

"Well, there ain't nothing to speak of resistance-wise on the ship right now. All the marines that aren't sick are on shore. They had to send some regular seamen over to your ship, Nolan, to take your watch. Don't know how that turned out. The rest that are here probably wouldn't put up much of a fight. Everyone's scared of the yellow fever. Too many to count's held up in their hammocks. I don't think any of 'em's really got it, but I told 'em they did."

"How many men do you have?" From the sound of Bellamy's voice, he had already moved to the door.

Nolan remained silent, glad to let his old mentor take over in this respect. His only goal was to get out of here and get to Jewel. He'd never be glad to serve under Bellamy again, but when it came to surviving, Bellamy Leggett was your man.

"Only ten, but I figure we can rid ourselves of some of the seamen quiet like. Don't have to be an out and-out fight. I already took care of the fellow with the keys. One of my crew's paying a visit to the captain in his cabin right about now."

Nolan didn't have to wrestle with the idea of slitting the throats of men unawares. He'd do whatever he had to do to get off this ship and find his wife. "Agreed. Do you have weapons for us?"

The door opened and light flooded the cabin. "A couple knives right now, but we'll pick up more as we go along." Jack stepped out of the cabin.

Bellamy blocked Nolan from following. "You get off first chance you get and go find Jewel."

Nolan studied Bellamy's face, searching for the hook in his bait. Bellamy nodded, and Nolan could find only one conclusion. The old captain said, "That's right. I care about her, too. Not as much as you, that's true, but I don't want her to come to harm. Never did. Even when I gave her the map, I never intended to tell anyone else."

Nolan nodded and followed Bellamy from the cabin. Jack had already made his way up a moonlit passage. Bellamy paused one more time. "And instead of thanking me, you can just have my hunk of the treasure ready when I find you again."

Nolan smiled for the first time since he'd agreed to fight to the death the father of the woman he loved. This was as close to a truce as he and Bellamy were ever likely to come.

Wayland grabbed the first rung of the rope ladder that hung over the *Neptune*'s side. The ship seemed to have lanterns on every rigging. The girth of the vessel outlined in light made it its own constellation in the murky night, bloting out the moon and stars. Jewel wondered if the extra lanterns were merely an illusion created by the fact that they had doused the torches on the beach, or if the crew of the *Neptune* expected them. Wayland continued to hover above the skiff and stared up at the ship, and she suspected he pondered the same question.

Shadows danced across the tall masts, signaling a flurry of activity. Maybe it was just a luminescent reflection from the waves that lapped against the side. Jewel secured another button on the red coat she wore. She tried to reassure herself with the fact that they'd plunged the beach into darkness the moment they relieved the soldiers of all their weapons. The *Integrity*'s crew had made quick work of wresting the British of their coats and tying them up. They'd not bothered finding the group of soldiers that still lingered at the waterfall, but left the beach as soon as possible, taking all the longboats with them. Even if they did choose to swim back to their ship, which she doubted they'd be able to do in time to fight, the soldiers couldn't do without their muskets.

Wayland glanced down at her from his dangling position on the rope ladder. He had two muskets slung over his back and wore a red coat like the rest of them. Parker and his group used the same ploy to approach the *Integrity*. Hopefully, watches on both ships would think they were their own men returning.

"Stay in the boat until I give you the signal to follow," Wayland whispered in a croak. None of the five crewmen, who included Jewel, raised a voice to agree. She'd been surprised how many wanted to join her and Wayland on the risky mission aboard the *Neptune* to rescue Nolan. After all, the treasure remained on the *Integrity*.

"Well, let's go then," said Wayland, before he quickly made his way up the ladder.

Jewel grabbed the rung and hurried up after him, gripping a sword in her hand. At Wayland's insistence, she had another sword hanging at her hip, but she'd refused to carry a musket. She didn't know how to shoot, and this didn't seem a good situation in which to learn. The hem of her petticoat caught under her feet as she maneuvered on the ladder. She should have at least taken the opportunity to shorten its length, even if she hadn't had the time to wrestle breeches from a soldier.

Once she cleared the *Neptune*'s railing, she discovered her fears about the circumstance in which she might find Nolan were not nearly as dire as the scene before her. Nolan and Bellamy had their backs to each other, swords raised, engaging no fewer than seven men at once. Clanks and shouts warned her that other battles raged around her, but only this one captured her interest.

Luckily, if there truly was any in the situation, the group of men didn't seem happy with their overwhelming advantage. One or two would advance, and a swift parry and riposte from Nolan or her father would send them back to a safe distance. The fallen bodies she saw scattered about the deck might have something to do with their reluctance. That, and the fact that none of the men, who all wore sailor's attire rather than soldier's uniforms, appeared to be very skilled in combat.

Jewel advanced, after a quick glance to Wayland for some sort of last-minute instruction. She paused when she found him with his musket raised, aimed above Nolan and Bellamy's heads. She swung her glance to the sailor standing on the roof of the companionway, a net poised to drop over them.

Wayland's musket exploded, creating a sharp pain in her right ear, but Jewel didn't pause to give it much thought. The old pirate hit his mark, causing the sailor to drop the net and slip from his perch. The tangle of rope landed on three of the British engaging Bellamy, giving him a momentary advantage. Jewel rushed to Nolan's side and met the blade of the man who turned to face her at the sound of the musket.

His feeble attempt to block her thrust showed her that he'd not had much experience with the weapon. The idea of merely wounding him crossed her mind before he made a wide target of his midsection and she drove her sword home. She withdrew her weapon and found a new opponent before she had time to regret his likely fatal wound. She'd done what she had to do.

After a few passable parries, Jewel's next opponent swung his sword at her head, forcing her to duck or be decapitated. When she straightened, eager to return the favor, the man stared at her in stunned horror. She followed his gaze to the end of the cutlass that stuck from his belly. Nolan removed his sword from the man's back and only gazed at her briefly over him before turning to engage another opponent. Not that she could tell absolutely, considering the circumstances, but he didn't seem particularly upset to see her. In fact, she thought she caught a hint of a smile in his eye.

Jewel turned to find another man to engage and noticed some of the sailors had dropped their swords, their hands raised in surrender. Wayland and Bellamy herded them together and forced them toward the ship's stern. Jewel scoured the deck, averting her gaze from the litter of fallen men and the red stream of blood that had begun to make the deck slick.

With a will of its own, her gaze paused on a particularly mangled individual. On closer inspection, she noticed the worst of his wounds weren't recent. His nose and a good portion of his lip were missing. The thick red pool beneath him, along with his vacant, unblinking stare, left no doubt that he was dead. Jewel recognized the pirate who'd boarded the *Integrity*, intent on stealing the map. Nolan's compassion in letting Handsome Jack go might have come back to haunt him, but Jack Casper had got what fate intended in the end.

A cannon blast shattered her speculation, and instinct forced Jewel to crouch. She glanced toward the deafening sound to see Bellamy pull his bloody sword from the back of the man who'd lit the fuse.

"Damn it! The bastard signaled the marines on the beach. Nolan, get Jewel out of here. I'm going to cut anchor before they make it back," yelled Bellamy.

Wayland and a few others who didn't look as if they belonged with the British crew rounded up the sailors who no longer had the will to fight, who appeared to be all that was left. She searched the deck for Nolan and found him striding in her direction. "Let's go." He wrapped an arm around her and started dragging her to the side.

"There's a ladder. Don't jump," she said, and dug her heels into the deck, reliving a similar moment with no intention of repeating it.

He paused to kiss the top of her head but didn't loosen his grip. "I'm aware of that."

They reached the railing, where Nolan's men were already finding their way down. She didn't know if Wayland had told Nolan that the commanding officer, as well as the majority of the marines, were tied up on the beach, nor did she know how long that would remain true. The cannon no doubt alerted the men at the waterfall to return to the beach, if they hadn't already done so. Besides, she wasn't sure how Parker was faring, and she feared he might need their help.

Nolan shoved Jewel to the ladder in front of the next man waiting to go down. She spared a brief glance at her father. He stood at the helm brandishing his sword. "Join or jump, lads. Name your poison," he shouted.

Jewel didn't have another moment to spare; she hurried down the ladder with Nolan right behind her. Once they settled in the skiff and untied the line, she realized they had forgotten Wayland. Oars were thrust into water and furiously worked, sending them farther from the *Neptune* with each passing moment. Apparently no one wanted to take the time to count men.

Jewel struggled to keep silent, and to keep the surge of emotion that warned her she might cry at bay. Even if she mentioned it, she doubted anyone would be eager to turn around and retrieve Wayland. Bellamy deserved to be left behind; in fact, she didn't doubt he preferred it. And perhaps Wayland did, too, though the closest thing she'd ever had to a father figure had mismatched eyes and more gum than teeth.

A white bundle tossed over the *Neptune*'s side forced her from her melancholy. The male scream that echoed over the water immediately before the splash warned her that the jetsam was human. Lieutenant Greeley floundered in the water, a nightshirt billowing around him.

"Hey, Nolan!" Wayland appeared at the railing, assuring her he had encouraged Greeley to abandon ship. "You take care of her, or you'll be answering to me when I see you next." He waved, then disappeared.

Jewel glanced in Greeley's direction once more to find him swimming toward the beach with even strokes. The scattered lanterns on the *Integrity*'s rigging grew closer, while the *Neptune*'s blaze faded farther into the distance. A flare on the beach dragged her gaze in its direction. Soldiers were filtering onto the sand.

Nolan must have seen it, too. "We have no idea who has control of the *Integrity*?"

"I'm sure Parker is doing his best," she said but realized she didn't sound hopeful. She'd been placed in the front of the longboat, and another man blocked her view of Nolan.

"I imagine once they untie him, Devlin will be mad enough to swim to our ship and wring someone's neck."

Jewel braced herself on her elbows. He'd been told what happened, probably by Wayland in between cutting down the seamen. The old salt had been gushingly proud of her ingenuity. Though Nolan's voice sounded stern, she thought she heard a hint of amusement, maybe even pride as well. She had been positive that if they got out of this alive, Nolan would flail her for taking such a risk.

Either way, she didn't have the strength to defend her actions. "I guess we'd better get out of here, then."

"I guess we'd better." An undeniable note of humor softened his voice.

"How did you and Bellamy get out of your chains?" Jewel asked. Crowded in a boat full of men and still in fear for her life, she had just discovered a new form of intimacy with her husband.

"Jack Casper rescued us, which was considerate, since he was the one who turned us in. I'm afraid his plans went considerably awry."

"I noticed that." Jewel struggled to see around the crewmen blocking Nolan from her view. "Good thing *my* plan didn't." She caught only a portion of Nolan's face but the crinkles around his bright eyes warned her that he couldn't suppress a smile.

"Yes. Good thing."

Nolan didn't say anything else. They were swiftly approaching the *Integrity*, and everyone knew to be silent without being told.

Jewel still clutched her sword in her fist, and had unconsciously cradled it in her lap. They passed a body floating facedown in the water. It was too dark to identify without flipping the man over, and Jewel was relieved when Nolan guided them toward the rope ladder instead. The *Integrity*'s deck loomed silent, giving no clue as to what lay in wait. Jewel mustered her strength for a fight she knew she wasn't ready for.

Nolan pulled himself up the first rung, then, when Jewel followed, didn't say a word. She wished his acceptance of her as a part of his crew hadn't come when she wasn't sure she could continue to lift her sword. He proved much swifter than she and cleared the railing while she still hung near the water. She had almost reached the top when he thrust his head over the railing, panic in his gaze.

"Hurry," he called.

She pulled herself up the next few rungs and when she was close enough, he lifted her over the ship's side. For a moment she didn't know what had caused the anxiety in Nolan's voice. The crewmen who had left the beach for the *Integrity* rushed across the deck in obvious preparation for them to set sail. Then she spotted Parker braced against the main mast. He clutched his bloodied sword in one hand, much paler then when she had seen him last. He appeared as if he was about to faint, which didn't surprise Jewel in the least.

She strode in his direction, Nolan on her heels, but obviously letting her have the lead. "You did it, Parker. You took back our ship."

He let his sword clink to the deck. On closer approach she noticed that the red coat he still wore wasn't buttoned, but blood, the same hue as his jacket, covered a good portion of his chest. His heavy-lidded gaze warned her that it was his.

"I request to be relieved of command," he said before he crumpled onto the deck.

Dawn eased over the horizon in a pink fog that lit the tired lines around Jewel's mouth. She sat on a crate, her knees on her elbows, and watched Nolan steer. The ocean's calm rocked them with a sleepy rhythm and the warm trade winds ushered them forward with a gentle but persistent nudge. Neither land nor ship showed on their starboard, leeward, stern or bow. Tranquil blue waters, with only lazy waves to break the monotony, surrounded them as far as the eye could see. Even as he heard the *Integrity*'s sails struggle to breathe, Nolan thanked his good fortune.

"Why don't you check on Parker again and then get some sleep?" he said to Jewel, softening his voice so as not to startle her.

She stretched, still wearing the red coat over her chemise and petticoat. Though he'd enjoy tossing the reminder of how much danger she'd been in over the side, the British uniform would no doubt be of service to him in the future—a military future that wouldn't begin until he had his letter of marque. His other future, the one that mattered most, was sitting before him.

"Last time I slipped into his cabin, he was sleeping and I woke him. He'll be fine. I think he fainted from exhaustion and shock as much as blood loss. You should really teach him how to use a sword."

"I think you'd be much better at that, Mrs. Kenton." Nolan kept his gaze on the horizon, but he could see the tilt of her head and her curious smile in his peripheral vision. He still needed to explain himself, but he hoped his casual claim would ease his way. At least she didn't balk when he claimed her as his wife.

"You're right about Parker," Nolan continued, as if

he didn't notice her questioning stare. "Though let's not tell him that. He wouldn't appreciate it."

Parker's wounds had looked far worse than they were. He'd been nicked in more than half a dozen places. Only one, a slash on his hip, had needed stitches. With Wayland gone, Jewel had performed the task with skill and patience, while Nolan felt a little faint himself. He'd excused himself to see to the navigation while she did the worst of it.

Now Jewel nodded, then let her gaze drift to the searching rays of soft yellow that reached out over the ever-lightening sea. Her apparent exhaustion, which was no surprise, gave him an excuse not to speak his mind, but he chose not to take it. She needed to be reassured, or at least given the opportunity to reject him.

"Thank you for what you did tonight. You've saved my life twice now." Nolan took a breath before he continued. "I wish you hadn't done what you did to Devlin."

Jewel's gaze swung in his direction, a look of hurt in her eyes, and he quickly continued. "Though I'm grateful. I want you to know something, and not just to clear myself of wrongdoing in your eyes. I know I have much to account for. But I couldn't kill your father. I laid down my sword before the British came."

Jewel stood, sauntered behind him, then wrapped her arms around his waist. "I know. Wayland told me. And that you won."

Nolan was glad she couldn't see the satisfied grin that pulled at his mouth. "But did he tell you why I laid down my sword?"

She squeezed his waist. "I think I know." She cushioned her head against his back, letting him know he didn't have to continue.

"It's because I love you, Jewel. No matter what Bellamy has done or been, he is your father, and you're too kindhearted not to care for him. I'll not tread on those feelings again."

"Thank you, Nolan," Jewel said. There was a hint of tears in her voice.

"Would you like to steer?" he asked, not wanting her to be upset.

She straightened, and slipped in front of him without any more encouragement. "I'd love to. I've been wanting to from the first day on board."

"Why didn't you ever ask?" He slipped his arm around her waist. "Never mind. Don't answer. I know why. From now on, you can ask me anything. Especially about the ship. You're going to have to learn to sail."

She gripped the varnished wheel. "Where are we going, anyway?"

"To St. Lucia. I think it best if we rename the ship. I don't think our British friends will be leaving the island anytime soon, and I'd rather not have the entire Royal Navy after us."

Nolan felt Jewel stiffen. "But they accused you of treason. When Devlin is rescued—"

"By that time, if not already, the war will have begun, and I'll be a privateer for my country," he said. He wasn't as sure as he hoped he sounded, but he didn't want her to worry. "There's another reason I want to stop at St. Lucia. I want to marry you again."

"You don't have to do that," she said, but he could hear the pleasure in her voice all the same.

"Yes, I do. I want to have a piece of paper to show your father next time we see him." He brushed the hair from the back of her neck and kissed her there.

"You don't have to worry about Bellamy. I don't know if we'll ever see him again."

"We'll see him again." Nolan didn't want to tell her about his promise to give her father a portion of the treasure in order to escape with her. "And don't think you're going to be rid of Wayland."

"I hope not." She laughed. "He's definitely grown on me."

Nolan took a deep breath. He'd gotten this far, and he could say the last of it. "And of course, if you don't want to marry me again, I'll consider it my just due. You'll have your share of the treasure to do as you please."

She laid her head against his chest. "My treasure is right here."

CHERYL HOWE
The Pirate &
THE PURITAN

In her youth Felicity was swept off her feet by pretty words—but though that time in Boston felt so right, the man was so wrong. Now she's sworn to bury her sensuality under somber clothes and a rigid lifestyle; religion is the cure for future mistakes.

In Barbados, Felicity finds her father's cronies worse than expected. Worst is the infuriating Lord Christian Andrews—with his strong jaw; lean, muscled body; and that diabolical glint in his eye conjuring all the reasons she's renounced pleasure. But sneaking onto Drew's ship to prove his depravity, Felicity is again swept away. The man has only a heart of gold . . . and a nature bent on uncovering her own buried passion.

AFTER THE ASHES
CHERYL HOWE

A stagecoach robbery is the spark that sets fire to Lorelei Sullivan's plan for the future. She and her brother moved to New Mexico Territory to escape the past, to ranch, but Corey has destroyed all hope of that. Lawmen now want him—and Lorelei won't see the boy hang.

Yet defying the law places her between two men she can't trust: her sibling and Christopher Braddock, who is her brother's one shot at redemption—a hard, silent man who lights a fire inside her. And as his kiss fans the flames of desire, Lorelei wonders whether she will be consumed by this inferno or rise reborn from its ashes.

I Do

MIMI RISER

"Florrie or Dorie—'tis such a wee dif'rence. Dinna ye fear, lassie, Alan'll still wed ye," declares Angus MacAllister, chief of the Texas branch of the Clan MacAllister. And with these words, the mixed-up mayhem begins. When Dorcas Jeffries offers to temporarily stand in for the bride in a ridiculously archaic arranged marriage, she never imagines she will find herself imprisoned in an adobe castle or being rescued by the very man she is trying to escape. She is sure her intended bridegroom will be the worst of an incorrigible lot. But what do you say to a part Comanche Highlander whose strong arms and dark eyes make you too breathless to argue? What else but "I do"?